RED MENACE

A NOVEL

Jeff Kildow

Blackside Publishing

Colorado Springs, CO

Connect with Jeff
Website: www.jeffkildow.com
Twitter: https://twitter.com/jeffkildow
LinkedIn: https://www.linkedin.com/in/jeff-kildow-a66b9026/
Facebook Author Page: https://tinyurl.com/Jeff-Kildow-Historical-Fiction

Blackside Publishing
www.blacksidepublishing.com

Cover and Interior Book Design: Scoti Domeij

Red Menace: A Novel/ Jeff Kildow. -- 1st ed.
Trade Paper: 978-1-68355-020-4 1-68355-020-X
E-pub: 978-1-68355-021-1 1-68355-021-8

What Others Are Saying

Like to read? You'll love this! In Red Menace, author Jeff Kildow scores a trifecta of storytelling: an adventurous, fast-paced plot; intriguing characters; and excellent craftsmanship. He weaves imagination, history, and military factoids—oh, the planes and weapons!—into a fascinating what-if scenario that brings the world to the brink of war. And it's not only the toys and action that'll keep you flipping pages faster than an M2 machine gun, but the characters: a menagerie of corrupted souls bent on destruction and those with the grit to try to stop them. This one's a definite must-read!—Robert Liparulo, bestselling author of *Comes a Horseman, Germ,* and *The 13th Tribe*

Congratulations on an exciting, well-written novel. Your timing and descriptions are very well done. I had a hard time leaving my computer, wondering what would happen on the next page. Well done.—Randall Meathrell, Pilot, Retired Aerospace Engineer

Joel Knight returns in this exciting sequel to *America Under Attack*. This time, the stakes are much higher. The action takes place in the fledgling nuclear age in the midst of Chinese, Korean and Soviet intrigue. With a healthy dose of history and aviation technology, Jeff Kildow provides tension, excitement and fascinating alternate history. The characters are believable, the action tight!—Michael Carroll, Author and Science Journalist

Jeff Kildow demonstrates his story telling talent in his alternative history novel, *Red Menace*. As a historian and recognized expert on the American Civil War, Jeff's story captured my interest. As a reader, I know the trick to writing alternative history is to make the story plausible, as if it really happened. This reads like the real deal and Jeff pulled off this Christ-centered saga, masterfully; so much so, as we see history about to repeat itself on a global scale. Jeff's story could soon become our reality. Well Done!—Charles J. Patricoff, Author, *Destination Hope* series.

This book is dedicated to my daughter J. Robyn Hesse
for continuing, cheerful encouragement.

"If you're going through Hell, keep going."
—Winston Churchill

ACRONYMS AND MILITARY TERMS

AIR CORPS: Aviation branch of the U.S. Army until 1947, when it became the United States Air Force

AVGAS: Aviation gasoline

BBC: British Broadcasting Corporation

CAA: Civil Aeronautics Administration American, predecessor to the Federal Aviation Administration (FAA)

CHEKA: Soviet Secret police under the Tsar, predecessor to NKVD and KGB

CHIANG KAI-SHEK NATIONALISTS: Members of a Chinese political party, known as the Chinese Nationalist Party or Kuomintang, whose leader was statesman and soldier Chiang Kia-shek.

CIA: Central Intelligence Agency

COD: Carrier On-Board Delivery. A class of U.S. Navy cargo planes designed to land on an Aircraft carrier

COMPACFLT: Commander Pacific Fleet U.S. Navy acronym

COMRADE DEPUTY CHAIRMAN: The honorific for the head of the Soviet government

CPO: Chief Petty Officer U.S. Navy NCO

DISTINGUISHED FLYING CROSS: A military decoration awarded to any officer or enlisted member of the United States Armed Forces who distinguishes himself or herself in support of operations by "heroism or extraordinary achievement" while participating in an aerial flight, subsequent to November 11, 1918.

FTD: Foreign Technology Division: U.S. Air Force organization charged with analyzing foreign aircraft and missiles

FUSILIERS: Units of British line infantry. The name harkens back to the time when muskets were fired by burning fuses.

G-2: Military Intelligence Division U.S. Army

GAZ: Russian motor vehicle manufacturer

GCA: Ground Controlled Approach

GI: Government Issue; slang for a soldier

GREAT WAR: A term used to refer to the First World War (WWI) prior to the Second World War (WWII).

GROUND EFFECT: In fixed-wing aircraft, ground effect is the increased lift and decreased aerodynamic drag that an aircraft's wings generate when they are close to a fixed surface. When landing, ground effect can give the pilot the feeling that the aircraft is "floating", and can result in overflying the runway.

GRU: *Glaunoye Razedyatel'noye Upraleniye.* Soviet Army intelligence service

KGB: *Komtitet Gosudarvennoy Bezopasnosti.* Russian Committee for State Security; the secret police

KIM II-SUNG: The first Communist leader of North Korea. Born: April 15, 1912 Died: July 8, 1994

KPH: Kilometers per hour

LSO: Landing Signals Officer. Formerly, the man on an American aircraft carrier who signals an approaching pilot via flags whether he is level, in line with the deck, or must 'wave off' and try again.

MATS: Military Air Transport Service U.S. Air Force

MLADSHIY SERGEANT: Soviet Army junior sergeant, a rough equivalent to a U.S. Army 'buck' sergeant with three stripes

NAS: Naval Air Station U.S. Navy

NATIONALIST CHINESE ARMY: The military arm of the Chinese Nationalist Party, commanded by Chiang Kia-shek

NCO: Non-Commissioned Officer. Enlisted soldiers in the U.S. Army who are noncommissioned officers with the ranks of corporal, sergeant, staff sergeant, sergeant first class, master sergeant.

NKVD: *Narodnyi komissariat Vnotronnikh del.* Refers to the original Soviet Secret Police, the predecessor to the KGB.

OOD: Officer of the Deck U.S. Navy

ORDER OF THE RED STAR: A military decoration of the Soviet Union recognizing a soldier for bravery

OSS: Office of Special Services, predecessor to the CIA

PO: Petty Officer

POLITRUK: Communist Party Representative, Soviet Army

RED ARMY UNIFORMS: Red Army uniforms were simple and functional. Traditional titles and insignia were reintroduced in 1940, and modified further in 1943. There was no unit identification, only branch of service devices and colored piping on shoulder straps and collar tabs. The infantry used raspberry piping, but no branch insignia like the other branches. By 1944, uniforms were dark olive-green. Head gear included the *pilotka* or side cap and the popular overseas style field cap, often with an olive-green star with a raised hammer and sickle. Also used was an enameled red star with a hammer and sickle. Officers wore a *budionovka* or peaked cap, a round service cap with a black visor. Excerpted from "Soviet Rifleman 1941-45" by Gordon L. Rottman, pp. 18-19, Osprey Publishing, 2007.

RED ARMY: Shorthand for the Army of the Soviet Socialist republics.

RED WOUND RIBBONS: A Red Army award for wounds suffered in battle equivalent to the Purple Heart.

REVETMENTS: A parking area, or an aircraft 'foxhole' for aircraft along flight lines at forward operating bases. Surrounded by blast walls, a revetment protects parked aircraft from damage by enemy fire or an explosion and blast fragments from nearby.

RIF: Reduction In Force: A policy created by Congress following WWII to reduce the number of troops in U.S. forces involuntarily.

RON: Rest Over Night

RUSSIAN DECAPOD 2-10-0: An American-made freight, steam engine built for Soviet railways. This locomotive was the predominant freight locomotive that powered the far-flung lines of Asiatic Russia.

SAR: Search and Rescue

SAS: Special Air Service, British Army; similar to U.S. OSS

SCR-284 (C): A fictional version of the widely used U.S. military radio

SECNAV: Secretary of the Navy U.S. acronym

SILVER OAK LEAVES: Insignia of rank for Lieutenant Colonel, U.S. Army (and later Air Force) and Marine Corps, and Commander, U.S. Navy

SSB: Single sideband modulation is a form of radio wave modulation used to transmit information, such as voice or Morse Code

STARSHINA: Sergeant Major; highest non-commissioned officer rank in the Soviet Army

TNT: Trinitrotoluene; a powerful explosive used in mining, farming, and the military

UNREP: Underway Replenishment U.S. Navy. Term used for the replenishment of a ship's fuel, food and other supplies while the vessels are underway.

USAF: United States Air Force

USMC: United States Marine Corps

USS CABOT: CVL-28 WWII U.S. Navy Independence-class aircraft carrier. In *Red Menace*, the ship was converted for use as an anti-submarine warfare ship.

USS CALOOSAHATCHEE, AO-98: WWII U.S. Navy Cimarron-class fleet oiler completed too late for action during the war. It subsequently served well into the Cold War Era.

USSR: Union of Soviet Socialist Republics

VSI: Vertical speed indicator. An aircraft instrument that indicates upward or downward motion of the aircraft by the position of a needle which is level in level flight.

YEFREJTOR: Corporal, Soviet Army

ZIL: Russian truck and heavy equipment manufacturer

ZIS: Russian truck manufacturer

CAST OF CHARACTERS

AMERICANS/UNITED STATES

COLONEL JOEL KNIGHT: USAF, West Point graduate, WWII ace, part-time CIA operative. Code name "Edward Teach," radio call sign "Pirate."

DR. SUSAN KNIGHT: Joel's wife. PhD, OSS/CIA psychologist who specializes in predicting behavior of U.S. enemies.

MAJOR GENERAL GARRET "RED" MCNEIL: USAF, Joel's mentor, boss, longtime friend, and CIA contact.

LT. COLONEL DEREK "CHAPPY" CHAPMAN: USAF, retired; Joel's WWII deputy commander; copilot of the converted Lockheed Typhoon

COLONEL LOUIS "CAJUN" FONTAIGNE: USAF, retired; crack navigator

CIA EXTRACTION TEAM

JAMES "JD" DEREK MONROE: Ex-U.S. Army sergeant, 10th Mountain Division; awarded Bronze Star and three Purple Hearts, head of the CIA extraction team.

BAILY "FELIX" SINCLAIR LOWELL HARRISON III: Ex-U.S. Army paratrooper, 101st Airborne with 10 combat jumps; the team's Mr. Fix-it with his 'bag-o-tricks.'

REGINALD "REGGIE" HARRISON SYMTHE: Ex-Warrant Officer, His Majesty's British Royal Fusiliers; former SAS operative, expert in explosives and locomotives.

JOHN "SMITTY" SMITH: French–Moroccan, ex-French Foreign Legionnaire. Expert in Russian weapons, a sniper.

TOM LONG: Ex-U.S. Army Master Sergeant; expert on organization and logistics.

MURPHY "MURPH" MCGREGOR: Captain, USMC, retired; Ace fighter pilot in Pacific; expert radio operator.

RUSSIAN SCIENTISTS

DR. ILYA FADEYKA KALUGIN: Head of Soviet team sent to Siberia to test nuclear weapons. A top ranking Russian nuclear scientist, who wants to defect to U.S., but only if his wife and son come too. He suffers from a heart defect that the Russians can't treat.

DR. DAVID YAKATOV: Kalugin's deputy. A PhD mathematician with people skills, whose slight build and quiet, bookish demeanor hide a courageous heart and steely resolve.

DR. ANNA KASANA BAKHTINA: Former WWII nurse from sturdy peasant stock. Holds a PhD in nuclear physics.

DR. VALENTINA RAHIL TUMANOVA: PhD in physics, nicknamed the 'Ballerina.' Astounded her former professors with her quick mind.

DR. HEINZ LUTHOR BERTHOLD: PhD; Former aircraft designer in Nazi Germany, kidnapped by Russians and forced to assist Dr. Kalugin's team. Brilliant, sarcastic, suffering from dwarfism. Holds PhDs in both engineering and physics.

SENIOR TECHNICIAN KONSTANTIN YASHA DUSHKIN: Non-scientist technician assigned to Kalugin's team. Possible KGB informer.

RUSSIANS/SOVIET UNION

LAVRENTI PAVLOVICH BERIA: Deputy Chairman of *Sovnarkum*, known as the Council of People's Commissars of the Soviet Socialist Republics. Deputy Chairman was commonly referred to as "premier." The former NKVD head murdered his way to the premiership of Soviet Union after the 'accidental' death of Joseph Stalin.

COLONEL IVAN SEMYON YABITOV: Army of USSR. Beria's sycophantic aide, sworn enemy of Joel Knight.

COLONEL BORIS KOSTENKA TSARSKO: KGB, Beria's senior trouble shooter. A vicious, amoral killer known for transporting his enemies to Moscow in body bags.

STARSHINA (SERGEANT MAJOR) PYOTR YAKOV BORODIN AKA SERGEANT ROGER ALEXI DUBOV: Holds the earned rank of Sergeant Major in the Army of the Union of Soviet Socialist Republics—U.S. Army, deep cover CIA agent.

URI JEIRGIF DERIPASKA: Commissar of Red October Collective Farm. Ardent, secretive anti-Communist.

YAKOV DERIPASKA: Twenty-year-old son of Commissar Deripaska, guide for Joel's group.

ILYA DERIPASKA: 16-year-old co-guide with his older brother, Yakov.

IGOR YAKOV DERIPASKA: Yakov and Ilya's wily, world-wise great uncle who knows how to spread "Russian oil."

SERGEANT TOKAREV: Innovative aide to Colonel Tsarsko. Distant cousin of the gunmaker.

SERGEY SAUCHENKO: KGB Chief of the Committee of Information, also Chief of Internal Security. Holds the rank of General Lieutenant [two star general)

MONGOLIANS

COURIER-CORPORAL TSAKHIA GANTULGA: Motorcycle courier

LUTHOR TÖMÖRBAATAR: Mongolian trader

KOREANS

JUNG KIM: Korean finance expert, resident of Inchon City. Has wife Cho, daughter Sun, and son Gi.

SYNGMAN RHEE: President, Republic of South Korea

KIDNAPPED

Sunday, 13 October 1946
Berlin, Occupied Germany

Dr. Heinz Luthor Berthold, PhD, tugged on his worn coat, working the mismatched buttons into their frayed holes. A tired fedora rested on his oversized head. Wisps of graying hair escaped like smoke from under the brim.

His thoughts flitted to his mother, his only surviving family member. *She bears the suffering of the war that never ends for the living or the dead. When I saw her yesterday, she was so thin. I hope she eats what I took her, instead of giving it to her neighbors again. Even when starving, she shares with others. She's the kindest woman I've ever known, the only person who ever loved me, the only person who touches me.*

"Very well. I am ready now to depart." Two young American soldiers rose from the tattered sofa, and snubbed out their cigarettes. They gathered their M1 Garand rifles to escort Berthold to the train station. The Nuremburg Tribunal demanded the brilliant, diminutive aircraft designer to testify against Goering and other high Luftwaffe officials. Again.

The diagnosis of achondroplasia at birth resulted in his adult height of less than 4 feet, six inches, and a right leg shorter than the left. He walked with a swooping cadence, using a stout, metal-tipped cane. The American Corporal led. The private followed. Berthold's cane clacked against the stone steps as he trudged down the street.

"Come on, old man. Hurry!" The Corporal snapped.

Berthold stopped. "I walk slow. You know this. I suggest, Corporal Wilson, that *you* explain to the lieutenant why you started so late."

Wilson groused under his breath. "Just hurry it up, see?" The private smirked, then slung his rifle strap over his shoulder.

A brisk October breeze chilled their backs. The staccato tap of Berthold's cane accented each step. Sporadic military traffic rumbled past. The rubble of destroyed buildings buried the sidewalks, forcing them to walk in the street.

Berthold snorted with disgust at the debris littering the street. *More than a year since last the bombs fell. The streets still aren't clean.*

The alert private interrupted the old man's thoughts, "Vehicle."

A black, 1937 Buick Roadmaster sedan raced around a corner and roared toward them. The wheels screeched to a stop, the rear doors flew open. Two men barreled toward them. One fired his Russian Tokarev TT-33 semi-automatic pistol. A sharp crack echoed off the nearby buildings. Wilson collapsed, mortally wounded.

The private swung his M1 Garand rifle off his shoulder. Two more bullets cracked through the air. The metallic tinkle of the brass shell casing bounced on the street, jangling Berthold's frayed nerves. The private's rifle clattered on the pavement as the young American crumpled in a sodden, bloody heap.

In Russian-accented German, a man ordered, "Come with me, you little . . . " The man thrust his coarse, rough hands toward Berthold.

Berthold's mind flashed to the bullying and torment he endured as a scrawny, handicapped kid. He learned how to defend himself then. Ever since he maintained a rigorous exercise regime each day. His powerful arms and upper body belied the weak appearance of his short, bowed legs.

"I think not." His cane whistled through the air. The heavy, polished steel tip smashed into the abductor's kneecap with a *crack*. The Russian doubled over screeching curses. Berthold's cane thudded across his back. The Russian gripped his ugly pistol, then lunged toward the Berthold with lightning speed.

"Don't shoot him," the driver shouted in Russian. "Seize him."

Berthold's black walnut cane swished through the air and shattered the man's wrist, then ricocheted off his rib cage. The Russian howled in pain, grabbing his broken arm. His pistol skittered into the rubble.

The driver leapt from his seat and raced to aid his comrade. Berthold spun toward him too late. Raising his hand to resist, the flash of the leather-wrapped sap caught him off balance. The lead shot inside the leather sack whacked the side of his head. Fiery pain dissolved into blackness.

✕✕✕

The moving car bounced, jostling Berthoud to a head-throbbing consciousness. The stiff, wool mohair upholstery scratched against his cheek. The rope tying his hands behind his back chafed his wrists. Through slitted eyelids, he glimpsed black curtains concealing the windows.

The Russian beside Berthold whined as he nursed his broken wrist. "Since when does Moscow need German dwarfs? Don't we have any of our own?"

"This man is high on the list, a genius, an airplane designer. He'll design for us, or stand against a wall." The driver's coarse, barking laugh grated on Berthold's ears. "Filthy Nazi. He'll pay, like all the others."

CHAPTER 2

SIDETRACKED

Colonel Joel Knight mulled over last night's conversation with his wife, Susan. *We want to start a family. Heaven knows, both sets of in-laws keep dropping enough hints.*

The corners of his mouth raised thinking about the love of his life. *The CIA hired her when the OSS disbanded after the war. If she gets pregnant, there's no guarantee they'll keep her on—psychology PhD or not.* Joel smiled at the thought his upcoming assignment as Aviation Attaché at the Moscow Embassy and of creating a baby with Susan.

"The General will see you now, Colonel."

Colonel Joel Knight, USAF, rose to his full six-foot, two-inch height, straightened his blouse, and swapped the smile on his face out for a deadpan look. He entered the room and saluted smartly.

)O(O(

Major General Garrett "Red" McNeil returned the salute as he studied the intense colonel. *As usual, Joel looks like a recruiting poster. How many men will Congress force us to lose with this stupid RIF (Reduction in Force)? Especially men like Joel.*

The Command Pilot's wings pinned on the Colonel's uniform gleamed over rows of ribbons. *And how many are West Point grads with a degree in aeronautical engineering, plus aces with a Silver Star awarded by the President himself? I'll keep him, if he'll go along.*

"Take a seat, Joel. How'd Syracuse treat you?" The general asked his old friend.

"Sir, I picked up Russian quick enough, so I better *need* it, but they can have their New York winters. I thought I knew cold growing up in Colorado. That place is something else. The weather's almost as painful to endure as language school."

McNeil laughed. "I read the report about your close call on your test flight of the Heinkel HE-162 Volksjäger back in October. Sounds like you dodged a bullet."

"Couple more minutes, I'da bought the farm. The right outboard aileron hinge almost broke loose from the wooden aft spar."

"Your experience made the difference. How many different planes have you flown?"

"Including the captured ships? Fifty-seven."

"I can only claim fifteen." The General shifted in his chair. A downward curve of his lips replaced his welcoming smile. "State Department has delayed your assignment as Aviation Attaché at the Moscow Embassy for at least a year. Some idiotic political wrangling about the guy you'd replace. Nothing to do with that little incident after the Bolshoi." *I can't tell him about the Soviet's strenuous objections to his nomination.* "Instead, I have a Special Assignment for you."

"No, no, General, please, not *that* kind of special assignment."

More often than not, "Special Assignment," was a nasty euphemism for make-work jobs. It was given to officers awaiting a post-War RIF, signaling the end of their careers.

"Hear me out, Joel." Without thinking, Red's fingers massaged the scars on the side of his scalp through his short, graying ginger hair. He searched Joel's face, watching for a frown of anger or head shake of denial. "We're temporarily assigning you to the CIA. They need a senior pilot for the second half of an ongoing mission, which is classified Top Secret Compartmented . . . flying into a somewhat belligerent country undercover as a civilian." Left unsaid was the fact that, if captured, Joel would be shot as a spy.

Joel's skeptical squint glinted with a hint of apprehension. "I'm not sure about the mission, Red. Am I guaranteed reinstatement on active duty afterward, sir?"

Red McNeil paused, considering how to answer. "Yes . . . we'll give you a written agreement to take you back. We're talking China. Your cover is a war veteran pilot-for-hire. I can't tell you more until you sign on. Trust me on this: The mission is crucial to the military security of our country. If everything goes perfectly, you'll return home in six weeks, no longer than two months."

"Why me, Red? What do I bring to the party that a hundred other pilots don't, sir?"

"Fair question. First, you're available and still in the Air Force. We don't want the complications of using a civilian. Second, you've flown many different aircraft. You'll be a quick study to operate the aircraft involved. I can't tell you much more until after I read you into this mission. If you decide it's not for you, we can recover. However, you're better off declining right now, rather than later."

The General leaned back in his chair and fixated on the lean Colonel's body language. *He's almost convinced. Wish I were going, but I can never do that again.*

"Here's the thing, Joel. If you pull this off, success *might* help you earn a star, if that's what you want. Of course, you can never talk about the assignment. Nonetheless, the people who make career decisions are fully aware. Accomplishing this mission can work to your advantage. More important, you'll perform a great service for your country. This is less risky than fighting German bombers or flying captured fighters, that's for sure. On the other hand, you can stay where you are, and hope everything works out, that somebody finds you a new assignment." His sales pitch ended, the general leaned forward in his chair, steepled his fingers, and waited.

)()()(

Like many active duty military flyers, Joel suspected war would soon come to Korea. Conflicted, Joel weighed his options. *Susan and I talked about starting a family just last night. Susan and I celebrated when I was nominated and accepted as Air Attaché— a dream job now gone. If the flag goes up in Korea, I'll be in the thick of things as a spy. If the ChiComs catch me, they can legally shoot me. Red says this is crucial. I've never refused an assignment.*

"What about Susan, Red? What can I tell her? I can't just disappear for six weeks."

"Susan's been part of this operation for months, Joel. She doesn't have any problem with you joining. She's a key factor in the government deciding this is the real deal. A reminder, though, you can't discuss the mission with her until you're formally introduced by your CIA contact, and then only in a secure location."

"This won't put me in charge of ground troops, will it? You know I hate that."

"This is a flying job, pure and simple," General McNeil assured. Red shoved the highly classified paper across the desk toward Joel.

Joel stared at the document. *Long ago I reconciled myself to the rigors and morality to maintain secrecy. The harsh penalties for revealing the slightest mission detail? Prison for decades. Fines enough to impoverish a rich man, let alone a mere colonel. But this . . . the only thing new is how seriously they're taking it. Man, they really don't want this mission compromised.*

Joel shifted in his chair, then signed the document, closed the classification cover, and slid it back to Red.

"OK, Joel, welcome aboard PROJECT JUBILEE." The General beamed with success. "You *will not* use that compartment name outside this office, or any other designated secure facility. You will discuss this with someone *only after* being introduced by a third person you personally know is cleared to the program. Without such a personal introduction, speak to no one. Period. If you must refer to PROJECT JUBILEE in unclassified messages, refer to it as BASKET. Your personal code name is JUMPER.

"You're part of the CIA's Special Activities Division, and no smart remarks about SAD sacks. Here's the backstory: Eighteen months ago, a high-ranking Soviet scientist contacted our agent in Moscow about defecting. He's number three in the Soviet science hierarchy working on atomic bombs. The Soviets obtained a lot of our atomic bomb secrets from two American traitors."

"Yeah, the Rosenberg's."

"Yep. The Attorney General is prosecuting them under federal espionage statutes. The administration intends to ask for the death penalty, and a lot of us think they'll get it. The defecting Russian scientist is Dr. Ilya Fadeyka Kalugin, code named ROVER. He's got a heart condition only we can treat. If we agree to treat him, he'll tell us everything he knows about the Soviet program, with one stipulation: his wife and young son must also escape."

Red leaned forward in his chair. "The plan is for Mrs. Kalugin and her son Pasha to travel to Finland by train under assumed names. We'll meet them, and transport them to the American embassy, as Dr. Kalugin leaves for Siberia on the Trans-Siberian Railway. He's scheduled to leave around the fifteenth of next month. We're talking Russia here, with a fudge factor of a few days on either side. Kalugin is part of an advance team testing atom bombs somewhere in Eastern Russia."

"We'll take him in Siberia?" Joel asked.

"Yes. A CIA extraction team will remove Dr. Kalugin from the train near a remote town called Petrovsk."

The general swiveled his chair and pointed to a map on his

wall. "From Petrovsk, it's three-hundred-and-twelve miles south to the little Chinese town of Hami." He locked his eyes on Joel. "That's where you come in."

Apprehension engulfed Joel's thoughts: *Spies, nuclear weapons, kidnappings. This is socio-political machinations on a grand scale, far beyond anything I've ever participated in.*

"Wow, Red, I expected secrets, but this . . . " Joel rubbed the back of his head. "How will I know whether they transported him to—what was it? Hami? And where is that?"

"You don't need the details." The tip of Red's pencil zeroed in on a dot on the map. "Hami's in central China, in the desert north of the Himalayas. As soon as you arrive, you'll be informed about the doctor's status, his location."

The General tapped his pencil on the map, accentuating Joel's disquiet about the mission's risks.

"As part of your cover, you'll fly in civvies in a modified airplane and cross into China to Baotou—a Communist stronghold. Don't worry, that's covered. You'll refuel and continue on to Hami, 762 miles, and pick up your passenger, then fly to Tashkent. On the last leg of your mission, you'll hop over to Tehran where CIA officials will take Dr. Kalugin off your hands. You'll deliver the airplane to the Iranians, then, come home via military transport. Sweet and simple."

CHAPTER 3

REFITTED

Friday, 14 July 1950
Major General Garret "Red" McNeil's Office

J oel chuckled as he eyeballed his old friend. "Simple? We both know there's no such thing as a 'simple' mission, General, sir. And this one definitely isn't simple. Tell me more about this 'modified' airplane."

"It's a surplus Navy Lockheed PV-2 Harpoon. Ever flown one?

The Lockheed PV-2 Harpoon was a fast, sophisticated, second-generation modification of the pre-war Lockheed Lodestar twin-engine airliner. Equipped with twin tails and two powerful Pratt and Whitney R2800 engines, the Harpoon served as a reconnaissance and patrol aircraft by U.S. Navy in the Pacific theatre.

"No. I clocked a few hours in a Lockheed Hudson, though. Close enough?" The Hudson was an earlier modification to the Lodestar.

"That'll do. We'll check you out in the Harpoon soon enough."

"Where do I take off from?"

Red cocked his head. "Ever flown off an aircraft carrier, Joel?"

"You want me to take off from a *carrier*?" Joel's back stiffened. "I don't think that's possible with a Harpoon. I mean, remember the trouble Doolittle had flying from the *Wasp*—his B-25s had what? A sixty, sixty-five foot wingspan? The Harpoon is closer to eighty. Plus, the B-25 has a nose wheel. The Harpoon's a tail-dragger."

"The ship was the USS *Hornet*, not the *Wasp*," McNeil corrected.

"You're right. The Harpoon's wingspan is over seventy-five feet compared to about sixty-five for the B-25. How to take off from a 'Jeep' carrier with a long wing tail-dragger is one of several small obstacles we left for you to resolve, Colonel. Let me tell you about the plane's modifications.

"All the armaments are gone and the interior aft of the spar has a flat floor. There's a new airliner-style door, and six fancy leather chairs and a couple of tables, like a Deluxe Pullman car. Your cover story is the Shah of Iran bought this plane as a personal transport for a high-ranking muckety-muck, which is true. You're simply ferrying the Harpoon to the Shah's buddy. Forward of the spar, where the bomb bay was, is a compartment with a hidden access, where our 'passenger' will ride. The compartment looks like a big internal fuel tank from the outside. Pretty clever."

Joel considered. "With no armor and guns, that lightens the plane. Does that increase her speed much?"

"So far, she's done a twitch under 300. Probably cruises at 285 or thereabouts. Not bad."

"I take the plane has civilian registration? U.S. or Iranian?"

"Iran. The new number, EP-ZED, is an official number registered with the CAA [Civil Aeronautics Administration]."

Joel mulled over what the General described. "Wait . . . you said 'Jeep' carrier? Those are narrower than a regular flattop."

"Thought I slipped that one by." Red McNeil chuckled with amusement. "Here's the deal: Navy is loaning us some deck space on USS *Cabot*. She's already steaming her way to Hawaii, transporting forty F-84s to Inchon, Korea. You'll meet her at Pearl Harbor where they'll hoist the PV-2 on board."

"You'll fly off *Cabot* in the Bay of Korea—the Gulf of Chihli." He pointed to the spot on the map. "It's a straight shot to Baotou, with one exciting leg north of Peking."

"So we modify *Cabot* to make the Harpoon fit and . . . "

"Nope. No way. Navy sank a boatload of money into *Cabot* making her a sub-chaser—lots of new radars, sonars, and the like. We'll make any necessary mods to the PV-2. Don't worry, I'm sure you'll think of something."

"What about a copilot and a navigator? You don't expect me to fly this solo, do you, sir?"

"No, no, we sure don't expect that." The red-haired general sported a sly grin. "You'll meet your copilot and navigator soon." The General's desk drawer screeched as he opened a wooden drawer to remove documents. The drawer clunked closed as he thrust the documents toward Joel. "Here are your civilian credentials. The passport and flying license are in your new name, Edward Teach, nickname "Pirate." You separated from the Air Corps in '45."

Joel inspected the documents as Red continued, "You recall I told you that Dr. Kalugin heads east in about a month. Given the Soviet's old steam engines and their track conditions, we estimate about five days, give or take, to arrive in Petrovsk. We're guessing another five or six days to make your way to Hami. That gives you about six weeks to transition into the Harpoon, learn how to take off the carrier, hitch a ride with the Navy to Korean waters, then fly to Hami. A MATS C-54 leaves for 'Frisco at 0530 hours tomorrow. Here's your ticket. One more thing: Susan's down the hall waiting to brief you." He pushed the button on his intercom. "Send Captain Jacobs in, please." An Air Force Captain with the rope of a general's aide stepped into the room.

"Colonel Joel Knight, meet Captain Ron Jacobs. This is an official PROJECT JUBILEE introduction. Captain Jacobs will escort you to your wife and introduce you. If there's nothing else, Colonel, you're dismissed. Best of luck."

CHAPTER 4

THREATENED

Friday, 14 July 1950

Norton Air Force Base Headquarters, Room 2A115-3

Susan flipped her blonde hair like a frolicking palomino. "Hi, flyboy. Wanna show a girl a good time?" Susan giggled as she posed on the edge of a desk, swinging her crossed legs like a warbird-pinup girl.

"Susan, you little prevaricator. You said you'd be shopping in LA." Joel loped toward the desk, saddled up to his wife and wrapped his arm around her waist.

"Well, as soon you're on your way, there *is* a darling little dress shop in Beverly Hills . . ." Susan tilted her head and swiveled her hips and chest toward her husband.

Captain Jacobs cleared his throat. "Sorry to interrupt, sir, Dr. Knight. I must formally introduce you two."

Joel tightened his arm around Susan's waist, pulling her closer. Susan kissed Joel's neck. The captain's cheeks flushed red.

While Captain Jacobs introduced them Joel mused on Susan's unique qualifications: *When I met her during the war, she'd already earned her PhD in Applied Psychology from the University of Wisconsin. Man, she's good at analyzing and predicting our enemies' behaviors. The OSS even hired her, one of only a few women they employed during the war.* He smiled to himself. *She looks more like a Hollywood star than a shrink—tall, slender blue-eyed, blond, gorgeous. A lot of guys underestimate her. Too bad for them.*

After their 'introduction,' Captain Jacobs excused himself and closed the door with a firm thud. Susan shifted from the desk to a large, comfortable leather chair. Her work face replaced her flirt face. "Have a seat. We need to move along. You still need to go home and pack. I'll meet you there later. My staff and I pulled together information on three people you need to be aware of."

"First is Dr. Ilya Fadeyka Kalugin." She handed Joel several large, glossy color photographs from a thick, red-striped envelope. "The defecting scientist."

The middle-aged man appeared "academic," with rounded shoulders and a thick mustache. Gray hair encircled a shiny, brown-speckled head.

Joel eyed the photo. "This guy's worth all the time, effort, and risk?"

"He's a brilliant physicist, a nuclear weapons expert. Kalugin's done innovative work on the Soviet's nuclear weapons development. To keep his job, he joined the Communist party. He's terrified Premier Beria will employ the weapons against innocent civilians. Kalugin has no stomach for the political intrigues and power plays necessary to maintain a senior position in the Soviet bureaucracy."

"So, his conscience motivates him?" Joel questioned.

"He's in severe moral conflict. He's tired and desperately wants out."

"Red told me about helping his wife and son escape through Finland. Why can't he leave that way as well?"

"He's watched *very* closely."

"Hence the elaborate ruse to extract him?"

"Yes."

"He's the real deal, not just playing us?" Joel asked.

"As real as the bombs he's helping the Soviets build," Susan said. "We collected information corroborating his story. I studied everything about him, including his personal correspondence over the last six years. We've monitored private phone conversations. To prove himself, he's already provided highly secret material, at great personal risk. Grabbing this man will be a major intelligence coup. Besides, extracting him will slow down their atomic weapons program to a considerable degree, and possibly save hundreds of thousands of lives."

Susan stared into Joel's eyes. "Keep in mind, Joel, this man is betraying his country. He's fully aware his relatives will pay a steep price for his defection. He's leaving everything he's ever known to come to a place he's never visited. He can never return. He'll experience immense psychological pressure. He may show signs of deep remorse, anguish, regret, and sorrow. You and your team need to provide a lot of support and encouragement."

"So I'm babysitting, too?"

"Whatever you call this, your role is vital. And something else to watch out for: occasionally in cases like this, the subject is so overcome with emotion that he may attempt to renege on the bargain and run back to what's familiar, even when it means imprisonment, torture, death."

Her face tightened with sternness. "If Dr. Kalugin attempts that, you *will* use physical force to keep him in custody and bring him to the U.S., regardless of his wishes. Handcuffs, blindfolds, gags, drugs—whatever's necessary. He's too valuable, his knowledge too critical. Once he's in our custody, we can't let him back out."

"And if nothing we do to restrain him works?"

"Do you want me to say it?"

Joel swallowed. "So I'm supposed to kill him? In cold blood?"

"I pray to God, no. And it's not in cold blood, Joel, this is war. A cold war, maybe, but war nonetheless. The harsh reality is, Dr. Kalugin's life isn't worth the destruction he'll cause by staying in Russia."

Her expression softened. "Joel, if it comes to that, you must kill him. If you can't, we'll scrub your part of the mission and find another way, which will prove difficult at this late date. I must know that you can do this."

"I'll do my duty, of course."

"I'm sorry to be so blunt, Joel. This is the real world, the cold, hard reality."

Changing the subject, Joel asked. "You said I needed to know about three people?"

Susan shot him that I-know-what-you-just-did-look, then continued, "The second goes by the Russian name Pyotr Yakov Borodin. His real name is Roger Alexei Dubov. He's a U.S. citizen, born in Milwaukee to Russian immigrant parents. He's been deep cover since 1944. During the confusion surrounding the fall of Stalingrad, he infiltrated into the escaping Soviet army."

Joel flipped to the next photograph: A hard-looking man in his thirties, with a short, military-style haircut, and piercing grey eyes. His thick neck, and crossed, muscular arms conveyed power and strength.

"He speaks perfect Russian with an accent traceable to the region his parents immigrated from. His cover's birth village changed hands several times between the German and Russian armies before disappearing under tank treads and boots. The name, Borodin, is common in the area. No one questions his authenticity. His war wounds from D-Day at Normandy he attributes to Stalingrad. A Russian secondary hospital treated him, and we made sure his records survived. The Soviet's awarded him the Order of the Red Star and three Red Wound Ribbons.

"He stayed in the Red Army after the war and rose to the rank of Sergeant Major without our help. His service branch is Infantry, the most respected in the Red Army. He has excellent small arm skills. His spycraft is second to none. With help from us, he came to the attention of the third person you need to know about: Colonel Ivan Semyon Yabitov, senior aid to Premier Beria."

Susan sipped some water, then pulled more photos from the red-striped envelope. "Colonel Ivan Semyon Yabitov. You'll recall him as the drunk who crashed the Secretary of State's car after the Bolshoi."

Joel recognized the skeletal-thin Yabitov, his cheekbones in sharp relief over a sallow complexion. A pointed nose presided over his narrow chin.

"Oh, yeah, I remember this character," Joel said. "You and I were in DC for meetings. Red gave us tickets to the Bolshoi. Can't believe this dope crashed his car into the Secretary of State's limousine."

"Injuring both the Secretary and his wife."

Joel said, "Yeah, I stopped him from trying to shoot the Secretary's driver. Drunk as a skunk, Yabitov fought me like a mad dog. I hit him hard enough to make him stay down until the cops arrived."

"He threatened you, remember?" Susan asked.

"Yeah, said he'd hunt me down and kill me because I besmirched his honor or something. What an idiot."

"Well, he's a *dangerous* idiot." Susan warned. "He's a genuine loose cannon and about as likeable as a cornered rattlesnake. You remember Stalin's Red Army purges in the '30s?"

"Yeah, Stalin, another idiot. Killed more than seventy-five percent of his senior military staff from sheer paranoia, leaving him without seasoned leaders when the war began."

"When the purges started," Susan continued, "Yabitov's father was a Red Army Colonel with impeccable military credentials. A chance conversation with a tainted General resulted in his arrest. Yabitov's father was shot without a trial. The effect on Yabitov—only fifteen? Catastrophic. To this day, Yabitov's sycophantic to his seniors, fearful they'll come after him too. He drives himself hard and the people under him harder. He strikes fear into his subordinates by his inability to accept anything less than his idea of perfection. His superiors love what he accomplishes. His men detest him."

"He's a drunk." Joel's tone sounded as hard as the ice in Yabitov's vodka.

"He binge drinks. He's a teetotaler, then falls off the wagon, usually after an assignment," Susan amended.

"How's he involved in this mission?"

"He oversees the atom bomb testing."

She stopped, her beautiful face a study in concentration and concern. "When this prize scientist defects, you can bet Yabitov's reaction will be quick, violent, and far reaching. Won't matter the distance apart. Yabitov will almost certainly launch Tsarsko, his KBG puppet, to capture you. Sorry, no photo. Tsarsko is a cross between a rabid pitbull and an enraged alligator, with no redeeming virtues. He'll find and kill you, or literally die trying. He's ruthless, merciless, and intelligent. Watch out for him—*please*."

CHAPTER 5

OBSTACLES

After packing bags, a lingering goodbye left Joel groggy from a sleepless night. Joel boarded a noisy C-54 in Southern California and arrived at Moffett Field Naval Air Station south of San Francisco. Chief Petty Officer Gavin met Joel with a sunny smile stretching toward his eyes.

"I haven't drunk my morning coffee yet." Joel commented with a slight hint of grump from a lack of sleep and caffeine. "Where can I grab some coffee to jump-start me?"

The curly haired NCO said, "Here take mine, I haven't drunk from it yet. It's genuine U.S. Navy coffee."

"Looks like bunker oil," Joel mumbled.

"Naw, Colonel, bunker oil is thinner and less oily. I'll orient you, then maybe you can take off a little early this afternoon and grab some shut-eye before we check out the Harpoon and begin logging flight time."

Joel sipped on the muddy cup of Joe as Chief Petty Officer Gavin escorted him to Commander Carter's office. An experienced Navy Lieutenant Commander, Carter checked Joel out in the modified Harpoon, signed off his log, and grabbed drawings of the *Cabot*'s deck. Carter's signature qualified Joel to fly the Harpoon.

Chief Petty Officer Gavin, Commander Carter, and Joel strode out to the tarmac. The royal blue stripe down the airplane's fuselage and the strange series of letters—the registration 'number'—attracted attention away from the stealth-gray and white Navy aircraft parked around the Lockheed PV-2 Harpoon.

After taxiing the Harpoon to an unused section of the runway for takeoff practice, Carter pointed at the runway. "We painted the outline of *Cabot*'s deck, Colonel. Five-hundred-fifty feet, five-inches long by seventy-eight feet, seven-and-a-half inches wide. The mock-up of the island limits your deck space. Can you take off in that distance?"

Joel remarked, "Not a chance. No catapult in the world could launch an aircraft as heavy as the Harpoon off the deck of a light aircraft carrier. Even if a catapult existed strong enough to launch a Harpoon, the plane's simply not stressed for the structural loads a catapult imposes."

The sunburned Lieutenant Commander scratched his short, blond hair, then affirmed Joel's observation. "If you check page eighty-four in the *Pilot's Handbook*, figure forty-six—the "Takeoff, Climb and Landing Chart"—even at low weight, you need at least five-hundred feet. You'll never get her airborne in three-hundred feet, especially with full fuel tanks."

Joel didn't argue. *He's logged 2000 hours in the Harpoon and he's a check pilot. He knows this plane better than the Lockheed design engineers.* "OK, Instructor Pilot, how can we use more of the deck? Can we take off at an angle, to miss the island?" Joel asked.

Commander Carter, Chief Gavin, and Joel poured over drawings of the *Cabot*'s deck.

"If you start at the fantail on the starboard side and head toward the port bow, there's two or three feet clearance going past the island, Colonel," the Chief said.

"Not enough," Joel said.

"What if we removed the wing tips?" Carter suggested. "They're not structural, just there for streamlining. We'd gain about eight feet of clearance in total."

"That kind of change to the aircraft might draw unnecessary attention," Joel said.

Knowing the aircraft and his mission had to remain secret, the Navy men accepted Joel's comment without question.

Chief Gavin spoke up, "Sirs, what about this? Instead of going down the *center* of the deck, what if we offset the plane to port? We'd gain ten or fifteen feet of clearance for the right wing tip, and still have—I'm guessing—about twenty-five feet from the plane's left wheel to the edge of the deck. I could paint a line to follow."

Carter recalculated. "Yeah, that'll work, at least on paper. Colonel, is ten feet of clearance enough?"

"Barring a crosswind, that's plenty," Joel said.

Chief Gavin added, "No crosswind, Sir. *Cabot* will head straight into the wind for your take off."

Joel paused. "OK, how do I follow the Chief's painted line, especially at the start of the takeoff roll? I'll still be sitting on my tail and the nose blocks my view."

The two Navy men considered the remaining obstacle.

Joel snapped his fingers. "I know. If I run up the engines to takeoff power with the brakes locked, I can fly the tail using the elevators. I've seen it done at air shows."

"Hmmm," Carter said. "Let's give it a try."

CHAPTER 6

SUCCESS

Saturday, 15 July 1950
Moffett Field Naval Air Station, California

Two hours after their first takeoff, an ear-to-ear grin split Carter's face. As they taxied in, Carter exclaimed over the engine noise, "That's fun. Too bad the Navy won't let us do this."

"I think flying the tail is the only way I can follow the painted line," Joel said.

"Sir," Chief Gavin said, "the carrier deck moves up and down. Be careful the props don't hit the deck. It'll spoil your whole day."

"Chief's right, Colonel. Let's try using the elevator trim tab to remove the human error," Carter added.

"First time in a long time I've been accused of being human," Joel joked.

Joel annotated in his dog-eared copy of the PV-2 *Pilot's Handbook*: A three-degree nose-up trim tab setting allows the big twin to fly its tail before the start of the takeoff roll.

"How many knots will the ship make when I take off?" Joel asked.

"She's capable of thirty-two knots, sir, about thirty-five miles per hour. If there's a breeze, the wind speed over the deck could be as high as fifty miles an hour," the Chief said.

"Good. I only need to gain an additional twenty-five to thirty miles per hour to takeoff, according to our Instructor Pilot's famous figure forty-six."

By the time the crimson sunset turned bluish purple on the western horizon, Joel had logged more than a dozen takeoffs, gaining confidence in the airplane and the unorthodox technique. The last several takeoffs saw the big Lockheed airborne as much as twenty feet before the end of the painted faux deck.

"OK, pilot," Carter commanded. "I want you here at 0530 tomorrow morning to practice more takeoffs. We've only got tomorrow to make you competent."

"Aye, aye, sir, Instructor Pilot, sir." Joel quipped, saluting.

CHAPTER 7

CLEARED

B efore the sun peeked over the pre-dawn blue horizon, Joel stood on the runway taking in the calm morning. Sea gulls soared overhead on their squawky search for breakfast in the nearby salt marshes.

In the distance, he recognized the thunder of an engine being run up. A briny breeze blowing in from San Francisco Bay smelled of oil and gasoline. A smile of satisfaction stretched across his face, as dawn's soft orange and yellow smile urged its way above the skyline.

Joel strode toward the waiting aircraft to perform a thorough walk-around inspection of the PV-2. CPO Gavin and Lt. Commander Carter arrived in a gray Navy Jeep.

Carter glanced at his watch. "Tell ya what, Joel. After two or three takeoffs, if the Chief says you're lifting off okay, we'll break for breakfast. Then, at noon you'll leave to rendezvous with *Cabot* at Pearl Harbor."

"I thought we had all day."

"That's what we thought, too, Colonel. *Cabot*'s Air Boss radioed. Their departure from Pearl was pushed up twelve hours."

"Then I'd rather skip breakfast. Let's do this," Joel said.

By noon, Joel accomplished twenty more takeoffs, surmounting the challenging obstacles of taking off. His carefully lettered notes on engine RPMs, manifold pressures, mixture settings, supercharger settings, and flap and trim tab settings filled the margins of his pilot's manual.

After taxiing in for the last time, Carter, sitting in the copilot's seat turned to Joel, "Colonel, Chief Gavin has a work detail ready to prep this ship for your hop across the Pacific. A car will drive you to Captain Bergeron's office for a briefing." He thrust his hand toward Joel. "It's been nice flying with you, sir. Good luck on your mission."

With two firm shakes of their clasped hands, Joel replied, "I appreciate your help, Commander Carter."

A sailor transported Joel to Captain Bergeron's Moffat Naval Air Station office building fifteen minutes early. Joel hopped out of the Navy Jeep, "Thanks for the ride," then headed into the cement-grey building to await his briefing.

"Sir, the Captain will see you now." The sailor escorted Joel into Captain Bergeron's office, then closed the door as he left. Two men stood with their backs to Joel, speaking to a serious looking, grey-haired Navy Captain seated behind a metal desk. Both wore Army A-2 leather jackets, and civilian slacks and boots.

"Colonel Knight reporting, sir." The two men turned to face him.

"Chappy," Joel exclaimed. "I thought you separated from active duty in the Army."

During the war, Lieutenant Colonel Derek "Chappy" Chapman was Joel's deputy commander at Millville Army Air Field, New Jersey. When Joel was promoted to command the Air Defense District, Chappy became wing commander. The men and their wives were friends. Joel noticed the post-war years had not diminished the physical condition of the five-foot, ten-inch former college fullback. An excellent pilot and a resourceful, dependable leader, his brown eyes still snapped with humor and intelligence.

Chappy clasped Joel's hand and pounded his back. "Great to see you, Joel. I did get out, right after the war. I've done some . . . ah . . . *freelance* work ever since. They tapped me as your copilot on this mission." Shaking his head in false shame, Chappy quipped, "Playing second fiddle to you again."

The two laughed until the stern-faced man behind the desk stood and cleared his throat, "If you don't mind, gentlemen, there's a mission to plan." He stretched out his hand and power-gripped Joel's hand, shaking it with vigor. "Welcome aboard, Colonel Knight. You obviously know Mr. Chapman. This other gentleman is Mr. Louis Fontaigne, your navigator."

Fontaigne's slender build, perhaps five-foot-five, stood ten inches shorter than Joel. Tanned, with short black hair, his intelligent grey eyes appeared perceptive, his handshake firm. "Nice ta meetcha, sir." A distinct Cajun drawl flavored his speech.

Captain Bergeron interjected, "First, let's take care of security. I personally vouch for everyone in this compartment. Everyone here is cleared for PROJECT JUBILEE. This is your formal introduction to your crew, Colonel. Besides the four of us and General McNeil's staff, only the Captain and the Exec of USS *Cabot* are briefed to your mission. You *will not* speak of the mission outside this compartment." Bergeron's penetrating stare into the eyes of each man reflected the seriousness of the mission.

Bergeron continued, "We received word this morning. The Russian half of this mission is scheduled to leave Moscow with the scientist in about ten days. Our inside man heads the security detachment. The intercept team is moving into position, so we must be sure you and your aircraft arrive quickly. You'll receive an updated brief on board *Cabot* at Pearl. Your transit time to Pearl Harbor is about ten and one-half hours. Chief Gavin phoned. Except for changing a main gear tire that'll take forty-five minutes, your ship is tuned up, fueled, and ready. Mr. Fontaigne did weather checks and everything looks perfect. I trust you have your personal effects and civilian clothes, including your new passport?"

"Yes, sir," Joel replied.

"When we finish, change in the officer's head. Leave your uniforms here."

He handed Joel a small, heavy pouch. "Here's $500 in gold coins for emergencies. This wallet has $15,000 in U.S. currency. Share this with your crew and use some, or all, as needed. Sign here."

That done, Captain Bergeron handed Joel a small photograph of an unsmiling Chinese man. "This is your contact in Baotou. He's a civilian airport employee with 'Mr. Wu' embroidered in English on his shirt pocket. He'll say, '*It is a fine day to fly.*' You'll reply, '*Only if the sun keeps shining.*' He'll answer, '*The sun will shine on white birds.*' Refuel and continue on to Hami to pick up your passenger, then fly to Tashkent.

"If Mr. Wu says anything else—*anything*—that's your signal the mission is off. Refuel and continue to Hami according to your cover story. Understood?"

"Yes, sir."

"Do *not* ask about the Russian." In a stern tone, Bergeron ordered, "Repeat the signs and counter signs again to me. They must be perfect."

Somewhat flustered, Joel obeyed. Chappy and Fontaigne watched closely.

After Captain Bergeron briefed Chappy and Fontaigne on contingency plans, his face softened. He turned toward Joel. "Colonel, both men have memorized the responses and counters, too. You're a team. Back each other up. Don't worry."

Sounding like a "famous last words" curse, he added, "This mission is a piece of cake."

CHAPTER 8

UNLEASHED

Sunday, 16 July 1950

The Kremlin, Moscow, USSR, Office of the Deputy Chairman

Lavrenti Pavlovich Beria, Deputy Chairman of the Council of People's Commissars of the Soviet Socialist Republics, strode into his office. His custom-made Italian shoes clacked with fury against the polished parquet floor.

The slam of his fist on his desk echoed in the empty room. Beria ranted, "When I ran the KGB at Lubyanka Square, my word *was* law. No one dared question me." His balled anger struck the desk again.

"I did as I saw fit, eliminated problems, solved 'em. But now—*now* I must to deal with these quivering, fearful Politburo fossils who hold hidden, or not so hidden, agendas, who are like insolent children. I am Chairman! I *expect* resistance from the *military*. They are always conservative, careful until combat. Then they follow orders, like good soldiers.

"But these fools? How can I allow the head of the Agriculture Committee to delay things? And that whimpering, senile idiot at Gosbank, 'We can't afford another war?' Increase taxes. Force the peasants to work harder. What's the problem?'

"How can I allow the Chairman of the Rivers, Harbors, and Railways Committee to interfere with the destiny of Mother Russia?"

The door opened interrupting his bitter soliloquy.

"Sir, Comrade Chairman Ivanov of the Factories and Production Committee asks to speak with you. I believe he has good news."

Beria pivoted to face his aide, Colonel Ivan Semyon Yabitov, the thin-as-a-rail, occasional drunk who possessed an excellent mind. Best of all, from Beria's perspective, this excessively sycophantic man remained slavishly loyal, carrying out any order like a snapping turtle that refused to let go.

His visitor—Chairman Ivanov—another faithful supporter, cleverly manipulated Beria's Politburo opponents.

"Da, Ivan Semyon, send the Comrade Chairman in. Stay to listen."

A stereotypical Russian, Ivanov's dark hair and bushy eyebrows framed his expressionless face. His suit, a shapeless, gray utilitarian lump bearing no style, drooped on his solid body. On the right breast, he wore, as always, his gaudy medals from the Great War. He was, after all, a Hero of the Soviet Union.

"Comrade Deputy Chairman, thank you for seeing me. I just participated in extensive . . . *discussions* with the dissenters, especially Comrade Khrushchev." His fat hands rubbed together like a capitalist merchant closing a deal. "He has seen the light, let us say, and agrees to influence the others. At tomorrow morning's vote, the Politburo will be favorable to your plan."

"Excellent, Ivanov," Beria spread his hands in question. "How *did* you accomplish this miracle?"

Ivanov's shrug appeared almost Gallic. "This is not so difficult if you know which lever to pull, Comrade Deputy Chairman . I simply mentioned the *inappropriate funds* that built Comrade Khrushchev's dacha and he became cooperative."

"Well done, Ivanov." Beria poured his guest and himself vodka, ignoring Yabitov, too minor a player to acknowledge. The two men lifted their glasses to nose-level in a toast.

"To Mother Russia."

"Mother Russia."

Yabitov waited in silence unnoticed to the side.

After Ivanov left, Beria paced, thinking, plotting. *My plans are coming together. I'll send troops to the North Korean border, use the Chinese and Koreans as minions, provoke the Americans to fight. Then! Then, I'll unleash the Chinese against the Americans and give them a taste of their own atomic bombs. Already, we are slipping oblique references to Chinese bombs into dispatches the Americans intercept. They'll blame the Chinese, of course, and they'll fight, with Russia waiting to pick up the pieces. Then, I'll be leader of the world! My plan is perfect!*

With a dismissive wave in the air, he discounted North Korean Kim Il-Sung as a credible military leader. *Kim is a reliable Communist. He fought well in China and rose to the rank of Major in the Soviet Army before I placed him in power.*

"Yabitov, here is a task for you. Kim brags he'll sweep his army down the Korean peninsula. When he drives the hapless U.S. Army into the sea in shame, the grateful South Koreans will rise in joy at their 'liberation.' I doubt this greatly. Investigate Kim's claims before you leave for the east."

"Yes, sir," In a precise salute, Yabitov raised his right hand, palm down, to his right temple not quite touching it.

Beria dismissed Yabitov from the room with an irritated wave of his hand.

With a sycophantic curvature of his spine, Yabitov backed from the room.

CHAPTER 9

HAWAII BOUND

Sunday, 16 July 1950
Moffett Field NAS, California

Carrying box lunches and two large coffee Thermoses, Joel, Louis Fontaigne, and Chappy walked toward the civilianized Harpoon. Joel recalled Chappy's piloting skills as among the best. Knowing trans-Pacific flights were notoriously difficult, Chappy's meticulous walk-around reassured Joel.

"With our fuel weight, we'll need a lot of runway to get this bird airborne, Joel, even without armor and guns. I suggest the long runway."

Joel also recalled that Chappy's outlook was often a little dour. "You might be surprised," Joel said. "Ready for engine start?"

XOXOX

The powerful engines roared. Joel released the brakes when the tail flew, and with a slight bobble, the Harpoon raced forward.

The entire dash down the runway, Chappy repeated, "*What? . . . what're you doing? . . . what . . . ?*" When his mouth wasn't forming words, it gaped open.

The plane leapt into the air.

"What's the matter, Chappy? Haven't you ever seen a *real* pilot take off?" Joel laughed as he retracted the landing gear. "Retract the flaps, if you'd be so kind, Mr. Copilot."

"Holy Smokes, is that how we're taking off from the carrier?" Impressed, Chappy lifted the lever, moving the flaps into place.

Joel glanced at Chappy. "With a slight offset to the left—that is, port—to miss the island."

As the California coastline disappeared, navigator Louis Fontaigne gave Joel a heading. He set the autopilot and asked Fontaigne, "Do I call you Louie or Lewis or what?"

"Colonel, I been called a lot of t'ings, but mostly, dey jus' call me "Cajun"."

"Cajun works for me." Joel said. "What's your background?"

"Sir, I—"

"Stop calling me sir, will you? I'm Joel. No, no, check that. My cover name is Edward Teach, nickname "Pirate"."

Cajun's guffaw cut through the wind noise. "OK, 'Pirate.' Seem like a funny name, but if ya say so."

"The mission rules say so."

"I join da Army Air Corps 'bout a month before Pearl Harbor. Washed outta pilot training. So, dey sent me ta navigator school. I guess I'm pretty good, ya know? Dey made me head over da school, den sent me to Tactical Air Command when dat started. Den I got RIFed. CIA, dey offer me work, so I come on board. Been doin' dis spooky stuff 'mos' three years."

"He's too modest, Joel—er, *Pirate*," Chappy said over the more muted engines. "A thousand guys worked for him and he was a light colonel to boot. If you're ever lost in the back woods, this is the guy who'll get you home. He's done some scary stuff in places without names, all over the world. A couple of medals hang on the wall at CIA headquarters with his name on them. They offered me my choice of navigators on this job, and I picked ol' Cajun without a second thought. He's the best. Besides, he always buys the beer."

✗✗✗

Hours later, Joel finished switching fuel tanks and watched to be sure everything was OK. The reassuring drone of the engines continued. He compared his watch to the instrument panel chronometer. A glance over the nose revealed a gorgeous tropical sunset streaked with red, orange, and pink just transitioning to twilight blue.

"We're about three hours from landing, guys. Ever done an approach to NAS Ford Island in the dark, Chappy?" Joel asked.

"I can probably land without killing us all. Navy has a pretty good GCA [Ground Controlled Approach] there. Want me to take her in?"

CHAPTER 10

OFF THE RECORD

Monday, 17 July 1950
The White House, The Oval Office

President Harry S. Truman assembled his cabinet for an off-the-record briefing on the disturbing CIA intelligence report. He watched as Vice President Alben Barkley, Secretary of State Dean Acheson, Secretary of Defense Louis Johnson, and Army Chief of Staff George C. Marshall entered the room. Also in attendance was Rear Admiral Roscoe Hillenkotter, Director of the CIA. To the side of the room stood an Air Force major.

Truman glanced at the quiet Air Force major. A sense of anxious anticipation seeped through the tobacco haze enveloping the crowded Oval Office. Truman glanced at a bookish, thirty-five-year-old CIA man, who briefed Truman in private earlier. Shifting from foot to foot, Dr. Simon Rathman the CIA guy adjusted his horn-rimmed glasses.

"Boys," the President said, "this meeting is unofficial and all this is Top Secret, so I don't want to see *anything* in the papers tomorrow. Keep your yaps shut. I want you to know what I know, so when decision-time comes, you can help. Go ahead, son."

"Mr. President, gentlemen," the bespectacled man said, "I'm Dr. Simon Rathman, Director of the Far East Desk at the Central Intelligence Agency. My brief this morning concerns the buildups in far Eastern Soviet Union and Northern China, as well as North Korea."

He uncovered a large easel-mounted map and tapped it with a pointer. "Here in Mongolian Russia, we observed many infantry, armor, and artillery units moving in. I'll cover these in a moment.

"First, the air forces: In the last three weeks, a dozen major Soviet Air Force units arrived. There may be as many as ten units each roughly equivalent to one of our bomber wings. We're seeing the TU-4 copies of our B-29 as well as the Tupolev TU-270 copies of the six-engine German GO-460 flying wings. There may be as many as three hundred heavy bombers—almost two-thirds of their known heavy bomber fleet. Rumors of large, jet-powered bombers, are as-yet unconfirmed. Obtaining intelligence from an area this remote is difficult."

Truman watched the group as they listened. *Marshall and Hillenkotter are skeptical. Interesting. Hillenkotter disagrees with his own man. Johnson seems shocked and Barkley disbelieving.* With a derisive shake of his head, Truman realized his Vice President appeared disconnected and befuddled, as usual.

"At a base we're calling Base One, since we don't know its name yet, the numerous fighter units include many Lagg-7 and MiG-3 propeller planes we thought the Russians retired after the war. Base One includes about two-hundred-and-fifty MiG-9 Fargo jet fighters, nearly their entire force of these planes. Performance-wise, they're roughly equivalent to our Lockheed F-80 Shooting Star. Considerable support forces accompany all these fighters. And I mean more than just refueling and armament units. We're seeing heavy maintenance groups equipped to do engine changes and the like. We interpret this to mean they're planning to be there for a significant period of time. Furthermore—"

"Dr. Rathman," Secretary of State Dean Acheson interrupted, his head cocked in a skeptical way, "are there any of those new MiG-15 Fagot jet fighters we've been hearing about?"

"Yes, sir, about a dozen, with many more on the way. But because of their short range and short-lived engines, they may be shipping them by train, not flying them in."

"You're sure of this?" Acheson asked.

"Our sources are reliable, Mr. Secretary."

"Why does this information contradict what General MacArthur's G-2 Intelligence Section told him and us?" Acheson's question ratcheted the tension in the room.

Truman cleared his throat and intervened, "General Marshall, please introduce your guest."

"Yes, sir. Mr. President, gentlemen, may I present U.S. Air Force Major Barton Thomas? You will recall Major Thomas and his crew went missing in Russia after their RB-50 photo plane was shot down several months ago. He returned after an incredible ordeal, the sole survivor. He has corroborating information for us."

"Go ahead, Major," Truman encouraged.

"Thank you, Mr. President." Thomas tugged at the collar of his shirt as he shifted from foot to foot not knowing who to address. He jerked his head from the President to General Marshall, the Army Chief of Staff.

"As the President said, I commanded the RB-50 photo recon ship the Russians shot down. I observed large groups of Soviet aircraft on new air fields. Heavy bombers of several types—I'd guess hundreds. Even more fighters. MiG-9 Fargos shot us down. I saw no MiG-15 Fagots. Nearby, I saw an army camp of several divisions. Tanks, artillery tubes, and many, many trucks. I regret our film, which was quite convincing, didn't survive."

"So you saw just the one air base, is that right?" The Secretary of Defense asked.

"No sir, I spotted another new base some distance away, also well organized, with paved cross-wind runways and a control tower. I detected aircraft on the field, but the distance was too far to identify them, sir."

"You are experienced at observing air fields, are you?"

"Sir, I am. This mission was my twenty-third. I'm sure of what I saw."

George Marshall added, "Major Thomas is well thought of by his superiors. His Efficiency Reports always rate him highly," then he turned to Thomas, "Any of the aircraft Chinese?"

"Sir, the only aircraft I identified as to country of origin were the MiG-9s. If I may anticipate your next question, sir, I understand the differences in markings between the Soviet and Chinese air forces." He stood with his hands behind his back, unconsciously at Parade Rest.

General Marshall prodded, "Major, in your opinion, were these facilities temporary, consistent with forces on maneuvers?"

"No, sir, General Marshall. They're as permanent as they come. The base closest to us had concrete runways, sir, and many paved roads."

After a moment's silence, Truman said, "Any other questions for the Major? Very well. Major Thomas, I extend to you my most sincere condolences on the loss of your crew and my hearty congratulations on your promotion to Lieutenant Colonel."

The President reached for a box containing silver oak leaf emblems and pinned them onto the dumbfounded Thomas' uniform. *This'll show 'em I'm in agreement with him and not MacArthur.* "And here's something else I'm proud to award you, a Distinguished Flying Cross. Well done, Colonel." As the President finished pinning on the medal, applause rang throughout the room.

The flustered and surprised Thomas saluted the President. As the new Lieutenant Colonel was escorted from the Oval Office, Acheson asked in a firm voice: "Dr. Rathman, I repeat: Are you aware that what you told us contradicts General MacArthur's G-2? Why is that?"

"I'm sure I don't know, Mr. Secretary." After a tense moment, the CIA Director of the Far East Desk regained his composure. "In terms of ground forces, reports are mixed. The picture isn't clear yet. May be as many as ten divisions of Red Army troops. We haven't discovered who's in command. Several of the known units are well-trained, with combat veterans. New conscripts man the majority of the units, which are an unknown quantity, militarily."

The skepticism deepened on the faces in front of Rathman. *They don't believe me.* "Train loads of artillery tubes were moved in along with at least two hundred T-34 tanks. We haven't observed T-54 tanks yet. There are many trucks and Jeep-style vehicles, perhaps thousands, along with supply vehicles. In at least some cases, new rail lines were laid to bring in large quantities of ammo."

Some men's mouths tightened in a grimace, while others shook their heads from side to side. Rathman pressed on, "Turning to the Chinese, there are major movements with them as well. Since the take-over by the Communists, our intelligence gathering has fallen off, especially in the region south-west of the North Korean border, so this is more speculative: As many as twenty divisions of crack, combat-experienced troops, who are well-equipped with Russian arms, are being or have moved into assembly areas north of the North Korean border. Their complements of artillery and tanks are less than what we consider adequate. However, they are well-trained, disciplined troops led by highly competent generals. We consider them at least an equal threat as that posed by the Russians."

General Marshall's curt tone sliced through the tension, "Why do you believe they're equal to the Russians?"

Rathman replied in a low-pitched voice, "Because they defeated the Nationalist Chinese Army."

Secretary Johnson cleared his throat. "Go on."

"Lastly, the North Korean Army comprises about ten divisions, with little or no armor, and minimal artillery. They fought alongside the Chinese. They're almost as experienced as the Chinese. While their leadership is far less professional than the Russians or the Chinese, they're tough, resilient soldiers. Their air force has about 200 aircraft."

"This sounds pretty ominous to me." The President directed his question in the direction of the Army Chief of Staff. "What does MacArthur say?"

An awkward silence pervaded the room as General Marshall squirmed. He licked his lips in caution. "Mr. President, General McArthur's Chief of Staff, Colonel Willoughby, reports the North Koreans are no threat. He thinks the Chinese are doing 'maneuvers for effect.' Even if the North Koreans attack, he believes the Chinese don't dare do so. He says they're afraid of General MacArthur's forces. He didn't mention the Russians."

"I take it you don't agree with that assessment, General."

"Mr. President, I don't wish to cast aspersions on the commander on the scene. However, it appears to me the intelligence from General MacArthur's G-2 section is pretty benign in its implications." He hesitated. "This isn't scientific, sir, but my gut tells me that when potential enemies gather forces as large as what the CIA says, they aren't just for maneuvers or demonstrations."

The President shifted in his chair. "Do you think this Willoughby is downplaying the intelligence, then?"

"It feels that way, sir."

"What does MacArthur say?"

"General MacArthur informed us that he's too busy organizing his forces to take time to comment, sir. He refers all questions to Colonel Willoughby."

Truman stared at Marshall in stony silence. In a flinty, cold voice, the President commanded, "Send MacArthur a message that specifically demands *all* his intelligence, and *his* assessment. Identify the message as coming from me, a direct order."

"Yes, sir."

"Dr. Rathman, with Admiral Hillenkotter's agreement, I want a summary of everything you presented today on my desk tomorrow morning. Is that possible?"

Rathman glanced at his boss, who waved his hand in agreement.

"Yes, Mr. President."

CHAPTER 11

USS CABOT

Monday, 17 July 1950
NAS Ford Island, Pearl Harbor, Territory of Hawaii

Chappy made a smooth landing on runway 040 at NAS Ford Island in the center of Pearl Harbor, touching down on a dark airstrip, slick from a passing shower. They taxied to a hard stand. A flashlight-waving sailor in dungarees guided them to a halt.

The pungent scent of gasoline and the sea spoiled the fragrant aroma of orchids and other tropical flowers wafting in the warm, damp air. Nearby, sailors with a Navy airport tug and a tow bar waited to transport the Harpoon to the USS *Cabot*. Once a sour-faced Petty Officer convinced Joel that his men knew what they doing, Joel and his crew gathered their belongings and strolled toward the light aircraft carrier.

They hadn't walked twenty feet when a Navy Lieutenant in a sharp uniform stopped them. "Mr. Teach? Messrs. Chapman and Fontaigne? Mr. Smith sent me to escort you to *Cabot*."

Joel remembered that "Mr. Smith" was the local CIA chief.

The Lieutenant pointed to an awaiting, shiny Navy blue '48 Chevrolet sedan and then drove them to the ship looming over the dock. He led them to *Cabot*'s gangway and saluted the ship's flag and again in the direction of the Officer of the Deck (OOD). Turning to the Ensign at the desk, he said, "Lieutenant Fogerty with three visitors for Chief Conroy."

"Aye, aye, sir. Welcome aboard, gentlemen. The Chief will arrive shortly." The Ensign reached for a ship's phone.

Joel squirmed, knowing that military and Navy protocol required certain actions on his part when he boarded a U.S. Navy ship. Yet, he needed to conduct himself as a civilian. To quell his agitation, he said, "We request permission to come aboard, Ensign."

"Granted, sir,"

The dozens of shrouded Air Force F-84s crowding the huge deck impressed Joel. *I wonder where they're going to put our PV-2.*

A graying man with smile lines circling his eyes strode toward them. "Gentlemen, I'm Command Master Chief Conroy. Follow me, please. Watch your heads and knees as we pass through the bulkheads. The Captain is waiting. A sailor will take your bags to your stateroom."

※※※

"Gentlemen, welcome aboard *Cabot*. I'm Captain Franklin Seavers. This is my Exec, Lieutenant Commander Delron Van Greuter. Kindly introduce yourselves."

Joel introduced himself, as did Chappy and Cajun in turn.

Seavers, a no-nonsense man, said, "After the crew hoists your aircraft onboard, secures, and shrouds it, we'll depart. In the meantime, this conversation is Top Secret JUBILEE. Commander Van Greuter and I are briefed to your mission and know our parts." Seavers looked toward Lieutenant Commander Delron Van Greuter. "We are the only men aboard this ship, besides you, with such awareness. My crew will be curious about the aircraft and why you're aboard. You will answer *no* questions beyond your approved cover story. Furthermore, you will restrict yourselves to your assigned state room, the ward room, and the flight deck. If you need access elsewhere, you will contact either me or Commander Van Greuter, and we'll provide an escort. That is *not* negotiable. Understood?"

The three agreed in chorus.

"Gentlemen, I have work to attend to. The commander will brief you on our sailing plan." He exited the compartment, closing the door with an unmistakable clunk.

"OK, gents," Van Greuter said, "welcome aboard *Cabot*. We'll do all we can to make your trip comfortable and launch you safely. I prefer that you *do not* bother the Captain with any requests—contact me or Command Master Chief Conroy and we'll handle things, whatever they might be. I repeat: *do not* contact the Captain. Is that clear?"

Another chorus of "*Yes, sirs.*"

"Now, how are you gonna get that big bird off my deck without scattering parts from Hell to breakfast, Colonel?"

Joel said, "Well, Commander—"

"Call me Van."

"I'm Pirate. This is Chappy and Cajun. No ranks, we're civilians."

"Right."

Joel described the takeoff technique and the need for a line to be painted down the port side of the flight deck.

"Hmmm," Van squinched his eyes and scratched his head. "You practiced this, right?"

"Of course, on a painted deck on Moffett's runway. The technique will work even better if you give me about thirty knots from the ship."

"That's not a problem, Col—uh, Pirate. *Cabot* just came out of refit and her engines are in top shape. You want thirty knots, you got thirty knots. As the Captain said, we'll depart Pearl as soon as your bird is shipshape. The President is leaning on SECNAV [Secretary of the Navy], and *he's* putting pressure on COMPACFLT [Commander Pacific Fleet], so the clock's ticking for us to sail to Inchon Harbor, Korea. Our Intel is full of contradictions. The situation doesn't look good. So, we'll be doing an UNREP—that's Underway Replenishment. We'll only refuel and resupply with food when we arrive in Korea."

He pointed to the Captain's wall map. "It's about 3800 miles from Pearl to Inchon. The Captain will push her hard, at around twenty knots, except for the UNREP. Then we'll slow to about ten or twelve knots, depending on the tanker. Count on ten or eleven days, to be conservative. Then we'll off-load the F-84s, steam into the Bay of Korea, and the Gulf of Chihli, and launch you. What are your preferred launch coordinates?"

Cajun said, "38 degrees 21 minutes North, 120 degrees 30 minutes East. Dat's 'bout 750 miles from Baotou, easy range for our plane, OK?"

"Let's see," Van spread out a maritime map of the Gulf of Chihli, also known as Bo Hai. "We'll need to watch for shallows." His finger moved around the map. "Yeah, shouldn't be a problem. It's a busy seaway, mostly little guys who'll give us a wide berth."

The USS *Cabot* cast off her lines and maneuvered with majestic ease around Ford Island, down the eastern passage, past the rusting hulk of the destroyed USS *Arizona*. An oily sheen lay atop the quiet water. In an act of defiance, a U.S. flag flew from the sunken wreckage. Solemn sailors in dress white uniforms lined the edge of *Cabot*'s flight deck and rendered salutes to the more than 1100 entombed Americans who lost their lives on board her nine years before. Joel rendered his own salute with a deep sense of reverence. This indeed, was a place for reflection and remembrance.

Clear of the harbor, *Cabot* rounded the south end of Maui. When she and her escorts gained open sea, the Captain gave the order and the big ship accelerated, headed toward her rendezvous with fleet oiler USS *Caloosahatchee*, AO-98.

CHAPTER 12

PREPARATIONS

Pyotr Yakov Borodin, Starshina [Sergeant Major], Army of the Union of Soviet Socialist Republics, scrutinized his new charges with suspicion as the conscripts surged into the train station annex. *They're so young. Despite their enthusiasm, they look like peasant farm boys.*

Their summer uniform with raspberry-colored collar piping, indicated their military branch: infantry. After nearly a decade in the Soviet army, the former U.S. Army sergeant lived his covert cover persona as naturally as he breathed.

Not an intimidating group. They'll frighten only old ladies and children. Thirty-eight men and the sole NCO's are two Yefrejtors [corporals] and one Mladshiy Sergeant [junior sergeant, the second-lowest, non-commissioned officer ranking]. Borodin's crossed, muscled arms, partially hid the double row of medals pinned on his uniform.

Sergeant Major Borodin scanned the men's chests for medals. Three sported sharpshooter medals. Only one man displayed the mortar specialist badge for grenade launcher proficiency. The rest? No awards.

No qualified machine gunners. Hmmm. The Mladshiy Sergeant wears a Party badge. He's the Politruk, the Party stooge. He bears special watching.

A tinge of sorrow tightened his throat. *I know only too well how combat treats the inexperienced and veterans alike. Their fates are surely sealed. Most will not survive. And those who do will bear scars on their bodies and their souls.* He pushed aside the images of lost American comrades flashing though his mind to avoid the pain. *Well, if there's a bright side to this sad display, my task will be easier with such inexperience. They'll never know their unwitting part in this act of international intrigue. A pitiful looking bunch. I hope my officers look better.*

They didn't.

A pair of frazzled lieutenants slouched into the transportation center with an unshaven major wearing a soiled, wrinkled uniform. His graying hair and dark, puffy bags under his dulled eyes revealed seniority well beyond the "mandatory" retirement age of 60. As he limped across the stone floor, a ragged shout of "Attention," echoed across the room.

Borodin inspected the lieutenants. *These men are no youths. Facial wrinkles etch their brows and sprinklings of gray hair speak volumes about their incompetency. I must be careful with these three.*

In the Soviet Army, the concept of a professional non-commissioned officer corps, common in armies throughout the world, remained unknown. Many Red Army officers didn't know what to do with men of Borodin's unusual, new rank. Lieutenants often performed the duties expected of non-coms in the American Army.

As they straggled closer, Borodin noted the telltale signs of recent heavy drinking—pasty complexions, bloodshot eyes, sullen expressions. The major and his two lieutenants appeared hung over.

Good. When the time is right, they'll be drunk again. The Politruk Sergeant fell in behind the officers, striding forcefully, as if their equal.

Standing at attention and saluting with practiced precision, Borodin said, "Comrade Major, I am Sergeant Major Borodin, at your orders, sir. The men are assembling. I haven't called the roll yet. Our equipment has arrived and is reasonably complete."

"Da, this is good, Comrade Sergeant Major Borodin. Assemble the men." His words tumbled out like gravel pouring from a dump truck.

Borodin bellowed, "Attention. Form ranks, now."

With a curt dip of his head, the Major acknowledged Borodin, then spoke to the men. "Comrades, my name is Major Vladik Gorshun. These are Lieutenants Sergeyev and Shirokii. Together, we will escort our brave Socialist scientists to the East to perform tests of their equipment to the glory of the Soviet Union. You will protect the scientists from all threats." The monotonic delivery of his command betrayed the fact that he expected none. "You will follow the orders of Lieutenants Sergeyev and Shirokii *and* Sergeant Major Borodin as if they came from me. You will be informed when our train will depart. Call the roll, Borodin." As he and the two Lieutenants ambled off, Borodin glanced sideways at the Mladshiy Sergeant. *Nobody likes Party snitches.*

As was the custom, Borodin called the roll in order of rank, beginning with the smug-faced Party Sergeant, who answered too quickly as he cold-stared Bordin through narrowed eyes. Borodin ignored him and proceeded down the roll. To his great relief and small amazement, everyone was present.

"Comrades, this trip will be long. I intend to conduct frequent weapon drills and reviews of Standard Orders. There will be live fire practice as the situation permits. There—"

The Party Sergeant interrupted. "There will be also daily lessons in Party Doctrine and Communist theory as well as—"

"Silence, *Mladshiy Sergeant*. You will wait until I finish speaking." *Thank you for giving me the opportunity to establish my authority.*

The Party Sergeant reddened and spoke again, "I was . . . ."

"Did I not make myself clear, *Mladshiy* Sergeant? Or must I impress upon you that *I am Sergeant Major*?" Borodin raised his voice and clenched his huge fist above his head. Violence from senior non-coms remained common in the Red Army. Borodin knew he could easily take the small-framed Party official.

I've knocked a few heads in my time. Putting the runt in his place now will make dealing with the other men much easier later on.

Borodin thrust his chest out, but resisted the urge to step toward the man. "*Do I?*" His booming command imperative reverberated off the walls.

"No, Sergeant Major. I was merely performing my duties as Party representative and—"

"Party or not, you *will* observe proper military courtesy in my presence. Is that clear, Comrade Mladshiy Sergeant?"

The party stooge gritted his teeth and glared straight ahead. Some men raised their eye brows and stared wide-eyed at Borodin, who recognized he'd made his point. *He* was in charge.

CHAPTER 13

DELAYED

Tuesday, 18 July 1950
Train Marshaling Yards, Moscow, USSR

Sergeant Major Pyotr Borodin smacked his right fist into his left palm in frustration. Their train formed up. His troops boarded, only to disembark and told to wait—again.

We're a full day behind schedule and haven't even left the vast Moscow train yards. Sweat stained the underarms of his uniform. *At this rate, I'll never meet the CIA team on time, or hand over my scientist, or inform the CIA team we're late.*

To distract his troops, he "supervised" as they checked their gear, cleaned weapons, and exercised. He watched over them as they ate. He stopped fights and harassed them just enough to take their minds off the delays.

As he surveyed the huge train yard, his take on the extended lines of flatcars loaded with military freight alarmed him. *T-34 tanks, no T-54s. Some T-34K Command tanks with dual antennas—that means the advanced R-113 radios. And hundreds of boxcars. Those segregated cars carry ammo and there are hundreds of them. I've never seen so many passenger cars, even some converted from boxcars. They could hold ten or twelve divisions. This is no exercise. What's happening?* His scientists and their tests faded in importance. *And everything is headed east. Korea?*

Finally, they re-boarded. He took roll, satisfied all his men were aboard, although several were far from sober. He scarcely finished when the train lurched. A small cheer rose from the men. He glared, stopping their ragged chorus.

The wheels clattered, as the train bounced over rough tracks for three hours, then slowed with a jerk. They screeched over a rusty switch and rattled as they shunted onto a weed-infested siding. A long train of tank-laden flatcars thundered past. Two Russian steam locomotives with trailing black smoke worked hard to pull the heavy load.

Eighty-seven cars. That's a long train even for the steppes. What'll they do when they arrive at the eastern hills? On the other hand, maybe that's why there are two engines. Hmmm. Haven't seen that before. He collected much Intel to reveal to the CIA.

Twice that day, they waited on a siding as trains loaded with weapons and troops rumbled past them, knotting Borodin's stomach. Night approached as he supervised the evening meal cleanup. Leaving a Corporal in charge, he went to the scientist's car. *I need to be sure he'll go through with this.*

✕✕✕

"I'm Sergeant Major Borodin, the contact you expected, Comrade Doctor," the man in the Soviet Army uniform said in an undertone. He bent over and looked into Kalugin's startled eyes, "The code word is *snowflake.*"

Dr. Ilya Kalugin's eyes dilated spooked by the Red Army man speaking to him. "You? But—but, you are Army."

"Did you think I would wear a khaki trench coat?"

Dr. Ilya Kalugin shifted in his seat and uncrossed his arms, then said, "Oh, the counterword is *feral.*"

"When the time arrives, I will inform you. The material is secure in your briefcase, and you are ready, yes?"

"Yes, it is all there, ready to kill me," Kalugin said.

Borodin smiled with confidence. "Do not worry, Comrade Doctor. Soon you shall leave behind all the glories of the Communist Motherland."

Kalugin grunted and turned away dismissing him.

Sergeant Major Borodin latched the door. The other scientists gathered around Kalugin.

"What did that soldier want, Ilya Kalugin? Was he NKVD?" They all feared NKVD, the original Soviet secret police.

"Nyet, not NKVD," Kalugin said, his voice tight. "Do not worry."

Ana Bakhtina—short, sturdy, and round-faced—looked at him with narrowed eyes. She'd known Kalugin for many years and shared the most difficult Soviet nuclear program problems with him.

"I know you almost as well as your wife, Ilya Kalugin. You are hiding something. What?"

"Da, I agree with Ana, Doctor. Your behavior gives you away. Valena Tumanova's direct approach distracted Kalugin more than her incredible beauty. I think you are hiding something important from us. What?" Light and graceful in her movements, Valena's nickname "The Ballerina" fit within days of joining his group.

The Ballerina has three great advantages in this world: great beauty, great intellect, and powerful connections. Still, I trust her after these years.

Kalugin glanced at their gifted technician, Dushkin. *Is Dushkin listening?* As usual, he stood aloof. His deadpan eyes missed nothing. Everyone else encircled Kalugin.

Konstantin Yasha Dushkin—what a mystery. So competent, yet quiet and separate, secretive.

To survive in a clandestine world, only a tiny number of scientists in the Soviet Union held the knowledge they knew. Yet, this whole different kind of secret could forever change his life—and theirs. With caution, Berthold chose his words, knowing deep in his gut that if any one betrayed him, he'd die. In a low, quiet tone, he explained, "The Americans are going to rescue me."

Astonishment rippled through the atmosphere. Dushkin's mouth sagged open. His raised eyebrows frowned above his wide-eyed stare. He stepped even further away from the group.

"This is wonderful," Dr. David Yetkatov exclaimed, then lowered his voice, "I must go also."

The others echoed Yetkatov's words. They all wanted to escape their tyrannical enslavement.

The scientists chattered quietly with excitement, intoxicated by the prospect of freedom—real freedom.

Dushkin shouldered his way into their circle, and planted both feet on floor, with feet and legs splayed out. Blood drained from Berthold's face. Gasps of fear escaped the scientists' gaping mouths as they stepped away from Dushkin.

Dushkin raised his hand. Berthold's shoulders cringed and his hands covered his face. The other scientists turned their heads and in unison crossed their arms over their chests.

Konstantin Dushkin spoke in a quiet, humble tone, "Perhaps—perhaps in America, instead of being forced to report to the KGB, I can obtain a real university degree and move above my role of technician." His eyes beamed with optimism.

As with one breath, all the scientists heaved sighs of relief. A fiery spark of hope glimmered in Dr. Heinz Berthold's eyes. "Such an audacious plan. Only Americans could dream such an exploit. Only Americans can make it reality. Such an opportunity will never come again. I must try to escape, even if the cost is—"

"You dropped these, Doctor." Berthold gazed into the smiling face of Ana Bakhtina, who held out a sheaf of his papers. As he reached for them, their hands touched. An electrical charge buzzed through Berthold's body.

Her touch was not accidental. Thanks to his deformities, women rejected him his entire life.

"Thank you." A warm red glow flushed his cheeks and ears.

"You are, of course, so very welcome." She shot him a broad smile, and turned to glide away. With a flirtatious glance over her shoulder, she winked at him. Again.

A puddle of emotions, Berthold watched Ana glissade away with balletic grace. *Her smile could liquefy a glacier.*

The unflappable German engineer who confronted senior Nazi and Soviet officials with boldness, backing down from none, stared nonplused as Ana sashayed down the aisle of the railway car.

Never has a colleague treated me so.

CHAPTER 14

ON TO INCHON

Sunday, 23 July 1950
Aboard USS *Cabot*, six days out from Hawaii

Joel surprised himself by adapting quickly to the ship's motions in the gentle Pacific. Chappy, on the other hand, suffered from seasickness—dizziness and nausea. Cold sweat beaded on Chappy's pale skin reflected a waxy discontent.

He's no sailor. Joel felt compassion for his friend.

An impeccably uniformed ensign entered the ward room and spoke to Joel. "Mr. Teach, our chief of aircraft maintenance requests permission to inspect your aircraft, sir. We'll verify your ship is in tip-top shape. Is that OK, sir?"

Joel smiled at the eager young Ensign. *I'll bet an inspection was his idea.* "Why, yes, of course, Ensign. Let me know if you find anything unusual."

An hour later, a Petty Officer Second Class in work dungarees entered the ward room. His eyes squinted, scanning the ward room. His pursed lips expressed intentness. "Mr. Teach?"

Joel raised his coffee cup. "Over here, Petty Officer."

"Sir, when we checked the number one magneto on your left engine, it acted kind of strange. May we have permission to test it in our shop? Did you experience any problems coming across from San Francisco?"

"Both engines ran perfectly. What do you think is the problem?"

"Sir, I suspect minor, internal short circuiting. That happens sometimes. If the magneto is too hot, the lacquer insulation breaks down. We can wind you a new armature if that's what's needed."

"Yes, OK. What else will you do?"

"The Chief says to change the engine oil, check all the hydraulic cylinders for leaks, fill the hydraulic accumulator, air the tires, and charge the batteries. Just like a *Phillips 66* station back home, sir."

Joel chuckled at the image. "Don't forget to wash the windshield."

"We'll wash the entire aircraft, sir," the Petty Officer replied with a serious tone, "after we strip off the cocooning. Chief Conroy says that'll remove the salt spray. 'Course, that'll be after we depart Inchon. I'll let you know how things are going."

"Well, well," said Cajun with a glint of humor in his eyes. "Somebody's really t'inkin' dis t'ing through. Salt spray could give us away, ya know?"

CHAPTER 15

TOP SECRET

Tuesday, 25 July 1950
Tehran, Iran, CIA Headquarters Briefing Room

Four silent men, unfamiliar to each other, occupied a single row of chairs facing Bruce Harrell, CIA Deputy Chief of Station. He'd interviewed each man in private. *Each man is a professional, serious, dedicated, able to kill if he must. Just what we need.*

"Welcome aboard, gents. I remind you that *everything* you hear in this room is Top Secret. If you leak anything, to anybody, at any time, we *will* find you and we will *punish* you." Harrell fired a hard stare at them. "That means 'termination with extreme prejudice'."

No one flinched.

"OK. Project JUBILEE. That name is classified, do *not* repeat it. The unclassified name is BASKET. Your team leader is James 'JD' Derek Monroe."

A thirtyish man of moderate height, curly dark brown hair, and piercing brown eyes leaned against the wall and waved acknowledgement. With a broad grin on his handsome face, JD said, "Gentlemen."

"To JD's right is Bailey Sinclair Lowell Harrison III."

"Call me Felix," the sturdy man said with a faint New England accent.

Harrell continued, "JD is an ex-Army NCO, 10th Mountain Division; has a Bronze Star and three Purple Hearts. He's fluent in five languages and understands several more. He's an old hand at infiltration missions into Russia. Felix: 101st Airborne, ten combat jumps. He's a jack-of-all-trades and master of several. He's the go-to guy for problem-solving."

The door burst open. A man strode with urgent steps toward Harrell. He bent down and whispered in his ear.

Harrell tilted his head, then spoke to the four men seated in front of him. "Sorry. Something's come up. JD and Felix will brief you on the plane. Collect your gear. Meet them at the airport tomorrow morning at 0400. Dismissed."

CHAPTER 16

EXTRACTION TEAM

Wednesday, 26 July 1950, 0400 Hours
Mehrabad Air Field, Tehran, Iran

The extraction team waited on grass beside the tarmac. A long narrow sliver of the sun's golden orange lined the dawn's night blue sky. Each man carried a duffle bag loaded with clothes, rations, and personal equipment. Their canvas weapon bags concealed their weapons and five hundred rounds of ammo.

Felix bore two duffels and an enigmatic smile. Although a light load for the aircraft, the copilot weighed each man and his luggage. Civilian planes required this procedure, plus they needed to maintain their cover.

The off-white, pre-War Douglas DC-2 carried fictitious *New China Airline* markings. When the men clambered inside, they found a large rubber fuel tank mounted on the floor.

JD said, "CIA souped this up with bigger engines to climb over the mountains. Our cover story is we're archeologists on a charter flight to Ulaan Baatar, Mongolia. They'll drop us as close as possible to where we need to be."

The sturdy DC-2 clattered out of Tehran airport on smooth air and into the pre-dawn, inky blue sky. It banked northeast toward the burst of golden-red seeping above the horizon. The smells of oil, raw gasoline, lubricating fluids, sweat, and unwashed men pervaded the aircraft's interior.

The forward portion of the passenger compartment contained 12 seats. JD and Felix sat on opposite sides of the aisle, as the other men found their seats behind them.

They motioned the man sitting behind them to come and kneel in the aisle between them as they reviewed his dossier.

Felix read: *Reginald Harrison Symthe III, nickname Reggie. Ex-Warrant officer, His Majesty's Royal Fusiliers, and SAS. Explosives expert. Can operate and immobilize American-made Russian steam locomotives.*

"Good day to you, sir," Reggie, a slender, fair-haired man, said with an English accent. His flamboyant, bushy mustache presided over a broad grin, exposing the gap in his teeth. Smile lines radiated from his clear blue eyes.

"So, Reggie, ever worked with C-3?" Felix asked, referring to the RDX-based plastic explosive developed by the U.S. after the war.

"Yes, sir. I've more experience with good old Explosive 808, of course, and the odd dynamite exercise. Not to worry, sir, SAS trained me on C-3 and other unpleasant surprise packages."

"Ah, yes, 808—smells like almonds. You had a problem once?" He pointed to Reggie's left hand which was missing his little finger and the top joint of his ring finger.

"Had a bit of a fright with a precocious Italian grenade. Things could've been worse, old boy. That's why they mustered me out of the Fusiliers, you see. Hasn't encumbered me."

"American locomotives? What's that story?"

Reggie leaned toward JD. The outer edges of Reggie's mustache twitched with his smirk. "SAS laid on an op in '47 that needed a Russian loco immobilized on the QT, right in the Moscow train yards. Sent me to Baldwin Locomotive Works in Philadelphia, and made me an expert on the so-called Decapod engines, the 2-10-0 arrangement. The Tsar bought hundreds of them from the Americans, you know, and the Russians still use them, especially on Trans-Siberian routes."

Felix leaned back, "Any medical training?"

Reggie's eyebrows flashed up, then down. "Only the odd combat first aid, learnt by hard experience. Nothing formal."

"Good enough. Please return to your seat," Felix dismissed him.

A second man, who moved with powerful, lethal grace, kneeled in the aisle vacated by Reggie.

Felix read his dossier: *'John Smith.' Yeah, right. Nickname 'Smitty.' A former French Foreign Legionnaire. An expert on Russian weapons.*

Smith's enormous, muscular torso loomed over Felix. His hands looked like they could crush granite. Sporting short, military-style hair, Smith asked in a French-North African accent, "How do you do?"

"Done any sniping, Mr. Smith?" Felix asked over the roaring engines.

A wide smile divided Smitty's dark-tanned face, exposing gleaming white teeth.

"Which weapons?"

"Russian Mosin-Nagant, American-made version's best. Lee-Enfield; Ross-Canadian, good rifle; M1903 Springfield; M1917 Springfield; M1C sniper."

"The engines . . . " Felix pointed to his left ear. "Louder, please. Is the M1C a variation of the M1 Garand?"

"Yes. Not known widely. The .30-06 round's better than .303."

JD liked Smitty's taciturn answers. *Mr. Smith prefers action to words.*

"Any medical experience, Mr. Smith?"

"Combat surgeon's assistant."

"I like your style, Mr. Smith. Glad you joined us. Return to your seat."

A slight smile flickered across Smitty's lips. With the quiet grace and stealthy ease of a black, prowling jaguar, he slunk toward his chair.

JD read the dossier on the next man: *Tom Long: ex-U.S. Army*

*NCO, college grad, history major. With Patton through Europe.
Good at organization and logistics. Umm, we'll need to control that
carefully on this mission. Difficult to re-supply in Russia.*

JD motioned for Tom Long to come forward. A handsome,
brown-haired man, JD watched Tom shuffled up the aisle. *Do I detect
a slight limp?*

"Good morning, JD. A pleasure to meet you," Long's erect posture
and strong baritone voice reflected confidence as he took a knee
beside JD.

"You were with Patton at the Battle of the Bulge?"

"Lost some good friends there."

"So did a lot of us, I'm sorry to say . . . you were wounded." Felix
stated the question as a fact.

"Yes, shrapnel in my right upper leg. Not a problem."

"How do you lead a patrol?" JD asked.

Long's intense gaze and answer was immediate. "The only way,
sir—from the front."

"Thank you. Dismissed."

The last man, Murphy McGregor, strolled toward JD with insolent
ease.

"Sir," Murph waved a salute as the noisy airplane bumped in a
desert thermal.

JD motioned him to sit as he perused the man's dossier. *Murphy
'Murph' McGregor, Captain, USMC. Flew F6Fs in the Pacific until
some Jap flak put a piece of Plexiglas in his right eye. Says he sees
OK, but the Marines grounded him. His real assets are his radio skills.
An expert on Russian radios and ours. He'll operate the customized
SCR-284(c) Shortwave radio to stay in contact with home.*

"Do you consider yourself a successful pilot, Murph?" JD asked.

"I have six kills, if that's what you mean." Murph leaned forward
like a predatory animal. "I wanted more."

Six kills. He's an ace. Less than ten percent of pilots in the Pacific gained that distinction.

"Are you current?"

Suspicion flashed in Murph's eyes. "I flew last week. Why?"

"We need to know all our people's skills. What'd you fly?"

"A CIA C-47. Yes, I'm current."

"Hmmm," Felix examined the pages on his lap. "Radios. How did you become an expert?"

Murph's eyes brightened. "I messed with radios as a kid in Michigan. When I was ten, I built a crystal set. Dad gave me a Hallicrafters kit on my thirteenth birthday. I built it and it was working in a week. I've been an active ham ever since, except for the war and missions, of course."

"What's your equipment and call sign?"

"A Hallicrafters Super Skyrider SX-28 receiver and a souped-up HT-4 transmitter. My call sign is K8QLNQ."

"What about single side band? How's your code?"

"I can work SSB. My code's a bit rusty. With practice, I could do thirty, forty words a minute."

"Do you speak Russian?" JD interjected.

The question caught Murph off guard. "I have enough problems speaking American. I can say 'vodka, stroganoff, and borscht.' A hint of a wry smile tugged at the left side of Murph's lip. "I do understand a little Russian."

"Thanks, Murph, a guy can hope. Please ask the others to join us."

Finished with the dossiers, JD stood and shouted over the engines, "If anybody has second thoughts after I explain the Project JUBILEE mission, you'll be put off at Tashkent and held incommunicado until the mission is over. Understand?"

All four men nodded their agreement.

"All right, here's the deal. We're going to illegally invade Russia, intercept a Trans-Siberian Railways train above Mongolia, and kidnap a scientist. He's defecting, but the Ruskies won't see it that way. If you're caught, you'll be tortured and imprisoned, if you're not shot first. So don't get caught.

"This scientist is *very* important. The Ruskies will not take kindly to our liberating him. In all likelihood, half the Soviet army will chase us, to say nothing of the friendly GRU and the KGB.

"Once we've rescued the scientist, we'll transport him to Hami, in Western China, where Americans flying a modified Navy bomber will meet us. They'll fly him to safety, along with me and Felix. You will escape however you can. I recommend returning to Iran ASAP, which means stealing an airplane. That's why Murph's along. Treat him nice, fellas. He's your ticket home. Questions?" JD asked.

After a moment, John Smith spoke. "That's a complex plan, over a great distance. How do we talk to the train to know where is it? How'll we tell the plane if we're late or are injured?"

"That's what Murph's custom radio is for. If the plan runs off kilter, our people, who are listening, will help us."

Silence reigned in the airplane, as the men stared at JD. Military radios held a reputation for being fragile. If this one broke, they'd be cut off.

Tom Long's rigid fingers and thumbs tapped together. "So, this important scientist is our main goal. Will he carry any baggage— papers or parts of a machine, anything like that?"

JD said, "That's perceptive, Tom. Yes, he's bringing papers and it's imperative anything he carries escapes. He's the most important person you'll ever meet. His life is worth more than yours or mine. He *must* survive. Protect him at all costs."

Long interjected, "Is he willing to leave? If he fights us, that'll make this mission a lot more difficult."

"He's willing. He can't back out."

Reggie's finger stroked his bushy mustache. "I say, do we know what sort of protection this chap likely has? Are we facing a company? A platoon? Body guards? Do we have anyone on board the train?"

"The train left Moscow with around twenty, green regular Red Army troops," Felix said. "The NCO in charge is undercover CIA. He'll incapacitate the troops and help with the escape." It was rare to expect inside help and Felix scrutinized the men's reactions.

"One more question," Long said. "You implied timing is critical. Tell us more."

"That's why we left this morning," JD explained. "We must meet the train at a specific location, where it slows for a steep grade. If we miss that rendezvous, the problem becomes a lot harder."

The men settled back in their seat as the plane climbed over the intervening mountains. A few hours later in Tashkent, the DC-2 made a smooth landing.

"Stretch your bones, boys, and grab some lunch," the pilot instructed, "while I pay off Customs and buy gas. I expect to take an hour."

Sixty minutes later, the white transport and waves of heat lifted off the blistering runway. The DC-2 with fictitious *New China Airline* markings bumped through desert thermals eastward, bound for Hami, China.

JD entered the cabin from the cockpit. "We're making decent time, boys," he shouted over the engines. "We'll arrive in Hami in about six hours. We'll stay overnight. The next leg will be rough 'cause we'll proceed north, real low over the mountains. They'll set us down in a field somewhere. Once we land, I'll 'procure' transportation to head toward the rendezvous."

CHAPTER 17

INCHON HARBOR

Wednesday, 26 July 1950
Aboard USS Cabot

Under the watchful eye of Captain Seavers, the helmsman steered USS *Cabot* into the west coast port of Inchon Harbor, Korea. With huge tidal surges twice a day, and a long, shallow channel, passage into the harbor was tricky.

Moments after *Cabot* passed through the narrow harbor entrance, the powerful handmaidens of the port chugged toward the *Cabot*. Two Type V tugs maneuvered her toward the scarce dock space and docked her.

The odd mixture of the sea, diesel fuel, old fish, rotting food, and night soil wafted over Joel and his men. These strange smells, their first impression of an Asian city, irritated their throats.

Despite cool temperatures in the mid 50's, the deck swarmed with busy sailors wearing white T-shirts and blue dungarees. They offloaded the F-84s. On the dock, another team in green Air Force fatigues waited with the ground support equipment.

"Look at that," Chappy pointed. A dockside crane hoisted a large net of food and provision boxes high over the deck, lowering them to waiting sailors. Within minutes, the ballet was performed several times with the smoothness born of experience. Before half of the F-84s were lowered to the dock, most of the provisioning was complete.

Olive drab tractor-like, airport tugs towed all the cocooned F-84s through city streets. Encased in white shrouds, the long line of slow-moving aircraft resembled mechanical mummies trailing behind the tugs.

Cajun pointed aft. "Say, look, dey're movin' our ship." A team of sailors rolled the PV-2 forward by hand to the center of the deck. "Guess dey can work on it easier."

"They couldn't work on the right wing because it was hanging over the edge of the deck," Joel observed. "These Navy guys have their act together. Since we came aboard, they've been on top of things. Kind of gives you confidence, doesn't it?"

"Yeah, well, let's hope their engine shop knows what they're doing," Chappy grumped. "If we lose an engine on the way, it's a long, cold swim."

CHAPTER 18

GULF OF CHIHLI

Saturday, 29 July 1950
Aboard USS *Cabot*

Under cloudy skies and a rolling sea, two escorting destroyers and the *USS Cabot* steamed out of Inchon Harbor, then angled southwest. The wooden flight deck vibrated under Joel, Cajun, and Chappy's feet as the ship's speed accelerated.

During their dock-side time, Chappy recovered and wasn't too thrilled about heading back to sea. Joel watched Chappy's complexion, but it didn't change to that greenish hue like before.

Command Master Chief Conroy joined Joel at the railing. "When you have a few moments, sir, we have a brief from the weather shop waiting for you. Looks like it will be a pretty clear day for your launch, but I need the meteorologist to tell you that."

"Let's go," Joel waved toward Chappy and Cajun.

They followed Conroy to the weather shop. A youthful lieutenant walked up to Joel to give the weather briefing. "Sir, as often happens after a typhoon, the seas will be gentle the next couple of days, including your launch day. The barometric pressure is high and the skies should clear. Speaking in general terms, the weather moving down from Siberia is benign this time of year. As we move closer, I'll give you a better forecast, though I doubt I'll tell you anything a lot different from today."

"Any idea about what winds we might see, Lieutenant? I'd sure like about twenty to twenty-five knots over the bow."

"Too soon to say for sure, sir. There's a good likelihood we can obtain at least ten or fifteen knots."

"Every bit helps."

Cajun entered the compartment. "I jus' finished talkin' to da ship's navigator. Nice guy. Taught his Annapolis instructor, ya know? He says no problem puttin' us right on da launch point day after tomorrow 'bout 0800. If dis beautiful weather holds, we lookin' good."

"Excellent. Chappy, are you satisfied with the shape the plane's in?" Joel asked.

"Aw, you know you can never be too ready. I ran-up both engines yesterday and nit-picked every detail about the aircraft's readiness. The sailors adjusted and tuned every item I found. If those swabbies polish that bird any more, they'll rub through the paint." His brows furrowed into a worried wrinkle. "I'm afraid if something goes wrong while we're in China, we can't fix it. God knows, we sure don't want to get stuck in China."

"Yeah," Joel agreed. "Not sure the State Department can do much, with all the anti-colonialism that triggered the Communist Revolution. This isn't a good time to be American guys with no way home."

They had to trust the Navy mechanics' word that the airplane was mechanically sound. To be sure no crew-related problem could cause a forced landing, Joel and his crew spent hours poring over the charts and graphs in the pilot's manual.

"If something goes south, we must react immediately. We won't have time to look anything up. We have one shot at doing this right, guys," Joel stressed. "The whole mission depends on putting this tin bird in the air."

Working with paint-splashed guides, the ship's crew painted the line to follow for takeoff. In less than an hour, the arrow-straight, foot-wide line stretched down the deck.

At the urging of the Air Boss, Joel reviewed his takeoff plans with the flight deck crew. The "tail up" takeoff process amazed the sailors.

One sailor commented, "I sure hope the water's not rough, sir. You might have a hard time keeping the props from hitting the deck."

"Man, you gonna need ta keep dat ol' bird in a straight line, boss." Cajun laughed.

"Isn't that the truth," Joel said. "Like a camel passing through the eye of a needle."

"Dere's a fact," Chappy agreed.

The launch officer turned toward Joel. "Your aircraft will be offset to port, sir. I'll stand to the starboard side of the plane." He pointed at Chappy. "That means you, sir, as copilot, will take my 'release brakes' signal, not the pilot. I'll time the rise and fall of the ship's bow and estimate how long it will take to reach the forward end of the deck."

They couldn't practice an actual takeoff. Based only on the launch officer's judgment, Joel worried about this takeoff more than any since his first Army solo.

With years of training and teaching, Cajun attempted to boost Joel's spirit. "Ya trained us to a razor's edge, Joel. Dis plane is fine-tuned. Ya done all y'all can. Da res' is in God's hands. Trust Him, man."

"Only God can help us now."

CHAPTER 19

THE REPORT

The Kremlin, Moscow, USSR, Office of the Deputy Chairman
Sunday, 30, July 1950

Yabitov entered Beria's office. As if rubber replaced his backbone, Yabitov's spine bowed low in feigned respect.

"Stand up, Yabitov," Beria ordered. "What have you to report? What of Kim's claims that he'll drive the U.S. Army into the sea in shame and the South Koreans will rise up to welcome his army?"

"You were right, of course, Comrade Beria. Kim over-estimates both himself and his army. They are experienced fighters worn down by years of fighting Chiang Kai-shek's nationalists. They are well equipped with Russian rifles, machine guns, and mortars, but possess few artillery tubes, virtually no tanks, and a borrowed air force. If Kim achieves complete surprise, they *might* make some gains against the Americans, who are a shadow of their greatness in the Great War.

"I estimate that unless Kim's army quickly wins *complete* victory, the Americans will reinforce, bring in vast numbers of troops and aircraft, and defeat him. We must remember the American MacArthur is there. A formidable enemy, as you often say."

Beria yielded a grudging acknowledgement to only two American generals: Douglas MacArthur and George Patton. Both American Presidents, Roosevelt and Truman, forestalled MacArthur and Patton's desires to expand the war, reinforcing Beria's belief: Americans have no belly for a real fight.

CHAPTER 20

OFF TO CHINA

Sunday, 30 July 1950
Airborne

Joel, Chappy, and Cajun chowed down a hearty breakfast, then carried their gear and coffee and box lunches provided by the mess cooks to the plane. Like himself, Joel noticed his crew slept poorly. Chappy fussed over the fuel and oil. Cajun checked and rechecked his charts.

Everything was ready.

The ship's weatherman gave them good news. "Sirs, the seas are calm, with winds out of the north north-west at about seven knots, gusts to fifteen. Winds aloft are also north north-west at about thirty-five knots. Scattered clouds occurring at 10,000 to 12,000 feet are fair weather clouds. You'll have a smooth flight to Peking."

"Very good." Joel resisted saying they weren't going to Peking. The three went to the flight deck to wait for the ship to arrive at the launch location.

"*Cabot'll* be in position in about fifteen minutes, sir. The Captain would like to see you."

Joel waited on the bridge for Captain Seavers. The man graced him with a smile. "Well, good luck to you and your crew, Mr. Teach. I trust the ship's company treated you well?"

"We couldn't have asked for more, Captain. I'm sure you'll be glad to be rid of us."

"This has been an unusual experience for *Cabot*, one we'll long remember, even if we can't talk about it. God speed, sir." The Captain grabbed Joel's hand in his palm and squeezed it with strong grip.

A tinny loudspeaker announced, "Pilot and crew, man your aircraft." Joel and his men strode to the plane with parachutes slapping their backsides. The gleaming white Typhoon rested at the far aft end of the deck with the tailwheel only feet from the stern.

The day before, a skilled sailor painted an Iranian Imperial crest on each rudder, and repainted the Iranian registration number EP-ZED on the fuselage sides with the Farsi equivalent below.

On the bridge, Captain Seavers issued his orders: "Officer of the Deck, bring her into the wind. Full speed ahead."

"Aye, aye, sir, into the wind, full speed ahead."

Chief Conroy insisted they wear life vests, no matter how stiff and awkward. "If you splash that thing, we want to pluck your sorry butts out of the water in one piece. If we let you drown, it's bad for ship's morale, you know."

Joel noticed blank spaces where the ship's name and 'U.S. Navy' were removed from the vests. *It's that 'non-attribution' thing. If we crash, the Chinese can't tell how we arrived. Isn't that comforting?*

The seas remained low, with few white caps. The bow rose and sank with stately rhythm. In the air was the clean, clear, salt smell only found at sea. Hyperaware, Joel noticed the oil stains and tire marks on the wooden deck appeared stark, rougher—more vivid. The painted line gleamed ruler-straight, white and bright. Sweat moistened his palms and armpits. The big moment loomed only minutes away.

Curious sailors gathered to watch, anticipating a spectacular show. Joel noticed Chappy's mission-focused quietness. No gloomy comments this morning.

Chappy knows everything must be done right. Cajun's unflappable. Guess he's used to the flight deck crew doing the worrying. His work starts after we're airborne.

The Navy deck crew performed a walk-around. Chappy and Joel performed their own meticulous inspection. No one took offense: Their lives were on the line. As they finished, the ship completed its turn. The wind blew in gusts down the deck. *The weatherman delivered on his promise.*

Once in the cockpit, Joel strapped in. The familiar actions and practiced routines, focused his mind, easing his tension. Step by step, he and Chappy went through the pre-start checklist. They signaled the deck crew: Ready for engine-start.

The Pratt and Whitney R2800 engines started and settled into the characteristic, loppy idle of all big radial engines. Joel exercised the controls, exaggerating the motions in all directions. Everything moved freely.

"Cylinder head and oil temps are in the green, Joel. We can take off when you're ready," Chappy said.

"OK, Take Off Check List. Ignition check."

Chappy cycled the magneto switch between each engine's pair of magnetos, watching for a drop in RPMs. Both engines passed. On through the lengthy list they went, item by item in deliberate, careful steps, voices crisp, concise, professional. Tension built as each item was crossed off and takeoff loomed.

"Parking brake?" Joel asked.

"Off." Chappy replied, his voice tense.

"Tailwheel?"

"Locked. We're ready, Joel."

"Roger. Signal the Launch Officer." Joel's gut tightened. His mouth became dried out as if filled with desert sand.

Chappy formed the "OK" signal with his thumb and finger through the open cockpit window.

A green-clad man on the deck twirled his hands in an exaggerated circle.

"Wind 'em up," Chappy said, not looking away.

Joel held the brakes tight with his feet and advanced the throttles. The RPMs and manifold pressures jumped. The engines roared like artificial thunder. The aircraft vibrated under restrained power, lunging against the brakes like a lurking lion ready to pounce on its prey.

The tail rose. The control wheel juddered in Joel's hands from the propellers' powerful gale. The gusty wind tempted the nose to bob up and down. The engine instruments stabilized.

"We're in the green," Joel shouted.

Chappy signaled the flagman again.

The flagman's hand rose as he watched the bow's rise and fall to calculate the timing. Abruptly, he swept his hand forward.

"Go!" Chappy shouted.

CHAPTER 21

FIRST GLIMPSE

Sunday, 30 July 1950
Over the Gulf of Chihli

Time slowed for Joel. For the first few feet, the aircraft crept along the flight deck. The white line appeared *too* short. As they gained speed, the tires bumped over the wooden deck seams. He corrected for the powerful engine torque with the rudder. His pulse throbbed in his throat.

"Airspeed 48 knots," Chappy shouted as *Cabot*'s island flashed by on their right.

Plenty of clearance, Joel thought.

"Airspeed 65."

The end of the deck raced toward them.

"Airspeed 80."

"Airspeed 90!"

"Airborne!" Joel shouted. He didn't know whether they took off or the deck dropped out from under them. Either way, the big white Typhoon was in the air.

As the plane began a slow climb, Joel licked his dry lips. The airplane was barely above stalling speed. *We'll never gain enough speed.* Joel's sweaty hands gripped the control wheel. From the corner of his eye, Joel noticed Chappy concentrating, watching the altimeter and the Vertical Speed Indicator (VSI). The roar of the engines faded as Joel concentrated. He touched the brakes to stop the spinning wheels.

"Gear up." The landing gear settled into the wing with satisfying clumps, and two green lights. Their airspeed increased. The VSI showed a slow climb.

"Flaps to ten percent."

"Flaps ten percent," Chappy responded. Their speed increased.

Joel lifted the nose for a gentle climb. *Our speed must be faster.*

"Flaps up."

"Flaps up."

When 120 knots registered on the airspeed indicator, Joel began a climbing turn toward China. *Cabot* and her escorts arced away, leaving behind broad, white wakes.

As the engines roared, Joel's heart rate slowed. The brown line on the horizon announced mainland China.

Chappy puffed out a deep breath. "Well, we cheated death this time."

"Don't jinx us," Joel grinned.

"Mr. Pilot, sir, turn ta headin' 272 degrees true," said Cajun. "Next stop, China."

Ten minutes later, they climbed through 10,000 feet. "Chappy, Cajun, take off your life vests and hand them to me." Joel slipped from his life vest.

Both complied and Joel clipped all of them together.

"Chappy, you've got the airplane. I'm going to dump these."

Joel forced the sliding cockpit window open against the powerful slipstream and shoved the vests through the window. In seconds, they plummeted out of sight, into the sea.

By the time they crossed China's coast at 13,000 feet, Joel instructed everyone to put on their oxygen masks. He trimmed the aircraft, shifted the props into cruise mode, and put the superchargers into "HI" blower. Moments later, he engaged the autopilot and stared at the mysterious land of China.

CHAPTER 22

INSERTION

Thursday, 27 July 1950
China's Gurbantünriggüt Desert

The choppy air over the Altai and Hangayn mountain ranges exhausted the DC-2's cockpit crew. The former airliner
lurched and rattled in the thermals rising from China's
Gurbantünriggüt Desert floor. The white knuckled CIA extraction
team and crew rode the unseen air rapids.

Using powerful binoculars, the copilot spotted the southern end
of Lake Khövsgöl. "There's the lake. Turn five degrees right to 012
degrees. We'll fly between two mountain ranges, which are . . . " He
consulted his map. "Ah, there: the Khamar-Doban Mountains on the
left and the Buteeliyn Mountains on our right. The next landmark will
be a river, the—uh, the Tennik River where it joins the Selengu River.
Gotta love those names. Anyhow, near their confluence, we can land
on a flood plain and unleash these tigers."

"How far?" The pilot asked as the off-white, pre-War Douglas
DC-2 dropped and shuddered again.

"Two hundred miles, at most." The copilot's voice wobbled.
"Another hour, I guess."

An hour and a half later, they found a flat field in the river's flood
plain. The sturdy DC-2 absorbed the landing without complaint,
despite a single, jarring bounce.

"Man, that trip defines rough." JD groused, rubbing his backside as
he stepped onto the dry, grass-covered field.

"Yeah, and they probably lost our luggage, too," quipped Felix.

The six men unloaded their gear with practiced efficiency, hiding everything in nearby trees. Felix retrieved a battered bicycle from the airplane and pedaled toward the small town they spotted from the air.

The DC-2 took off in a cloud of gray dust and rumbled toward Ulaan Baatar, Mongolia. The men laid in the shade, enjoying the cool silence. Within minutes, most fell asleep.

Forty-five minutes later, they woke to the growl of an engine and a jaunty horn honking. Felix grinned behind the wheel of a dark green Red Army truck with a red star painted on its door.

"That looks familiar," Tom Long inspected the boxy, canvas-covered, cargo bed.

"It should," Felix climbed out of the square cab wearing a 'borrowed' Soviet Red Army uniform, displaying the proper cloth unit badges and pips (shoulder board), should he encounter anyone. "This's an exact copy of a 1932 American Autocar, Model CA. The Soviet name is ZiS-5. Won't win any races, but the thing's tough as nails and as dependable as sunrise."

"Yeah. I remember," Long said. "My dad owned three Autocars for his wholesale plumbing business in Baltimore."

"Cut the chit-chat," JD ordered. "Load the gear and we're outta here."

As if filled with cotton and not a hundred pounds of equipment, Smitty lifted a duffel bag in each hand and hauled them to the truck.

CHAPTER 23

THE HUNT

Saturday, 29 July 1950

SW of Ulan-Ude, East Siberia, Russia, Trans-Siberian Railway

Felix connected alligator clips to the telegraph wire. He inched down the telephone pole, making sure the reel of wire on his back didn't snag on anything.

Felix stepped off the pole and unstrapped the climbing spikes. "Here you are," he handed the wire reel to JD sitting in the back of the stolen Red Army truck.

Felix climbed under the canvas cover of the cargo bed. JD's telegraph repeater clattered. JD and Felix leaned closer, listening with intent concentration. The others lounged under the canvas, while maintaining a careful watch.

JD thought, *Supposedly, they update the train schedules every fifteen minutes or so. In reality, it's an hour or more.* By regulation, the rules for each regional control center along the Trans-Siberian railway demanded they provide regular telegraph information about the trains in their region.

JD listened for "his" train's identifier. *Some CIA genius developed a clever code that lets us send simple messages imbedded in those updates. Any Russian who reads the message will think the words are scrambled, an example of the old concept of hiding in plain sight. We just gotta be careful not to overuse the technique.*

The Eastbound train schedules also used a separate wire from the Westbound trains, an arrangement JD found clumsy and baffling. *To understand the traffic situations in both directions, the Russians have to listen to all the message traffic on both wires.* At choke points, confusion reigned, which—along with broken switches, drunk trainmen, and bad weather—accounted for a lot of wrecks. Encountering long delays on the Trans-Siberian railway was common.

So many screw-ups are in the system. I hope they'll mask what we're doing. With the lousy roadbed maintenance, I'm amazed they transport as much rail stock as they do. "That's no way to run a railroad," Felix said out loud, to his own amusement.

After many long minutes, JD jotted down the distinctive letter-number-letter-number-number symbol for the scientist's train.

Felix laughed as he read JD's writing. "Hey, guys, the train's more than a day behind schedule and three-hundred miles west of us. They've stopped to let another troop train pass. And," Felix said with relief, "our guy *is* on board."

JD estimated a twenty-five mile jaunt to the interception point on the primitive 'road.' "OK, Felix, that God-sent delay is just what we needed. Still, it'll be a hard drive to arrive on time at the rendezvous point. Install the cutter. We'll hit the so-called road," JD ordered.

Felix and Smitty, the ex-Legionnaire, mounted "borrowed" horses to ride ahead of the dark green, Red Army truck to set explosive devices. JD jumped in the cab. Everywhere they stopped to listen, Felix fastened a small, innocuous brown box next to a telegraph wire insulator. Each box held a rugged, reliable Swiss-made, wind-up clock mechanism and a detonator for two ounces of C-3 explosive. He set each box to random denotation times over the next three or four days. The exploding charge would sever the telegraph wire—to say nothing of the top half of the pole—leaving train schedulers in the dark until somebody located and repaired the destruction.

With luck, finding and repairing the damage would consume days, covering their trail. In a burst of diabolical ingenuity, Felix installed a couple of boxes to detonate within hours of the planned interception. He also set others to detonate hours and days afterward. To add further confusion, he set several devices on the westbound wire. Reggie Symthe added his own expert touches, setting explosive charges on switches and random stretches of rail.

"There'll be so many outages it'll take them hours before they notice our train has stopped," Felix predicted.

"Yeah," said JD, "we'll see."

"And man, we found a perfect spot half-across bridge," Smitty told JD in his French/North African accent.

"When does it explode?" JD asked.

Reggie said, "As we hit our train. That little pop should nicely spoil some engine driver's day. Smitty found a marvelous hiding place. Quite secure, actually, under the trestle."

"When it blows," Smitty's huge hands waved in demonstration, "the train derails and takes down the bridge."

"Pity we won't be round to watch the show." The smile beneath Reggie's bushy mustache revealed the archetypal gap between his teeth.

"No doubt, time to check in." Murph handed Tom a linen-covered kite. "Launch that kite in the air while my set warms up."

Murph opened a steel container twice the size of an ammo can and switched on the transmitter. He took out a compact headset, and a telegraph key from a compartment, then inserted a crank into the side of the box. He pulled a flash-paper code book from his shirt pocket.

"How's this?" Tom shouted. The kite bounced on the breeze, fifty feet in the air.

"That'll do. Bring the wire to me," ordered Murph.

The kite's "string," a strong, fine wire, connected to the shortwave radio as an antenna. To generate power, Smitty rotated the crank.

"Remember the WWII emergency radios they gave aircrews in the Pacific? This is like them, only with 1949's best improvements." Smitty grunted and cranked.

Murph flexed his right hand to prepare for the frantic action with the telegraph key. In thirty-seconds, he sent a condensed, coded report and shut down the equipment.

"Thanks, Smitty. Reel in the kite, Tom. Let's blow this juke joint."

With the horses tied behind the truck, the men bounced in slow motion along the barely distinguishable track, heading eastward toward their rendezvous with the train. Hours later, the truck bumped to a halt under a cluster of trees. Reggie, Smitty, and Murph climbed out and looked at JD and Felix in expectation.

"OK, everyone, gear up. We'll take the train at the top of that long hill," JD's thumb pointed over his shoulder. "Felix has your uniforms. Somebody untie the horses and let them feed."

Felix lugged a duffel from the truck and dropped it with a thud. "Read it and weep, gents, here's what we're wearing. Everybody gets a uniform, a balaclava, and a watch cap. Don't let me catch you *not* wearing these until I say so."

As Murph dressed, he asked, "Why do they call you Felix?"

Felix grinned. "Remember Felix, the cartoon cat? He always escapes trouble by grabbing just the right thing from his 'bag of tricks'." He patted his duffle. "That's me—and my bag o' tricks."

"I hope so," Reggie grimaced as he grabbed a uniform.

Tom Long held up a coverall-style garment. "Whose uniform is this? I don't recognize it."

JD laughed. "Didn't think you would, Tom, and neither will any Russians. They're Danish work uniforms."

"Danish?" Murph asked.

"They're surplus, never issued, from before the war—as anonymous as they come. I doubt anybody here has ever seen a Dane."

CHAPTER 24

ENCOUNTER

Saturday, 29 July 1950
East of Ulan-Ude, USSR

*P*oor, tough Mr. KGB man can't handle a little train ride. Olaf Kazakov, the train's engineer, smirked through the graying stubble covering his ample, double chin. He shifted his heft on the steam locomotive's hard seat and stared at the shining track ahead. With no wheels under the cab, he barely noticed the bouncy, bobbing ride from his engine. Equipped with a pair of wheels in front, and five sets of driving wheels under the engine, the arrangement, called a 2-10-0 or Decapod, met the need for the twisty mountain roadbeds ahead. Their sharp curves would derail a conventional locomotive.

On the plains the constant pitching and nodding—like a small boat on choppy water—bothered some people, like the pale KGB man sharing the cab with him and the fireman.

Kazakov glanced at the 'fireman'. *Fireman. Ha. Since all these steam engines converted to burn oil 30 years ago, all he does is sit on his rump, fiddle with valves, and wipe leaks.*

On most national railroads, regulations required the engine crew to be relieved after a certain number of miles or hours on duty; not so in the Soviet Union. Once at the controls, Kazakov held responsibility for the train until they reached their destination. On long trips, he used a relief engineer to catch some shut-eye. Still, like a ship's captain, he remained always on duty, always responsible.

Two hours earlier, the train entered the west-facing foothills of the vast mountains in the country's Eastern Republics. Kazakov worried. *I know this engine, it's worn out, tired. Doesn't matter that this train has but ten cars, the inclines will give us trouble. I hope the old girl is equal to the task.*

He snorted with typical Russian irony and resignation: *Those Politburo fools think they save a few Rubles by delaying repairs, year after year. Soon, this poor machine will grind to a stop. They can blame no one but themselves, which of course won't stop them from blaming me, or someone else who couldn't do anything about it.*

Kazakov's thoughts reflected reality: Dozens of water, oil, and steam leaks revealed years of neglect. The flash boiler tubes choked on scale. Loose packings on the main driver cylinders leaked almost as much steam as they used to turn the driving wheels. The entire engine rattled and clattered in a cacophony of noise. Due to the bearing wear, the axle journals dripped grease in ugly streams. The leakage and inefficiency meant the worn engine worked much harder, requiring more frequent stops for water and oil.

He frowned, thinking of a certain seven-kilometer-long hill ahead with a five percent grade. *That's a tough pull for a* new *engine. When we crest that hill, this old girl will barely be crawling, if something doesn't break first.*

✕✕✕

JD and Felix's binoculars scrutinized the hill that worried Kazakov. The Autocar/ZiS-5 hid fifty yards away, under the appropriated Red Army camouflage netting. The waiting extraction team checked and rechecked their weapons, rehearsing their roles in the upcoming attack.

"Looks pretty good," JD said, "When the train tops the rise, it'll be inching along. The track ballast is flat and solid. Reggie should have no trouble climbing aboard."

"I still think I should back him up," Felix said. "What if a relief engineer or some KGB lookie-loo is in the cab? Let me board from the other side. If he doesn't need me, no sweat, I'm ready to help with the scientist. What'ya say, JD?"

"Yeah, better to be safe . . . "

"*You* better be ready for those KGB guards. They won't be unprepared like those green troops." Felix checked the messages on the East-bound telegraph wire and read the code: *KGB, 6 men. Neutralizing forces in two places on the train spreads us thin.* Although the message didn't say so, he knew the KGB occupied the front car. The closer to the front, the more powerful the passenger.

XOXOX

Their covert insider on the train, Sergeant Major Pyotr Borodin, sweated, and not from the heat. The sun lingered on the horizon. At the last stop, he checked the station's teletype messages, and deciphered the cryptic message: *Hill 12,747 under repair:* his signal. He didn't know the location of the hill, just that he must disembark with the scientist and move away as quick as possible.

With any luck, tonight will be moonless. What'll they do when they find out there's not one defector, but six? And KGB aboard? Hope they received my message. This whole thing could unravel at the seams like a cheap suit. They probably can't extract more than the two of us. The rest will be left to be shot.

XOXOX

JD reviewed the modified, simple plan. *Reggie and Felix will jump aboard the creeping steam engine cresting the hill, capture the engineer and anyone else in the cab. Next, Reggie stops the train and stands ready to send it on its way when they're finished. With no one at the controls the train will go through the towns ahead under its own power. Of course, derailing or running into another train is inevitable. I hope that'll be many miles away. The rest of the team hits the fourth car, where twenty, untested soldiers are travelling. They're supposed to be drunk, along with the three officers, thanks to our man onboard. If he hasn't done that . . .*

CHAPTER 25

REDIRECT

Saturday, 29 July 1950
Baotou, China

The Harpoon cruised along on autopilot. Joel watched the unfolding countryside, confident in Cajun's navigation. To his right, Chappy held the controls and scanned the instrument panel. *So far,* Joel thought with contentment, *this mission is going great.*

Two hours later, Cajun jerked upright, pressing his headphones to his ears. He spoke rapid Chinese into his microphone.

Joel checked his watch—*yes, we're close enough to Baotou for initial contact, if—wait. The Chinese don't have radar. How do they know we're here?* A wrinkle formed a deep trench between his furrowing eyebrows. Joel raised one eyebrow and flashed a Cajun 'what's-going-on' hard stare.

With a slight bow toward the radio, Cajun finished. "Well, boss, dere's dis tiny wrinkle in our nice flight plan." He held his thumb and fingers an inch apart. "Baotou says American Consul General, he wants ta talk with ya. Dere's a change in plans, man. He won' say what."

Joel bit his lip. *Has the mission been called off? No, Captain Bergeron said if they cancelled the mission, the man wouldn't give the passwords. He didn't say anything about meeting a Consular official. This doesn't feel good.*

As Cajun translated the instructions from the Baotou tower, Joel lowered the landing gear and flaps for landing. The air field appeared to be a WWII Japanese military field.

They glided past a handful of Soviet-built light bombers and cargo planes and clunked to a landing on a worn, potholed runway. Joel followed a nondescript 'Follow Me' truck displaying a ragged red and white-checkered flag to an unpaved parking area near the terminal.

As Joel stepped out the plane's door, a dusty pre-war Chrysler sedan flying an American flag from the front bumper crunched to a stop on the gravel.

Great, a Consulate flunky, Joel decided. *Guess we don't rate a meeting with the Man himself.* He offered his hand. "I'm Captain Edward Teach. What's this all about?"

"Paul Higgins, Deputy Consul, Captain," the young man wiped his forehead. "I'll make this quick. You're being redirected to Ulaan Baatar, Mongolia, sir. I don't know the reason, just something about undefined complications regarding your rendezvous." His shrug communicated just relaying orders. "They want you there ASAP."

"Wait a minute." Joel raised his hand. "I don't take orders from just anyone." He waited to see if the man knew the code word.

"You don't—?" The man blinked. "Oh, yes, ah. . . *Mr. Smith* sent me with your written orders."

"Look, I don't know about this. Can that airport even support a plane this large? Do they have sufficient fuel stored? 110-130 octane gas?" He gestured toward the Typhoon's engines.

As Joel and the Deputy Consul Higgins spoke, Chappy pounded a steel spike into the ground with a wooden mallet, then clipped on a wire, grounding the aircraft. To prevent a spark from setting off a fire, the highly combustible avgas fumes necessitated the aircraft be grounded before refueling.

A Chinese Army truck clattered to a stop in a cloud of dust and oily smoke, followed by a small, square sedan. The troops riding the truck gawked at the Americans. A short, slender man approached from the car. A young woman followed behind. Her quick, tiny steps reminded Joel of a Chihuahua.

The man spoke in Chinese to Joel, and gave a slight bow. The girl translated: "Mr. Chang says welcome to Baotou. Your passports, please."

Joel shoved their passports toward her. "The aircraft is ready for his inspection."

The Customs man squirmed at Joel's stern countenance. He glanced at the passports, stamped them, and left. A battered, ex-Japanese Army fuel truck rolled toward them.

The Deputy Counsel warned, "We collected some maps for you. Again, I urge you, depart as soon as possible. We cowed that Customs man this time. If his superior arrives before you leave, well, that could be another matter."

"No," Chappy said with blunt emphasis, looking at Joel. "Flying a high-powered airplane at night, over unknown terrain, to an unknown destination, using maps you've never seen, when your crew is fatigued is a recipe for disaster, sir. We will R-O-N and leave at first light tomorrow."

"R-O-N?"

"Rest Over Night. We're spending the night."

Joel's fists clenched in frustration at not being able to continue, but he offered no objection. *Chappy's right.*

The Consulate official looked like he just swallowed a sour pickle. "The Consul General said—"

Joel crossed his arms. "I will not risk the lives of my men. You tell Mr. Smith we leave at first light."

Worried about the condition of the fuel, Chappy raised a sample to the sun in a slender glass cylinder, checking dye color, eyeballing the liquid for contaminates.

He discovered tiny rust flakes and ordered the Chinese men to strain the fuel through his chamois. They hand pumped the fuel from the truck and finished as the sky burst into rich hues of crimson orange and purples.

XXXX

They spent the night in the airplane, standing guard in two-hour shifts. Joel awoke to discover Chappy had disconnected the ground wire and nearly completed a preflight check using a flashlight. Cajun poured over the maps using another flashlight.

"We gotta leave, boss. Chief Customs guy's on da way."

"OK," Joel said, "I'll walk the props through on number one. Chappy, you do number two. I'll prepare for engine start."

In ten minutes, they belted in as Joel primed, then started the left engine. The high-pitched starter whine echoed in the early morning stillness. The engine backfired, popped, then chuffed to life with reluctance. When the idle smoothed, Joel started the right one.

"Did you remove the chocks, Chappy?"

"They're stowed in the back."

"Cajun, see if you can raise the tower."

"Dey're sayin' stay where we are, Joel." Cajun reported. "Army wants ta talk with us."

"And people in hell want ice water, too. We're going."

He swung the tail around on the runway, blowing a cloud of dust.

"Trucks headin' our way, Joel." Chappy said, latching the tail wheel.

"Let them try to catch us."

The engines' idling rumble became a screaming roar, blowing clouds of dust over three trucks full of soldiers racing behind them. A red spotlight—indicating 'stop'—blinked in futile urgency from the tower. Joel ignored both and took off, then banked the Typhoon north.

He racked his memory: *Did I see any fighters on the airfield?*

CHAPTER 26

BEST-LAID PLANS

Saturday, 29 July 1950

A Hilltop in Eastern USSR

An age-old military adage holds that no combat plan survives contact with the enemy.

The engine wheezed as it climbed the steep hill, chuffing with all its might, barely crawling to crest the summit. Reggie and Felix sprinted in pursuit.

"Saboteur. Right side," the engineer shouted over the engine noise.

The dozing KGB man leapt to his feet, floundering for his pistol. Felix climbed into the cab on the left side, pistol in hand. When the Russian drew his weapon, Felix fired twice, the M1911 .45's report loud over the engine's clatter. The KGB man dropped like a felled tree.

The engineer spun toward Felix. Reggie's gun thundered from the right side of the cab, taking him down in a tangle of arms and legs. The fireman swung a big wrench at Reggie.

Reggie and Felix fired. In seconds, three men lay dead. Eye-burning cordite smoke mingled with the metallic smell of blood and burning oil.

"I'd rather hoped we wouldn't have to do that," Reggie said in a regretful voice.

Felix said, "Stop the train and set the brake. Start again on my signal."

Reggie replaced the partially empty magazine in his gun, then bringing the slow train to a halt, he checked its controls. *There, all set. All the chaps must do is give the signal and we're right as rain.*

At the sound of gunshots, two KGB men in the train's first car leapt to their feet. Their food tumbled to the floor. They raced for racked Kalashnikovs at the rear of the car. Before they reached them, the door burst open.

Tom Long was first. His M1911 .45, the automatic roared, bucking in his hand. Smitty fired from behind, a Colt in each huge hand. The guns' noise deafened them in the closed space. The rattle of brass shells and the biting smell of cordite failed to penetrate their adrenalin-soaked senses.

The senior KGB man alone wore his weapon. He rose from the table firing a 7.62mm Tokarev TT-33 automatic.

A bullet hit Smitty's left arm. He grunted in pain and dropped one weapon.

Long snapped off two rounds, missed. The KGB man fired and missed as well.

With blinding speed, Long ejected his magazine and slipped a full one into place. Wounded, the KGB man raised his weapon. Smitty emptied his second Colt's magazine.

In the rear car, three Red Army officers slouched drunk over the card table.

"That, I would not feed to a pig," one Lieutenant slurred, nodding with his bewhiskered chin toward the food tray.

"Da," said another. "Is insult to pig." They laughed. They finished their cheap vodka and drank from the bottle confiscated earlier from Borodin. Murph and JD entered the car to find all three men sound asleep from Borodin's powerful anesthesia.

"That's the way I like my enemies," Murph said. "Fast asleep."

"Tie their hands," JD ordered.

CHAPTER 27

STRATEGY CHANGE

Saturday, 29 July 1950
A Hilltop in Eastern USSR

As soon as the train stopped, Borodin leapt off the railcar, then froze. He blinked from a flashlight's blinding light as he squinted down the unmoving barrel of Felix's wire-stock M1 carbine.

In English Borodin said, "Salute the cat."

"Make the bed." Felix replied.

"Beethoven's Fifth." Borodin countered.

Felix lowered his weapon. "I'm Felix Harrison."

"Roger Dubov. Russians call me Sergeant Borodin." He pointed toward the rear car. "Most of the troops are drunk, but we'd better check."

"Need this?" Felix tossed Dubov his spare M1911 .45.

Dubov caught the weapon in midair.

All of Borodin's soldiers lay passed out drunk except the two youngest men who played cards. When Dubov and Felix entered the car, a soldier shouted, and leapt for his racked Kalashnikov.

"Don't!" Dubov shouted in Russian.

The second soldier lunged toward the rack and wrestled a Kalashnikov free.

"Nyet!" Shouted Dubov, too late—Felix snapped off two rounds. The soldier sank to the floor, moaning, bleeding.

"Drop the rifle. *Now.*" Felix ordered in barely-fluent Russian. The white-faced, boy-soldier with cowered shoulders stood stock-still.

Felix's heart hammered. *That was close.*

They tied the young Red Army trooper's hands and bandaged the wounds of his wounded comrade. Undisturbed by the commotion, the other soldiers slept on, snoring. A sober Politruk sergeant feigned sleep, observing Felix and Dubov through slitted eyes.

"Where's the scientist?" Felix said.

"*Scientists,*" Dubov emphasized the 's.'

"What?"

"*Six defectors.* If we don't take 'em, the KGB will shoot them on sight. They're sweating bullets in the car just ahead."

Felix and Dubov strode toward the scientists' car. JD joined them as they walked. Felix introduced them. The waiting steam engine chuffed fitfully in the darkness, catching its last breaths of life.

Felix said, "Got a problem, JD. *Six* scientists."

JD stopped. "No. The plane can't carry that many."

Felix said, "We gotta take 'em. Otherwise, they're dead."

JD tapped his foot. His eyes contracted to pinpoints. "What's going on?" His eyelids narrowed. "How did this happen, Dubov?"

"The scientist spilled his guts to his team. They've worked together for years and are close. When they heard he'd get out, they all wanted out as well. They issued an ultimatum—all or none."

"Dear God." JD ran his hand through his hair.

"We can't just leave them. Let's move them away from the train, then figure this out."

Dr. Ilya Fadeyka Kalugin stumbled in the darkness toward JD and Felix. The other scientists trailed behind him. JD shone his GI flashlight in the man's face. "My name is Dr. Ilya Fadeyka Kalugin. My colleagues *will* accompany me," he asserted, offering no compromise.

"Dr. Kalugin, I'm JD, the team leader. I don't know if we can accommodate all of you."

"Mr. JD, I think you *will* 'accommodate' us. If you do not, do you imagine that we can keep your secrets from the KGB? Do not insult us. You have no options."

"Who's that?" JD pointed at Berthold.

"Herr Doctor Heinz Luthor Berthold, an unwilling German guest of the Soviet Union," Dubov said. "Intelligence will be *very* happy to chat with him. He has enlightening insights into recent Soviet aviation advances. Isn't that right, Dr. Berthold?"

The diminutive man leaning on his cane stared into JD's eyes. "Indeed."

JD asked, "Who else is here?"

"Dr. David Yetkatov," Dr. Kalugin pointed at a slight, bookish man cowering in the flashlight's glow, "is my chief aide."

"Next, my trusted coworker, Dr. Ana Ksana Bakhtina who's been with me for eight years." Ana glanced at JD for a split second as she tilted her head and cast him a shy smile.

Kalugin waved his hand toward a tall, slender, beautiful woman standing bolt upright. "Dr. Valena Rahil Tumanova, an honors graduate of Moscow University and my colleague for four-and-a-half years."

"And, Senior Technician Konstantin Yasha Dushkin. He has worked with me for a decade. I trust him with my life."

A faint hint of a squint twitched in JD's eyes. *Yeah. Duskin's a ferret. I don't trust him.* JD's combat-honed first impressions proved accurate more often than not.

Felix interrupted, "What're we gonna do, JD? Times a-wasting, we gotta move fast."

"OK, people, in the truck and outta those white lab coats. You can see them for a mile."

"What about the bombs?" Asked Dr. Kalugin in a soft voice.

"The *what*?" JD's gut clenched. *A 'simple' mission, ri-i-ght.*

CHAPTER 28

SHOCKING NEWS

"Are there *atomic bombs* on this train? How big are they?" JD's brain scrambled for a plan, as he adjusted to the bombshell.

"An assembled bomb weighs somewhat more than 4000 kilograms. However, these are not assembled. The uranium is stored in crates, which we must take," Dr. Kalugin said.

"Can we move them and isn't uranium dangerous?" JD asked.

Sounding like a lecturing professor, Dr. Kalugin explained, "The uranium is shielded—as much to prevent any atomic reactions as to protect people. No one should be near it for more than fifteen minutes."

"How much does the uranium weigh?"

"With shielding, each fissionable package weighs 300 kilograms."

Felix calculated. "About 700 pounds. We can manhandle them off the train, backup the truck to the boxcar, and slide the crates into the truck."

JD eyed the scientist. "Will the uranium explode if we drop it?"

"Nyet, that's a myth. A wooden framework separates the nuclear elements, so they can't touch. Even should they do so, the reaction will produce heat only, perhaps fire, not explosions."

"Is the uranium safe to transport elsewhere?"

The scientist considered. "For a matter of hours only."

JD eyed Felix. "You studied the geography around here. Where can we stash this stuff?"

"I'll check my maps."

Ten minutes later, Felix's flashlight shined on the map. "Here," he tapped the map, "about six miles away . . . an abandoned mine with a six-hundred foot vertical shaft. Let's dump the uranium down the shaft, then use dynamite. Good chance they'll never find the uranium."

"That's the plan," JD scanned the area, "Where's Smitty?"

"He was shot, JD," Tom Long said. "In the arm. He's bleeding. Not sure how bad."

"Take everybody else to the boxcar ASAP. Take Kalugin, Dushkin, and Dubov to help. Felix, as soon as the truck's positioned, tell Reggie what's next."

As JD unloaded their duffle bags and supplies from the truck, the diminutive Berthold said, "I shall accompany you."

JD looked Berthold up and down, then glanced at his cane. The left side of his mouth twitched in a crooked half-smirk.

Berthold insisted, "I am an engineer. I can help them do the work. Only my body is crippled, not my mind."

CHAPTER 29

ANOTHER SHOCK

Saturday, 29 July 1950
A Hilltop in Eastern USSR

Waiting in the Russian Decapod locomotive cab, Reggie noticed a sharp pain and a blood-soaked, bullet hole in his left pant leg. Running his hand down his calf, a jagged piece of embedded shrapnel pricked his finger. "Well, then, I'm hoist on my own petard. Looks like a ricochet."

Felix climbed into the cab. "How bad?"

"Hurts rather frightfully, I must say."

Felix plucked the bloody, impaled fragment from the wound and held it in front of Reggie's ashen face. "Looks like a flattened .45 slug."

"I say, that does hurt awfully. Is the wound deep?"

Felix grabbed a knife from his pocket, and ripped a strip of cloth from Reggie's shirt. "I've cut myself worse shaving." Felix tied the makeshift bandage around Reggie's leg. "Listen, we have complications. This train is carrying *six* defecting scientists *and* two atomic bombs."

Reggie swallowed hard. "Bloody hell! I trust someone knows how to deal with those filthy bombs."

"We're gonna dump the bombs. They're loading them on the truck as we speak. Take about fifteen minutes."

CHAPTER 30

SNATCHING THE PRIZE

Saturday, 29 July 1950
A Hilltop in Eastern USSR

"No, no. You're holding the crate too high. Carry the box just above the floor. Otherwise you are tipping, not sliding," Heinz Berthold scolded, pointing his cane.

JD, Felix, and Murph lowered the box and struggled to manhandle the heavy crate across the boxcar's rough wooden floor. A flashlight on the floor cast strange shadows. The stolen Red Army truck shuddered as the hijacked crate dropped with a loud bang onto the truck bed.

"Now the other." The three men shoved the second crate that slammed onto the truck bed. "Good. Well done," Berthold beamed.

JD wiped his hands, then stepped forward. "Good work. Felix, take Murph, Dubov, and Dr. Kalugin with you to find that mine. Drive slow. No lights. I'll work with Smitty to uncouple the cars."

"May I suggest—?" Berthold started.

"Now what?" JD's tone reflected the tension.

"The bomb casings contain each several hundred kilograms of trinitrotoluene to set off the atomic explosion."

"How much TNT are we talkin' about?" JD interrupted.

"Perhaps 1200 kilograms of trinitrotoluene in each bomb."

JD whistled. "2400 pounds. Almost two and a half tons."

"Approximately so." Berthold continued, "Should we build a fire under the railcar to detonate the explosives? That will be sufficient, I believe, to not only destroy the car, but a section of track as well. The confusion about the damage will delay the inevitable investigation of our absence."

JD smiled a devious, icy snake's smile. "I like the way you think, Dr. Berthold. The longer they wonder about what happened, the more time for us to escape. We'll need a large fire to make it happen, do you agree?"

"Yes." Dr. Berthold waved his cane back and forth. "I see plenty of fallen trees here. Piled into a bonfire under the car, they will do the trick."

Smitty shoved a frightened brakeman toward JD. "Found this guy in the caboose." An ugly, bloody stain soaked Smitty's left sleeve.

JD's mind worked overtime. "Several soldiers who weren't wounded are still in the car, right? You—" JD grabbed the brakeman by the neck and twisted his arm behind his back. "Come with me."

He marched the railroad worker to the troop car with the remaining conscious soldiers. He thrust the brakeman into the midst of the frightened soldiers.

"You," In lethal-sounded Russian, JD pointed to the brake operator crouched on all fours. "The engineer's dead. Teach the conductor how to operate the brakes on this car. Do a good job. You're headed for a wild ride down the mountain. All that will save you is how well you use the brakes on this car and in the caboose. The ride starts in ten minutes."

CHAPTER 31

DESTROYING EVIDENCE

Saturday, 29 July 1950
A Hilltop in Eastern USSR

*N*o *time for finesse.* JD swung the sledgehammer with vigor. The coupler rang flat, like a bad bell, releasing the troop car and caboose from the train. The coach and caboose rolled backwards toward Ulan-Ude.

JD watched the train cars clatter down the mountain and into the night. *Hope the conductor and brakeman are careful using the brakes. If they aren't, well—not my problem.*

In spite of their wounds, Smitty used his good arm to gather a large pile of dry branches and small trees. Berthold supervised their piling under the bomb-filled car.

Smitty said, "I found this tin of kerosene for lamps in the caboose. Should make the wood burn hotter."

"Yes. Wait till I say to light it." JD commanded.

"Mr. JD?" Dr. Berthold said, "You are aware how large will be the explosions, yes? We should move everyone farther away, do you think? A half-mile, at least. We must concern ourselves with falling bomb parts, rails, and pieces of the rail car."

"Hold onto that thought, I'll be right back," JD strode to the steam locomotive. Reggie set the valves and pumps to provide plenty of oil to the engine's boiler. JD said, "That'll do, Reggie. I'll decouple the bomb car, then you can start." After a minute and some clanging of steel, JD returned. "OK, Reggie, send this Russian Decapod on its way. You good to jump off once the engine's moving?"

Reggie grimaced. "No."

"Show me what to do, then climb down."

Spinning its drivers to start, the work-worn, American-built Baldwin locomotive strained to move the shortened train. With huge clouds of steam, oily smoke, and a clamorous racket, the engine sitting on the crest of the hill accelerated with agonizing slowness. JD jumped, and rolled once. In moments, the forlorn engine with its cargo of dead men chuffed out of sight to its final demise.

The demolition team, Dr. Berthold, Reggie, Smitty, and JD trudged toward the improvised camp. The Red Army camouflage netting strung through the trees covered everyone. JD noticed the civilians wrapped in blankets against the chilly air. A small fire flickered, contributing a faint haze to the surreal scene.

When they approached, JD said, "OK, listen, everyone, we've sent the train on its way. We'll bury the uranium and burn the car carrying the bomb casings. They contain explosives, and we're too close."

"I scouted a trail," Tom pointed, "which slopes downhill about twelve hundred yards, then turns left. We can protect ourselves from the falling debris under a big rock overhang, which will also hide us from airplanes. A better place for the fire, too."

"This I approve," Berthold said before JD could continue.

JD chuckled. "Let's move. Tom, give us ten minutes, then tell 'em to light the fire."

An hour later, the night erupted with two massive, close-spaced explosions. Thunderclaps echoed and rolled off the surrounding hillsides. Unseen shrapnel rained on the forest surrounding the protective rock overhang.

CHAPTER 32

URANIUM DUMP

Saturday, 29 July 1950

An Abandoned Mine in Eastern USSR

The fingernail moon shed slivers of faint light among the shadows falling dark along the rutted, dirt road. Felix and Dr. Kalugin jostled back and forth in the narrow cab as the dark green truck inched forward. Dushkin and Dubov bounced hard against the hard truck bed. Holding themselves in place as far from the roped-down uranium crates as possible, they strained to see in the darkness, Felix recalled driving past an overgrown mine road on their way to the train.

Felix turned at a fading, wind-battered sign, which marked a long-empty, guard shack. Kalugin jumped out to open the wooden gate, which toppled with a slight shove. Felix strained to spot the mine entrance. Kalugin thrust his hands against the dashboard, when Felix hammered the brakes. The wheels stopped within inches of a precipice of a deep, flood-carved gulley cutting across the road.

Felix said, "We'll never cross that. We gotta find another way."

Dubov scrambled to the top of an embankment, his flashlight cut the dark air with stray strips of light. "An old rail bed leads to the mine entrance. Still some wooden ties, didn't see any rails."

Hoping to gain traction from the multiplied torque of first gear, Felix shifted the truck's transmission into granny gear, then gunned the throttle. Like a determined mountain goat, the ZiS-5 workhorse slogged to the top of the slope and onto the rail bed.

"Whew, that worked. Gotta drive slow now. We don't want to blow a tire on the ties. That'd cook our goose," Felix quipped.

Dushkin and Dr. Kalugin's furrowed eyebrows mirrored each other as they cocked their heads and glanced at each other. Bewildered, Dr. Kalugin asked, "Why do you cook a goose?"

"Just an expression, means we'd be outta luck."

"Ah," Dr. Kalugin stooped over and picked up a rusty spike. "We must watch also for these."

A reddish arch merged with the darker sky. Twilight announced the coming dawn as the truck rattled toward the mineshaft.

"In case the Reds send out a plane, we gotta finish this before sunup."

A slap-dash barricade of timbers blocked the entrance to the mineshaft. Felix nudged the barricade with the truck's bumper. The timbers clattered, banging against the shaft's black hole. "Stay back from the edge. We don't know how solid the ground is." He turned the truck around in the narrow space. Dubov waved him back toward the shaft, then thrust his palm into the air. Dubov dropped the tailgate.

Half-frowning, Felix bit his lip. "What happens if the crates break open, Doctor?"

"Sparks, small fires, possibly a nuclear reaction." Dr. Kalugin's touched Felix's forearm. "A *small* one, perhaps."

"Let's dump 'em and see." A loud sploosh released the tension gripping Felix's neck and shoulders.

"This is good. Water will modulate any reaction," Dr. Kalugin said.

"Modulate? That's good?" Felix asked.

"Da."

The second crate banged against the side of the shaft with several bright flashes of light, then splashed at the bottom.

Felix lay on his stomach, holding the explosives bag Reggie prepared. He inspected the mine shaft with a flashlight. "I can see a ledge about twenty feet down. I'll lower the package onto that. You guys move the truck."

Sweating, his breathing shallow, Felix played out the detonator wires with great care, lowering the package to the ledge. He moved back to the rear of the idling truck and attached the wires to a magneto box, then spun the knob. Nothing. *What's wrong?* Heart pounding, Felix reviewed a mental list what could be wrong: *bad detonator, broken wire, malfunctioning magneto, even bad explosives. Oh, man, I don't want to climb down that hole to check.*

Then he saw the problem. A loose wire slipped off its connector. He reattached the wire and tightened the connector.

"OK, guys, once more, this time with feeling."

He whirled the knob again.

A sharp jolt rocked the ground and the abandoned mine-head building. A basso grumble erupted as the mine shaft caved in. Timbers groaned and snapped. The decrepit building collapsed into the opening. The pile of rubble belched a plume of dust. The ground rattled again as the last of the shaft collapsed. Then, all they heard was the faint sighing of the wind.

With relief, Felix said, "That uranium is out of reach."

"This is good," Kalugin affirmed.

"Sun'll rise soon. We gotta hurry back to the others. The KGB won't take long to figure out where things went wrong."

Dubov walked behind the idling truck, sweeping away their tracks with an old broom. After fifty feet, he flung the broom into the truck bed and clambered aboard.

In the blue blush of early morning light, Felix drove the truck to a Red Army depot nearby and parked among rows of similar vehicles. A passenger bus and a battered pre-war Russian R71 motorcycle with a side car caught his eye.

Although the bus could carry sixty people, the seats were removed from the back third of the interior, leaving space for cargo.

CHAPTER 33

KREMLIN

Sunday, 30 July 1950
The Kremlin, Moscow, USSR

Lavrenti Beria's bleary eyes studied a report as he drifted toward sleep. His intercom buzzed. He gasped a breath of air and his eyebrows flinched, adrenalizing him into a wakeful alertness. He smacked the reply switch and bellowed, "What?"

"Sir, please forgive the interruption. Comrade Lieutenant Colonel Ivan Yabitov asked to see you. He says the need is urgent."

"Send him in."

Beria removed his reading glasses and cocked his head. "Well, Ivan Semyon, what is so important that I must tear myself away from the brilliance of this scintillating report on the shortfalls in corn and wheat production?"

Yabitov's lips, a thin line of terror, twitched. *I place my head in the lion's mouth with what I must say.* His pallid complexion faded to the color of fresh-laundered sheets.

"Comrade Chairman, I received a report. The 'special train' encountered some problems."

"Explain." Tight as an overwound spring, Beria appeared like a venomous snake coiling to strike.

"Comrade Chairman, the report says the rear of the train, with the guards aboard, broke away. It rolled down a mountain and crashed into another train near Ulan-Ude with casualties on both trains."

The snake glared at him with the prolonged, unblinking stare of a cobra. "What of the scientists? The bombs?"

"Unknown, Comrade Chairman. I believed it more important to inform you of what we know immediately, rather than wait for a full report, sir," Yabitov's exaggerated earnestness oozed from every pore.

Slight warmth crept into Beria's eyes. "Da, you did well, Yabitov. Inform me at once when more is known. Send Tsarsko at once."

"But, Comrade, for a mere train wreck?"

"Send him. Now."

"Right away, sir." Yabitov about-faced and exited the room.

Beria rose and paced back and forth behind his desk. His inborn sense of conspiracy, his Russianness, fueled his thoughts. *This is not an accident. I can imagine no accidental situation which would release the last cars of that train. They were deliberately—what is the word?—uncoupled. Somebody interfered with this train. How could they know which train? There must be a traitor.* His eyes widened. *Somebody is out to topple me.*

His right eye's involuntary hard blink unleashed a throbbing pain in his temples, flooding his head and neck. Again. A flashing blinded his right eye. His right arm drooped with weakness. He felt for his chair, sat down, and plopped his head on the desk. After the attack dwindled away, he returned to reading.

Three hours later, Yabitov tapped on his door. "Forgive my interruption, Comrade Chairman. I have more news about the special train."

"Yes, yes? What have you learned, Yabitov?" Drained from the terrible headache, Beria spoke in a less intimidating tone. He frowned at Yabitov, the toady. *Someone close to me is a traitor.*

"A Politruk, a Mladshiy Sergeant named Federov, survived

although severely injured. Before he died, he said masked, armed men in strange uniforms boarded the train. They killed his officers. The senior NCO, Sergeant Major Pyotr Borodin is missing. Federov believes everyone was somehow drugged, because most of the men fell unconscious before the raid occurred. He himself could barely stay awake."

"How can this be?" Adrenalized, Beria roared, leaping to his feet. His deepest fears became reality. "Attacked in our heartland? Who has done this? We shall kill them all . . . slowly." His eyes narrowed to small slits as he clinched his fist.

"Comrade Chairman, the Politruk's report remains unconfirmed. He may have hallucinated."

"What of our KGB informant, what's his name? Dushkin?"

"Comrade, we have heard no word from him since the train left Moscow."

Is he part of the conspiracy, as well? A sharp rap at the Chairman's doorway interrupted his thoughts. "Comrade Chairman Beria, a most urgent message from an Army detachment on maneuvers fifty kilometers east of Ulan-Ude, sir."

Beria snatched the message from the Red Army captain's hand. "How can this be? His neck flushed crimson as he read the message: The engine and first car of the train collided with a freight train at a switching center twenty-five kilometers to the east." *To the east? How could it be to the east?* He read on. "The engineer, fireman, and several KGB all shot. Both trains destroyed in an explosion of leaking aviation fuel.

"The serial number of the locomotive confirms the identity: the special train." Beria's headache reared like a feral beast, stalking him, waiting to pounce. "No mention of the scientists or the bombs." His raised voice ranted revenge. "If those crazy Mongol separatists took our atomic bombs, Yabitov, there will be hell to pay."

Yabitov's heart knocked against his ribs. "Comrade Chairman, Tsarsko has left for the scene, sir."

Beria spun toward Yabitov, "Send a full team to help him. I will order Marshall Orlov to provide troops to find the scientists. Go, go, make sure this happens at once."

)O(O(O(

A day and a half later . . .

A Red Army captain entered the Chairman's office, his hands shaking.

"Sir, I received this message from an Army unit searching for the scientists and the—cargo."

"Quickly, you fool, tell me."

"Comrade Chairman, they followed the rails east from Ulan-Ude to a steep hill where they found a large bomb crater. The tracks and crossties are blown away. Nothing is left of the railcars but splinters and pieces. Even destroyed the railroad bed, sir."

Beria's ruddy complexion paled. "Our bombs exploded? How? The—the parts are kept separate. This can't happen. Was this report from Tsarsko? Or Yabitov?"

"No, Comrade Chairman, an Army Major wrote the report. Comrades Yabitov and Tsarsko arrive tomorrow. The area is very remote."

CHAPTER 34

MONGOLIA OR BUST

Sunday, 30 July 1950
Ulaan Baatar, Mongolian People's Republic

Cajun shouted over the roar of the Typhoon's engines. "Hey, Joel, we cross into Mongolia, in two, two and a half hours."

Joel surveyed the endless succession of brown, rocky hills and small mountains stretching to the north as far as he could see: *A desert without dunes.*

"How did you figure that, Cajun? Those junky maps they gave us don't show landmarks."

A chuckle escaped through the Louisiana native's broad, toothy smile. "I shoot da stars with da sextant. Den, I use my handy-dandy World Almanac, ya know, an' estimate da Lat/Long of dis Ulaan Baatar. Once ya know Lat/Long for both Baotou and Ulaan Baatar, man, is easy ta plot course."

"Easy for you, maybe. Left to me, we'd land in Tokyo or the North Pole."

Chappy laughed. "Told you he was the best, Joel."

XOXOX

Ten miles east of the Ulaan Baatar airport they spotted the runway. The town nestled in a valley with rounded, brown, treeless mountains to the north and lower mountains to the south and east. Joel banked west and descended.

"You speak Mongolian too?" Joel said to Cajun.

"No need, boss. Mongolian upper class, mos' speak English, ya know? No problem."

A call to the tower resulted in a prompt English reply, with a strange accent.

The modern airport featured cross-wind runways and paved taxiways. A radio tower with a rotating beacon glinted in the sun. Several airliners rested near the terminal.

They landed with a slight bump. Joel took a taxiway off the runway. A shiny follow-me truck with the de rigueur red-and-white-checkered flags directed them to a paved parking ramp. A neat, uniformed man stood beside a bicycle, waiting. Joel searched for any military or police presence. A hot dessert wind dusted fine sand through his cockpit window.

That guy must be customs. Did Baotou call about our abrupt departure with three trucks filled with soldiers racing behind our unauthorized takeoff?

※※※

"Welcome to the People's Republic of Mongolia, Captain Teach. I am Comrade Inspector Tuul, Mongolian State Customs Service." Tuul pronounced each word with sharp precision. "I understand your flight is under the auspices of the American Department of State. Why does your aircraft have Iranian registration?" A shiny, enameled red star in the center of his cap reigned over his somber expression.

He appears curious, not suspicious. Joel replied, "We're on contract to ferry this reconditioned American aircraft to new owners in Iran. The American State Department detoured us to Ulaan Baatar. We'll continue to Iran when we learn what the Ambassador needs." *Why did they divert us? I need to keep things low key.*

The man stamped their passports and visas in an efficient manner. Moving closer, he handed the documents to Joel, then spoke in soft tones. "Comrade Captain, I most strongly recommend you and your crew leave this airdrome immediately."

Joel scrutinized Tuul's earnest, saffron-colored, round face and furtive eyes.

Comrade Inspector Tuul added, "'Mr. Wu' says it is prudent for you to do so." His intent, steady gaze was one as an equal, an informed insider, not as a minor civil servant.

A flush of fear tingled up Joel's spine, accompanied by icy sweat. His heart battered his rib cage: "Mr. Wu" was their contact in Baotou.

This is a warning, not a precaution. This mission has taken a strange, scary turn.

"Thank you."

With a slight bow, the man turned, mounted his bicycle, and peddled away.

Across the ramp, in a hangar's shadow, a Soviet-trained Mongolian photographer focused his telephoto lens. Every foreboding click of the shutter captured close-ups of Joel, Chappy, and Cajun.

CHAPTER 35

SUDDEN EXIT

Sunday, 30 July 1950
U.S. Embassy, Ulaan Baatar, People's Republic of Mongolia

A dark blue, dusty 1947 Ford four-door sedan arrived. A gold medallion on the door read "Embassy of the United States of America." Below, Cyrillic letters repeated the title. Two men exited the car and strode up to Joel. From their close-cropped haircuts and disciplined manner, Joel tagged them as enlisted U.S. military.

"Mr. Teach?" The dark-headed one asked.

"Yes," Joel said.

"Sir, welcome to Mongolia. We've been ordered to immediately transport you to the Embassy. Please bring your belongings, including the aircraft's documents."

Chappy and Cajun loaded their bags in the embassy car's trunk.

Joel said, "Put the chocks in place, Chappy. Tie the ship down—"

"That's not necessary, sir. The aircraft will be taken care of. Please, sir, we must leave *immediately*." The two enlisted men offered no explanations, just deepening furrows between their brows.

Without another word, Joel and his crew climbed into the Ford.

This 'simple' mission is becoming stranger by the minute.

The car sped toward the city on a paved, two-lane road. The hot, dusty wind blowing in the windows failed to cool them.

"So what's this about?" Joel demanded in his Colonel's voice.

"Sir, we were instructed to take you straight to the Embassy. Respectfully, sir, that's all we know."

A Marine guard waved them through the American Embassy gate. The driver veered off the curved driveway to the building's formal front entrance, drove around the side of the embassy to a large garage, and parked inside. The garage door closed with a bang. A sandy-haired man wearing nondescript civilian clothes snatched the car door open.

"Colonel Knight, I'm Lieutenant Colonel Tobias McGregor, Deputy Military Attaché." He flashed a quick salute. "Sorry for the abrupt treatment, sir. You and your men are in serious danger. Please put your things in this truck. We'll depart ASAP." The man in nondescript civilian clothes flashed a quick salute.

He didn't use my cover name. Strange. "What's going on, Colonel? Why the bum's rush?"

"Later, sir. We *must* leave immediately. Please, climb into the back of the truck, sir."

Joel weighed whether to demand answers. McGregor's anxious countenance convinced him to comply. They climbed into the canvas-covered back of a battered old truck with a faded business logo on the door, then exited the embassy grounds through a back gate.

They bounced on rough wooden benches in the canvas-covered cargo bed as the truck rumbled its endless way through Ulaan Baatar. *Heat, exhaust fumes, dust everywhere; this is no limousine ride.* The somewhat smooth city streets gave way to a rougher road. Joel heard gravel rattle against the truck's underside. *It seems to me we're climbing,* Joel thought as they twisted and turned.

"Colonel, I insist, where are we going?" Joel asked as an unseen obstacle jolted them.

The Lieutenant Colonel cleared his throat. "Sir, I'm not cleared to your mission. All I know is something has gone wrong with the arrangements for you to meet somebody. The attaché directed me to take you to the bus terminal north of the city. People there will explain." With that, McGregor stopped talking, leaving Joel to wonder about their fate.

CHAPTER 36

ESCAPE

Sunday, 30 July 1950

Bus Terminal North of Ulaan Baatar

The truck slowed, brakes squealing, made a sharp turn, and stopped. Joel started to raise the canvas flap.

"Not yet, sir. Please wait 'til we're inside."

The truck moved forward a few feet. The engine stopped. A wooden door banged behind them.

"OK, sir, you can climb down now."

Joel stepped into the gloom of a large, dirt-floored wooden building. The stale air punctuated by the musty smell of old oil and grease accentuated the confined feeling of a closed building in a hot climate. Light struggled to filter through high, dirty windows. The omnipresent Mongolian dust swirled in the thin streams of sunlight. A handful of naked light bulbs revealed disassembled buses and their parts cluttering the building. Outside, Joel heard buses arriving and leaving.

The truck driver and the embassy Lieutenant Colonel hurried through a side door. Joel heard an engine start. An engine revved and gravel crunched as the unseen vehicle drove away. In the garage, a Mongolian man drove their truck out the rear door.

Joel walked toward four men standing nearby. Chappy and Cajun joined him.

What's going on? Two of the four men appear to be wounded.

A man with headphones leaned over a military-style radio on a small table. Several people, including two women, huddled against the wall. Joel guessed from her heaving shoulders that the tall, dark one was sobbing. The other woman, ashen-faced with fear, comforted her.

What's this? A dark-headed man approached him. "Colonel Knight?"

"Yes, I'm Joel Knight." He felt uncomfortable using his real name. For a reason unknown to him, the mission was on hold.

"Good to meet you, Colonel. I'm JD Monroe, CIA. Felix Harrison, my number two. This is Roger Dubov, our undercover guy from the train. I'll introduce my team later."

"Nice to meet you, JD." He shook JD's hand and acknowledged the others. "Please tell me what's going on."

"We can talk here, this building's secure," JD said. "Our mission has gone south big time. We need to make some fast decisions. First, instead of a single defecting scientist, six scientists, including the two ladies over there, want to escape. This is an all or nothing package deal. The Russians kidnapped Dr. Berthold . . . " JD pointed to a small man leaning on a cane. " . . . in Berlin." A heavy sigh escaped the tension in his chest. "We encountered problems at the train, and killed several Russians—soldiers *and* KGB. We divided the train into three parts, the front and back of which were sent away to crash. We destroyed the third part." He cast Joel a grim look. "The third part contained two atomic bombs."

"*Atomic bombs?*" Joel gasped. "Are you sure?" He raised his head. "Dear God in heaven, be merciful. Where are they?"

"We disposed of the uranium deep in an abandoned mine shaft. They'll never find it. When we set the bomb casings on fire, they exploded, destroying a large section of track. That's the good news."

"And the bad?"

"Despite our attempts to make everything look like the scientists perished on the train, Moscow knows better. We've been reading their messages. Do you know a Red Army colonel named Yabitov?"

The hair on Joel's neck and arms stood to attention. Yabitov, the drunk Russian who crashed his car into the Secretary of State's car in Washington DC.

"Yes. Nasty guy." *Susan warned me . . .*

"Well, Beria handed this over to Yabitov. He assigned his number one henchman, a malicious thug named Boris Tsarsko, to our case. He's utterly amoral, a sadist, has the reputation of bringing his quarry back to Moscow in shrouds. He's flying into Ulaan Baatar with a KGB commando team called Red Star. They're some *real, nasty* monsters."

Just like Susan said when she briefed me. Joel exhaled. *This is out of control.* "Let me review what you just said. We kidnapped six scientists out from under Russian noses, killed several Red Army *and* KGB troops, stole and hid two Russian atomic bombs, and destroyed the train transporting them. Beria's siccing his worst guy on us, along with Soviet commandos. And, instead of flying out two people, there are *six*?"

Before JD could comment, several deep, rolling booms echoed and re-echoed in the distance.

"Make that twelve people, Colonel. The six men on my team need to be evacuated, as well. We—"

A thin, mustached man limped up to them. "I'm quite afraid things are worse than that, JD," an English-accented voice interrupted. "We're in a bit of a spot, actually. Those bangs we heard came from the airport. A couple of Russian Air Force transports on the tarmac are right next to what *used* to be your aircraft, Colonel."

"Used to be?" Joel snapped.

"I'm quite afraid they've blown it to bits."

Joel blinked, trying to absorb the news. "My plane? How will all fifteen of us get out of here?"

"Better make that sixteen, flyboy."

Joel spun around, heart pounding. "Susan—" Joel almost screamed. "What are you—why are *you* here?"

She kissed him warmly. "Perfect timing, I guess. I just happened to be in the Philippines when Felix radioed about the extra scientists."

Fear clenched Joel's fists. "Do you know how dangerous this is? What idiot let you come?"

She smiled, unconcerned. "I couldn't wait to start my interviews, so I insisted they fly me in. I arrived by bus. So what'll we do without your airplane?"

Before Joel replied, a side door clapped closed. A man Joel hadn't seen before ran to JD. Around his neck hung a huge pair of binoculars.

"JD, bad news. The Russians transports are full of troops. They're loading onto trucks."

In the background, the radio chattered briefly, unintelligibly.

"What is it, Murph?" JD asked.

"Trouble, JD. They think we're here."

"This bus terminal?"

"Yeah. And they're coming like the hounds from hell."

WAR COUNCIL

Sunday, 30 July 1950
Mongolian Countryside

The metallic smell of urgency and fear tingled in Joel's nose. "JD, get us outta here, *now!*"

"Felix, quick. Drive your bus in here ASAP," JD ordered.

In authoritative Russian, JD ordered those crouching along the wall, "Gather your belongings. We're leaving."

With a mechanical growl, Felix's bus rumbled into the garage.

"Load everything in the back. Hurry!" JD directed the men like a traffic cop. "You civilians, into the bus, right now."

The scientists collected their few possessions, scurried toward the bus, quietly queued and boarded the bus, leaving the front seat open for Dr. Berthold.

Susan placed her hand under Dr. Berthold's elbow to steady his balance as he climbed the steps and turned into the aisle. He turned and smiled. "*Danke.*"

The extraction team loaded the bags and containers into the back of bus. *Efficient*, Joel thought. *Even the wounded men are helping.*

Felix waved his hand and shouted, "Grab a seat, people," as he drove through the garage's rear door, "Everybody, lie down on the seats until I tell you otherwise."

Joel pressed his face against a seat across from his wife. Thoughts of capture raced through his mind. *They'll know who I am within hours, if they don't already. I'm in civvies, using a phony name, so they'll treat me as a spy. That means torture and death, and even worse for Susan. To them, she's a spy too. Oh, God have mercy on us.*

Beads of sweat ran across his forehead and dripped onto the seat. He gritted his teeth with a fierce determination to avoid everyone being captured. Another thought struck him. *JD thinks I'm in charge. I don't want to command these CIA soldiers or the Russian civilians either. But duty calls . . .*

Susan perceived Joel's conflict and understood his quandary. *This is his worst nightmare coming true. He's forced to lead men into a dangerous situation again, just like at West Point.* She recalled Joel telling her about commanding a group of cadets on a wilderness training exercise. He got them lost. *With pure pigheadedness and youthful conceit, he denied the facts. Two cadets attempted to remedy their plight by rafting a dangerous river. Both drowned in the swift current. The regular Army men responsible for the cadets' safety, who should have intervened, were court marshaled for dereliction of duty. Joel still blames himself. He's hated leading troops ever since. The difference is, there's no one else to rescue us, and no guarantee we'll survive.*

JD interrupted Susan's musings and announced in English and Russian, "It's OK to sit up."

Joel noticed they'd entered low foothills. "Where are you taking us, JD?"

"Don't know. Where are we going, Felix?"

Over his shoulder, Felix said, "Colonel, we're going as far to the northeast of Ulaan Baatar as we can in an hour or so. Unscheduled buses like this run all over Mongolia, so that'll give us a little cover for a while. See that ridge line? On the other side are more trees. As soon as I find enough, we'll pull off and camouflage this baby."

JD spoke up, "Once we're safely out of sight, you can decide what comes next."

"So, JD, how did you come to be in Ulaan Baatar?" Joel inquired.

"We intercepted the train inside Russia right where we were supposed to. Our plan was to take Kalugin and Dubov, head south and meet you and the plane in Hami. After killing the soldiers and KGB, and with the additional scientists, the plan failed. They sent us to Ulaan Baatar to meet you after the embassy diverted you. The Russians found out, and you know the rest."

As the bus drove further into the wilds of Mongolia, the terrain became more mountainous, less desert-like. Huge, scattered boulders and random trees reminded Joel of southern Wyoming. The narrow, bumpy road angled toward the opening of a canyon. Two vertical rocks straight ahead appeared too large and close together for anything less agile than the wild goats watching them.

They topped a ridge line and began their descent. The narrow road tapered to a sliver of rock clinging to the steep canyon's side. As they progressed, jutting rocks scraped the roof. After a few hundred yards, the road dropped to the canyon floor, bumped along for half a mile, then climbed the opposite side, and resumed its bouncing, meandering ways.

At last, Felix said, "That'll do." He drove the bus off the road into a grove of fir and beech trees. They jostled to a halt. JD's team disembarked in disciplined haste.

Tom Long shouted, "Move her another twenty feet, Felix. The trees are too thin here."

The civilians clambered off the bus and gathered by a Siberian fir tree as they watched JD's men cover the bus with the camouflage netting. One man hacked off a fir branch, then scurried to the road to sweep away the bus tracks. Felix laid out wooden ramps and unloaded the motorcycle.

Thankfully, these guys know how to get things done, Joel thought. *Hope they're just as good at improvising great escapes.*

JD announced, "OK, we need a council of war, Colonel. Gather around everybody. Colonel, my people all understand Russian. What about yours?"

To Joel's surprise, both Chappy and Cajun understood the language.

"And you, Colonel?"

"I speak and understand basic Russian. Just don't talk too fast." He glanced at Susan who slightly shook her head. Taking her cue, he lied. "Susan doesn't."

"You can translate for her. Let us know if we're going too fast."

"You're in charge, Colonel," JD added, "however, I'd like to give you my advice, if I could."

Joel winced at JD's assumption. "Sure, go ahead."

"We oughta split in two, with Russians in each group and Dr. Kalugin's papers divided between them. One group goes south into China, and then to Tehran like the original plan. The other group goes to the Pacific coast, hoping for help from the U.S. Navy. That makes the Reds search twice as hard, and doubles our chances of the information getting out."

"I object," Dr. Kalugin pointed to himself with his thumb, and then waved his pointer finger toward the other scientists. "We are not mere *objects* you can divide at will. I demand we have a say-so in these decisions. Our lives are at jeopardy too."

Time to take charge. Joel said, "Dr. Kalugin, of course you'll all have a say in the decisions. JD is an expert in this tricky business, and we'd be wise to follow his recommendations."

Fluent in Russian, Susan scrutinized the Russians, pretending she couldn't understand. She waited for someone to say something important. Her psychology training analyzed the group: *Two are uncomfortable about deciding their fate. The one named Ana keeps shaking her head. She's not coping well with the situation. Dr.*

Berthold is reserved, dubious. We need him to participate. He's far too important to risk alienating.

Joel said, "The first thing to do is find out whether we've eluded the Russians. Who can reconnoiter?"

"That'd be me, Colonel," Felix raised his hand. "I'll put on a Mongolian coat, and take the motorcycle for a ride."

Joel frowned. "Do you trust any of the Mongolians at the bus terminal enough to ask what's going on?"

"Yes," JD answered. "The Soviets took away their surnames when they invaded. The Mongolians share a strong sense of national identity."

"Took away their *names*?"

"Yes, banished their ancestral family names. They even seized their centuries-old family trees sewn into silk to erase family ties and tribal identities and make them all good little socialists. Under the surface, Mongolians are brave and fiercely proud of their heritage. I admire them. Many will risk everything to stymie the Soviets. Felix knows several men at the terminal who are part of an underground rebellion. I think he can gather some good Intel."

"And, Felix," JD added, "we need supplies—food and something for shelter."

CHAPTER 38

INFECTED

Sunday, 30 July 1950
Mongolian Countryside

"**J**oel, something's wrong with Smitty." Susan pointed at Smitty lying facedown, unconscious on the ground. JD sprinted to him and rolled the big man onto his back and checked his eyes, which were rolled up under his upper eyelid. "They shot him during the train raid. I didn't think it was serious."

"Let me see," Ana Bakhtina, pushed past JD, Joel and Susan stooping around Smitty. "I was nurse during the war. I can deal with combat wounds."

JD jerked off Smitty's left sleeve, revealing a bloody, discolored bandage wrapped around his huge bicep.

"Here, take this." Tom Long handed her a combat first-aid pack.

Ana used scissors from the pack to cut off the stinking bandage.

"It's infected. Why didn't you care for it?" Her accusing stare fixed on JD.

"He never complained," JD said. "I just assumed . . ."

"He has a fever." Huffing her disapproval, Ana cleansed the wound. "Is there any anti-bacterial cream? Penicillin is better." She didn't glance away from her work. Wiping the wound with alcohol, she trimmed away the putrefying flesh with alcohol-sterilized scissors, exposing the actual wound. Lifting his huge arm, she treated the exit wound.

Tom Long handed her two packages. One held surgical dressings and sutures, the other a small container with penicillin vials and a glass hypodermic needle.

"Is there morphine?"

"Right here."

She sutured both wounds and administered the penicillin and the morphine. She wrapped the wounds with skill. "Let him sleep, but watch him carefully."

She stood and wiped her hands. "Sterilize that." She thrust the hypodermic needle toward Tom. " . . . and the scissors."

"Thanks," Joel looked at JD. "We have two wounded men. She needs to attend to the other one, too."

Reggie limped over and raised his left trouser leg for Ana's inspection. "Just a bit of a scratch, actually, not a proper wound like poor Smitty."

Ana removed the makeshift bandage. "No, you are wrong. This also is infected, just not as bad. I must clean it and cut away the necrosis. This is going to hurt."

CHAPTER 39

DIRE NEWS

Sunday, 30 July 1950, Late Afternoon
Mongolian Countryside

Felix returned from his reconnaissance mission a few minutes after Murph announced he spotted a motorcycle coming from his perch on the canyon wall.

Felix reported the dire news, "Colonel, Tsarsko and Yabitov ordered about three hundred Red Army soldiers to scour the countryside. Three truckloads are headed this way. We need to leave, pronto."

Joel said, "We gotta go. Leave as little evidence as possible."

JD ordered in a quiet voice. "You heard the man, people. Load your stuff and don't make any noise."

"JD, Joel," Felix grabbed Joel's arm. "There's more. My airport buddy told me a Red Army general is flying in to see Yabitov for a couple of days. The Army may be recalling their troops."

"Why would they do that?" JD asked.

"Something big's up." Felix steepled his fingers, then tapped his fingers together. "Maybe we can steal the guy's plane."

CHAPTER 40

OUT FOR BLOOD

Monday, 31 July 1950
A Siberian Hilltop in Eastern USSR

During a brief fueling stop at Ulan-Ude, travel-weary, Colonel Ivan Semyon Yabitov called Chairman Beria.

"Sir," Yabitov said with a shaky voice, "I sent you facsimile photographs from the Ulaan Baatar airport. Three Americans landed yesterday in a civilianized American bomber."

Yabitov's face flushed scarlet. "I know one of them. He pretends to be Edward Teach, but I know him. He is American Air Force Colonel Joel Knight. He assaulted me in Washington. This man hates Russia. He is an enemy of the People. He is not in uniform, Comrade Chairman." His voice rose to a shout. "He is a *spy!*"

"American spies? They dare to invade our ally Mongolia? Go to Ulaan Baatar at once, Yabitov. Take personal charge of this." Beria's voice bore a lethal hiss. "*Do not* kill them. I will interrogate them, in person. Afterward—you may take *your* revenge."

Lavrenti Beria hung up and lumbered to his private washroom. He heaved his breakfast into the toilet bowl. With an unsteady gait he returned to his desk. His head pounded, the vision in his right eye blurry. He dropped a pen and grabbed his screaming head.

CHAPTER 41

THE SNUB

Monday, 31 July 1950
A Siberian Hilltop in Eastern USSR

Yabitov frowned as Boris Tsarsko surveyed the still-smoldering crater with narrowed, practiced eyes. *Tsarsko has authored much explosive mayhem himself. He knows what to look for.*

"Where is the radiation detector?" Tsarsko ordered. "I've never seen an atomic explosion, but I do not believe this to be one."

A gruff man with huge hands inked with prison tattoos, held the Geiger counter like it was the Tsar's Fabergé Imperial Coronation Easter egg. With a Kalashnikov rifle slung over his shoulder, he shuffled back and forth, like a fine tooth comb, through the smoking rubble and into the crater. Watching for the slightest quiver of the instrument's meter, the Geiger counter's distinct crackling, popping, and clicking remained noiseless.

"Comrade Tsarsko, no unusual radiation is here, in any of the bands generated by a nuclear weapon. An atomic bomb did not detonate here."

"I thought not." Tsarsko scoffed. "This was a large, conventional explosion. Search for parts of crates or containers. Perhaps the blast threw the bombs aside."

"Over here. Come, see," Kiryl Pavlovich Lebedev shouted.

"What did you find?" Tsarsko demanded.

Ignoring Tsarsko's question, Pavlovich said to his superior, "Look here, Boris Arkady. These are recent truck-tire tracks someone tried to sweep. Over there . . . footprints from children or women."

Tsarsko interjected, "The group included two women scientists. Maybe they were captured. Follow those tracks."

Kiryl Pavlovich cast Tsarsko a murderous glare, then trekked off into the wilderness with blood thirst coursing through his veins. A sniper and an experienced big game tracker and hunter, he loved to stalk his prey, whether man or beast.

Several hours later . . . he returned to camp, his tired, dirty face bore a triumphant look. He strode past Yabitov, ignoring him, and marched up to report to Boris Arkady. The KGB had its own chain of command. "The tracks went southward toward Ulaan Baatar."

Yabitov's upper lip twitched. Angered by the snub, he snapped, "Quick. Take the men to Ulan-Ude at once."

CHAPTER 42

THE RISK

Tuesday, 1 August 1950, Mid-Morning
The Mongolian Wilderness

Riding on the pilfered motorcycle, Felix led the way ahead of the bus on a one lane dirt road deeper into the Mongolian larch, birch, and fir forest. A vulture swooped overhead as the weary bus sported its scrapes and dents as a heroic medal testifying to the rigors of their escape.

Staying off the main road avoided locals or Soviet scouts. As they drove further into the endless wilderness, Felix, JD, and Joel searched the landscape looking for a temporary sanctuary for the group. As they rounded a bend, Felix slowed the motorcycle to a stop. He pointed at long, sloping hillside with a meadow filled with deep purple-blue Siberian columbines and surrounded by a grove of birch and fir trees.

JD said to Joel, "We can hide from planes in those trees."

Joel added, "The meadow's our runway. That gentle slope uphill to the northeast will slow a plane landing and help accelerate one taking off."

The bus pulled into a narrow opening between the trees. JD and Joel hopped from the bus to survey the meadow.

"Think its smooth enough, Colonel?"

"From here it seems smooth enough, JD. The columbines dangling on their delicate, almost invisible stems remind me of birds in flight.

We should check for rocks and stumps, but I think this'll do. If the Russian plane isn't too big, this beautiful meadow appears fine."

Joel and JD clambered back onto the bus. "Everyone," Joel said in Russian, "we might be able to obtain an airplane to fly about eight of us to China. Felix and I will try to steal one tonight. I agree with Felix that by dividing our group, we double the chances of one group escaping. Plus, we'll confuse the Russians in the process. Chappy will fly the plane. If we manage to steal it, those going must board right away and leave immediately, before the Russians or Mongolians react. I expect the plane will be on the ground no more than five minutes. Those going on the plane with Chappy are Dr. Yetkatov, Konstantin Dushkin, Dr. Berthold, Tom Long, JD, Reggie Symthe, and Smitty. Considering the Russians use this type of plane as a medical transport, it's fitting. Reggie and Smitty will arrive at a hospital sooner."

Joel continued, "The nine people going overland to the Pacific coast will be Dr. Kalugin, Dr. Ana Bakhtina, Roger Dubov, Dr. Valena Tumanova, Felix, Cajun, and Murph McGregor, Susan, and myself. Murph will drive the bus. So eight will leave on the plane with Chappy and nine will go on the bus."

Dr. Kalugin spoke up, "Should all the women remain with you, Colonel? Would it not be better to divide them as well?"

"I will go on the plane," Valena Tumanova proposed on an impulse, and then glanced at Dr. Yetkatov.

"If Valena wants to switch, that's fine. Anyone else want to change?" Joel asked.

"Herr Colonel, I prefer to accompany you," Dr. Berthold volunteered.

Joel said, "Fine with me."

Dr. Berthold continued, "We must admit that the odds against either group successfully escaping are high indeed, do you agree?"

"Yes," Joel admitted. "We might not be able to steal an airplane.

However, if we do nothing, no one will escape. Can you suggest a better idea?"

"*Nein, nein.* I wanted to be sure we all have clear understanding of the risks that lay in front of us."

As Joel continued to lay out the plan to everyone, Susan observed the Russians with a clinical eye, noting each person's reaction. *Dr. Yetkatov nodded immediate agreement to Joel's list. Yetkatov and Dr. Kalugin are equals in leadership and project knowledge. Seems logical to separate them. Both wounded men appear relieved. They're still in pain. Bless them. The sooner they receive medical care, the better.*

Dushkin brightened when they called his name to take the plane. He's eager for a new life. I suspect his old one was none too pleasant. Valena was quick to volunteer, she has her eye on Dr. Yetkatov. Ana appeared less panicky when Dr. Berthold asked to stick with Joel.

With resignation, everyone filed from the bus to set-up a stopgap camp. Ana checked on Smitty. His fever raged. After Felix started a small fire, Ana said to Felix, "I want to make a poultice from the Siberian columbines for Smitty's fever." As she mixed and warmed the healing dressing, Felix prepared the bubbling rations. Ana rubbed the medicinal remedy on Smitty's arm and wrapped it. Then with an air of nonchalance, she strolled over to a fallen log and pretended to sit beside Dr. Berthold by accident.

Joel and Susan held hands, and Joel quietly prayed, "Heavenly Father, thank you for our successful escape. Stand guard around us and protect us. Thank you for this food. In Jesus' name, Amen."

Unsure of what she just witnessed, a stunned Ana observed Joel pray to a God the communists insisted was dead.

CHAPTER 43

GRAND THEFT

Tuesday, 1 August 1950, Early Evening
Ulaan Baatar Airport, Mongolia

As the sun slipped below the horizon, the airport came into view. Felix drove the motorcycle with Joel riding in the sidecar.

Joel observed, "That fence keeps out only cattle and camels, not people stealing airplanes."

Felix chuckled. "Not quite prepared for us, are they?"

They stashed the motorcycle in a shallow ravine, hidden in the abundant, wind-blown weeds. Felix said, "I hope the dust doesn't choke the engine. We might need our trusty transport." Without heroics, they stepped between two strands of barbed wire.

"Not many lights. That's good," Felix whispered. "My guy said they only patrol the perimeter." He shifted the canvas sack with his bag of tricks from one shoulder to the other.

Joel pointed. "Let's sneak behind those hangars and work our way to the flight line. If they have guards, they'll keep watch around the planes."

A half-moon brightened the area, so they skulked in the shadows of the hangars. Half an hour later, they examined a row of modern twin-engine transports. To one side loomed a big, strange-looking three-engine, heavy transport.

"Those twin-engine planes are Ilyushin IL-12s," Felix said, "with Aeroflot Airlines markings. They're Soviet Air Force, of course. They carry about thirty troops each. The big, three-motored outfit is a converted WWII German JU-252 with Russian engines. No units except the Red Star Commandos use them."

"The IL-12s look like American Convair 340s," Joel said.

Felix laughed. "Yeah, some guys call them Martin 404-ski's."

They eyeballed the control tower, a stark, unpainted three-story wooden affair. The glass of the cab at the top angled outward. They detected dim lights inside. A pair of flood lights shone indifferently on the parked aircraft, leaving large areas in shadows.

"A controller is on duty around the clock. If we're quiet, he'll never know we're here," Felix continued in soft tones.

"It's the random patrol I'm worried about," Joel said.

They moved closer to the line of aircraft.

"That's the plane I mentioned, Joel, on the end."

The strange-looking plane featured a sleek, shark-like fuselage that curved upward at the rear. It rested on its tail wheel, with gangly, fixed landing gear stretching from the high-mounted wing. A pair of small engine nacelles sprouted from the wing on each side, forward of the landing gear struts. The aircraft sported rudders on the tips of the horizontal stabilizer.

Joel had never seen such a bizarre airplane. "What the heck is *that*?"

Felix chuckled. "It's a Shcherbakov ShchE-3. The Russians call it 'Pike,' because the body looks like a fish."

"An insult to the fish of the world. That thing is *ugly*."

"The Soviet Air Force has a bunch of them. During the war it transported wounded soldiers from the battlefield and spare parts to repair combat aircraft. Thing's fabric-covered, except for the body, which is pressure-formed plywood, kind of like the WWII British Mosquito, you know? The engines are about a hundred-fifty horsepower each. The top speed is about one-fifty, and has a range of about four-hundred miles, give or take."

"Can it fly off grass?"

"Yes, virtually everything the Reds fly can. They say these are tricky to take off, but then fly OK once airborne. Let's take a look."

They scampered to the aircraft's side door. "Unlocked," Joel whispered. They climbed aboard.

With a shielded flashlight, Joel scanned the interior. "There's room enough for our purposes, even with that . . . desk or whatever."

"A bar. Remember, this is a general's plane."

Joel moved to the cockpit. "Here's the pilot's manual. Hope my Russian is equal to the task."

"I'll see what I can find to create a diversion when we take off." Felix left Joel to read the manual by flashlight. Joel studied for about forty minutes.

The aircraft rocked slightly as Felix climbed in. Felix smirked, "I untied the plane, but I'll need your help, 'cause I think I've found the perfect distraction."

"OK, I'll start the engines, you start the timers. When things start happening, we'll hightail it outta here."

"Be right back," Felix said.

Joel primed the carburetor on the Pike's first engine and breathed a little prayer. The engine started instantly, sounding loud on the quiet air field. A moment later, the other engine sprang to life.

Heart pounding and palms sweating, Joel watched the temperature gauges and waited for Felix.

Twenty minutes later, Felix flung himself into the copilot's seat and yelled, "Go! Let's get outta here." Joel advanced the throttles and began to taxi. Using the brakes with a gentle touch, he taxied out of the parking spot.

Felix radioed the tower in Russian: "Fire! The tanker truck is on fire! I'm moving the general's plane." Then he pulled out the radio's circuit breaker. Whatever the controller yelled into his mic, Joel and Felix couldn't hear. A big red searchlight flashed at the moving plane.

Joel shouted, "Hang on." The engines roared. The plane raced to the far side of the runway. The airfield behind them erupted in explosions. A siren split the early morning air. An antique fire truck chugged toward the flight line. The blaze hurled flames high in the sky. Fire engulfed an airplane parked next to the escaping Pike. Mere feet away, flames enveloped the fuel tanker truck.

Felix shouted over the engines, "I'll ride the motorcycle back. See you there." He jumped from the co-pilot's chair, ran through the cabin, closed the door behind him, and raced away.

Joel turned onto the runway, groped for the tailwheel lock, and advanced the throttles. Once airborne, Joel's heart slowed as he wiped his sweaty palms against his pant leg.

That was a tricky takeoff. Thankfully Felix warned me about the sluggish acceleration and low rate of climb, or I'd be dead. I forced this thing to reach takeoff speed and climb out of ground effect. What a strange beast. Once in the air, it's as tame as a pussycat.

He ran his eyes over the unfamiliar gauges and banked the plane eastward as the sun frowned red on the horizon. He checked Cajun's compass heading—a few degrees to the north put him on the right track.

Next! Find the meadow.

CHAPTER 44

HASTY EXIT

Wednesday, 2 August 1950
A Mongolian Meadow

The rising sun sparkled on the diamond dew droplets gracing the Siberian columbines. The high-pitched chip of the song of the warblers reverberated in the air, breaking the tranquility. A lone woodpecker drummed on a birch, as the Mongolian marmots rustled in the feathery grass. JD spread a red cloth blanket atop the Siberian Columbines in the shape of an arrow.

JD shaded his eyes and scanned the sky trying to locate the drone of aircraft engines. *Soviet airplanes are unlikely to fly over us . . . if one does, we're exposed big time. If it's a fighter, and he strafes us . . .* JD's jaw clenched as he ground his teeth. His arms and shoulders tightened. JD shoved away his negative thoughts and scoured the sky. *I have no idea what kind of plane to look for.*

Ana pointed. "There's a plane." A two-motored plane with gangly landing gear hanging like a giant, misshapen mosquito flew over the meadow. It banked and soared into the sun's light and out of sight.

It's flying away.

The cool morning breeze swooshing through the birch trees and the peaceful meadow evoked JD's feelings of smallness and insignificance in the vast, timelessness of this rugged terrain.

CHAPTER 45

DETECTED

Wednesday, 2 August 1950
Another Mongolian Meadow

Mongolian People's Courier-Corporal Tsakhia Gantulga adjusted his uniform as he walked toward his motorcycle. Nature's call interrupted his courier mission to Ulaan Baatar. With no postal system, his county's provincial and national governments depended upon couriers to transport important documents and small packages.

His rank allowed him to choose the best routes for himself. This smooth road to the capital was better than any in the country. As he slung his leg over his motorcycle, the sound of airplane engines cut through the air. He spotted the source—a strange looking, low flying machine turning north, slowing, and preparing to land.

No air fields are nearby.

The Russian-marked aircraft puzzled him. Groping in his satchel, Courier-Corporal Gantulga retrieved his prized possession, a scarred, WWII Japanese pocket compass. Glancing at his watch, he jotted in his spiral notebook the time and the airplane's estimated, original course and its new one.

I'll report this to my Lieutenant. Being extra observant often produces positive effects on promotions. Perhaps this will lead to more finances to allow me to marry my pretty girl.

CHAPTER 46

DESPERATION

Wednesday, 2 August 1950
A Mongolian Meadow

Joel scrutinized the landscape below for the broad, open meadow filled with purple-blue, Siberian columbines. Landing a strange airplane for the first time on an unprepared, grassy strip was for the desperate, not the timid. Joel spotted the crude, cloth blanket arrow JD spread in the meadow below. He circled, slowed, followed the arrow, then flew slowly over the meadow, deciding how to land.

On the third pass over the open meadow, Joel thought, *Here goes nothin'*. The funny little flaps slowed the Shcherbakov ShchE-3 as the Pike descended. Keeping the handbook's *"stall speed with flaps: 72 KPH"* in mind, Joel aimed toward the wildflower and grass runway.

The airplane wobbled on the final approach. Unfamiliar with the slow-flying the plane, the fish-shaped plane stalled about three feet high, then dropped hard onto the ground. The leggy landing gear absorbed the shock and rebounded with a small bounce.

Whew! Down in one piece.

Joel taxied to the top of the meadow and rotated the aircraft around with the left brake. He set the parking brake, shut down the engines, and swiped beads of sweat from his brow.

In his best Gary Cooper imitation, he said, "This here's a tricky little filly to wrangle, ain't it?"

Climbing from the plane, he fired orders. "We need someone to collect the blankets and stow them in the plane. Where's Dr. Yetkatov?"

"Here, sir," Dr. Yetkatov stepped toward Joel.

"Make sure your people are ready. Everyone on the list goes. JD, refuel the plane from the jerry cans inside the plane. Top off both tanks. Save two cans for the bus, and leave the rest for Chappy."

Chappy found a folding ladder tucked in a compartment along with some wheel chocks.

"OK, that lets us reach the wing gas filler caps, but we need a funnel," Murph said.

Dr. Berthold suggested pulling sheet metal from the side of the bus and rolling it as a funnel, which did the trick.

With the work under way, JD asked Joel, "Any problems?"

Joel slapped his thigh. His torso rocked as a deep horselaugh blasted across the grassy meadow. "You'd be amazed, JD. Felix did a number on them. He's driving back on the motorcycle. They parked this shark-faced plane at the end of the ramp, next to a fuel truck, right next to the fuel tank farm. I mean only a few feet away. Stupid place to park a plane. We filled a dozen jerry cans with gas, loaded 'em, and moved the plane, then Felix opened a drain valve on the fuel truck. The gas streamed straight toward the tank farm, neat as you please.

"He set a couple of timed igniters . . . and *boom*. The gas truck exploded and destroyed a couple of Russian transports. Then the tank farm exploded. The noise reverberated in the air, miles away. That was one big bang, I tell you. The firefighters will have their hands full for hours. They didn't send any planes after me. I flew a long way south before turning north, to throw off anybody watching." As Felix rumbled into camp on the motorcycle, Joel added, "I think Felix stows magic in his sack. He'll take good care of you and your people."

CHAPTER 47

ONE SHOT

Wednesday, 2 August 1950, Midday
The Mongolian Meadow

Satisfied with the refueling progress, Joel said, "Chappy, in the cockpit ASAP. I want to check you out." They settled into the cockpit, Chappy on the left.

"These are the throttles. Those are the mixture controls," Joel pointed at the oddly located controls. "Whoever laid out this cockpit never flew much." He methodically reviewed each control and instrument. Chappy paid strict attention to everything Joel told him.

"Watch for the red 'low fuel' marking," Joel warned. "When the needles reach to the top of that zone, put this thing on the ground, you're about dry. The pilot's manual says there's virtually no reserve."

Chappy said, "So when you're out, you're *out*? I don't like the sound of that."

"Not much we can do."

With only one shot to lift off from the meadow, Chappy's tongue stuck to the top of his parched mouth. He wiped his sweating hands, and asked to Joel to repeat the instructions again. "OK, Joel, show me again, what's the startup procedure?"

Joel showed him, then said, "Watch out. This thing doesn't like to fly out of ground effect. You've got to really horse the elevator when your airspeed is about 104 KPH. That'll pop you out of ground effect, just don't overdo it. Keep an eye on those trees, you may need to dodge them. Once airborne, this ol' Pike flies pretty well. Tom reads Russian. He can help with the pilot's manual. Of course, in a pinch, there's the native speakers. Let's find Cajun. He's working on the maps. He'll want to see these new ones and plot the course."

※※※

"T'anks, man," Cajun welcomed the new maps Joel found in the Pike. "Deese aviation maps much better, ya know? An' Joel, I t'ink dis general, he plan ta fly ta Kamchatka or somewhere on da Pacific coast. Several of dem are for dat area. Dat's the direction we're headed. Don' ya t'ink we should keep deese?"

"Good idea, Cajun."

Consulting the old map, Cajun transferred some points to the new one. "We're here, Chappy. Distance aroun' 800, 850 miles ta Hami. Dat probably means a refuel stop. What's its range, Joel?"

"Book says 475 with a light load, 425 miles close to gross. Terrain'll be a concern, Chappy. Finding a place to land may be a bit spotty. The ground is pretty rocky most of the way. How much gas remained after the tanks were topped off?"

Felix said, "We saved two jerry cans for the bus, that leaves eight. They're forty liters each, about eighty gallons total. Should half fill the tanks."

The hair on Chappy's neck rose. "No matter how you slice it, I'm still short by several hundred miles. Any place we can tap some gas?"

Tom Long said, "In Övörhangay Province, the small town called Arguut has a training airport for Mongol pilots where they refuel the provincial government's airplane. They'll refuel for gold." He stretched his arm past Chappy's shoulder and pointed to the tiny town on the map. "Looks like it's about half-way to Hami."

"How do you know that?" Joel asked.

Tom shot a smug look at Joel. "I have my sources."

Joel and Chappy performed the walk-around together to verify the rugged plane shook off the landing. Pulling grass and wildflowers from the tail wheel, Joel patted Chappy on the shoulder, "You'll do fine. *Fly* the airplane, don't force it. We'll pray for you."

"Nothing like leaping off into the unknown with a planeload of innocent souls."

With the walk-around complete, Joel shouted, "Everyone on board." As everyone lined up, Joel shook hands with Dr. Yetkatov, Dr. Valena Tumanova, Konstantin Dushkin, Tom Long, JD, Reggie Symthe, and Smitty before they climbed into the plane.

Chappy said to Joel. "Good to work with you again, Joel. I hope we meet again soon." Lines of deep concern radiated around Chappy's eyes.

Joel shook his hand, then patted Chappy on the back, knowing full well this might be the last time he'd see his friend.

Susan hugged Chappy and said, "Get yourself home safe to that wife and baby of yours, you hear?"

Chappy grinned. "Ronnie's almost six, Susan. He'd throw a fit over being called a baby."

Joel closed the door behind Chappy. Susan and Joel walked to the edge of the meadow and waited for the engines to start.

CHAPTER 48

TAKEOFF

Wednesday, 2 August 1950, Midday
The Mongolian Meadow

The engines on the Shcherbakov ShchE-3 Pike ran smoother as they warmed. Chappy jazzed the throttles a couple of times to check responsiveness. He shifted the control wheel through its range of motion, then blipped the throttles again and moved the tail a bit, to maximize the distance to the trees.

"Tom, watch the airspeed indicator, there. When you read 105, yell *speed* as loud as you can, OK? When we take off, don't let me slow below sixty. If I'm getting close, yell again. OK?"

"Got it." Tom white-knuckled the sides of the copilot's seat. Despite his combat experience, he'd never shared the responsibility of flying a plane before. "I despise flying. Seems unnatural, to hang in the air with no support or anything."

Chappy's heart raced. Dry as the Mongolian dust, Chappy rolled his rough tongue around his parched mouth. He glanced out the window. Joel gave him a thumbs-up. Chappy sucked a deep breath into his lungs, slammed the throttles to their limits, and released the brakes.

The Pike bounced twice as it accelerated down the sloping meadow, flattening the wild flowers as it picked up speed. *Hold the tail down, maximize the speed.* Chappy hyper-focused as the plane bounded across the grass and the controls came alive. *The trees, the trees are almost on top of us.* Adrenaline screamed through his body like a jolt of electricity. His jaw clamped, grinding his teeth.

"Speed!" Tom shrieked with crackly terror.

Chappy pulled the control wheel back. With a slight hesitation, the Pike jumped off. The trees loomed like a wall. *We're not high enough.* His heart jackhammered against his ribs. He pulled back harder.

Tom bellowed, "Speed! Speed!"

Hot sweat drenched Chappy's underarms. Chappy lowered the nose and rolled right. A tall tree flashed by under the left wing. A clipped tree branch plunged downward. Then, clear air. The sloping ground fell away. The Pike climbed into the spacious Mongolian sky. Chappy raised the flaps. The nose lowered. The airspeed indicator sped faster. The altimeter read five hundred meters. A guttural victorious laugh escaped deep from Chappy's throat.

"Just like taking off from LaGuardia." Tom snorted and rolled his eyes.

Everyone on the ground suspended their breathing as the awkward airplane leapt skyward and banked to miss the tree. Everyone shouted in triumph. As the Pike disappeared, a stab of emptiness welled and caught in Joel's throat. His heart palpitations failed to settle down as the engine noise faded.

"He's been my dependable right-hand man and good friend. Now, he's headed to China without me. I'm alone . . . responsible for all these people." Joel didn't hear the contradiction. His fear of failing again, of leading men into disaster gnawed at his confidence.

Susan slipped her warm hand into his. "God's covering us, Joel. All of us. And you know He's given you everything you need to figure all this out. Trust God—and yourself."

He opened his mouth to say how much he appreciated her. Thinking better of it, he stopped searching for the right words. Joel leaned down, tipped her head up, and felt her breath upon his lips.

CHAPTER 49

NOSE UP

Wednesday, 2 August 1950, Mid-afternoon
Somewhere over South Central Mongolia

JD chose the seat behind Chappy's in the lumbering Pike. Through the cabin windows, a movement caught JD's eye. "Fighters, off the port tail! Yak-9s!"

Chappy responded with combat-honed reactions: Instantly lowering the nose and banking hard to the left. *Not too hard, Chappy. This thing's a transport, not a fighter. Don't pull the wings off.* Chappy's adrenaline surged. His heart battered his chest.

Shouts of surprise and panic sprang from his passengers as his maneuvers tossed them about in the rear of the cabin. Their shrieks stopped as the Soviet fighters roared past.

Few airplanes can out-turn a Yak-9, Chappy remembered, *and they're fast, over 400 miles per hour. Fighters mean they know we stole this plane. There's no sense pretending. We're easy pickin's for 'em.*

"I'm not makin' it easy," he shouted in defiance, twisting the control wheel again.

A Yak-9 thundered past, guns blazing—missing. Chappy banked away and spotted other fighters coming toward him.

"Divide and conquer, huh?"

He feigned turning right just before they passed and grinned with satisfaction that all three took the bait. When he banked to the right, an awful pounding roar enveloped them. The left engine exploded like thunder, spewing parts that rattled against the fuselage. Chappy saw the smoking 37mm Nudelman-Suranov cannons on the Yak rocketing past only feet away. Sweat poured down his face. His plane dying, the controls jerked in Chappy's hands.

JD grabbed his gun duffle. In one smooth motion, he yanked out his M1 carbine, and shoved in a fifteen-round magazine. He smashed the window beside him and fired four precise, three-round bursts at another Yak. Smoking brass clattered on the floor. The Yak jerked away, oily smoke pouring from its engine.

Powerful hammer blows juddered the plywood fuselage with violence. Another Yak concentrated its firepower on the Pike's tail. The raw smell of human fear mixed with cordite and cannon smoke.

Absurdly neat, round holes appeared at the rear of the cabin. The smell of fresh-cut wood and smoke filled the cabin and cockpit. Valena Tumanova screamed in pain. A man howled in pain, his voice unrecognizable.

Impossible to control, the limp control wheel flopped in Chappy's hands. Fire erupted from the left wing. The elevator failed to respond. Another Yak roared behind the plunging Pike. The nose of the Yak's hollow propeller shaft spat out a dozen rounds from the powerful cannon.

The wild beat of Chappy's heart matched the thunder of the steel-tipped ammunition blasting its metal storm of destruction. The violent jerk of the engine in its mounts, rattled it apart. A huge chunk of the three-bladed prop careened away.

The tinge of terror tingled up Chappy's spine. *I longer control this plane.* The powerless Pike twisted sharply left. The huge rocks below appeared scattered about like playthings for a giant child. The plane hurdled toward dun-colored rocks.

Adrenalin surged through Chappy's muscles. He yanked on the control wheel with hysterical strength, then suddenly released his pressure. Chappy yanked again. Somewhere in the tail section, the elevator control cable snapped away from the broken longeron that jammed it and pulled back into the pulley groove.

"There. Now, I've got you." His thick arm muscles bulged in desperation as he strained to raise the nose. Chappy yelled the second-to-last thing Tom wanted to hear, "Pray." Then Chappy shouted to a terrified Tom Long, "The flap lever, pull down the flap lever."

Long grabbed the lever as if it were the handle to salvation itself, and yanked. Hard.

The stricken craft grudgingly responded to the nose-up commands. With agonizing slowness, the Pike pitched toward a more-or-less, wings-level configuration.

Somewhere in the back of Chappy's consciousness, he heard more cannon rounds. *The ground's sloping. Get the nose up, Chappy. If I can pull it up a little, the space between those big rocks . . .*

CHAPTER 50

MURDER

Wednesday, 2 August 1950, Late Afternoon
Ulaan Baatar, Mongolia, Colonel Ivan Semyon Yabitov's Office

Lieutenant Colonel Ivan Yabitov tried to make sense of the reports about the huge fire and explosions at the Ulaan Baatar airport. He hazarded a guess to Boris Kostenka Tsarsko, "I'm convinced the Mongolian Courier-Corporal saw the general's plane. There was no wreckage of general's aircraft, so someone flew it away. The obvious conclusion, then, is the Americans stole the Pike and escaped with the scientists. Since that aeroplane has limited endurance, what would be their destination? We can find them, don't you think?"

"Yes, Comrade Colonel." Yabitov's smug supposition irritated Tsarsko. He repeated Yabitov's speculation in a monotone. "We shall find them. The Red Air Force and the Mongolian People's Army Air Forces continue searching. "

"I share your confidence." Yabitov's telephone rang. "Send him in."

The office door opened, admitting a young, frightened soldier. "A message for the Comrade Colonel from the officer at the airport, sir."

"Speak."

"Sir, our gallant Air Force fighter pilots report shooting down an aircraft of the type being sought sixty-five kilometers southwest of Ulaan Baatar. No survivors reported, sir."

Yabitov rose. "Excellent. Tsarsko, go to the crash site at once and verify everything. Wait—a Major Vassily Petrov is among the general's men, an expert on aeroplane crashes. Take him." Yabitov released a long sigh. *"Finally, I can brief the general."*

XOXOX

Tsarsko rubbed his sore backside, the sluggish pace of the bumpy drive to the crash site took forever. He held a handkerchief over his nose and mouth against the choking stench of burnt bodies and the ever-present Mongolian dust. He scowled at the peasants wandering through the wreckage.

"Who's in charge here?" Several peasants glanced at Tsarsko and continued poking through the wreckage. "Get them out of here," Tsarsko roared the order for everyone to hear.

A man confronted Tsarsko. "My name is Mongolian People's Army Captain Nicholas Batbayar, in charge of this investigation. Who are you and what do you want?"

In a guttural, authoritative tone, Tsarsko retorted, *"My* name is *KGB* Colonel Boris Tsarsko. I will investigate the crash of this *Soviet* airplane. Remove your people—*now."*

"No," the captain's firm reply reduced Tsarsko's pupils to pinpoints. "This is the territory of the Mongolian People's Republic. It is *my* responsibility to investigate. With respect, Colonel, step aside until we complete our investigation."

Major Vassily Petrov broke into the conversation. "Colonel, they are disturbing vital crash evidence. I must view everything where it lies, without disturbance, if I'm to provide an accurate report."

Tsarsko loosened his pistol in its brown leather holster. The spotlight of Tsarsko's unwavering glare into the Mongolian captain's face accompanied his measured, cold command. "Captain, remove your people, immediately, or suffer the consequences."

The captain crossed his arms. "I will not."

"Then I will remove you." Tsarsko's pistol cracked. Two high velocity bullets hissed through the air.

The Mongolian captain writhed as the ground sucked up his life blood. All the Mongolians froze in place.

"All of you—*leave*."

The eyes of one man standing near Tsarsko flitted from side to side, seeking someone to tell him what to do.

The 7.62 mm Tokarev TT-33 automatic pistol jerked in Tsarsko's hand twice more. The brass striking the ground struck an almost musical note. The Mongolian lay face down, unmoving.

"Interrogate them. See if they found something. Major Petrov, begin your investigation."

A broad-faced Mongolian soldier said, "You have no authority here. I will tell you nothing."

Pistol shots echoed off the near-by hills. The soldier's lifeblood saturated the Mongolian dust.

"Now then, who will speak with me?"

CHAPTER 51

MOVE OUT

Wednesday, 2 August 1950, Late Afternoon
The Mongolian Meadow

Felix said, "Move out, folks. We gotta leave, fast." The scientists climbed aboard the bus in less than ten minutes. Despite earlier objections, the scientists had reconciled to dividing up. Lifetimes of conditioning shaped their compliance.

Bumping along the meadow toward the road, Felix drove past a gentle slope, the perfect place to drive onto the road. He shifted into reverse, backed onto the road, then said, "I'm going to spread confusion."

The tracks left by the bus curved toward the Mongolian capital. "When they find the tracks, they'll think we headed toward Ulaan Baatar. Give me a second to sweep away our reversing tracks. About five or six miles down this road we'll turn north for a couple of hours, then park, and do some head-scratching."

Three hours later they bumped off the road into a thick birch grove and climbed out and stretched their tense, stiff joints. While Murph assembled his radio, Felix directed everyone to cover the bus with the camouflage netting.

After they finished, Felix pulled Joel aside, "Boss, we need to talk. My friend at the airport told me about a guy who'll trade horses for the bus. I could ride north to make contact. We might need to throw in a few gold coins, too, but it'd be worth a few bucks to rid ourselves of this rig."

"Yes, the bus is too easy to spot from the air, even camouflaged," Joel agreed. "With horses and local clothes, we'll blend in."

Murph counted. "We'll need nine horses, plus a few to haul our stuff."

Dr. Berthold offered, "I will, of course, experience great difficulty getting on and off a horse." Ana Bakhtina rubbed his shoulder with compassion. Berthold smiled in spite of himself.

"Dis bus worth enough ta buy all da horses we need?" Cajun asked.

"Don't count this bus out," Felix said. "It looks beat up, but it offers a lot—a new engine and tranny, six new tires, and new upholstery."

Dubov said, "We'll need tents, and maybe livestock to blend in."

Felix glanced at Joel, "If you'll pay with gold maybe we could buy a yurt—easy to carry, weather resistant, and big enough for us all. And they attract about as much attention as a rock."

Joel said, "OK, I'll give you what you need. But we'll keep a reserve for contingencies. Take the motorcycle, find this guy, and see what kind of deal you can make."

Dubov said, "Let me go with him, Joel. I speak Russian like a native. That might convince him to deal with us."

"Along with the gold," Felix added.

"Offer them the motorcycle, too. How long do you think it will take to make the deal?" Joel asked.

Felix said, "They don't do business slam-bang like Americans. They'll get to know us first to see if they can trust us. I'm guessing about a day's ride, a day of initial discussions, and a day or two, maybe three, of nitty-gritty negotiations, another day back here. So four days, maybe more."

Joel bit his lip. "All right. Leave at first light. We'll hide the bus better and organize ourselves. If you're not back by Monday, we'll leave without you and drive the bus as far as the gas takes us, then figure out what to do next."

CHAPTER 52

DIS-INFORMATION

Thursday, 3 August 1950
Early Morning under the Birches, Eastern Russia

The coral dawn peeped above the horizon and faded into the blue-violet atmosphere as Dubov and Felix climbed onto the motorcycle. Roger rode in the sidecar with a gas can on his lap. Felix kick-started the engine, which roared to smoky life. "See you in a few days, folks."

Despite the early hour, everyone saw them off. "Be careful," Ana Bakhtina said with a fearful tremor in her voice. "Our lives are in your hands."

"God bless you," Susan said. "Goodbye."

They rumbled off followed by a cloud of dust.

Joel said, "OK, everyone, there's work to do. Dr. Kalugin, help Murph camouflage the bus. Use tree limbs to break the outlines so the bus can't be spotted from the air. You know what I'm talking about, Murph."

Murph gestured a thumbs-up to Joel.

"We need to inventory our rations. We'll need to hunt."

"I've seen rabbit and deer around, even a wild boar," Dr. Berthold said. "We must be mindful of the carnivores—wolves, lynxes, and bears. They will find us soon if not already."

"Good points. The last thing we need is to lose our meager rations to a wandering bear." Joel wrote on his notepad to hoist the food high in a tree, on a slender limb.

Cajun cocked his head. "I'm pretty good hunter. A rabbit stew taste pretty good 'bout now, don't ya t'ink'? Jus' don' wanna blow 'em apart with a .30 caliber or a 7.62mm."

Joel said, "Yeah. Inventory the weapons and ammo, then we'll turn you loose on the unsuspecting local game."

Murph said, "Felix has a .22 in his bag of tricks. Will that work?"

"If he has ammo," Cajun said.

"If Felix has a gun, he has ammo."

As the sun rose, Joel looked over his handwritten list, then said, "Ladies, please inventory the food and decide what we can cook in. We need something to boil water in." He stopped. *Where's Susan?*

Just then, she emerged from the trees, her face white and her eyes red. Susan wiped her mouth and said in apology, "I'm afraid something in last night's supper didn't agree with me."

Joel rushed to her side. "Are you OK?"

"Feeling better." Susan waved him away.

Ana Bakhtina stepped beside Susan. "I'll see to her, Colonel Joel."

Still worried about Susan, Joel continued. "Dr. Berthold, please help me and Cajun plan a route to the Pacific coast. These aviation maps aren't the best, but we'll make do. Murph, when you finish with the bus, we'll send a radio message out about what's happened."

Ana nudged Dr. Kalugin. "First, Colonel," Dr. Kalugin said, "Are you aware the Russian Army has other such bombs as those we destroyed? Ought not we inform your . . . listeners?"

"*What?*" Joel said. "Where?"

Kalugin raised his chin a little, "My colleagues and I saw components for several more, perhaps a dozen. They assemble them in secret, outside of Moscow, not at our laboratories. I don't know where."

"This just keeps getting better and better," Joel muttered with a hint of sarcasm. His gut clinched. *Hope I'm not getting an ulcer.*

Joel wrote down what Dr. Kalugin just revealed, then walked over to Murph and handed him a note. "Radio this to Washington, to update them on what's happened since JD's team arrived at the bus depot."

"That's a lot, Joel." Murph stroked his bewhiskered chin. "We don't dare send that in a single message. Tell ya what . . . I'll confuse eavesdroppers by breaking the message into several short one or two-sentence signals. I can imbed in the first message that we're going to use short messages, and throw in some 'random' frequency changes too. I'll use shorthand code words to shorten everything." He rubbed his fingers back and forth across his lips. "Maybe I'll send a couple in Chinese or Russian, that'll throw them off. Can we spread this over several days?"

Joel considered Murph's suggestion. "They need to know about the additional bombs ASAP, and to expect Chappy and his people. That's the absolute minimum. The rest we'll send later. Can you code our location if Cajun does a star fix tonight?"

"We gotta be *real* careful with that, Colonel. If they break the code, they'll know *exactly* where to find us. Maybe an offset—" Murph's voice trailed. "Yeah, I'll put an offset clue in one message, then the doctored location in another. Even if they break our code, they still won't know where we are."

"Offset? You mean sending wrong Lat/Longs?" Joel asked.

"Sure. If I tell 'em the offset, they'll make the corrections." Murph shot Joel a shrewd look. "You'll want to tell them every time we move, won't you?"

"Yeah, probably. But if we're moving every day or so, maybe we should restrict our messages, and not send them on a schedule. Sooner or later, especially when we're closer to the coast, I think they'll send a recon plane to check on us."

Susan and Ana completed the food inventory. Susan frowned. "Joel, we only have forty-seven C-rations of the hundred and fifty that

JD left. At three meals a day for the seven of us, that's just over two day's worth of food remaining."

Joel's left cheek contorted up, closing his eye. Wrinkly creases shot across his forehead. "Well, if Cajun can bag a rabbit or a marmot or two each day, we can make things stretch. Roger and Felix are due back tonight."

Susan's sweet smile melted Joel's grimace of concern. "God will provide."

"I pray you're right, beautiful lady. I pray you're right."

As she walked away, Joel's lips pursed and furrows lined his forehead. *I wish I knew what's wrong with her; she's been sick every morning. It's not the food. The rest of us are fine.*

CHAPTER 53

SOMBER NEWS

Friday, 4 August 1950
In the Birch Grove, Eastern Russia

The next morning, Murph found Joel chopping firewood. "Joel," Murph addressed him in a flat, emotionless tone. "There was a message from the airport."

Joel lowered the ax to his side, then looked at Murph, "And?"

"Bad news. The Russians shot down the Pike. No survivors. Tsarsko's at the crash site."

Joel gasped and dropped the ax. "No survivors? Oh, no. Chappy. Hopefully it was quick." A sharp ache in his heart filled his eyes with tears. He and Chappy shared a close friendship and the terror of combat. Joel stood for a long moment, head down, until the first wave of anguish passed.

"We need to tell the others."

As they trudged back into camp Joel dreaded what he must say. *I want to find Susan and hold her close.*

"Everyone, there's bad news." Joel's voice cracked. "The Reds shot down Chappy's plane. Everyone . . . killed. No survivors. They're all . . . gone."

Like a death rattle, the sharp, agonal breaths of everyone vibrated in their throats. Susan moved close to Joel and clung to him. Salty sorrow trickled down her face.

More alone than ever, everyone looked horrified as they realized their tenuous hopes for the others vanished. The question left unsaid hung in the air. *And what of our fate?*

The weight of the responsibility to get out alive niggled at Joel's doubts.

The blood drained from Dr. Kalugin's face. "I never dreamt such a thing could befall us. All gone? I do not know what to say. Trusted colleagues, friends, suddenly lost." With a dizzy gait, he searched for a log to sit on.

Dr. Berthold gave Joel a studious look. "Colonel, could they know how large our number was to start? If not, they may think we all perished. We know there were seventeen of us. Is it reasonable they might assume all of us were on that plane?" Dr. Berthold asked.

"I don't know." Joel warned. "Don't underestimate them. They may connect the disappearances of Chappy, Cajun, and me with the others."

With the back of her hand, Susan swiped away the tears on her cheeks. "Psychologically, Yabitov will want to believe we all died. That would tie up all his problems with a tidy bow. The fly in the ointment is Tsarsko. He never takes anything at face value. He may decide there aren't enough bodies." Her shoulders and chest convulsed, as gasping sobs engulfed her. Joel pulled her tight against his chest.

Joel looked over Susan's shoulder and eyed Murph. "We can't delay that message to Washington any longer."

CHAPTER 54

CODED MESSAGE

Saturday, 5 August 1950
Washington, DC

T he Deputy CIA director strode into the Oval Office. "Mr.
President, we received several coded messages from our people
in Mongolia."

"Give me a summary, please."

"Yes sir, Mr. President. A total of seventeen people escaped from
Ulaan Baatar. Three Russian scientists, four of the CIA extraction
team, and one aircraft crewman attempted to escape to China in a
stolen airplane. They were shot down. No survivors. We only know
the numbers, no names yet."

Truman's breath caught in his chest. "That's awful." His shoulders
sagged under the responsibility of both missions he authorized. His
mind flicked ahead to the sad letters to write to their families.
"Was Dr. Kalugin a survivor? He's the reason for this risky and
costly operation—be almost too much to bear if he didn't make it."

"Sir, we don't know for sure who was killed. The surviving group
is somewhere in far eastern Russia, far from the Mongolian border.
They encoded their location in a transmission we haven't deciphered
yet. I'm sure you understand they must be careful how often they
transmit and for how long. The Soviets monitor every transmission
in their territory."

"Of course," the President said. "Anything else?"

"Sir, a senior Russian scientist said the Red Army has at least six more A-bombs, maybe as many as eighteen. He believes they'll replace the ones our men destroyed. He still insists his mission was simply to test the bombs. At this point, sir, there's no contradictory information. I personally place a high level of credibility on the report, since it was sent over Colonel Knight's signature."

Truman stroked his face, deep in thought. "Despite what Admiral Hillenkotter said, I was sure they had more than the two bombs we destroyed. Damn. He's wrong again. I want to discuss this with your people and the Chiefs. Schedule a meeting. Listen, those survivors are in a real pickle. How can we help?"

CHAPTER 55

BODY COUNT

Monday, 7 August 1950
Ulaan Baatar, Mongolia, Colonel Ivan Semyon Yabitov's Office

Boris Tsarsko sank in a weary heap into the proffered chair and dropped a dingy canvas bag on the floor. He slapped at his dusty uniform. "What a miserable, god-forsaken country."

"I do not need a commentary. What did you find?" With an irritable sweep of his hand, Yabitov shoved papers aside on his desk.

Tsarsko said, "The crash site is about sixty kilometers from here as a crow flies. Of course, on these pitiful, primitive so-called roads, we travelled more than 120 kilometers."

"What *did* you find?" Yabitov's tone sounded less than congenial.

"We confirmed it was General Lobov's airplane. The manufacturer's works plate and serial number are proof. The wreckage appeared smashed, broken, burned. I hate airplanes, do you know? The wreckage was scattered everywhere. The fuselage broke into three parts. Even the bodies were burned."

"How *many* bodies? Whose are they? How many persons aboard?" Yabitov insisted.

Tsarsko twisted in his chair. "That's a difficult question, Colonel. The bodies were charred beyond recognition. Some remains only broken skeletons." He shivered in revulsion.

"That Red Army major you asked me take along says six to eight people. Expert. Bah. He only guesses. Must have been at least ten people, from all the body parts. He poked and sifted through them, disturbed every one. He's a ghoul." Tsarsko almost spat, but thought better at the last second.

"What evidence of who they *were*? What proves that it was the Americans and the scientists?"

"This . . ." Tsarsko opened the canvas bag and pulled out a book with the stark Russian words *Highest State Secrets* printed on the cover, "was found in the scattered debris."

Yabitov snapped opened the book smelling of smoke. It contained page after page of technical drawings and mathematical calculations. "This is meaningless. I'm a soldier, not a scientist. Wait . . . Dr. Ilya Kalugin signed here. This is it. Here is proof—these *are* the papers of the traitor Kalugin." He snapped the page with his finger.

"There is also this." Tsarsko held up a small piece of scorched pasteboard. "The Party Membership card of Dr. Valena Tumanova."

"Hmmm. Good. This is good." Yabitov rubbed his hands together. Being afraid of rejection, of being wrong, made him overly cautious.

"You're sure? No survivors? Were there any witnesses?"

Tsarsko's bushy, caterpillar eyebrows crawled down the bridge of his wrinkled up nose. He tugged his upper lip above his gum line. "Mongolians are repulsive. They did not cooperate at first."

"At first? What have you done, Tsarsko?" Yabitov asked with more than a hint of ice.

Tsarsko peered at him with merciless eyes. "It is nothing. After I shot one, the others cooperated."

"You shot one, you fool? You've no authority here. No legal right to detain them, let alone shoot them. They are our 'Fraternal Socialist Brothers,' do you not remember? How will you explain this?" Yabitov's words chilled the air.

"Do not worry, Ivan Semyon, no one will miss two or three of these ignorant savages."

"Two or three? What *have* you done? No one authorized you to take such actions, *Comrade* Tsarsko. If you are lucky, you *may* avoid formal charges." His frigid tone became as hard his glacial glare. "Do you know how close Mongolia is to open revolt? The last thing Chairman Beria needs on the eve of our actions in Korea is an uprising in Mongolia. If that happens because of you, you will find yourself standing against a wall."

"What?" Tsarsko asked, unbelieving. "After all I've done for the Motherland, for you? You abandon me over some *Mongolians*?"

Yabitov's lethal eyes fired at Tsarsko. "This time, you must face the consequences of your constant over-reaction and rash decisions. *You* will brief General Lobov and tell him exactly how you gained your information." An echo of the grave rang through his words.

Fear and rage surged through Tsarsko's veins. *Yabitov throws me to the wolves, over some worthless Mongolian peasants?* A cold chill prickled down his spine, accompanied by icy sweat. *Yabitov will do anything to save himself. If he so much as mentions this, I'll be shot.* His mind scrambled for a way back into the mercurial colonel's good graces.

Before he could react, Yabitov's adjutant knocked on the door. "Comrade Doctor Major Vassily Petrov, sir."

Yabitov scowled at Tsarsko, then sneered, "I dislike these technical officers, especially, so-called 'Doctors of Pathology' who are also aeronautical engineers. They dishonestly obtain rank." He paused, glowering, then sighed. "Send him in."

Tsarsko realized, *I am to say nothing.*

Major Petrov saluted. "My initial crash scene analysis is complete, Comrade Colonel." He carried a small sheaf of typewritten pages.

"On my desk, Comrade Major. A summary. *Now.*" Petrov appeared unfazed by the cold, intimidating imperative.

"Of course, sir." He stood with his hands behind his back in the approved Red Army semi-attention stance. "The subject aircraft, a twin-engine Shcherbakov ShchE-3 serial number AE17F3974, crashed

in the Middle Mongolian dessert at approximately Latitude 46° 37'
North, Longitude 106° 17' East in the Mongolian province of Dundgovi
as the result of concentrated cannon and machinegun fire from Yak-9s of
the 303rd Fighter Air Division. At the time of the crash, both engines
stopped turning due to damage from cannon fire. The crash impact
was severe, breaking the fuselage into three large pieces."

Petrov's intelligent, brown eyes gleamed behind circular, gold
wire-frame glasses. "The right wing was substantially destroyed by
impact. The left wing survived, but burned completely after impact.
The remaining wreckage was heavily burned both prior to the crash
and as a result of the crash. I experienced difficulty, therefore, in
ascertaining the pre-crash condition of the aircraft."

"The passengers?"

"Injuries to all were consistent with either large caliber gunshot
wounds or blunt force trauma due to severe impact, or both. Several
may have been dead prior to the crash. All injuries, whether from
gunshot or impact, were not survivable. Only the copilot's body
remained intact, although badly burned. All the other bodies suffered
dismemberment. The crash and subsequent fire were not survivable."

Yabitov hid his surprise at the detailed, dispassionate report
Petrov delivered without notes. "We must know how many bodies
you found, Major."

"Comrade Colonel, without proper clinical facilities and
formal autopsy procedures, I cannot be precise. My educated
estimate based on preliminary examination is one female and
approximately six males."

"*Approximately* six males? Can you do no better?"

"No, sir. I was presented with multiple dismembered and burned
bodies, with the single exception I noted."

"Why can't you just count them?" Yabitov asked with irritation.

"Colonel Yabitov." The major donned the tone of a bored professor
answering a dull student's self-evident question. "At a major crash,

sir, one finds it difficult to determine which piece of leg bone, say, belongs to whom when there are multiple victims. Aviation gasoline burns at a high temperature, leaving little."

"You are positive there was but one woman?" Yabitov struggled to find a question that didn't make him appear the fool.

"Yes, sir, quite positive. You see, a female's pelvic structure is quite different from a male's, easily distinguishing them. The female was tall, slender, long legs, mid-thirties."

"Tumanova."

Tsarsko's left eyebrow raised with question. Yabitov flicked a finger, giving him permission to speak.

"Tell me, Major," Tsarsko interrogated, "did you discover a dwarf among the male bodies?"

"No, absolutely not."

Tsarsko faced Yabitov. "I submit to you, Comrade Colonel, that this aircraft was *not* carrying all the scientists. Had it been, you would have found two women's bodies, not one. Where is Ana Bakhtina's body? Where is the German dwarf? Both are distinct enough."

"Da, that is so. I would have found a second woman or a male dwarf immediately. They were not in the crash remains," Petrov confirmed.

As Yabitov's scrupulous construct wrapping up the case collapsed, his shoulders twitched. A scant trace of a smirk twisted Tsarsko's left lip as he recognized Yabitov's quandary. *Time to turn things to my favor.*

"Sir," Tsarsko said with feigned thoughtfulness, "the Mongolian Courier's report. Didn't he say he could identify the place where the plane landed? Perhaps the other traitors await its return."

Yabitov's eyes widened with eagerness. "Yes, that's what he said, Tsarsko. In fact, he said it boldly. Order him to take you there and search the area."

CHAPTER 56

SECOND LOOK

Wednesday, 9 August 1950
On Road A-137, Mongolia

"So how will you find this place, Courier-Corporal Gantulga? From memory?" Tsarsko asked.

"Oh, no, sir. I recorded the information in my journal—date, distance from my depot, time, and the course changes I observed. I am Junior Sergeant-Courier now, sir." His chest extended with pride, showing his shiny-new collar badge.

Tsarsko couldn't read the Mongolian's scratching. *I hate taking the word of a mere underling.* In his coldest, most threatening voice he demanded, "Take me to this place, Comrade *Junior Sergeant*."

"Of course, sir. The location is about one hundred twenty-eight kilometers from this depot, taking the A-317 road."

Tsarsko turned to one of his men. "How can we measure distance, Ivan?"

"We can't, sir. Our trucks measure time of operation, not distance traveled."

"Sir," Gantulga said with enthusiasm, "if you give me authorization, I can take my motorcycle, which has an odometer."

Four jarring hours later . . . Gantulga waved them to a halt. The Junior Sergeant-Courier parked his motorcycle by a ditch, removed his goggles, and walked back to Tsarsko in the lead truck. "This is where I relieved myself, Comrade." He pointed toward a clump of bushes. "I observed the aircraft flying on a course of . . . ," he glanced at his journal, "about 127 degrees. The aircraft then made a turn to the north and flew on course 019 degrees, and dropped from sight behind those trees on the ridge." He pointed to the long, sloping hillside, at a line of birch trees, three-quarters of a mile away.

"How did you determine these courses, Gantulga?" Tsarsko challenged the man who was not his equal.

"Using this, sir." Gantulga held out his battered Japanese compass.

Tsarsko grunted. *So far, this sounds reasonable. Woe to him if he is lying. I will take great pleasure in shooting him myself.*

Tsarsko ordered his men, "Go to that hill and investigate. You . . ." He waved his arm at Gantulga. "Wait here with me."

Gantulga cocked his head to the right side as his right shoulder rose in acquiescence. He marched in obedience back to his motorcycle, and shut off the fuel petcock, per regulations, lest the carburetor become flooded. He leaned against the side of the seat, and waited.

An hour and a half later . . . Tsarsko noticed his senior KGB Red Star NCO descending down the hillside. *They found something so quickly?*

"Well?" Tsarsko demanded.

"Comrade, There is no doubt an aircraft landed and took off in the meadow. We found truck tire tracks and evidence of people as well. I would say at least a couple were women, perhaps more than two. They camped here, although animals disturbed the site. We also discovered motorcycle tracks."

"Did you ride to the meadow, Gantulga?"

"No, sir," the Mongolian replied. "It is forbidden to drive my machine off the road."

"Boris Kostenka," the NCO said, "my men are following the truck tracks northeast." The gruff man pointed in a northern direction.

"Gantulga, is there another road nearby?" Tsarsko's eyes narrowed with cruel intention.

"Yes sir, the B-223 road, a secondary road, not so good as this. B-223 joins this highway twenty-five kilometers to the west, sir. We passed the junction on the way here."

)O(O(O(

Two hours and fifteen minutes later . . . a sweating man bearing an aggravated frown crossed the ditch and approached Tsarsko. "I followed the truck tracks as they left the meadow, Boris Kostenka. They led to a road, as the Junior Sergeant-Courier said. There's something about this I don't like."

"What is that, Sasha?" Tsarsko trusted the man's instincts.

Sasha swiped the sheen of sweat from his forehead. "The tracks indicate the truck headed toward Ulaan Baatar. But the tracks seem *too* plain to me, as if they want us to think that. They tried to hide them. The tracks stopped and reversed before going onto the road, as if they missed the turn, but . . . "

"But, what?" Tsarsko interrupted.

"Boris Kostenka, if you drive a truck off the road, you must drive very slow and it is a rough ride. Then why would you drive *past* this obvious place to get back on the road? I think they staged this. I think, in fact, they drove the opposite direction."

CHAPTER 57

ESCORT

Wednesday, 9 August 1950, Late Afternoon
In the Siberian Birch Grove, Eastern Russia

D r. Kalugin sprinted toward the bus from his sentry post near the road. Short of breath, he gasped for air, then called out, "Colonel Joel, Colonel Joel, a motorcycle is coming. Could be Roger and Felix. I saw also a car not far behind, so it may not be them." He stopped and sucked in more air to ease the tight sensation in his chest.

"Go back. Shout if there's a problem." Joel said to the others, "Pick up your weapons and take your hiding spots. Leave your safeties *on* until I say otherwise, or until you hear gunfire."

A motorcycle engine revved twice above the chirping of the birds, then revved two more times—the agreed-to signal. In moments, a grinning Felix wheeled the dusty Russian R71 and its empty sidecar into the clearing.

"Hey, folks, back like a bad penny." He pulled off a leather pilot's cap he'd never worn before.

"You made it back just in time. Today was your deadline to be back before we moved out. Where's Dubov?" Joel asked.

"He's with Yakov in the car."

"Yakov?"

"You'll meet him in a minute. I told him to park beside the road. We don't want to scratch that thing or his dad will tan his hide."

Roger Dubov ambled into camp followed by a handsome, dark-haired, young man about twenty. A second man, a bit older, more Chinese-looking, followed him. Susan scrutinized them. *I can't figure out their ethnicity. These young fellows could be Mongolian, Russian, Chinese, or all three.*

"Folks, this is Yakov Deripaska. He'll escort us to his dad's collective farm. His dad wants to buy the bus. This is Yakov's cousin, Vitenka."

"Good day to you all," Yakov said politely in educated Russian. "My father recommends you quickly follow me home, to prevent detection." He nodded toward Susan and Ana. "Ladies, you would honor me if you permit me to drive you in my father's automobile."

The experienced group loaded everything into the bus posthaste. In fifteen minutes, everyone sat in their bus seats, except Susan and Ana.

"If you ladies are ready, please follow me," Yakov bowed and smiled, revealing the dimples in his cheeks. He picked up their luggage and walked toward the car. Utterly charmed, both women giggled and followed him to the car.

"I'll help," Joel said, anxious about being separated from his wife. They plodded to the road where an unusual, blue car waited.

"Looks like an old Chrysler Airflow, except smaller." Joel examined the four-door sedan in disbelief. "What in the world is it?"

A laugh from the young man's belly broke the somber atmosphere. "My father's pride and joy, Mr. Teach. This is a 1936 Toyoda of model AA style. The Japanese held great admiration for the artistic design of the Airflow automobile of Chrysler. They copied the design, but made the car smaller for their roads. The automobile runs well and rides comfortably. My father has owned it since 1940. Parts are somewhat difficult to obtain these days, but he has managed. I should tell you, it is to honor you that he allowed me to bring it here."

Yakov loaded the suitcases into the trunk as Joel opened the back-hinged "suicide" rear door and peered inside. He helped Susan settle into the plush mohair of the upholstered seats. Then he walked to the other side of the car and opened Ana's door.

Yakov's cousin Vitenka and Joel boarded the bus. Murph hopped into the driver's seat, cranked up the engine, then inched out of the birch grove and onto the road. Felix pulled the motorcycle between the bus and the imitation Airflow. They both followed the diminutive Toyoda on the bumpy, dusty road. To the west, the sun slipped below the horizon.

Vitenka spoke to Joel. "In about twenty-five kilometers, sir, we will take a turnoff to enter the repair barn from the rear."

An hour and a half later . . . the Toyoda slowed to a stop. The glare of the headlights revealed a farmer's gate.

Yakov boarded the bus and said to Murph, "I'll open the gate and close it behind you. See you at the repair barn in fifteen minutes." Yakov exited the bus as quickly as he boarded, then lifted the elongated gate and swung it open. He waited until the bus drove through the gate onto what appeared to be open prairie.

Joel watched Vitenka for any indication of an ambush or trap, his hand not far from his M1917 .45 revolver. But the young man appeared unconcerned as he directed Murph into the deepening darkness. The headlight beams bounced in an erratic fashion over the hummocky ground. Joel noticed tracks from previous vehicles. Conflicted, his thoughts ping-ponged between a sense of comfort and sensing something ominous.

At the top of the rise of a low hill, they noticed lights glowing on a cluster of buildings. In the center, tall doors on a metal building stood open, beckoning. Murph drove inside without stopping. The doors closed behind them.

CHAPTER 58

WELCOME

Wednesday, 9 August 1950, Evening
Red October Collective Farm, Eastern Russia

"Welcome, welcome to Red October Collective Farm. It is my pleasure to greet you. My name is Commissar Uri Jeirgif Deripaska, your host." A large, solid-built man with a Fu Manchu mustache and work-hardened hands splayed his arms in welcome. A broad smile creased his sun-darkened face. "Come, a feast waits for you, my friends."

Joel glanced at a small group of men nearby.

Deripaska detected Joel's glance and said, "My men will disassemble the bus. By morning, nothing will be left but scattered parts."

"I'm Edward Teach, in charge of this group." Joel offered his right hand to Deripaska. "Forgive me, I thought you needed a *bus*." Deripaska's hearty handshake reminded Joel of his rancher father.

"Just its parts, especially that new motor and transmission. We will use everything. We waste nothing." A sly smile crossed his face. "Besides, it is much more difficult to find a bus that does not exist, yes?"

Joel chuckled. *The bus can't exist. The Soviets allow no private property. Reducing the bus to salvage eliminates the possibility of ownership.*

Deripaska intuited Joel's thoughts. "We sometimes make our own rules in the wilds of the far-away east, just to get by. What works in Moscow . . . " His shoulders and palms lifted up as his lips turned down. "Doesn't always work here. So, please, come. We will eat and talk."

"Oh, please, could I bathe first?" Ana asked.

"Oh, yes," Susan seconded. "We haven't bathed in days. I'm dying to wash my hair."

Deripaska's bushy eyebrows raised in amusement. "Of course, dear ladies. How rude of me not to realize you must first freshen yourselves." He bowed. "Our ladies will escort you to the baths. You gentlemen may avail yourselves of our shower facilities, as well."

Two hours later . . . Deripaska rubbed his hands in anticipation in a private dining room off the huge dining hall. Joel noticed opaque curtains covering the windows, separating their group from the main dining room.

"Now, dear guests, a true Russian feast: a variety of fine meats—goat, ox, sheep, caribou, wild boar. Is there bear this day?" He asked a primly dressed worker in a white apron.

"Sorry, no bear today. Also chicken, duck, goose, pheasant, and potatoes. What Russian feast does not include potatoes? Carrots also, and cabbages, turnips, beets, beans. Tea, vodka, and beer also, if you like."

"I'm overwhelmed, Uri Jeirgif," Joel looked hungrily at the steaming dishes. "Do you always eat like this?"

Deripaska's laugh rumbled from his chest. "No, my friend. Very seldom, in truth. But we do not often entertain such distinguished guests, and we Russians never pass the opportunity to celebrate, yes? We are proud to show what a *properly* run collective farm produces. Now a select few of my family and workers will join us. But until we decide who we shall say you are, we shall restrict the access of others."

He waved to everyone. "Come everyone, let us eat and honor our guests." Everyone seated themselves as workers in white aprons served steaming potatoes, vegetables, and meat.

Susan said, "Oh, Joel, try this wild boar. It's good." She dropped a portion on his plate. "A lot better than C rations, I must say."

Joel tried the roasted boar and smiled his approval. "Delicious . . . don't forget, I need your observations." *Susan looks radiant with her blond hair tied up on her head, but then she looks great under any circumstances.*

Deripaska raised a glass of vodka. "To our honored guests." Mumbled thank-you's circulated the room, accompanied by warm smiles and uplifted glasses. Joel toasted with a glass of water.

Dr. Berthold flushed crimson when somehow, again, Ana found a seat next to him. After a few moments, she said to him, her voice soft. "May I ask you a question, Heinz Luthor?"

"Of course, yes." *No one in Russia ever uses my first and second names the way the Russians are accustomed to when they are with friends or family.*

Her steady, warm eyes stared into his. "Have you ever—please excuse me for being blunt—been friends with a girl or woman?"

"Well, my mother . . . " The worry clasping his heart plucked his heartstrings and he changed the subject. "My early education was at home by tutors, you see. At university, I kept apart from others. Girls found me . . . repulsive," he stated as a fact without any pity. "My relations with female colleagues are cordial. But as friends? No. As much as I know about many things—physics, ballistics, atomic energy—the opposite sex confounds me."

Ana's dimples dotted her cheeks near her upturned lips. Then allow me to be your friend. I will teach you."

Embarrassed, Luthor squirmed in his chair, then turned his attention to Deripaska who was downing another vodka.

"Let me tell you of our farm, Edward Teach. We hold fifteen hundred hectares, give or take. That is about thirty-two hundred of your American acres. About five-hundred hectares is under cultivation, the remainder is grazing lands or idle."

Joel whistled. "Back home in Colorado, my dad's ranch is a little over two sections, or about thirteen hundred acres and that's considered large. This place is huge."

Deripaska's ample chest swelled with pride. "Da. Everything in Russia is huge, or so we maintain." He winked at Joel and Susan. "Most of what you eat tonight we raised on the farm, or obtained nearby. We do not operate as do the collectives in the west. I refuse the limitations of quotas. We raise what we can for each other and provide the surplus to the Communists. Well, some of it.

"Like other collectives, we pretend to meet their quota, and they pretend that we have done so. That keeps the Party happy, and they mostly leave us alone." His eyes sparkled with mischief. "We often invite a Party observer to winter over with us. They don't acclimate well." A chuckle rumbled deep in his chest.

"You are self-supporting then?" Joel asked between bites.

"Yes, very nearly. You see, this is more like a small town than a typical collective. Because we are so isolated, we have a tannery for shoes, boots, belts, and tackle. We grind our own wheat and bake bread. Our property is forested, so we mill our own lumber. To the east, are nut and fruit orchards.

"We grow hay for winter feed for more than three thousand heads of cattle. We maintain a slaughter house and smoke house. Our cannery preserves meat, vegetables, and fish from our streams. We generate electricity hydroelectrically and heat many buildings with steam from the hot springs nearby.

"My second cousin's daughter went to university and is our resident doctor. Our medical staff includes a dentist, as well. Our veterinary clinic is the largest in the region. We operate a modern breeding program.

"To accomplish all this, we're forced to venture outside to obtain parts, fuel, and lubricants for over fifty trucks and tractors, and other machinery."

Joel said, "You run this like an American farmer or rancher. Are you a secret capitalist, then?"

"Ah, you show good insight." A self-satisfied smile brightened Deripaska's face. "Yes, as much as I think I can sneak by the officials. I operate so people who work gain the benefit. Is that not right? Those who work harder or smarter gain more. But of course, no one starves. After all, most of these people are my relatives. Still, if you do not work, you are granted subsistence only. Non-workers have no claim to the benefits going to those who work hard."

His smile slumped to a frown. "I only pretend to be a Communist. I hate them and everything they represent. I should not speak so. I could be overheard."

He's slurring a little, Joel noted.

Susan leaned forward. "This is delicious, Uri Jeirgif, thank you so much. May I ask why are you are entertaining us? Isn't that dangerous for you?"

"Your lady is as direct as she is beautiful, Edward Teach. Here is why, my dear guest. My ancestors lived here for more than two thousand years, long before the Bolsheviks. We shall be here, still living in this God-blessed land long after *they* are but distasteful memories.

"Let me say also, you are not the first, hmm? During the Great Patriotic War, we helped several Allied aircraft crews, escapees from a closed gulag nearby. I do not underestimate the power of the Party or the Army to crush me and everything here." Deripaska slapped his palms on the table. "Nevertheless, I don't avoid any chance to work toward their demise. I may not live to see freedom in my land again, but surely, my sons shall." Defiance danced in his eyes.

Susan said, "You're not surprised by our presence."

The genial man leaned back, spreading his arms. "My dear, do not be misled. We are *geographically* isolated, but we are well aware of what goes on in the world. A thirty-meter-tall antenna is nearby. It's one of the most powerful radio transmitter-receivers for several thousand kilometers. We monitor Radio Moscow and repeat the 'news' locally each day at 6 a.m. and again at noon. Remember, we are six time zones ahead of them. More important, we monitor continuously the short wave broadcasts of station Radio Free Europe and station Voice of America.

"In wintertime, we often receive commercial broadcasts from America. Can you believe we can hear KNX radio station in Los Angeles, California, KOA in Denver, Colorado, and WLS in Chicago, Illinois? Each month, if weather permits, at least one of my many sons travels to China, and sometimes to South Korea and Japan. We have contacts also in Singapore and Hong Kong."

Murph caught Joel's eye. The two exchanged knowing nods. Murph needed access to the radio.

That sly smile snuck across Deripaska's lips. "I have also my own spies—shall we call them—in the Soviet Army, and elsewhere: Family members or former farm workers. I know a great deal about the escape of these scientists and the sabotage team who, shall we say, interrupted service on the vaunted Trans-Siberian Railway, no?"

Joel glanced at Susan's rapt attention. *Susan is intrigued with this man. I hope she remembers to watch for clues to what he really thinks.*

Susan said, "How do your sons move in and out of the country, Mr. Deripaska? I believed the USSR far more controlling of their citizens' movements."

Deripaska's smile flatlined. "I can thank my late departed first wife, Alina—that means *beautiful*, you know. During the thirties, she witnessed the chaos as the Communist Party tried to gain control here. They never really did, you know. She obtained passports from Hong Kong and Singapore, for herself, our three sons, and me. Wonder of wonders, we are allowed to renew them and add many others by spreading a little 'Russian oil'—a few Rubles here, a few Rubles there—but no problems."

While Deripaska and Susan chatted, Joel caught Felix's and Murph's eyes. He lifted his glass, looked at the glass, and shook his head back and forth. No matter how generous Commissar Uri Jeirgif Deripaska was with their drinks, Joel needed his men clear-headed tonight. *We'll take turns standing watch tonight, despite the cordial reception. It's way too soon to trust these people.*

Deripaska pushed his chair away from the table and stood up. "My farm livestock workers and I begin our day at 0300 and eat a hearty breakfast before starting work. Please excuse us as we leave to go to bed." Joel shoved his chair back and Deripaska patted his shoulder. "No, stay. Eat and drink all you want. Maybe you join us for breakfast, yes?"

Susan interrupted, "We're tired and 0300 is terribly early."

Deripaska chuckled. "Our livestock workers need a second breakfast and eat with the rest of the staff at 0800. Please rest and join us for breakfast at 0800."

Joel said, "Yes, I understand. That's how my dad runs our family's Rocking K ranch back home."

CHAPTER 59

COLLECTIVE FEAR

Thursday, 10 August 1950
Eastern Russia Red October Collective Farm, Eastern Russia

The long night passed with no signs of threatening activity. Joel, Murph, and Felix rotated three-hour tours as sentries, monitoring the men and women's dormitories. Felix drew the last tour, reporting bleary-eyed to Joel at 0600.

"Didn't see anything, boss. Nobody went in or out of the ladies' dorm, and the guys who came into this building a couple hours ago went right to bed."

"OK, get some rest and join us for the second breakfast. Remind everybody to assume they're being watched and listened to." Joel murmured to avoid waking the others.

Joel gathered their group and headed to breakfast. When he saw the cafeteria, he said, "Ah, a *real* breakfast."

"I'll say," Susan said. "Look at that food."

The cooks served mountains of eggs, meat in thick slabs, sturdy porridge, piles of aromatic still-warm bread, and huge jars of jam in many colors. Tubs of butter beckoned near the bread. Cheese in several varieties enticed with sharp aromas. A pile of smoked fish tempted the hungry visitors.

Dr. Kalugin gestured toward the griddle, with a glint of pride in his eyes. "Ah, true Russian delicacies, *blini*, traditional yeasty Russian pancakes. Wonderful." Dr. Kalugin helped himself to a steaming stack. He pointed. "Those are farmer-style *syrniki*, hearty cheese pancakes filled with tea-soaked raisins. Both delicious."

A large, green glass jar held hardboiled eggs. The smell of strong brewed tea rose from several huge samovars. Joel searched for coffee in vain, settling for the strong tea thinned with boiling water.

As he downed his porridge, fried eggs, and syrniki, the scuffing of a chair caught his attention. Turning, he noticed Susan headed out the nearest door, her hands over her mouth. He rose and darted after her.

)O(O(

Uri Deripaska found Joel after breakfast. "So, Edward Teach, come to my office and let us conclude this. Let us be quick, so you can depart."

Joel smiled, raising his hands. "A great democrat like you should know, I don't *command* this group, I lead them. We all need to vote on any decisions."

Deripaska's brisk attitude infected everyone. Joel rounded up his people. Uri's sons scurried to find enough chairs. Half an hour later, everyone gathered in Deripaska's office. "Yakov, please close the door. Thank you. We will not be disturbed. This office is, shall we say, *isolated* from KGB recording devices. There is no time for pretense or subtlety. I know exactly who you are, Colonel Joel Knight, Dr. Kalugin, the rest of you, and why you are escaping."

As if on cue, the eyebrows of everyone in Joel's group shot up. Wrinkles branched out on their foreheads. The whites of their eyes and their o-shaped mouths revealed their shock. Ana Bakhtina covered a small gasp with her hand. Felix and Murph tensed like over-wound springs.

"KGB has not yet discovered where you went after leaving the meadow where the airplane landed. They will divide their forces to search for you. They will almost surely come here, because we are the largest settlement in the region."

For the first time since their arrival, Deripaska's intense gaze and stern tone unsettled them. "Very few people know you are here and very few will know when you leave. I will not pretend no informers are here. We endure the official politruks, of course, whom we can manage. Those who go behind our backs—those we worry about. Once the KGB arrives, I will do all I can to obscure your whereabouts and delay their pursuit. You must depart, no later than tomorrow morning."

Ana grabbed her knees, pulled them against her chest, and rocked back and forth, whimpering. Susan knelt beside her, and whispered soothingly in her ear. *If she doesn't gain control of herself, this could be a real problem here.* The subtle change in the room's tension about-faced from fear of immediate capture to a palpable concern about getting away.

Joel said, "Yuri, you should know, our goal is the Sea of Japan, as soon as possible, by whatever means you can place at our disposal." He waved his index finger toward the scientists. "The crucial thing is making sure these people escape safely. The stakes are very high, Mr. Deripaska. Not just for them, but for the world."

"Da," Deripaska's face soured. "I hold a good idea of Moscow's intentions. I do not want another war, not with America, not with anyone."

"Do you recommend that we head straight east to the coast? The terrain and primitive roads expose us to aircraft."

Deripaska said, "I am thinking it unwise for you to venture into Chinese Manchuria. Perhaps a feint turn in that direction, and then, how do you say? Make a U-turn toward the air field."

"Air field?"

"Ah, you do not know. Our Soviet Air Force built a large base about eight hundred kilometers from here, near Magdagachi. They are training pilots, there many planes, even—," he waved his hand dismissively, "those screeching ones . . . *jets*, aren't they called?"

"Why there? Isn't the chance of being discovered even higher near the military?" Murph asked in an anxious tone.

"Two of you are pilots. Why not journey to where there are airplanes to . . . ah, borrow?"

Deripaska amazed Joel and Murph that he knew so much about them.

"Won't they guard their airplanes, since they know we're at large?" Susan asked.

"You don't know the Soviet military, my dear lady." Deripaska lifted one bushy eyebrow. "At such an isolated location, it would surprise me if there are *any* guards not on discipline duty. Most are drunk. Vodka is cheap, even there. And what do they guard against?" He spread his hands and tilted his head to the side. "They go through the motions. Besides, KGB will not dare reveal they lost civilians they supposedly already captured."

"Fighter planes seat two at most. Are there cargo planes at the air field?" Joel said.

"Oh, do not worry, my dear Colonel. The Soviet Air Force colonels and generals must travel in comfort, yes? And many important supplies—like vodka—are transported by airplane because of slow trains. So, at Magdagachi Air Field are many two-motor transports. Occasionally, even four-motored ones. Some of the older bombing planes also carry people. You have many choices."

CHAPTER 60

DETAILS

Thursday, 10 August 1950
Deripaska's Office, Eastern Russia

"Details," Deripaska said. "Please exchange your clothing with us. We admire such stylish garments. If you dress in our mundane clothing, you will be less obvious."

Joel asked, "You mentioned a physician. Before we leave, could some of my people see a doctor?"

"Da. Doctor Lyudmila Kazakova, my second cousin's daughter. Competent, and pretty, too. Who wishes to see her?"

Susan, Ana, Dr. Berthold, and Dr. Kalugin raised their hands.

"Very well. I think she shall come to us, to draw less notice," Deripaska said.

Joel's turned in eyebrows twitched up. *Maybe we'll discover why Susan's sick all the time.* "We're lightly armed and can't defend ourselves. Do you have weapons or ammo for us?"

Deripaska's eyes crinkled with warmth. "Joel Knight, we have an excellent arsenal. I can give you more than you can carry." Identifying both CIA operatives, Deripaska suggested, "Mr. Felix and Mr. Murph can help you choose."

Yakov spoke up, "Father, I wish to ask your permission . . ."

With a slight frown of displeasure, Deripaska turned toward his son. "Permission for what, Yakov Evgenii?"

"Father, these people may never find the air field if they travel into the wilderness alone. Worse, Army patrols might discover them. I ask your permission for Ilya and me to escort them to make sure they reach the air field in safety. Besides," Yakov's head tilted forward and his eyes widened, "It's time I accomplished something more useful than counting cows." His brother Ilya's face radiated with the promise of adventure.

"Oh, it is, is it? We shall see."

Deripaska will give them a hard time. Joel recognized the same indulgent smile on Deripaska's face he'd observed on his dad's face. *He's already decided to let them go.* Joel added, "That's a great idea. We could easily become lost even in a small forest. Taking on a rugged forest this large without expert help seems foolish. If someone's watching, your sons will change our body count, which could help throw off Yabitov." Yakov flashed Joel a grateful glance.

"So. You conspire against me with my own sons, do you?" He laughed. "Of course, you need expert guides, and sending them saves me the nuisance of going. So, get ready, you young whelps."

Grinning, Yakov scurried from the room. Ilya stayed to snatch another syrniki.

"I intended to ask them to accompany you," Deripaska winked at Joel. His smile faded as he slipped a huge ring of keys from a locked desk drawer. "Please, follow me to the armory. You too, Ilya."

Felix and Murphy trailed after Joel and Deripaska. Deripaska unlocked a heavy steel gate and strode down a cement ramp into a large, half-round, soil-covered building that looked like an American ammo dump. A pair of massive, steel doors at the base of the wide ramp opened to row after row of brand new, large, heavy trucks.

Deripaska chuckled at Joel's unasked .question. "After the war, trains continued shipping American lend-lease supplies eastward from Vladivostok. With our war ended in so sudden a fashion, we received no orders about what do to with such wonderful vehicles. Of course, an official collective farm has many uses for such trucks, so

I obtained a few. More than fifty, to be precise. On those same trains we discovered American war supplies intended for the Army. In such confusing times, someone needed to place them into protective custody, yes?"

He strolled past the gleaming new two-and-a half ton GMC CCKW 352 trucks to a dirty cement block wall. His shoved a broken cinder block out of the way with his foot and stepped on a hidden pedal. Without a sound, the wall moved aside. Deripaska flipped a light switch. Joel whistled at the racks of M1 Garand rifles, M1 carbines, and M1A1 Thompson submachine guns, still in Cosmoline. Stacks of cased Colt M1911 .45 pistols rose high above his head. Browning .50 caliber machineguns gleamed under the naked light bulbs. Wooden cases marked "Browning Automatic Rifle (BAR) U.S. Caliber .30 M1918A2" comprised another tall stack. Nearby shelves held hundreds of wooden ammo boxes.

Deripaska said, "Heavier guns are nearby—howitzers, anti-tank guns, anti-aircraft guns, bazookas, and mortars in several calibers. If revolution comes, we are ready, my friend. Will you want some of these?" He pointed to the Thompson submachine guns.

"No," Felix piped up. "They waste ammo. We need carbines, M1911 .45s, and ammo. What about 7.62R rounds for our M1891/30 Mosin-Nagant?"

"Got any grenades? Cleaning kits?" Murph interjected, "We'd like some .38s for the ladies."

"Of course, everything is here, everything. Ilya, collect what these gentlemen need. Do you prefer Russian or American grenades?"

"Both," Murph said.

CHAPTER 61

COLLECTIVE MINDS

Friday, 11 August 1950
Hangar G-1, Ulaan Baatar Airport

Boris Tsarsko waited as the KGB Red Star Battalion filed through the large sliding metal hangar doors into the drab aircraft hangar. With a sense of pride, he stared into the scarred faces of tough men who'd never failed him. *They are without fear and follow every command to accomplish the job. What a joy to work with them.*

"These are all the men available, Comrade Tsarsko," said a stern-faced Lieutenant.

"Thank you, Comrade Lieutenant." Speaking as their equal, Tsarsko's voice echoed in the large hollow expanse. "Comrades of Red Star, we were successful in destroying the traitors' stolen aircraft. We killed at least six or seven. Your proud combat history has sharpened your powers of observation and I need to know what you observed to decide whether to search for additional traitors and spies. The smallest fact may help. What did you see?"

Tsarsko gathered these hard men together to compare notes and impressions. Their collective knowledge always amazed him. Little things added together created a sum that equaled success. He set out to build a good reputation with these men. Tsarsko respected them and valued their contributions, no matter how insignificant. If he remained patient, a picture of the situation would not escape them.

Yabitov sneered with disdain. "You will find nothing useful from peasants, they are cannon fodder, not intelligence gatherers."

"Nevertheless, I shall do this, Comrade Colonel. I always work with them in this manner. And please, I request that you do not attend. Your high rank intimidates them."

Yabitov's neck and face reddened. His jaw clenched as he scowled at the men standing stiff at attention. A stony silence descended upon Hangar G-1. Yabitov shifted his glare to Tsarsko. As an aircraft taking off interrupted the silence. Yabitov stomped away. Tsarsko knew Yabitov didn't dare oppose him. Someone with the Chairman's ear, like Tsarsko, always carried the Chairman's implied authority.

A corporal raised his hand.

"Comrade Corporal?"

"Comrade Tsarsko, at the bus terminal, I overheard someone say a collective farm bought an old bus. There's no collective farm, yet the bus disappeared. A Mongolian said something about a foreigner."

"What foreigner?" Tsarsko leaned forward.

"The man was vague, sir. He thought the buyer was a foreigner because of his accent."

Tsarsko jotted down the corporal's comment in his notebook.

In the front row, a grizzled sergeant frowned, then raised his hand.

"Comrade Tsarsko, the Mongolian Secret Police reported several people at the bus terminal walking from the waiting area to a nearby garage. Sometimes passengers use the toilet facilities, if the terminal is crowded, but there was no crowd that day."

"How many people?"

"Perhaps ten, including at least two women."

A second corporal interjected, "Also at the bus terminal, sir, I spotted a woman with blond hair. She may be the woman spotted at the American Embassy a few days ago. Blond women are uncommon here, perhaps she's the same person?"

Tsarsko pointed. "You two step aside and discuss this and establish the time of these events. I must know when the missing bus left, and if that happened before or after people walked to the garage."

Tsarsko began another tack. "Did anyone hear anything about the crew of the American bomber we destroyed?"

"We know they went to the American Embassy by official car, sir. I know of no sightings since." The lieutenant confirmed Tsarsko's suspicions.

"What do our embassy spies say?"

"Our senior KGB man said there was no official record of them arriving, sir."

Tsarsko's eyes narrowed into horizontal strips, like a snake focusing on his prey. His lips stretched across his face into a thin, tight strip. "What else?"

Another said, "A maid who cleans visitors' rooms said none of the rooms appeared slept in."

"They did not sleep at the Embassy? Did anyone see them leave the grounds?" The only response Tsarsko received was dead air. *They need more urging.* "Either they remain in the embassy in a secret area, or they escaped the embassy without our knowing. What surveillance do we have of the embassy?"

A slight sound of turning pages broke the stillness. A sergeant said, "Sir, I obtained the KGB embassy surveillance logs. They record the arrival of the aircrew at the embassy. Then about ten minutes later—" He flipped pages back and forth between the entries from two observers in separate logs. "According to our observer at the rear of the compound, a local grocer's truck departed through the rear entrance and turned north onto the Khoroo 9 road." Tsarsko recognized him from the meadow as the Red Star soldier who pointed out the bus's tracks heading toward Ulaan Baatar.

"What's your name Sergeant?"

"Sasha Demyon, sir."

"Where does this road lead, Sergeant Demyon?"

"Toward the bus terminal, sir."

Tsarsko said, "The common factor is the bus terminal. Anything else?" The two corporals he sent to confer together returned. "Well?"

"Sir, we believe the bus left the garage *after* the people walked to the terminal. They may have left *on* the bus."

The other corporal turned to his comrade, "What sort of bus did you see?"

"Explain what you mean." Sasha interrupted as Tsarsko listened.

"Sergeant, Mongolians use many different types of vehicles as buses, from six-passenger converted automobiles to great, clumsy contraptions made from army trucks, and regular Russian-made buses. Which kind was sold to the false collective?"

The corporal who reported the bus sale said, "Sir, an actual bus, a factory-made bus, about two-and-a-half or three-metric tons in size."

The rear door of the hanger opened. A Red Star man wearing an aviator's coat and the red imprint of flight goggles on his forehead walked in and stood in silence.

"How many passengers could this bus carry?" Tsarsko asked.

"In its original configuration, perhaps sixty passengers," the corporal added. "It was missing several rear seats, leaving space for cargo."

Sasha asked, "Was it equipped with two tires on the rear on each side or just one?"

Tsarsko made a mental note to himself. *This young sergeant seems unusually astute.*

"Two tires on each side at the rear."

Sasha spun to face Tsarsko. "Sir, I think it possible, even probable, this stolen bus made the 'truck' tracks at the meadow. I couldn't tell the difference."

Tsarsko's heart pounded—*the whole picture appears.*

"I have something, too, Comrade."

Tsarsko pointed to a private at the rear. "Comrade?"

"Sir, we found buried food containers at the meadow, American Army 'C-Rations.'"

Now we are getting somewhere. Tsarsko said, "We found similar containers near the sabotaged train . . . more evidence the Americans invaded our homeland. Who has the containers?"

"The KGB, sir," the Private said. "They're comparing them to the others from the explosion site. Americans mark their containers with the production date. If these reveal similar dates, it's probable that they are from the same production lot, which could mean the same people ate from them."

"Good deduction, Comrade Private. Anything else?"

"Yes, sir." The Private continued, "The trash inventory is incomplete, but we found both American and Russian cigarette butts, and a scrap of paper perhaps from the same laboratory book we found at the airplane crash. If that proves true, we can confirm that the people at the meadow are connected to those on the airplane."

"Bravo, Private. This man deserves a promotion, Lieutenant."

"Yes, sir, right away," the lieutenant said.

"One last thing, if I may, sir?" I found indentations in the ground at the meadow, along with the footprints, indicating a person leaned on a cane. Doesn't the German dwarf use a cane?" asked Sasha.

"Indeed he does Sasha," A smug smile widened Tsarsko's thin lips.

The man in the flying jacket raised his hand. "Comrade Tsarsko, I bring news. My pilot flew several kilometers north-east of the grassy meadow, where the road forks to the north. He landed nearby and I spoke with several locals. Two men reported seeing a northbound bus. There's no bus service in that area. Perhaps it's our missing bus, sir?"

"Excellent, excellent. I'm impressed by your good observations."

CHAPTER 62

WHAT HAPPENED?

Friday, 11 August 1950
Meeting at The Kremlin, Moscow, USSR

More than a month had passed since Beria's last headache. Beria recognized the symptoms and this one was worse. His right eye blinded as he stood to walk to the washroom. His hand grasped in the air for his desk to steady his balance, but he missed the desk's edge, and collapsed. Uncontrollable vomit soiled his suit. His right hand twitched, then became unresponsive.

Seized with terror, thoughts flashed through his mind. *Why can't I move my hand? What is happening?* His heart thumped in his ears. *Am I dying?*

Embarrassed, the Politburo members meeting with him squirmed from side to side in their chairs. Beria loved his vodka—but drunk in the morning? They glanced at each other, then called Beria's aide.

The aide rushed into the room and lifted the confused Chairman to his feet. He draped Beria's arm around his neck and half dragged, half walked Beria to a private room. The Politburo members rose and shuffled from his office hushed-murmuring among themselves.

Two hours later a doctor arrived only to receive a shout down from the now-recovered leader. "No, you may not examine me. You are too late. Go, go, I feel fine. Go—*now*."

CHAPTER 63

STARTLING

Friday, 11 August 1950
Red October Collective Farm

Joel's ragtag group gathered in the maintenance building draped in their disguises, shapeless, grey-green shirts and trousers. Clunky, nondescript brown boots laced-up below their knees. Long scarves dangled from Susan and Ana's necks.

Joel stared at his beloved A-2 leather flying jacket that he'd worn since he first pinned on his wings, then stuffed it into a bag. He reminded Dubov to safekeep his Red Army Sergeant Major's uniform.

Deripaska gave them a yurt, then said, "You'll ride in a truck to an orchard on the far eastern reaches of our collective and stay overnight. Then you'll start on your journey with horses and three oxen to carry your provisions and baggage. We'll transport the animals in a truck by another route and meet you at the orchard."

Joel noted Ilya and Yakov's mounts were well-bred riding horses, not working animals, like the others. Joel and Murph distributed the guns. Dr. Kalugin held his Colt M1911 .45 automatic like a venomous snake, afraid of the weapon. Dr. Berthold cleared and checked his M1911 .45, loaded a magazine, and put on the safety. He repositioned his shoulder holster and secured the big automatic.

Dr. Berthold noticed Joel watching him. "This is not my first time to be armed, Colonel."

With a matter-of-fact grip, Ana Bakhtina spun her Smith and Wesson Model 10 .38 revolver's cylinder to verify it was loaded, and set the hammer on an empty chamber. She tucked the gun into her sturdy purse with a handful of cartridges. Her past as a combat nurse accounted for her familiarity with handguns.

Joel whispered to Susan, "She appears competent, but frightened."

Susan murmured to Joel, "Shoulda given her a gun sooner."

Still carrying their own weapons, Dubov and Cajun gathered ammo. Felix's .22 and Smitty's Mosin-Nagant sniper rifle both needed rounds. They each pocketed a hundred rounds. Joel grabbed a new M1 carbine with a box of .30 caliber rounds, plus a hundred-round box of .45 ACP ammo for his M1917 revolver. To his surprise, Deripaska even had C-clips for speed loading the revolver.

Susan nestled her Smith and Wesson .38 in a waistband holster, then elbowed Joel's arm. "We *must* talk."

"Let's wait. We'll talk in the truck."

Leaving no room for discussion, Susan insisted, "This can't wait." She pulled him aside and leaned close to Joel. "Look at me, Joel." Her big, clear blue eyes sparkled with an anxious, yet joyful look. "I've been sick in the mornings because . . . we're going to have a baby."

Overcome with an irresistible need to protect her, his knees turned to jelly. "*What?* Are you sure? When—"

"Our goodbye when you left for China."

"Oh. . . uh. . ." *We both wanted to start a family. Heading overland to the Sea of Japan will be hazardous enough, but this—how can I keep her safe? Oh, Lord, how can I protect her?* "You can't ride a horse—"

"Of course I can, silly. I'm not crippled. We just need to get on with this so our son—I'm sure he's a boy—is born in America."

"A baby." Joel swept her into his arms. "What wonderful news in such a dismal place."

She snuggled in the warmth of his arms. "A spark of light in the darkness."

Joel closed his eyes and held her tight, then stepped back and held her at arms length, "We need to leave." *We look like worn-out workers catching a ride home,* Joel helped Susan climb onto the open truck bed as the earth's purple-gray shadow rose on the horizon. Joel glanced at dusk's haze resembling an approaching storm, then clambered aboard and settled beside her.

The rolled, canvas-wrapped yurt took over the right side of the truck bed, crowding the refugees and Deripaska's sons to the left. Dr. Berthold sat near the front to disguise his size and crippled legs, even though the growing darkness camouflaged him.

Joel's crew shared the truck bed with boxes of saws, pruning shears, and other implements to enhance the deception. At Deripaska's recommendation, their bags and weapons traveled with the animals. Orchard workers didn't carry extra baggage or guns.

Susan leaned against Joel's shoulder and dozed as the truck bounced and lurched over the rough and dusty backwoods trail. Wide awake, Joel tried to wrap his mind around Susan's revelation. Resisting the urge to feel desperate, escaping gained a new level of importance.

Two hours later, they arrived at the orchard. A rough-hewn, one-story log barrack awaited. Joel and Susan shared a room alone, the first time since her arrival.

Joel asked her, "Which bed do you want?"

"Ha." She smiled, leaving much unsaid.

CHAPTER 64

TREKKING

Saturday, 12 August 1950
The Orchard, Eastern Russia

Before Joel awoke, Cajun knocked apologetically on their door. "Sorry, y'all. It's 0500, an' we gotta eat before we leave."

The chill of the Siberian morning, prompted Joel and Susan to speed dress, then gobble down breakfast.

Joel announced to everyone, "Let's mount up." *Well, I'm relieved Susan made it through breakfast with no problems. We'll see how she handles riding horseback.* With dogged looks on their faces, each person trooped out the door and traipsed to their horses.

Before Joel could give Susan a hand, she grabbed the reigns with her left hand and a tuft of mane with her right hand, positioned her left foot in the stirrup, swung herself up, and settled into the saddle. With an air of pride, she smiled and patted her mare's neck. Joel heaved himself into the saddle and moved his horse alongside Susan. Two oxen shared everyone's bags. The third carried their yurt.

With the confidence of an experienced horseman, Yakov rode over to them. "Colonel Joel, today we travel about ten kilometers. The ground ahead is heavily wooded and rocky. I don't want to push too hard."

"You're the expert." The young man pressed his leg against the horse's girth, then cantered to the front.

After four-and-half-hours of tackling the rough terrain, Joel called a halt for lunch. "How's everyone doing?"

Joel rubbed a sore spot on his posterior and chuckled as he noticed the stiff gaits of several people. *Long time since I spent a day in the saddle.*

Dr. Berthold said, "Colonel, I need a better way to grasp my saddle, yes? I can't reach the stirrups and the pommel is too small to give me enough leverage. I almost tumbled into that stream we crossed."

Ilya Deripaska inspected Berthold's saddle. "Sir, are you right-handed or left-handed?"

"Right handed."

Ilya disappeared into the dense Siberian larch, Scots pine, and birch forest. Within moments, they heard the sounds of a handsaw. Ilya returned with a two-inch diameter pine branch with an angled end, looking somewhat like the top of Berthold's cane. "Try this." The boy handed the branch with the short, angled end to Berthold, who grasped the shortest end of the branch. Ilya pressed the other end of the branch against the front of the saddle. "Hold on like handlebar."

The angle made for a comfortable grasp for Berthold's left hand. "Ah, I see—this you will attach to my saddle to stabilize me. This is good empirical engineering, young man."

"Thank you, sir," the boy beamed. "So I will secure the brace under the leather and to the wooden base of your saddle. My brother has a saddle repair kit. We'll shorten the stirrups."

When Ilya completed modifying Berthold's saddle, everyone saddled up and continued their arduous journey. They stopped again at a small stream with grassy banks to water their mounts. Yakov and Ilya unloaded the animals and led them to the water. Cajun, who worked with horses and oxen in Louisiana, helped the brothers.

Before they left Deripaska's Red October Collective Farm, the brothers' father agreed to broadcast an innocuous statement as part of the daily "news" on his radio station to inform Joel and his team about the KGB. Deripaska's suggestion to copy the BBC's technique to send messages to the French underground during WWII met with quick approval.

Murph assembled his radio and put Dr. Berthold to work cranking the magneto. Within minutes, he approached Joel. "No news from Deripaska about the KGB. In about forty-five minutes, I'll listen to Voice of America's evening news." Murph added, "We need to stay on top of what's going on in Korea, which is a powder keg."

CHAPTER 65

FIRST NIGHT

Sunday, 13 August 1950
Far Eastern Russian Wilderness

The yurt impressed Joel. Nomads, who followed sheep, goats, and yak across wind-swept steppes bordered by jagged peaks, created the three-thousand-year-old, circular yurt design. *Instead of analysis, those ancient wanderers tweaked their portable homes until their dwellings worked in the harshest of climates.*

Despite the traveling shelter's roominess, there was only enough space for everyone to sleep side by side. Yakov delighted the women with a theatrical performance revealing a pair of folding beds. "See, they stack one over the other."

"Bunk beds!" Susan burst into laughter. "Thank you."

Joel gathered the men, "Tonight, we'll rotate sentry duty on two-hour tours. I'll start in the 2000-2200 slot. Ilya and Yakov, I'll include you in the rotation. Murph, what's the radio-monitoring schedule?"

"Mornings at 0600, afternoons at 1200."

"Good. Cajun, your sextant chronometer is our most accurate timepiece, so we'll set our watches by that. Take a star-fix tonight, so we know our starting point. I'll keep a log to chart our path."

"Will do, Joel." Cajun turned to the brother. "Ilya, Yakov, how do we protect our food from da animals?"

Proud to be invited in their inner circle of trust, Yakov straightened his back and pushed his chest forward. "We must collect everything edible and hoist the food high in a tree. I brought a canvas bag, and—Ilya, where is the steel cable?"

"Here, brother." Yakov's sixteen-year-old brother lifted up the steel cable. "This one's three meters long, with hooks, so the bag hangs above reach of animals."

Cajun, Yakov, and Ilya strung a metal cable between two trees to hang the food bag from.

Joel asked Dubov to remount his horse and to retrace their steps, watching for signs of the KGB. Joel told everyone, "If we keep the smoke down, I think we can use a cook fire."

Cajun agreed. "With all deese trees, nobody see da fire. An' if we use dry wood, should be minimal smoke."

With the animals fed and bedded for the night, the others started to pull together the fixings for supper. Adept campers in the wild, the Deripaska brothers set about building a fire pit with a rock lining. They fashioned branches into Y supports, which they placed on opposite sides of the fire. The cooking pot hung neatly over the fire from a steel rod nestled in the supports.

As usual, Joel and Susan returned thanks before eating and Ana studied them. Over supper, the group continued planning around the crackling fire.

Ilya said, "The food my father gave us will last only another day or so, Colonel Joel. We must hunt."

"Cajun, will you be our hunter-in-chief?" Joel asked.

"'Course," His grin spread almost to his ears. "Love ta."

"Please, no more marmot. I've 'enjoyed' enough rodent meat," Murph joked.

"Don't worry," Ilya said. "This area has many red deer. One should feed us for several days."

"I've never heard of red deer," Joel said.

"They're basically elk, Joel," Dubov said. "Five hundred pounds or so, dressed out."

"Elk? That'll be a treat. The best T-bone steak I ever ate came from an elk, and that's coming from a cattle rancher."

The blazing oranges and reds streaking the sky faded to a sleepy purple-blue. The damp forest mist drifted into their camp, towing in an autumnal chill. Roger Dubov rode into camp at 2130 hours.

"Nobody else's in these woods." A dark grey, half circle of exhaustion drooped below his eyes. "I saw wolves who seemed pretty interested in my horse. They followed me for a while. We need to watch the animals tonight."

"If these wolves are anything like those at home, they don't need to stalk horses. There's plenty of game in the forest, right Yakov?"

"This is true, Colonel Joel," Yakov said. "Unless these wolves crave horseflesh, they'll leave us alone, but, still, we should watch."

CHAPTER 66

THE SEARCH

Monday, 14 August 1950
Yabitov's Headquarters

"**W**e must search all directions," Colonel Yabitov insisted. "Split your forces into four groups."

Convinced that searching to the west, south, or east would prove a waste of time, Colonel Tsarsko withheld his comments. *Better to humor this Colonel than oppose him on something minor like this.* "Very well, Colonel Yabitov, I'll send teams toward China, Ulaan Baatar, and Ulan-Ude. I'll send my best men to the collective farm. I believe our greatest hope lies there."

Later in the afternoon parked beside the road heading north, a KGB man stuffed a telephone handset into his vest and climbed the phone pole to tap into the single telephone wire and called Tsarsko. "Nothing has been found so far."

"Yabitov orders you to continue on to the collective farm. If you find nothing, you are to return," Tsarsko said.

The sergeant grimaced. "We'll stay here tonight and continue to the collective tomorrow. We could have a hundred miles to go, for all we know. No sense wandering in the dark."

He climbed back down the pole, turned to his men, and clapped his big hands. "Who has vodka?"

CHAPTER 67

DOOMED

Thursday, 17 August 1950, Early Evening
The Camp, Far Eastern Russian Wilderness

Weary from the last four days hard ride, Joel worried about Susan and the baby. *What if Susan falls off her horse? What if she loses our baby? What a trooper.* Susan never complained and pitched in to help every night they pitched camp. This morning was no exception. She smiled while helping others pack up to set out again.

As Joel packed his bedroll, Murph sprinted toward him and interrupted his thoughts. "Colonel, Deripaska just sent the code phrase. The KGB is at the collective farm. He added "departure imminent." They're headed our way."

Joel's gut tightened. "'Wonderful.' Let's hit the road."

At the noon stop, Joel told Dubov, "Backtrack and look for those KGB guys. If you spot them, hightail it back to us."

"Right, boss." He mounted his horse and galloped back in the direction from which they'd traversed the last few days.

That evening after sunset, the deep cover CIA agent's horse slogged into camp. Dubov sagged in his saddle, fatigued from the hard ride. He slid off his panting horse as sweat drenched his steed's coat.

"Found 'em, Colonel, ten KGB Red Star Brigade troops, armed to the teeth. They're also pretty stupid and contemptuous of us, or both. I snuck in close at nightfall and heard them bragging about how soon they'll find us and what they'll do to our women. Disgusting. I stayed until just after dark—they never posted sentries. They're drinking a lot and seem convinced they'll find and kill us with ease."

As everyone gathered, Joel asked, "No military order?"

"None. They're in two big trucks and a Gaz 67 Jeep. They sound like charging elephants, crashing through the woods." His weary eyes expressed anxiety. "They're about ten miles behind us, Joel. With this tough terrain, their trucks can't move as fast as our animals."

Joel rubbed his chin. "Good work, Roger. Grab some chow and some sleep."

Cajun grabbed the reins of Roger's horse and patted its neck. "I'll tend ta his horse."

"Great," Joel said, "Everyone else, conference time." Joel scanned the grim faces by the light of the campfire.

Dr. Kalugin's jittery hands shook. "We are doomed. They will catch us and kill us." The other Russians murmured in nervous agreement.

Cajun said, "We have *skills* dey don' know 'bout. We can defen' ourselves against drunk Russians any day."

"Right," Joel said. "We'll take care of them, maybe that'll buy us enough time to ride to the air field."

"What do you mean, 'take care of them'?" Dr. Kalugin asked.

"Kill them, of course." Dr. Berthold replied in an edgy tone.

"Yes, that's what I mean." Joel sighed.

"Even if they are drunk or sleeping?" Dr. Kalugin quizzed.

"Yes, even then," Joel said.

"But . . . is this not murder?"

"No, Dr. Kalugin, murder is illegal. Killing enemy soldiers on the battlefield is legal. It's war—them or us." Susan cradled her pregnant belly. "Don't deceive yourself. If they catch us, they'll kill all of us. Is that what you prefer? We're weaker and less skilled. We must use guile and surprise to level the battlefield."

"We'll only have one chance to take them out," Joel warned. "If we don't, they'll kill us. Our mission is to survive—it's that simple. Now, here's the plan . . . ."

CHAPTER 68

KGB ENCOUNTER

Friday, 18 August 1950
On the Trail, Late Afternoon

"Wait. What was that?" Felix lifted his hand above his head. Everyone reined their horses to a halt, straining to hear. The animals huffed and snorted. "Truck motors, boss, a mile away, maybe." Felix pointed southwest. "That way."

"My ears aren't the best anymore. Too many hours next to loud engines. Gotta be them. Dubov, check 'em out. We'll wait," Joel ordered.

Dubov clicked his tongue and his horse galloped toward the noises. Everyone dismounted and led their horses down to the stream to water them and camouflage their presence in the surrounding dense wooded area. Each person checked his weapons. All carried extra magazines or rounds in coat pockets, within easy reach.

Forty-five minutes later, Dubov returned. "It's them. Ten, as I said. They're already drunk. They're cooking game stew. Good time to move into position."

"Here's an idea, Joel," Felix said. "No matter how we kill these guys, sooner or later, somebody'll find 'em, right? Instead of the obvious, why not spread confusion and discord. They're drunk as skunks . . . skunks with hand grenades."

CHAPTER 69

AMBUSHED

The KGB troops camped in a small opening in the forest, below a slight ridgeline. A fire crackled in a rock-lined pit. Empty vodka bottles lay strewn around. Past the ridgeline, Joel spotted their haphazardly parked trucks.

Joel counted nine loaded men lazing around the stew pot, preparing to eat. As the tenth man pulled a battered mess kit from a pack, Joel signaled his men to take positions around the Russians.

When they were in position, he gave the signal. Each man pulled a pin from his hand grenade, and tossed it toward the campfire. Joel's grenade flipped end-over-end in the air in slow motion.

From the corner of his eye, he noticed Felix's grenade lope through the air. To his amazement, Joel's grenade plunked into the bubbling stew pot, splashing the Russians with boiling liquid. Before they reacted, both grenades exploded, a powerful double clap of thunder in the silent forest. Seconds later, another grenade boomed.

The hole-riddled, stew pot rolled to a clanking stop. A bloody charnel house of skulls, appendages, and body parts catapulted around the clearing. A sickening mist of dust, stew, and blood drenched the air.

As the echo of the explosions faded, the sharp crack of a pistol punctuated the air. The lone KGB commando, who survived the explosion, wasn't fortunate enough to avoid Cajun's *coup de grâce*. Bloody mercy spurted from his head, and he toppled over.

Joel struggled to keep his stomach under control. "Clear out, men."

Without pulling the pins, Felix tossed a few Russian grenades around the Red Star's camp to give the appearance that the drunk, dead men had played with grenades and blew themselves up.

)O(O(O(

After Joel and his team retreated from the Russians' camp, a Siberian brown bear stopped and sniffed the air. The smell of smoke stiffened the hair on his powerful neck. Every creature, large and small, sensed terror when encountering the huge fires that periodically swept this forest.

The bear tossed his huge head and sampled the breeze. Usually by August, he'd filled out his winter gauntness. Despite his best efforts, he hadn't consumed enough to regain his weight this summer.

Last night, he caught a foolish goose and devoured the bird, feathers, feet, honk, and all. Still hungry, the omnivorous beast lumbered toward the smell of fresh meat. His skin, still loose from hibernation, bounced and rippled. His wobbling run looked like a man clambering about in an over-sized, fur coat.

He reached the wrecked KGB camp within minutes. The smell of men mingled with raw meat. Wary, he hesitated, sniffing. The foxes fled. Crows flapped up and away as his cautious amble entered into the chaos of the ruined camp. He lapped some stew meat. Another chunk of stew meat caught his eye.

His right front foot stepped on something. Recognizing the grenade as something reeking with the stench of man, he halted, then swept the interruption aside with his huge paw. His six-inch claw caught the loop of the hand grenade's pin. Irritated, he hurled the annoyance free.

A thunderous explosion eviscerated the bear's body, launching bear bits into the air. The lifeless animal's body smacked to the ground with the soggy slap of wet carpet.

CHAPTER 70

RUBICON

Hours later, no one spoke until they rejoined the others. Joel's tortured eyes announced to everyone gathered the lethal outcome of their mission, before Joel even spoke the words: "They're dead. We tried to make everything look accidental."

Joel straightened his shoulders bent low from what they'd accomplished to stay alive. "We've 'crossed the Rubicon,' people. Any chance for mercy died with those men. Now, we must ride like the wind to that air field as fast as our horses can fly. The farther away from those bodies, the better. We'll leave at sunup, and push hard until sundown or the horses give out. Now let's set up camp, eat, and rest before our long trek tomorrow."

Everyone worked together to set up the yurt. Yakov and Ilya caught thirty lenok trout while Joel's men were away. The brothers dug a small pit by the stream and smoked the fish. Everyone ate dinner in a sober silence, then headed to bed.

The next morning, a sliver of orange peeked above the horizon. Joel pushed the sleepy refugees to rise, eat more smoked trout, and then mount up.

Cajun rode ahead, scouting the escape route. Around noon he returned. "Colonel, da shallow stream ahead will hide our tracks. Let's ride upstream as far as we can, den go on."

Joel leaned forward in his saddle and shouted, "Follow the stream, folks. We'll ride up the creek bed to cover our trail. Take things slow so your horses don't slip." Joel looked back at Susan, praying her horse didn't stumble.

They splashed along and caught up to Cajun. Sporting a big smile, he reported to Felix, "'Tonto, da Forward Scout' reportin', sir. Dere's 'nother stream over to da right. Ya know what? Da streams, dey split in two, on dat ridge, ya know why? 'Cause dere's a natural dam." His powerful arms stretched out as far as possible. "Big fallen tree blocked by debris dammed da stream. Dere's a hun'erd-yard-long pool behind all of it. I t'ink if we blow da dam, the water'll wash away our tracks."

"I have some C3 in my bag," Felix grinned and pointed. "And there's a big, flat rock under that tree to reflect the blast. I only need one package of C3."

Joel overheard Cajun and Felix and diverted everyone up the hill and told them dismount. "Hide your entire body behind a tree trunk. Protect yourself from the deadly rock and wood fragments propelled outward and away from the explosion."

Felix trailed the wires. His muddy hands placed the charge. Murph fastened the wires to the charge box.

"Fire in the hole!" Murph hollered into the wilderness and twisted the knob. A heavy *whomph* silenced the chirping birds, buzzing insects, and croaking frogs. A tall water geyser gushed into the air. A loud, tortured groan reverberated from the splintered white spruce. With a roar, a flash flood of gushing water jetted through the blast opening, emptying the small lake in minutes.

"Washed our tracks clean away," Ana observed, impressed. "You can't tell we were ever here or even that a tree dammed the stream."

CHAPTER 71

DISCOVERY

Sunday, 20 August 1950
The Red Star Camp

"We found the Red Star camp, Colonel." The telephone connection squawked and squealed, terrible, as usual.

"Speak louder, man," Tsarsko shouted.

"They're all dead, sir," the KGB man reported.

"Dead? How?"

"We can't tell, sir. The bodies are scattered. There's a big bear's carcass, too. I don't know what happened. Animals—fed on them."

"Were they shot?"

"I don't think so, sir. Empty vodka bottles, unexploded grenades lying around. Other grenades exploded. We're trying to find out . . . "

"Leave—*now*. Touch *nothing*. Move *nothing*. I'll send investigators. I'll be there as soon as I can." He slammed the telephone receiver into its cradle with a violent curse.

"My team is dead, Colonel. That fool I sent to find them is telling a fairy tale about hand grenades and bears. I think this is a plot."

"All dead. Your *best* men. What now, Tsarsko?" Yabitov jeered with biting sarcasm.

Tsarsko ignored the gibe. "Colonel, I'm going to this 'Red October' collective farm. Their communications equipment is better. May I suggest you accompany me? We can fly and land at a small air strip."

Yabitov loathed flying with an abiding, primal fear, especially small aircraft. Pride overpowered his fear. "How soon can we leave?"

CHAPTER 72

EXPERT REQUESTED

"Comrade Deripaska, we need trained criminal investigators," Tsarsko demanded.

Deripaska responded with equal force. "There is a *fine* police force here on the collective, Comrade Tsarsko and—"

"I want trained investigators, not country bumpkins," Tsarsko interrupted.

Deripaska ignored him. "Two of my policemen graduated from the All Union People's Criminal Investigation Academy, sir. One, a private, but two years ago. The other, Corporal Boris Lakitov, three years ago. Both received top honors. They obtained the skills you require."

Tsarsko withheld a sarcastic remark. Deripaska ignored Tsarsko's vicious glare.

Suddenly, he needs me. Deripaska mused. *We will 'help' him investigate and pass the findings on to my escaping friends.*

CHAPTER 73

STENCH

Tuesday, 22 August 1950
The Destroyed Red Star Camp

People's Police Corporal Boris Lakitov read his precise notes. "Comrade Colonel Tsarsko, I believe the soldiers in the clearing died as the result of one or more standard issue hand grenades exploding, one within the cooking pot. The bear died as a result of a hand grenade explosion as well."

The violent scene shook the battle-hardened Tsarsko. "I've smelled dead bodies before, but what is that hideous smell?"

"Wolverine, sir. They fed on the dead."

"When did my men die?"

"I can only estimate the time of death, sir. From their bodies' decomposition, I estimate the men and the bear died between two and five days ago."

Lakitov's partner whooped from the slope below the camp. "Over here. Come see." Tsarsko and Lakitov scurried down the hill with Yabitov trailing behind. The young police private pointed to a shattered human skull half buried in rotting pine needles. "This skull rolled down the hill from the camp. Animals and insects stripped the bone of its skin and internal parts. Much of the lower jaw and several teeth are missing, consistent with a grenade explosion. That was not, however, the cause of this man's death."

"What killed him, then?" Tsarsko's eyes darkened with rage.

"This, sir." The police private pointed at a neat hole appearing under the right eye socket with a stick. "He was shot, sir, by a large caliber round, bigger than 7.62mm, perhaps .45 caliber."

"You are sure of this? My men carry no such weapons."

"Yes, sir. I used this gauge—" He pulled a tapered, graduated stainless steel rod from a side pocket. "When I inserted this into the entry wound, I measured .45 caliber, sir."

Tsarsko bellowed to his men. "Look around, see what else you can find." An hour later, Tsarsko's man yelled, "I found a shell casing."

Corporal Lakitov walked to his position, knelt, and inserted a pencil into the shiny brass cartridge. Standing, he sniffed the open end. "Fired within a week." Turning the cartridge to see the base, he said, "Colonel, the markings say ".45 Caliber U.S." in English."

"Well done, Comrade Police Corporal. I shall recommend a commendation for your excellent work." Then he shouted orders to his men. "Find the escapees who shot him. The murdering imperialist Yankees surely left tracks." Tsarsko whirled around only to encounter Yabitov within inches of his face. Drawing in a deep breath, Tsarsko summarized their findings, "Colonel Yabitov, our men died from hand grenades, except one who died of a gunshot wound. We think he was wounded, then assassinated. We found evidence incriminating the Americans. My men are searching for their tracks. I'll send for dogs."

"This is good, Comrade Tsarsko," Yabitov said with formality, certain someone listened. Someone always listened. "You and your men must act quickly. The Americans and the traitors have several days' head start on you."

"Of course, you are right, Comrade Colonel. We shall begin at once." Tsarsko closed his eyes and sucked in a long, deep breath. *This fool has the gift of seeing the obvious.*

CHAPTER 74

WASHOUT

Thursday, 24 August 1950

Washed Out Dam, Far Eastern Russian Wilderness

Colonel Tsarsko and a KGB private named Kaminski stood below the washed-out dam. "Sir, they entered the stream here. So far, we cannot find where they came out again. Their tracks just disappear. We found no evidence they went upstream. This soft mud ought to show their animal's tracks. Perhaps they followed the stream downstream," Kaminski said.

Tsarsko slapped the back of Kaminski's head. "You waste my time. Check upstream as well, at least a full kilometer."

An hour later, the private returned with a broad smile plastered across his face. "Sir, you were right. About three kilometers upstream, we found tracks. They changed direction as well, sir. They're headed north."

"North? What's north of here?" Tsarsko asked.

"Far as I know, sir," Kaminski waved his arms at the forest. ". . . just more of this."

Tsarsko almost struck the man again. "Get me a map. *Now.*"

CHAPTER 75

EASTWARD

Thursday, 24 August 1950
Deep In the Forest, Far Eastern Russia

With Colonel Tsarsko hot on their trail, the nine fugitives rode three hours in the post-dawn sunlight. Yakov consulted Ilya, then said, "Colonel, it is time to turn east."

Joel said, "Lead the way, gentlemen."

Last night, the young men approached him, recommending they continue north fifteen kilometers to avoid a rocky ridge to the east.

"The ridge is not high, sir," Yakov said, "but is steep and rocky. Possibly too hard on the horses and—"

Joel stopped him with a raised hand. "You're the guides."

While this detour added time to their journey, Joel was thankful the ground they covered today proved safer, especially for his pregnant wife.

By noon, they stopped for lunch. Ana surveilled Joel and Susan as they held hands and bowed their heads. Ana, the former WWII nurse who also earned a PhD in nuclear physics, approached Susan and said, "Do you *really* think God can hear you?"

"Yes, I do. Thanking God before Joel and I eat reminds us that it takes more than food to stay alive."

Before Ana replied, the basso notes of thunder rumbled through the forest. A billowy tidal wave of gray clouds roiled ominous.

Yakov rushed over to Joel, an urgent look on his face. "Sir, we must make camp quickly. Storms this time of year are quite strong."

"Yes, our animals could use a break anyway." Joel ordered, "Erect the yurt in that clearing."

A brilliant blue flash of lightening split apart a tall tree a few hundred yards away. The thunder roared like a dragon chasing the full-throttled flash of death. Large raindrops splattered cold on their faces.

Yakov, Ilya, and Cajun unsaddled the horses and unloaded the oxen. They secured the steaming saddles under a waterproof tarp. A pile of bags awaited transport to the yurt.

Joel and Felix fought against the wind and intensifying rain to expand the yurt's framework. Dr. Berthold stood off to one side. With the framework in place, everyone else helped place the felts that covered the yurt. Dubov spread carpets inside. Before the final covers lay in place, Susan and Ana dragged the drenched bags inside.

Hunched over, Murph clutched against his chest his precious SCR-284(c) radio—their only link to the outside world. Dr. Kalugin held a protective piece of canvas over Murph as he carried the heavy, vulnerable radio. Murph moved inside the yurt before the others, wiping stray raindrops from the set with a grateful nod to Dr. Kalugin.

The young Russian brothers dashed inside. "We tied the animals under some trees," Yakov reported. "Mr. Cajun is calming them."

The cascading rain thrummed against the resilient yurt's roof. The felt walls jitterbugged in the rainstorm's fitful wind. Cajun popped in, dripping wet, but smiling. "Deese horses y'all gave us, good animals, ya know?" He turned toward Yakov. "They settle right down, no problem."

"And the oxen?" Joel asked.

"Oxen always placid, ya know? Be good for dem, dis rest, I'm t'inkin'."

CHAPTER 76

STALEMATE

Thursday, 24 August 1950

Deep In the Forest, Far Eastern Russia

*W*e are crawling. Tsarsko's fists repeatedly clenched, then unfurled. "We must move *faster*." His trucks struggled to pass over the same ground the horses traversed with ease. To clear a path, the singing crosscut saws and the snap of felling trees were more frequent than the rumble of truck engines. Tsarsko ground his teeth in frustration.

"Where are the dogs I ordered?" Tsarsko said to no-one. He cursed the forest, the clumsy trucks, the saws and axes. Boris Tsarsko saved most of his vitriol for Joel Knight and the scientists. His obsession with Joel grew by the day. Spittle spewed from his mouth as he ranted.

The primal grumble of thunder in the distance interrupted Tsarsko's maddened musings. As a gentle drizzle alighted like soft kisses on his men's cheeks, Tsarsko commanded his men to forge forward.

Jagged forks of lightening radiated from the clouds. A sheet of light illuminated the sky. On the horizon, Tsarsko glowered at another cloud-to-ground flash of intense light zigzagging toward the ground.

"The weather, the roads, the rugged terrain is beyond my control. I'll never catch him. Never have I failed in such a mission." The lack of control and fear, both unfamiliar reactions, gnawed at Tsarsko's gut. Gentle droplets from grey clouds turned into hard pellets racing down from angry, roiling clouds. The drenching downpour saturated his men's uniforms further enraging Tsarsko's already surly mood. A violent gust of wind discharged wave after wave of diagonal sheets of pelting rain, saturating the men's uniforms. The ground wallowed in mud.

"We make no progress during this storm. The rain washes away their tracks." Compelled by the squall that paralyzed the prowess and potency of his men, Tsarsko commanded the soaked-to-the-skin men to stop their endeavors. They scurried to the trucks to find protection under dripping canvas covers. Tsarsko slumped in the lead vehicle, his Soviet GAZ 67 4 X 4 Staff Vehicle. He fumed as the rain drummed its mournful rhythm on the canvas roof. Pounding hail bombarded the glass windshield like foreboding bullets.

Stopped in their tracks, Tsarsko's grip on the steering wheel tightened. "How am I to explain all this to Yabitov or Chairman Beria? They accept nothing but results, not excuses, not even Mother Nature."

The group's senior sergeant sat silent in the passenger seat. *For a sergeant, the only safe response is no response.*

After a few moments, the sergeant spoke. "Comrade Tsarsko, this is not the worst thing to happen, sir. The men can rest and regain their strength. Surely, this storm will also stop the traitors."

Tsarsko grunted. "You're right, Comrade Sergeant Tokarev. Cook them a hot meal tonight. We'll begin anew come dawn. Order that worthless Private Kaminski and another man to scout a route our trucks can drive over. We must avoid anything that can stop us, even if we don't follow the traitors' exact path."

CHAPTER 77

THE MARKER

Friday, 25 August 1950
Deep In the Forest, Far Eastern Russia

Around midnight, furious flashes of lightening and a long, rolling clap of thunder signaled the storm's final fury. The puffy banks of storm clouds cleared, exposing brilliant stars sparkling against the pure night sky. The Milky Way appeared so close that Joel felt he could almost reach out and play with the glittering crystals. Joel nudged Cajun. "Cajun, get up. Please take a star fix."

Afterwards, Joel and Cajun settled in their rough-and-ready yurt, as the world—refreshed, clean, and beautiful—rested for the night. The curtain of night lifted and dawn awakened Joel and the others. Peach and yellow streaks seeped across the horizon.

The morning star faded as they ate the remaining red deer meat for breakfast.

Joel rose and pulled Cajun, Dr. Berthold, Yakov, and Ilya aside. "Let's study the map to figure out how far it is to the air field."

Using Cajun's Lat-Long numbers, they bent over the map, searching for their location in the vast Mongolian wilderness.

Dr. Berthold spoke first. "Precision is difficult using this crude map. The Lat-Long markings are vague, but it appears we're here, approximately."

Yakov squinted at the spot where Dr. Berthold pressed his finger. "Then we are within forty kilometers of the B-143 road between Chita and Mogocha. As we continue east, the forest will thin out. We should reach the road tomorrow afternoon."

Yakov lowered his head in deference. "Sir, may I suggest you contact my father about trucks for you? Ilya and I will meet livestock trucks from the Cooperative Farm later, and take the animals home."

Joel tensed, uneasy about giving away their location. He locked eyes with Murph, who blinked in recognition of Joel's concern.

Murph said, "I can send Deripaska our location in fewer than sixty characters, twenty-five seconds, tops. I pre-arranged with Deripaska's radio guy a one-time code so obscure by the time the Ruskies break it, we'll be long gone."

Joel's eyes narrowed in thought. He hesitated, then said. "While you and Dr. Berthold radio the message to Deripaska, the rest of us will tear down the yurt, and pack and load our gear."

As they finished breaking camp for the last leg of their journey, Ana approached Joel and Susan. Dr. Berthold hovered within earshot.

"I do not wish to be offensive, Colonel, but I must ask again. Every time you and Susan eat, you pray to a god the communists say does not exist. I do not understand this."

"'Marx said religion is opium for the proletariat, right?" Joel quipped with a smile.

Ana looked at the ground and corrected almost in an embarrassed whisper. "Karl Marx actually said 'Religion is the sigh of the oppressed creature, the heart of a heartless world, and the soul of soulless conditions. It is the opium of the people.'"

Joel contemplated what Ana told him, then said. "Jesus put his life on the line for the oppressed. His suffering was hardly an opiate and hardly a life for the weak. Our faith gives us a real picture of injustice in our world." Joel's eyes softened as he looked into Ana's eyes. "That's one reason why I serve and am putting my life on the line for you and the other scientists."

"No one has ever risked their life for me, not even when I served as a nurse in the Second World War." Salty gratitude brimmed in Ana's eyes.

"Susan told me your Babushka named you Ana Ksana, because Ana means 'one who will be reborn' and Ksana means 'praise be to God.' In the midst of this harsh world, prayer is our daily reminder to praise God, whose name and character means faithful, dependable, trustworthy, and abundant in mercy. This may sound too good to be true, but God loves you, Ana."

Dr. Berthold's head bobbed in agreement. "*Jawohl,* this is truth, I remember from my Lutheran upbringing."

ЖОЖОЖ

Murph's hands covered his earphones as Dr. Berthold cranked the magneto. Murph leaned back, and a broad smile spread across his face. "Trucks will be waiting at the road."

"That's a long road, Murph," Susan said. "How will they find us?"

Yakov answered, "We'll hang a yellow cloth marker by the road. The trucks will drive until they find one."

CHAPTER 78

RAPID TRANSIT

Joel grimaced as he assessed the road from the cover of pines. "So, the "B" in B-143 means an "improved" road. Improved over what? This new road is less than five years old? Was it built with ox carts? The adobe roads my dad drives from his ranch to town are better than this."

The narrow, dusty road meandered in both directions and disappeared into the horizon's eternal blue sky. He spotted spine-jolting ruts from fifty feet away. *Still, at least we arrived at the road before noon.* Joel's unease about exposing everyone while they waited for the trucks to arrive resulted in his insistence that they wait behind a copse of pine trees.

Before walking to the side of the road with Ilya, Joel turned to Murph, Felix, and Cajun, "Keep your guns ready."

"I don't believe any check points are near here," Ilya remarked as they neared the side of B-143.

"*Check points?* How far apart are these control points?"

The slight tilt of the dark-haired youngster's head and his raised shoulders unconsciously imitated his father. "Every hundred kilometers or so. They attempt to catch smugglers."

"How often do they catch them?" Joel asked.

The boy's eyebrows twitched up as he tilted his head and shot Joel a sly side-eye. "That depends on what they are smuggling and how much 'Russian oil' has greased the works. Most check point guards are well oiled."

"I hope your oil is enough."

A long Red Army convoy rattled by, ramping up Joel's consternation. By mid-afternoon, the only other traffic consisted of two small groups of trucks that clattered past in the dust and ignored the yellow rag.

At last Ilya said, "Here come our trucks, Colonel Joel."

Five big trucks, including two GMCs, all with tall sheet metal cargo boxes, pulled to the side of the road. A Red October Collective Farm sign emblazoned the side of each vehicle.

Ilya's great uncle, a white-haired bear of a man with a mustache matching Ilya's father's FuManchu threw his arms around the boy and hugged him tight. He turned to Joel and crushed Joel's hand with a vigorous handshake. His chest sported ribbons and medals from the Great Patriotic War, a commonplace practice by veterans in the Soviet Union.

"Good to make your acquaintance, Mr. Joel Knight. My name is Igor Yakov Deripaska, Ilya and Yakov's grandfather's brother. Let us be quick."

Joel shouted, "Gather everything you plan to take, and line up beside the truck." The drivers grabbed the women's baggage and loaded them onto one truck. Joel, Murph, Felix, and Cajun grabbed everything else and pitched it into another truck. A driver helped the women on board. Another driver grabbed Dr. Berthold's cane and lifted him on board and into the tall aluminum box on the back of the lead GMC. The rest of the Joel's crew climbed in last.

"All of you," Igor Deripaska instructed, "sit in front, on the folding seats. Water and food is there. Open the ceiling vent for ventilation, yes? When you are in place, we will put this folding bulkhead behind you and reload our cargo. The guards know to ignore the bulkhead, if they want their oil."

"When we stop, I will slap the side of the truck twice. . ." He demonstrated a drum-like sound that reverberated in the cramped space. "This means all is well. If I slap three times, there is trouble."

"How long to drive to Magdagachi, Igor Yakov?" Joel already liked this big, genial man.

"To Mogocha, perhaps two days. To the air field in Magdagachi, another three hundred kilometers. We make perhaps twenty-five kilometers per hour on these rough roads. There are many stops for check points, refueling, and an inspection at Mogocha. So, from here to the air field, five days, maybe six."

"We stop at night then?"

"Of course. No one drives this road at night. Too risky—pot holes, unexpected bumps, wild animals. We stop at sundown, make a camp, eat, relax, perhaps a little vodka, sleep until daybreak, then awake and drive on. Now time to drive."

Susan nestled close to Joel and leaned her head on his shoulder. "This isn't too bad," Joel cast a glance at Susan. "How are you doing?"

"I'm concerned about Dr. Kalugin," she said in a soft voice. "He's exhibiting signs of depression."

The Russian scientist's hands held his bowed head. Shaking in despair, he muttered to himself. "We shall all die. We will all die."

Susan reached her hand out and placed it on Dr. Kalugin knee. "No, no, Dr. Kalugin, don't lose hope. Look, you must focus on the great progress we've made and how God has protected us since we left the bus station."

She lifted his chin and looked into his forlorn eyes. "I know you're weary and frightened, but God knows us far better than we know ourselves. He knows our dangerous condition. God will protect us. Meanwhile, you will see America, and your wife and son again soon. Believe that. Hold on to that."

"I greatly fear the KGB will catch us, torture us."

"Of course you are afraid," Dr. Berthold said with surprising gentleness. "You are far too intelligent not to understand the consequences of something going wrong. Only a fool would not be afraid." He gestured toward everyone. "We are all afraid. You must keep confidence in these Americans, my friend. Have you not seen how remarkable and resourceful they are? Do not forget, they risk their own lives too. These people, their God will bring us through."

Ana placed her hand on Susan's arm. "We Russians are a morose lot, aren't we? In times of stress and fear, we are always sure the very worst will happen."

Ana smiled with fondness at Kalugin. "My dear doctor, you must gather yourself together. Be strong. We look to you for leadership. You, after all, are the whole purpose of our daring escape. We must be sure you arrive safe and sound in America. You must allow us to help you."

"Listen," Dubov said, his voice low and urgent. "Russian or American, there's never been a better team than Murph, Felix, Joel, and Cajun. They've worked wonders bringing us this far. And know this, too, sir, we are all totally dedicated to getting you safely out of the Soviet Union. Without you, everything is a bit pointless, don't you think?"

In the dim interior of the truck, Kalugin glanced from face to face. A slight smile creased his face. "How can I not continue, with such good friends as all of you?"

CHAPTER 79

Saturday, 26 August 1950
Deep In the Forest, Far Eastern Russia

Eight miles behind Joel's team and the fleeing scientists, Tsarsko repeated his cursing performance with considerable flourishes and additions. The lead truck, a heavy, dual rear-axle, all-wheel drive military vehicle skidded off the long, muddy incline and slid backward down the hill. A large boulder stopped the truck with a loud metallic crunch.

Tsarsko leapt from his Gaz Jeep and slipped and slid down the muddy slope toward the disabled truck. Impatience and rain-slickened leaves hastened his graceless tumble facedown on the mucky hill. Sergeant Tokarev rushed to his side. "Leave me alone. I am *fine*," Tsarsko snapped, his face rage red.

Private Kaminski noticed Tsarsko's ID wallet tumble from his tunic. "Worthless, am I?" He mumbled under his breath. His lips twisted into a smirk as his boot kicked the wallet, which disappeared under the sodden leaves.

"The rear axle differential case shattered, sir," a corporal reported. "Even the ring gear is broken. We must abandon the truck."

"No, no, that's not necessary," Sergeant Tokarev said before Tsarsko's fury flared up again. "Comrade Colonel, we can winch the truck to the top of the rise, then remove the wheels and the drive shaft to the broken axle. Then, we'll take out the broken axle. That leaves the forward axle to support and drive the truck. We'll redistribute its load to the other truck while the mechanics work. It will take two or three hours, at most. While they remove the broken axle, Comrade Colonel, I'll order someone to climb a tree and scout the area."

"Good," Tsarsko replied. Tokarev continued to impress him.

Twenty minutes later, a soldier shimmied down the pine tree, covered with sap, resin, and blue-green needles. "Sir," he said, "There's a long, high ridge parallel to us. Three or four kilometers away, there's a pass. The forest thins, sir, and the land slopes downward."

Tokarev eyed Tsarsko. "Sir, they headed north to avoid the ridge, then east to use the pass." Turning toward his men, Tokarev asked. "Who is familiar with this area? What is to the east?"

A man raised his hand. "Sergeant, I was born a few kilometers from here. This ridge is the last we'll encounter going east. Perhaps twenty-five to forty kilometers beyond is the B-143 graded dirt road between Chita and Mogocha. From Chita, it goes south-east toward China, then turns north toward Mogocha. The distance between the towns is around five or six hundred kilometers."

"What is beyond Mogocha, Private?" Tsarsko demanded.

"Well, sir, the next town is Skovorodino and beyond that, Magdagachi, where the air field is."

A slow, smug smile upturned the edges of Tsarsko's lips. "The air field. Comrades, we have got them. Load up."

Tsarsko pushed his men hard. They bounced and jounced, and arrived at the B-137 road in filthy, battered trucks. Tsarsko sprang from his GAZ Jeep and shouted, "Spread out, see if you can find the crooked collaborators and Hitler's dwarf dog."

Within a few minutes, they found animal tracks and manure piles behind the copse of trees. Nearby, they discovered tire tracks.

Tokarev called out to Tsarsko. "I think they boarded a truck here, Comrade Colonel, perhaps a semi by the tire tracks. But, sir, our truck missing its axle cannot drive fast. Without the weight of a second axle, the rear springs are too stiff, making it bounce. That prevents the truck from driving much faster than in the forest."

Tsarsko's eyes narrowed. His eyes blinked, then his eyes rolled back and forth in thought. *I must have all the troops in the broken truck.* He believed with unquestioned certainty in the Soviet doctrine of always using overwhelming force. *I want to crush the traitors, not just capture them.* "By now, they must know we're following them. They don't dare speed, lest they attract attention. We will see how fast our broken beast of burden can travel. If the truck's speed is too slow, it can trail behind. We will continue ahead and wait until he catches us each night."

Tokarev said, "This is a good plan, sir."

They heard the radio squawk and walked back to their caravan. "This is Colonel Yabitov, your dogs arrived."

Tsarsko slapped his head in frustration and grabbed the mic. "Sir, this is Tsarsko. Joel Knight and the traitors boarded a truck on the B-143 road. We no longer need the dogs." He cleared his throat. "We believe they are going to the Magdagachi Air Field to steal an airplane. You must warn the base commander, sir."

Yabitov snorted. "Steal an airplane on a Red Air Force base? This is a ruse, Tsarsko. They continue to China, I am sure of it."

CHAPTER 80

NORTHBOUND

Saturday, 26 August 1950
B-143 Road Northbound

D espite the rough ride, after a while, the produce truck from the Cooperative Farm developed a rhythm of sorts. Everyone endured the partial darkness in silence. The warmth of the sun permeating the metal box lulled Joel into a drowsy state of semi-sleep.

With surprising abruptness, the truck down-shifted, jarring him to full alert. The truck lurched to a stop and the truck door slammed. The driver slapped the side of the truck twice—all good. Whoever Deripaska spoke with sounded disinterested, bored. The conversation faded as they moved toward the other trucks.

"I need another rest stop, Joel—soon," Susan whispered. They'd already stopped twice, both times for Susan.

At this rate, our secret's going to be revealed soon, Joel thought.

Ana glanced at Joel, then at Susan. Joel imagined the wheels turning in her head. *She'll be first to figure things out.*

Deripaska slapped the truck again and said, "We stop for the night in a few kilometers."

Joel said, "Susan needs a rest stop right away."

Deripaska hesitated, then said. "We will do this."

Minutes after restarting, the truck slowed, and jerked to a stop on the roadside. Deripaska's driver opened the rear doors and shifted the cold-storage onion bags, opening a narrow exit passageway.

Susan scurried to the privacy of nearby trees with Ana trailing behind. Ana said in a terse tone, "You don't a fool me. Your complexion is perfect. You've been sick in the mornings. You must relieve yourself often, and you are thicker around the middle than when we first met. You are pregnant, yes?"

"Yes, but I don't want to alarm anyone or add to our problems. I'll be OK."

"Your husband knows?"

"Of course. Joel was the first to know after the doctor's confirmation."

Ana didn't mind pregnancies. She just couldn't abide unnecessary secrets. Her tone softened. "Everyone must know, to protect you. For your good and the baby's. To reassure you, even though your delivery is a long way off, I trained as a mid-wife as a teenaged girl. I delivered six healthy babies."

"Good to know," Susan said with gratitude. "But I hope I'm home, safe in the U.S. when my baby arrives. I hope you'll be there, too."

XOXOX

The trucks circled to park for the night. Joel said to Deripaska, "This reminds me of the Old West wagon trains circling their wagons to create a makeshift stockade to corral their livestock."

"Da, is good comparison. We must sometimes protect ourselves against bandits, although not so often as during the war. Also keeps bears out."

"Do you post sentries?"

"Always. For protection of the cargo, yes?" His eyes sparkled as he gestured toward Joel. "Sometimes—*special* cargo."

Around the camp fire, Susan waited until everyone was served a plate of stew. "I want to make an announcement, I'm expecting a baby."

Dr. Kalugin coughed and choked on his food.

Cajun smiled. "I 'spected dat, ya know? Congrats, y'all."

Felix said aloud what most were thinking. "This puts us all at more risk. Susan's health must be a top priority. No matter what happens, none of us can ever, ever tell the Soviets. They wouldn't hesitate to threaten the baby's life to learn our secrets."

"Please, everyone," Susan said, "I'm not sick or an invalid. I'll manage just fine—we'll just—need to stop a little more often, that's all."

Murph spoke up, "To be frank, I welcome every chance to escape that metal box. I hate being closed in."

CHAPTER 81

THE RUSE

Monday, 28 August 1950
Beside the B-143 Road

Three days later, the little convoy pulled over and circled, the drive over for the day. Great Uncle Deripaska approached Joel. "Colonel Joel, I have been thinking. As we continue north, there are more towns—most small, and many more check points also. I worry some guards may not be so used to our Russian oil."

His wide FuManchu mustache twitched back and forth. "I sent a truck ahead—the one with frozen meats that must make its delivery on time. The driver will scout for us. We will remain here with 'engine' problems until he returns with repair parts and reports on what he found."

The old man ran his hand through his thick hair. "The thought also occurs that you will not just walk onto the air field and fly away with an airplane, yes? This may take a few days. After we deliver our goods, we are expected to return home straight away. So, we must hide you until an airplane is obtained, yes?"

"That would be perfect," Joel prayed everything would work out.

"I remember when the Army built the runways, they evicted many people. An abandoned house in the woods, overgrown by trees, perhaps one could be your refuge. We see what my man finds."

CHAPTER 82

CHANCE ENCOUNTER

Wednesday, 30 August 1950
The Circled Trucks

Deripaska chose an older Gaz truck as the "victim" of the breakdown. "This old warrior burns oil and needs overhaul anyway. We just do the work here instead of at home."

Joel learned that Deripaska's drivers first trained as mechanics. By mid-morning, the truck's hood lay on the ground and most exterior parts removed from the engine. As Joel watched, two men strained to remove the engine's heavy cylinder head. Sooty, black carbon crusted the valves, confirming the need for an overhaul.

His drivers carried the fugitives' belongings into a nearby grove. Deripaska made sure both trucks held nothing incriminating. Reattached to the truck's wall, the wooden seats appeared unused.

"We will be ready when the new parts arrive. If some nosy Army officer comes by, is obvious why we are here. We rest in meantime."

"What if Yabitov and the KGB show up?" Joel asked.

Deripaska rubbed his chin. "You would be safer in the woods, out of sight. If Army—or Yabitov—comes, we are just weary drivers with broken truck, yes?"

With Felix's direction, Deripaska's young drivers grabbed axes and saws from their trucks, then hiked into the grove of pine and birch trees. Enjoying the exercise after the long drive, they chopped tree limbs and branches and also scavenged for downed boughs. After they fashioned a wooden frame large enough to camouflage everyone, they laid a thick blanket of pine needles to cover the floor, to make their 'guests' accommodations' more comfortable. They laughed and talked as they wove leafy branches and boughs between the branches. A smaller hut housed their bags. Blending into the environment, their forest veil of protection was impossible to spot from the road.

Ana rested her head on Berthold's shoulder. In bewilderment, he let her, unsure what to do. Without thinking, he slid his arm around her shoulders, then jerked away in realization of what he'd done. Ana smiled and pulled his arm back into place.

Cajun borrowed Felix's beautiful Winchester Model 63 .22 rifle and headed out to hunt. He returned with several rabbits and three birds that looked like sage hens to Joel.

"You shot birds with a .22?" Joel asked. "I need a shotgun for birds. Even then I don't hit 'em most of the time."

"Wha' can I say, boss? Back home, shotgun shells too 'spensive, but not .22 rounds. One round each, all ya need." His eyes twinkled with feigned innocence as he tweaked his boss's bicep. He knew Joel made no pretense of being a sniper, but Joel was no amateur shooter either.

"Yeah. Next thing I know, you'll tell me you hunted turkeys with a hatchet to save bullets."

"As a matter of fact . . ." They both burst out laughing, relieving the tension they repressed all day only to be interrupted with fear again.

"Quiet. Trucks coming," someone shouted. Joel, Felix, and Dubov dashed to a ditch just inside the grove of trees, and laid low. In fear, the rest sprinted to the hut.

CHAPTER 83

DISABLED

Wednesday, 30 August 1950
The Circled Trucks

Tsarsko spotted several trucks parked in a circle and signaled his driver to pull off. He saw the Red October Collective Farm signs, but the name failed to register. Straightening his mud-spattered Army tunic, he strode toward the white-haired man who appeared in charge.

"Good afternoon, Comrade Colonel," the man said to him. "Are you having trouble with your truck?" He pointed to the truck with the missing back axle.

"That's no concern of yours." With the precision of a machine gunner, Tsarsko fired off a round of questions. "Why are you here? Where are you going? What is your cargo? What is your destination?"

"We stopped because that old geezer blew its head gasket." With a slight tilt of his head and a raised right shoulder, Deripaska waved a hooked thumb toward the disabled truck. "We stay to guard it. We carry foodstuffs to the Magdagachi Air Field. We sent a frozen meat truck ahead. He'll return with repair parts. These trucks carry cold storage apples, onions, and squash. That truck carries wheat."

"I will inspect that truck first," Tsarsko pointed to the lead GMC.

"Of course, Comrade Colonel," Deripaska replied in a cool, correct tone. He stretched out his tanned, muscled arm and unlatched the cargo door. "Here are fifty-kilogram bags of cold storage onions."

"Why is that wall across there? What is behind it?"

"Comrade, this is a removable bulkhead. In front, is nothing."

"Show me."

Deripaska clambered onto the truck, more agile than his age suggested. "Men, help me move these bags so I can show the comrade colonel what's in front." In moments, a narrow passage appeared.

"Here, Colonel, see for yourself."

Tsarsko shot him a suspicious glower, climbed inside the dusty, empty compartment, and challenged, "Why do you do this?"

"We have learned, Comrade Colonel, that certain cold storage vegetables do not like to be piled loose when transported. In the case of onions, they bump and bruise each other, making soft spots which rot. With a bulkhead, you instead pile them snuggly against one another. They do not bounce or bruise, and our comrade airmen enjoy onions that are not just edible, but delicious."

The old man's ramblings irritated Tsarsko. "What if you need the entire truck?"

"Then we remove the bulkhead. This is a simple change and saves the people's food." Tsarsko didn't notice Deripaska's eyes narrowing.

"Now, I inspect the other trucks." Tsarsko climbed from the truck, turned, and riveted an intimidating gaze on the mustached peasant.

"I do not think so, *Colonel,* if you are indeed a colonel."

Amazed anyone dared oppose him, Tsarsko thumped on the enameled red and silver badge with a hammer and sickle superimposed on a sword pointing downward. "You old fool, I am KGB!"

The old man swept back his coat and planted his hands on a pair of holstered Tokarev TT-30 7.62mm automatic pistols.

Tsarsko glared with a murderous white-hot rage. "I will have you shot—"

Deripaska's faint signal escaped Tsarsko's notice. "I think not." The statement carried the chill of Siberia in Tsarsko's ears that now rang with alarm.

Tsarsko flinched at the stark, metallic clash of cocking machine-gun bolts. He glanced at the roof of the nearest truck, and stared into muzzle of a post-mounted RP-46 company machinegun. A metallic belt of coppery 7.62mm rounds trailed to the side. The expressionless face of the man behind the gun discharged a Siberian cold front down his back. Tsarsko's dry tongue stuck against the roof of his mouth. He took stock of the other trucks—each one machine-gun-equipped.

Tsarsko's eyes hardened and his back stiffened rod straight. *We have walked into an ambush.*

"I am KGB." Tsarsko declared a little louder than he intended.

"No, I think not." Deripaska's eyes narrowed to mere slits. He drew his Tokarev automatic and shoved the cold metal against Tsarsko's temple. "You drive muddy, beat-up junkyard trucks. You wear a disgraceful uniform. I'm just an old infantryman, a mere corporal, yet I have more decorations than you . . . *Colonel.* I think you stole that KGB badge. Did you kill its owner? You are bandits. I think we shoot you to save the Army the trouble."

The words resounded with the cold pronouncement of death. Deripaska slammed back the action of the automatic, cocking the gun—the loudest, most frightening sound Tsarsko ever heard. His face went sheet-white, frozen in fear. In all his criminal career, he'd never let down his guard or confronted a situation like this before.

"Quickly, seize their weapons. Set them in my truck. Tie them while I decide what to do," Deripaska ordered. Several young men scrambled to relieve the stunned troops of their weapons.

"Army convoy coming," someone yelled.

"Well, isn't that handy?" His pistol never wavering, Deripaska stared Tsarsko eyeball to eyeball. His voice taunted with irony commanded. "Stop them. We have prisoners for them."

CHAPTER 84

HANDCUFFED

Wednesday, 30 August 1950
The Circled Trucks

The lead army truck ground to a halt in a swirl of dust. The brakes on the other trucks squealed. A Red Army major burst from the front truck and marched toward the truckers and their prisoners.

"What is the meaning of this? Why did you stop us? Who are you? And who is that?" He pointed to Tsarsko, kneeling with his head down and hands tied behind his back.

"Sir, I am Igor Yakov Deripaska. That is a bandit pretending to be a KGB colonel, Comrade Major. Just before you arrived, they tried to hijack us."

Tsarsko jerked his head up. "No! You must listen to me. I am KGB Colonel Boris Tsarsko. My men and I search for Americans and traitor scientists, enemies of the people and—"

"Silence!" Roared the Major. "You expect me to believe you chase *Americans* this deep inside the Soviet Union? Am I a fool?" He un-snapped the holster flap on his Tokarev TT-33.

Deripaska said, "See his uniform, Comrade Major—no markings except the KGB badge and colonel's emblems. He is filthy, unkempt. No true colonel would dishonor himself by wearing such a uniform. He wears no hat. His hair needs cutting. His trucks are wrecks. That one is missing an entire rear axle. Must the KGB stoop to using junkyard vehicles? Comrade Major, I served under many colonels in the Great Patriotic War. Never have I seen such a colonel, even in the worst combat."

"Show me your identification," the Major demanded, his voice burnished steel.

Tsarsko shook with terror, his face white. "I . . . I lost it several days ago—"

"No identification? Yet you *claim* to be a KGB colonel? You just earned a date with a firing squad." The Major's pronouncement hung in the air like an executioner's axe. "Comrade Deripaska, you have done Mother Russia a great service. I will take these renegades to the officials at Magdagachi Air Field. I will not delay my convoy to convene a Court Marshall here, no matter how quickly it would be over. Lieutenant, load these prisoners into a truck. Guard them." Turning to Deripaska, he asked, "Where did you serve, my friend?"

Deripaska pulled himself into a credible version of attention. "Sir, I had the honor of serving with the Second Rifle Company, Third Battalion, 15th Guards Rifle Division of the glorious 51st Soviet People's Army at Stalingrad, under General N. I. Trufanov. I was squad leader."

The major eyed Deripaska's medals. "You wear the Guards Red Banner, the Medal for Service at Stalingrad, *and* the Medal for Service to the Homeland in the Armed Forces, 2nd Class. Wounded *three times*? I honor you, sir. You served your homeland well."

The major pumped Deripaska's hand, then strode to his truck. As the Army convoy clattered into the gathering twilight, the stunned, handcuffed prisoners jounced against rough wooden floorboards.

Sergeant Tokarev leaned toward Tsarsko. "Don't worry, sir," he whispered. "We all kept *our* identification. We will straighten this out at the air field."

"Silence," a guard shouted.

CHAPTER 85

REPAIRS AND INTEL

Deripaska's men disassembled their truck's engine, displaying the parts for Joel to see.

"See, Colonel, the crankshaft bearings and rod bearings are worn. We will replace them. Should replace the piston rings, too, but that must wait for a proper garage."

"I'm amazed you do this on the side of the road, Igor Yakov. What about dirt and grit?"

Joel shifted from foot to foot. *Staying in one place makes me anxious.*

"We keep everything as clean as possible, then as the parts are installed, we wash them with gasoline."

A horn sounded twice, and the now-empty frozen meat truck rumbled into the clearing. Deripaska greeted the driver. "Do you have the parts, Vassily Fedor?"

"Yes, Commissar. I obtained a complete engine overhaul kit."

"Did you find a place for our friends to hide?"

"Yes, an abandoned house south of the air field, well off the road. I doubt anyone remembers this house."

"What 'bout da game?" Cajun asked.

"Plentiful, all kinds."

"Water?"

"A well. Nearby is a small stream."

Joel asked, "Is the house defendable?"

"Trees close to the house provide cover for attackers, although you might escape into the woods."

"Did you notice any Army patrols?" Joel asked.

"No . . . "

Felix interrupted Vassily. "What about the air field?"

"The air field is *much* bigger than last year. A sense of . . . of . . . urgency, of anxiousness, of something about to happen. Hundreds of airplanes. Many convoys. Long trains unloading tanks and trucks."

CHAPTER 86

SETTLING IN

Thursday, 5 September 1950
The Wilderness House

Three days later . . . at mid-morning, Deripaska pulled the convoy to the side of the road not far from Magdagachi Air Field. While Deripaska's men pretended to repair a flat tire, Joel's team transferred their bags to the abandoned house nearby.

Igor Deripaska clamped his arms across his chest and declared, "We must leave. Only in case of emergency will we stop on our return. We don't want to draw attention."

Susan hugged Deripaska. "Thank you, Igor Yakov. We couldn't have survived without you." She kissed his forehead. Crimson flushed from Deripaska's neck to his cheeks.

The men exchanged handshakes and goodbyes, then the Russians departed. A sighing wind replaced the melancholy sound of their departure. The Joel's dispirited group trooped in silence through the woods and entered the filthy house.

Ana grabbed an old, worn broom from the corner, and swept the dusty floors. Felix stopped her. "I need to collect what you sweep."

"Why would you want sweepings?" Ana asked.

"When we leave, I'll use the litter to hide any evidence of us. At every step, we want them to ask, 'Were they here or not?' While they wonder, we move farther away."

Joel spoke up, "Listen, everyone, I hate to tell you this, but we're not staying in this house."

"Oh, Joel, *why?*" Susan's eyelids brimmed with tears as she eyed the bed in the next room. "I can't *bear* sleeping on the ground any more."

"I understand and I'm sorry, Susan, but we don't dare. Finding this house was too easy, too convenient. While we're all comfy-cozy inside, the KGB might know right where we are. I'd prefer to be more comfortable, too, but my first responsibility is to keep us safe."

"I agree." Felix glanced at Joel. "To me, Vassily finding this house appeared to be a set-up from the start. We need to get as far away from all of this as fast as we can."

"You think Deripaska betrayed us?" Dr. Kalugin asked.

Joel said, "Maybe. He's in an impossible position, caught between helping us and drawing too much attention to the collective farm. He wouldn't be the first Russian to play both ends against the middle. He's protecting his family."

"Russians love conspiracy," Dubov spoke up. "Did you notice, several drivers are not Deripaska's relatives? Even if Deripaska keeps our secret, those men, outsiders, might not."

"Where will we go?" Ana asked in a little girl voice, tears running down her cheeks. Dr. Berthold moved close and rubbed her shoulder.

Joel asked, "Cajun, will you leave right now and scout for a place at least a couple of miles away? Felix, do your magic on the house. Hide signs we've been here, then follow behind and cover our tracks. OK, everyone, and let's move out."

Everyone grabbed their bags and trudged out the door. An hour later, Susan lagged behind. Drained of energy, she stumbled and Joel wrapped his arm around her waist to steady her. Joel said, "Let's stop to rest and eat lunch."

Joel pulled Susan closer and whispered, "I'm gonna keep you safe, beautiful lady, you and our child. Don't worry, I'll take care of you."

"I'm sorry. I just cry so easily since . . . " She rubbed her tummy.

He stroked her hair, murmuring into her ear, "I'm here, you're safe. Everything's gonna be OK." *Oh God, please help me. I've just got to get her out of here.*

As they ate a cold lunch, Felix rejoined them sporting a cheerful countenance. "I had no trouble making things look like nobody'd lived there in a decade."

"What about our tracks?" Joel asked.

"Covered them with leaves and pine needles."

Cajun strolled into the clearing as casually as if walking into his own living room. "I foun' us da place, Colonel, 'bout three miles, a nice dry limestone cave. Little tight, but workable. We can hide da opening, even has back way out and fresh water."

Two hours later, Joel scanned the cave. "Good job, Cajun. No animals in here?"

The haggard fugitives dropped their bags in the cave as the clouds overhead reflected glorious red and orange. Aircraft engines echoed in the distance.

Cajun cleaned his gun and grinned. "Jus' a bear. He's gone. I clean da cave a little, too."

Felix and Dubov pulled Joel outside. "We'd like to sneak into the air base tonight, in the dark, just the two of us," Felix said. "Deripaska's men said the fences are just for game, not security. We'll scope out the layout, size, what's going on. I'll find their central supply, too, 'cause my 'bag of tricks' is a bit low. We need uniforms."

Dubov said, "I still have my Sergeant Major uniform. Might be able to wear it to gather Intel."

"You *look* Russian and speak like a native." Joel said, "plus, you know the Army inside out. If anyone can infiltrate that base, you guys can. Pay attention to the planes. What kind. How many. How active."

"Give us a couple of days." Felix said. "When we return, we'll signal with this." He pulled child's toy from his pocket—a metal cricket, used by American soldiers to signal each other in Normandy's thick hedgerows during the D-Day invasion.

CHAPTER 87

SOMETHING BIG

Saturday, 9 September 1950
The Cave Near Magdagachi Air Field

The toy cricket click twice. Felix and Dubov entered the cave. Dubov dropped a canvas bag with a solid thump, grumbling about the weight of Felix's booty from the base's supply depot.

Both slumped to the ground. Felix breathed out a weary breath. "Joel, Deripaska's driver knew what he was talkin' about. Something big's about to happen. The place is huge, full of troops. To the north is a large Army base, probably five or six infantry divisions, with two or three tank and armor divisions, and more artillery than I could count."

"Airplanes?" Joel asked.

"More planes than I *ever* saw around Moscow." Dubov added, "At least two hundred transports. Fighters everywhere. Props and jets. Some I've never seen before. Don't know the types. Bombers on the north side, those B-29 copies—what do they call 'em? TU-something."

"TU-4, NATO code name BULL."

"That's them. Two hundred, at least. Maybe a hundred American B-25s, too. Weird to see red stars on them. The craziest, though, were the flying wing bombers. They looked like WWII German Gothas."

"*Jawohl,* this is so," Dr. Berthold said. "At the war's end, German defectors brought GO-460 aircraft and drawings to the Soviets. Tupolev produced them for several years as the TU-270. I designed some refinements. Total production, maybe 350. Russian engines not as good as German."

"TU-270, NATO code name BLAZER. Aren't they out of service?"

"We saw two hundred, maybe two-fifty, so I don't think so. A separate group of twenty or so TU-270s parked off to one side, behind the others. Jet engines under their wings," Dubov said.

"What? You know about this, Dr. Berthold?"

"Perhaps. There was a study, called TU-270j, to mount jet engines under the wings, outboard of the engines. They proposed Russian-manufactured BMW 003 jet engines. I recommended against it. The engines developed too little thrust and were unreliable. I thought they scrapped the project."

"There's something else, barbed wire separates the jet wings from the others," Felix continued. "And, there's a building we couldn't see into, with a rail line going inside and heavy lifting equipment. They patrol the area with armed guards."

"Inside the barbed wire?" Joel asked.

"Yeah. Remember, those are observations from a mile or more away in barley field. Hard to see details. If we return, we might come in from the north and sneak in closer."

"The runways?"

"Three big ones, in a triangle, old-fashioned style. The main runway is about four, four-and-a-half kilometers long. According to my compass, it lies on 093/273 degrees."

"About two-and-a-half miles long." Joel rubbed his pointer finger back and forth across his lips. "Something pretty heavy needs that much strip. Dr. Berthold, how much runway do ya think a fully loaded TU-270 needs for takeoff?"

The diminutive German considered the question. "Depends on the winds, temperature, density altitude, and how well tuned the engines are. At full load, I expect three kilometers, perhaps a bit more."

"About what a B-29 needs. So why do they need so much length?"

CHAPTER 88

BETRAYED

Saturday, 9 September 1950
Magdagachi Air Field

The Magdagachi Air Field KGB freed Tsarsko and his men after they got around to checking their credentials. The 'process' consumed hour after interminable hour. Still fuming, Tsarsko bathed and donned a new uniform. As he left KGB headquarters, a sergeant called out to him.

"What do you want?"

The sergeant waved some papers. "Sir, a report. A driver for the convoy that captured you revealed the escaping traitors and Americans rode in the trucks. They hide in an abandoned house."

"Where is this man? I will question him."

"Sir, he left with the convoy two hours ago."

"Why didn't you arrest him?" Tsarsko's eyes blazed with anger.

"Sir, he's a paid informant. He'll collect more information. Here is the location of the house just south of here."

Shaking with rage, Tsarsko snatched the paper and stomped from the building and found Tokarev. "Gather your men, weapons, and trucks. We leave at once."

"Sir, that will take some time. The base armory limits weapons to assigned units. I explained you are KGB on special assignment, but they were unrelenting. Perhaps the KGB *commander* can help, sir?"

A scarlet-faced Tsarsko stormed up the wooden stairs to the commander's office.

CHAPTER 89

SECRET ORDERS

Since his last humiliating headache, Chairman Beria's once powerful hand continued to lose its grip. Intermittent headaches still invaded his life. He limited how much he walked in the presence of others, lest their powerful, murderous lusts detected his weakness.

Exhausted, he nursed a glass of strong, hot tea, then slid his chair closer to his desk. With difficulty he uncapped his pen to review the secret orders.

Three squadrons of the TU-270j jet-assisted atomic bombers, accompanied by five squadrons of the conventionally-powered TU-270s transferred to air fields in north-eastern China.

The inviting United Nations targets in Korea lay within easy range. Before launching their attacks, they would replace the Soviet Air Force stars with Chinese markings. Beria congratulated himself on his cleverness.

Beria signed the orders, displaying as much flourish as his sluggish right hand could muster. A self-satisfied smile flickered across his face.

Chinese markings on the planes shifts the blame onto the shoulders of that smug Chairman Mao. At last, Operation October Victory is underway.

CHAPTER 90

HIGH TENSION

Monday, 11 September 1950, Early Morning
North of Magdagachi Air Field

In dark silence Joel and Felix circled the Soviet base. By 0200 hours they nestled north of the sprawling complex among the stalks of a barley field awaiting fall harvest. Alert for roving guards and dogs, the fall chill announcing the coming of winter shivered through their bodies. With the stealth of an Amur leopard, they crouched low to the ground and inched across the treeless terrain toward the flood-lit, aircraft ramp.

Joel used his 10x30 binoculars while Felix looked through his 3.5x scope on Smitty's Mosin-Nagant M1891/30 sniper rifle to observe the TU-270s.

"Jet engines, all right," Joel whispered.

Felix pointed and whispered, "That plane has the cowlings off. Can you tell the engine type?"

Joel squinted, adjusting the binoculars, thankful again for his extraordinary vision. "Looks like a British Rolls-Royce Nene."

"If you're right, Joel, that would be the Klimov RD-45, Russian version of the Nene, rated at 5900 pounds of thrust."

"Why do the Soviets need almost 12,000 pounds *more* thrust on the TU-270j which already has six powerful engines? Did you notice that all the jet-equipped planes have vertical tails near the trailing edge? Must require more stability. That'll help us ID these birds in flight."

Felix pointed to a large building. "If we move over there, we could see into the building . . . "

The shrill single-note of a steam engine's whistle exhaled a sharp shriek with a discharge of steam. Both men dropped flat onto the frost-glazed grass.

A stubby yard engine chuffed as it tugged a dozen flatcars toward a gate in the fence surrounding the TU-270j's. Soldiers swung open the metal gate. The train rolled into the compound. The wheels grated against the metal rails and slowed to a squealing stop outside the mysterious building.

"Look. . . what are those large cylindrical shapes on the flatcars?" Felix asked.

A burning cold surged through Joel's body. "Atom bombs!" He lowered his binocs, and rubbed his fingers in a circle against both his temples. "*That's* why the TU-270j needs so much power. The TU-270s can probably carry only two bombs. Those bombs weigh 8,000, maybe 10,000 pounds each. What are they planning to bomb?"

Felix, an experienced spy, studied the fence line, then pointed. "We can cross down by the tracks and move close enough to see inside."

Exposed, no one inside the fence noticed their nerve-wracking bellycrawl across the railroad tracks and their last few feet nearer the building. Joel strained to see inside the building.

"What do you see?" Felix asked.

Joel sucked in a sharp breath. "More than a *dozen* atom bombs."

As they watched crews unload atomic bombs, another engine's roar wreaked havoc on their nerves. Using hand signals, men waved the diesel-powered ChTZ S-65 Stalinetz tractor straight backward to tow a TU-270j toward a deep pit.

"What're they doing?"

"Same way we loaded B-29s for Hiroshima and Nagasaki," Joel whispered. "They placed bombs in the pit, parked the plane on top, and winched the bombs into place."

The metal whine of winches lifting a heavy weight clacked and clattered as the rising sun blazed on the horizon. Joel commented, "That one's different. Cement, maybe?"

"Well, you don't train with the real thing."

They watched the men sweat and strain, wrestling the concrete bomb into place into the bomb bay. When they finished loading the practice bomb, the bomb bay doors closed in silence. The powerful tow tractor hauled the plane to the runway, disconnected, and drove away.

The sound of aircraft piston engines running up echoed across the vast steppe. Joel and Felix spotted an open truck drive to the TU-270j. Several men climbed out, dressed in flight gear.

"There's the flight crew," Felix smiled. "Here's how to throw a monkey wrench into their training syllabus." He moved in closer to a spot behind low bushes on a slight slope at the end of the runway.

Howling jets joined the throb of the huge piston engines. The TU-270j began a slow, awkward, bobbing taxi toward the end of the runway.

Felix unsnapped a pair of tough bamboo rods clamped to the Mosin-Nagant's stock. A thin bolt fastened them, forming a rigid bi-pod support for the heavy weapon. He inserted the magazine, loaded with five 7.62mm rounds, then wriggled himself into a sprawled position, and uncapped the telescopic sight.

The Tu-270 taxied toward him, slowed, made a 180-degree turn to face down the runway. The pilot braked. The airplane's cobra-like nose bobbed. The nose wheels straightened, aligning with the runway's center.

Heat waves rising from the jet engines distorted Felix's view. All the engines roared, shaking the huge plane. Felix jacked a round into the chamber and flicked off the safety. The plane lurched as the pilot released the brakes. The huge aircraft rolled forward.

Through the telescopic sight, Felix fixated on the ponderous, accelerating bomber, waiting, waiting, not breathing. The aircraft gathered speed, the nose wheels lifted. He squeezed the trigger. His shoulder bucked, absorbing the recoil. The thunder of the roaring engines swallowed the noise of the shot. The brass cartridge dropped soundlessly.

The bullet struck the outboard tire of the TU-270j's right main landing gear. The tire deflated in a fraction of a second. A split second later, the inboard tire, carrying twice its normal load, blew out. The magnesium landing gear strut stabbed the concrete with a huge burst of incandescent sparks.

The aircraft spun to its right, causing the tortured strut to fail. The right wing slammed into the runway, flinging the smashed jet engine into the air like a demented Roman candle.

The TU-270j skidded to the right, smoke boiling off the tires. The aircraft's left main landing gear strut snapped as the aircraft swerved ninety degrees. The left wing tip smashed into the runway, demolishing the jet engine and shearing off twenty feet of wing in a cascade of sparks. The shattered wing stub stabbed the concrete runway like a pole-vaulter planting his pole.

Felix and Joel watched open-mouthed as the huge aircraft arced through the air and flipped over. As the light gray belly of the aircraft twisted into sight, the bomb bay doors shredded, a huge shape bursting through. The practice bomb spun in the air with broken pieces of mounting structure attached, and slammed onto the runway with a concussive thud.

Like grotesque, arthritic fingers, broken, bent propeller blades silhouetted for an instant against the sky. The airplane continued its death roll. Broken parts propelled into the air. A fountain of jet fuel and gasoline showered the runway. A monstrous cloud of orange-red fire billowed skyward with a basso roar.

The aircraft crashed onto its back. The sliding wreckage screeched a demon's howl across the airstrip like an insane monster's fingernails on a blackboard. The remnants of the upside-down aircraft twirled in torment, veering off the runway, hurling clods of dirt and a cloud of dust high into the morning air.

Towers of dense, black smoke erupted like released demons. The shattered left wing tip slewed to a stop two hundred yards down the runway, its battered jet engine pointed, lifeless, heavenward. A siren screamed.

"I just expected an aborted takeoff," Felix said. "If that had been a real bomb instead of a concrete dummy. . ."

"I don't even want to think about it. Let's move back."

Four hours later, Joel and Felix crept back and lay in the barley fiend near the edge of the ramp. The smoke from the crashed bomber still hung in the sky. Joel studied the parked airplanes.

He whispered, "This's a challenge, Felix. The big transports unload their cargo and depart at once. Even if we could pack everybody in, the range of the small ones is too short. An IL-12 fits the bill, but they keep them separated. I keep coming back to an Li-2."

"Can you fly an Li-2, Colonel?" Felix whispered back.

"I can fly a C-47, pretty much the same thing."

CHAPTER 91

FRUSTRATION

Monday, 11 September 1950
The Kremlin, Moscow, USSR

Beria shook his head back and forth in frustration as he read Yabitov's latest dispatch. *Always one step ahead, the Americans escape us. Why can we not catch them in our homeland? I must notify the commander at Magdagachi Air Base that the escapees may try to steal an airplane.* He grasped the phone to call Yabitov.

A crushing headache overwhelmed him, sabotaging the urgency to phone the sickening sycophant. He snatched the wastebasket to catch his supper. Intense pain blocked his thoughts. Confused and fatigued, he rang for his assistant to empty the foul-smelling wastebasket, the call to the airbase postponed.

Two hours later, rage at Yabitov's failure re-energized Beria with enough strength to dial the phone number for the commander's office at Magdagachi Air Base and demanded to speak with Yabitov.

Spooked by a call from the Deputy Chairman of the Council of People's Commissars of the Soviet Socialist Republics, he stuttered, "Y-y-yes, s-s-sir, y-y-yes, s-s-sir, I-I-I will g-g-g-et him r-r-right away, s-s-sir." The commander sprinted down the hall where Yabitov fumed about his next move.

Yabitov returned to the commander's office, picked up the receiver, listened, and repeated, "Yes, sir. Will do, sir." Unable to get a word in edgewise, Yabitov seethed and slammed the receiver back onto its cradle, his hand trembling more in terror than anger.

CHAPTER 92

THREAT

Monday, 11 September 1950
Magdagachi Air Field

Tsarsko stood at the top of the administration building's wooden steps with orders for trucks and guns from the KGB colonel in hand—at last. Colonel Yabitov, in full Red Army uniform, stood wooden-faced at the bottom of the stairs, hands perched on his hips. "We will talk, Tsarsko, *now.*" Yabitov stormed up the stairs and directed Tsarsko back into the building and led him to a small room. The wall shook as he slammed the door behind them.

"Chairman Beria is *not* pleased with your performance, Tsarsko. That means also he is displeased with *my* performance. You let those traitors escape. You destroyed our careers. Tomorrow, Sergey Sauchenko arrives to take up the search. He's KGB Chief of the Committee of Information and also Chief of Internal Security, with the authority of a General Lieutenant. They threaten to relieve me and you as well." His words, as cold as ice, fell heavy with threat.

"Will Sauchenko find the traitors with a crystal ball?" Tsarsko scoffed.

"Remember to whom you speak," Yabitov snapped.

Tsarsko replied in a deferential tone. "Comrade Colonel Yabitov, we know where they hide. It is just a matter of arresting them."

"Then why haven't you done so?" Spittle shot from Yabitov's mouth.

Tsarsko waved the paper work. "Sir, I only just obtained authorizations for new trucks and weapons. We can depart as soon as the Comrade Colonel desires."

CHAPTER 93

UNINFORMED

Monday, 11 September 1950
End of Runway 273, Magdagachi Air Field

Firemen labored to extinguish the raging fuel-fed fires. Once contained, the Magdagachi Air Field Chief of Aviation surveyed the smoldering wreckage. An ambulance carried away the crew's charred bodies.

The huge, black practice bomb lay half shattered in a pile of crumbled concrete. The contorted, aluminum framework testified to the powerful forces that tore it from the aircraft. A captain, who inspected the twisted landing gear assembly fifty feet from the main wreckage, shouted, "Sir, come look."

The Chief of Aviation's anger turned stone hard when he noticed the label on a blown-out tire: "German? What idiot put old German tires on this aircraft? Why weren't those dried-out tires from the war discarded? To lose a crew this way, someone will pay dearly for this."

The base commander's detailing the incident on runway 273 exemplified the Soviet bureaucratic "efficiency." As his comprehensive, on-the-scene, runway-level report rose through each department, every command level further condensed the specifics.

By the time the base commander's report reached Moscow, the specifics melted away. Reduced to a few statistics, it was combined with other monotonic statistics on that month's training crashes.

No matter the fact that the crash involved the TU-270j atomic bomber—Beria was never informed.

CHAPTER 94

RECONNAISSANCE

Wednesday, 13 September 1950

Magdagachi Air Field

Felix and Joel described their mission to Dr. Berthold who asked, "The practice bomb tore through the belly doors, yes?"

"Yep, ripped the support structure right outta the fuselage," Joel said.

"This must concern the Russians who suffered three in-flight structural failures before with TU-4s carrying practice bombs. Not an aircraft flaw. The over-stressed, attaching structure made them switch to the older TU-270s that can accommodate a heavier structure. This exposes a problem with the TU-270j's attaching structure, as well."

"If the structural integrity of the TU-270j is in question, can they use another aircraft?" Joel asked the diminutive German.

"*Nein*, no others can handle such payloads over a worthwhile distance. The Russians are clumsy, inelegant engineers, but they are tenacious. They could resolve this issue in short order."

Dr. Kalugin added, "Far more atomic bombs exist than we believed. We must send this information to the U.S."

Joel suppressed the urge to say, "*No kidding.*"

Felix said, "Our move to the base makes it easier to watch for a Russian Gooney. Let's send somebody every night to keep tabs on when a plane becomes available. When we spot our opportunity, we need to move fast. Next to Joel, Murph's the most knowledgeable about planes."

"Yeah. Send Murph, starting tonight," Joel directed.

"On my way, boss," Murph said.

CHAPTER 95

INCOMPETENCE

Wednesday, 13 September 1950

The Wilderness House

Yabitov and Tsarsko spent four hours prying loose two trucks and a Gaz Jeep from a sour-faced, motor pool captain.

"I own too few motor trucks, Comrade Colonel. These vehicles *must* be returned at once. My colonel of logistics has no sense of humor. The loss of two is unacceptable."

Yabitov glowered at the man. "We operate under the direct orders of Comrade Chairman Beria, Comrade Captain. Inform your colonel. The trucks will be returned when the KGB is finished with them. *Maybe.*" His tone brooked no argument.

The dour captain demurred. Some fights weren't worth fighting.

With the rearmed troops aboard, Tsarsko and Yabitov sped south through the Magdagachi Air Field gate. They spotted a polished Li-2 flaring to land, bright red and gold KGB emblems on its nose resplendent in the afternoon sun. On its back, a twin machinegun turret glimmered with a death-foreboding gleam.

"That must be KGB General Lieutenant Sergey Sauchenko," Tsarsko said in a flat, sober tone.

As they rushed to the abandoned house, Yabitov gloated, "We have them now." Yabitov's excitement of the pursuit built as they pulled to the side of the road. Pumped on adrenaline, he yanked the door handle and hopped out of the truck.

Yabitov and his troops stole through the woods silent as ghosts, using hand signals. A full company of highly trained, shock troops spread around the cabin in silence in perfect coordination. At Yabitov's signal, they stormed in with full force.

Empty.

Colonel Yabitov entered the cabin and whirled around enraged. "Those collective farm bumpkins played you for the fool, Tsarsko. This house has seen no occupants in years. Rodent droppings. Is that what you expected? What a waste of time. We still have no idea where they are. Let us hope that General Lieutenant Sauchenko is more understanding than his reputation suggests. If not, *you* will take the blame, Tsarsko. You alone."

Burning nausea irritated Yabitov's throat as his head unleashed pulsating pain.

CHAPTER 96

CONTEMPT

Wednesday, 13 September 1950
Magdagachi Air Field

An infuriated, full colonel was intimidating, and a two-star general at full song even more so. "I cannot believe your incompetence, Yabitov," Sauchenko's low, ominous voice reverberated in the room. He marched back and forth in front of the two men standing at attention. "From the beginning, you utterly mismanaged this. And Tsarsko, you are KGB. Your failure is incomprehensible. You let these soft scientists and amateur spies slip through your fingers? Are you *blind?* A Moscow tramp could perform better."

His lips sneered with the warmth of a hangman. "You are both relieved. If this does not turn out well, God help you, if there is a god. From here on out, your men are commanded by the local KGB. They are not at fault. They simply obeyed two fools and incompetents." His words dangled in the air like a death sentence.

He glared at the ashen-faced men whose expressions betrayed their thoughts. Sauchenko wasted no time in manipulating their thoughts against them. "I should shoot you. Immediately. Perhaps I will."

Calculated with an unhurried deliberation, he lifted a glass of vodka to his lips and rested his other hand on his holstered gun. Wagner's *Flight of the Valkyries* played softly in the background.

His fingers drummed an ominous rhythm against his leather holster. His snort of contempt echoed along with the rapping of his fingers boring into their psyches.

"If they left the decision to me, I would do so, right this instant."

Pausing to allow his statement to drill further into their anxiety, he glowered at Yabitov and Tsarsko. "But somehow, Chairman Beria is convinced you might succeed. I am ordered to release you, and let you continue your 'search.' Meanwhile, a division of *competently* led KGB troops will be arriving. If you are wise, you will die in the wilderness and save us the trouble of shooting you. Dismissed."

CHAPTER 97

#2 KGB OFFICIAL

Thursday, 14 September 1950
Magdagachi Air Field

Dark clouds scudded across the sky as Murph rubbed his eyes. "Magdagachi is a beehive, Joel. A shiny Li-2 with KGB badges is parked off by itself. Been there all day, and nobody bothered the plane. I eavesdropped on some mechanics. The Li-2 is General Lieutenant Sauchenko's. He's taking over some big investigation. They're worried the investigation is about them."

Murph chuckled. "GIs are the same everywhere, always sure the brass is out to get them." He winked. "'Course, they usually are."

Dr. Ilya Kalugin exchanged a knowing glance with Ana who asked, "Ilya Fadeyka, are you thinking what I am thinking?"

"I am, Ana Ksana. Colonel Joel, Sauchenko is the number two KGB official. We've experienced unpleasant encounters with him in Moscow. He must be here to find us. This is not good, not good at all."

Joel asked, "So you think Yabitov and Tsarsko are off the case?"

Susan interjected, "No. Tsarsko will hunt us until he succeeds or dies. His reputation, not to mention his ego, will be destroyed if he doesn't win. I don't know about Yabitov, except that he'll do anything to protect himself."

"I agree," Dr. Kalugin said.

"Doesn't matter, Joel," Murph said. "That Li-2 is ours for the taking. We can just walk through the fence and hop aboard."

"I appreciate your confidence, Murph, but that works only if we're all young, physically fit, and military. Unfortunately, we're not. We'd be spotted in an instant."

"How about this?" Felix interjected. "Dubov and I wear our uniforms, 'borrow' a truck and drive you 'prisoners' straight to the plane."

Dubov said. "Yeah. With so many troops on base, no one knows anyone. Soldiers don't challenge KGB, especially with Sauchenko hanging around. I can cow them as a sergeant major. I *can* find us a truck. We can pull this off, Colonel."

"I see two problems," Joel said. "One, if you can't find a truck, we're up the proverbial creek. Two, if that goes perfectly and then Sauchenko flies off into the blue, we're sunk."

"Sauchenko is Beria's fireman, so to speak," Ana added. "If he is here, he will not leave until the fire is put out."

Dr. Kalugin agreed. "Beria sends him to *finish* the job."

Joel mulled the situation over. "Traffic's heavy. We need to be careful to stay out of sight. When we seize the airplane, we must board quickly. Gotta disguise ourselves so it's not obvious who we are."

Felix laughed. "I snagged three Russian walkie-talkies other night."

"That'll help, for sure. But opening a channel has its own drawbacks," Joel said.

"We could speak only Russian, one word, something innocuous, never repeat, keep moving. They won't find us," Murph said.

Joel turned to Felix. "You guys sure you can steal a truck?"

"We'll walk through the fence before dawn, and blend in with the troops 'til we find the motor pool. If this rain continues, it'll provide good cover. Russians don't like to fly in heavy rain. Let's send somebody every night to keep tabs on the plane. We gotta know that Russian Gooney's still there."

Joel said, "Yeah, no escaping that. Use the crickets tonight. We'll save the walkie-talkies for when we actually secure the trucks."

CHAPTER 98

REGROUP

Thursday, 14 September 1950
Magdagachi Air Field

After their release from death's dart, Yabitov and Tsarsko teetered between relief and mortification. Both plotted their next steps to apprehend Colonel Joel Knight and the scientists. The gloomy wet weather permeated their imposed downtime. Yet, their savage passion and exhilarating hatred both bonded and compelled them in their personal war to exact a counterblow upon their sworn enemy, Joel Knight. This intermission in their chase to capture the traitorous turncoats gave them time to choose new NCOs.

"Sir, I recommend Sergeant Tokarev," Tsarsko said. "He has above average intelligence and capabilities. I think he should be an officer."

"Tokarev? Like the gunmaker who designed the *unwieldy* TT-30 pistol?"

"Yes, sir. They're distant cousins."

"Hope your Sergeant Tokarev is better at his job than his cousin. The TT-30 lacks a safety catch and can discharge when dropped or bumped."

Tsarsko ignored his barb. "There're a couple of corporals I'd like you to interview, too."

"Bring the corporals, I'll select one. The local KGB commander gave me the latest intelligence. After I've read the report, I'll decide what we'll do next."

Tsarsko squirmed in his chair. *Yabitov wouldn't recognize a great NCO or excellent intelligence if they sat in his lap. I'll agree with him, and hope I can steer us in the right direction.*

CHAPTER 99

INTEL

Friday, 15 September 1950
Magdagachi Air Field

Before dawn Felix and Dubov left the cave. The thick cloud cover delivered on its grim promise. Heavy rain, laced with lightning and thunder, poured from the overcast sky as they slogged toward the airfield. Both men crouched in the muddy barley field.

Drenched, Dubov shook the rain off his jacket and plopped on the ground as the gloomy, gray skies lightened somewhat with the rising sun. Felix dripped beside him.

Dubov said, "Stay here, I'll scout out the base." Within half an hour, he returned, "The coast is clear."

Both men moved closer to the base commander's office and crouched in the rainy shadows. Dubov moved to the base of the stairs and listened. No sounds. "Cover me. I'm going inside." Dubov crept up the wooden steps. When he disappeared from view, Felix scanned the area, then moved up the stairs.

Dubov peeked in the commander's door. Silent darkness greeted him. The office was vacant. Dubov swung open the door and walked in. With a slight grin, he scavenged documents from the desk.

Dubov poked his head back into the empty hallway and said, "The safe is an old Barrister."

Felix grinned, "A piece of cake."

CHAPTER 100

SITREP

Friday, 15 September 1950
The Cave Near Magdagachi Air Field

"**M**an, it worried me when the KGB Li-2 was missing, then we found it in a hanger, getting a right side engine change," Felix reported. "Otherwise, not much going on, Joel. No flying, rain's still too heavy, ceiling's too low. Heard racket over on the Army base, some tank exercise. Tankers love to slog around in the muck."

Dubov unfastened a pouch and removed a sheaf of papers. "Found these in the tower, Joel."

"You went into the control tower?" Felix asked.

"Just walked in, no locks or guards."

"And you found—?" Joel asked.

"Arrival and departure schedules for the next few days. Looks like General Sauchenko is gonna be at the base awhile 'cause his plane's not on the list, even after the work is scheduled to be finished. Got Sauchenko's call sign, too. "Chest Odin," which means "Honor One." Training missions and supply flights are all that's scheduled. The weather forecast says this rain's stickin' around another day or so, and another big front is coming in behind it."

"And here's what I found in the Base Commander's safe." Felix handed Joel some papers.

Dubov warned, "They're preparing for "Operation October Victory," Joel. That's not good."

CHAPTER 101

D-DAY

Saturday, 16 September 1950
Magdagachi Air Base

The weather cleared in the pre-dawn hours. An earthy smell permeated the pristine air, as the sounds of aircraft engines rumbled in the distance. Murph's morning trip to the base revealed the KGB Li-2 parked again on the ramp. He scurried back to the cave to report to Joel, "They completed the engine change on the Li-2. Today's the day, Joel. With flying resuming, the base is active again and we can blend in."

"All right, everyone, this is what we've been waiting for. Felix, Dubov, put on your uniforms and go." He glanced at his notebook, "Your walkie-talkie codes are 'BOOK' if things are OK and 'RIFLE' if not. Cajun, you'll monitor the airplane. Take the second walkie-talkie. Your code words are 'APPLE' if the coast is clear, and 'TIRE' if not."

"The code words for the rest of us are 'LIGHTBULB' if everything is OK, 'TRASH' if not."

Tension in the cave increased. Everyone understood this was an all-or-nothing venture.

"Felix, Dubov, Murph, set your watches by Cajun's chronograph. We'll clean the cave, try to lure a bear or wolverine in with some food."

"Why?" Anna's face registered disgust.

"Animals obscure evidence of us being here."

"Besides," Cajun winked. "Who's fool enough ta mess wit' a bear?"

CHAPTER 102

UNDERCOVER

Saturday, 16 September 1950
Magdagachi Air Base

Roger Dubov, uniformed as Sergeant Major Pyotr Borodin, and Felix as Junior Sergeant Antipov, walked onto the base unnoticed and joined men going to breakfast.

He overheard some soldiers discussing a test flight that afternoon for the KGB Li-2. *That's swell. When we take off, they'll think we're doing a test flight after the engine change. Perfect cover.*

After eating, Dubov left with Felix to appropriate a Gaz Jeep parked near the mess hall. At the motor pool, Felix leaned against the wall and watched with admiration as Dubov worked his magic.

After only moments of gruff insistence and KGB medallion thumping, he gained the cooperation of the lieutenant in charge. When Dubov dropped General Lieutenant Sergey Sauchenko's name, a new Gaz-51 two-ton truck appeared at once.

Dubov and Felix manned their vehicles and wheeled out of the south entrance of Magdagachi Air Base in a late model Gaz-69 Jeep and the new canvas-covered, Gaz-51 two-ton truck.

CHAPTER 103

MINOR THEFT

Saturday, 16 September 1950
The Cave, The Flight Line, Magdagachi Air Field

The walkie-talkie's scratchy voice announced "BOOK." Felix and Dubov secured a truck. The slow movement out of the cave by the group and the slow trudge toward B-143 tested Joel's patience. Joel's chest rose and dropped as he drew in deep breaths. *Easy, Joel. You've got a pregnant woman, a crippled man, and a middle-aged scientist with heart problems, plus the others. Don't expect them to move as quickly as you.* His mental lecture only helped a little.

Forty yards from the road everyone halted and lay out of sight in a ravine. The men cut pine boughs for Susan and Ana to lie on. Dr. Berthold cuddled Ana in his arms. Joel left Dr. Kalugin in charge, found an unobstructed view of the road, and settled in to wait. *At least this isn't boring.*

A long caravan of trucks carrying troops rumbled past. Dust billowed through the air, covering trees and plants along the roadside. Joel slapped himself clean. Twenty yards away, the yellow flag flapped in the breeze.

A Gaz Jeep and a truck drove into view. Joel keyed his walkie-talkie; "LIGHTBULB." The vehicles stopped next to the yellow flag.

In minutes, the women and scientists loaded into the back of the canvas-covered truck with nothing but a handful of bags and Dr.

Kalugin's precious papers. Felix heaved his bulging bag o' tricks into the truck, which served as a couch for Susan and Ana.

Joel changed into a sergeant's uniform as Dr. Kalugin and Murph changed into guards' uniforms. As they dressed, Felix laughed. "Those soldiers scampered to obey Dubov's orders. They're terrified of the KGB."

"Me too," Joel said.

Joel drove with Sergeant Major Borodin in the Gaz, while Felix drove the ZIL truck. When they arrived at the Magdagachi Air Field gate, the long convoy Joel observed earlier on the road waited on paper work at the gate.

At Dobov's urging, Joel waved to Felix to follow them. Both vehicles swung into the left lane. With presumptive authority, they bypassed the waiting convoy, and drove straight to the gate.

The harried guard extended his arm, palm out. "You there, what are you doing on the wrong side of the road? Wait your turn."

Dubov stood up in the open Gaz like a conquering Roman emperor and shouted, "KGB, official business. Do not block us or you will be sorry." He thumped his KGB badge. "Let us through at once."

The guard waved both vehicles through. With characteristic KGB insolence, the Gaz and the big Zil truck raced through the gate.

The two vehicles drove across the base and parked on the right side of the KGB Li-2. Cajun, who hid in the barley field, recognized Joel and Dubov in the Gaz. He said, "APPLE" into his walkie-talkie.

Mechanics working nearby decided they wanted nothing to do with this KGB business and leaned into their work, eyes wandering no farther than the nearest bolt.

Joel and Dubov marched to the rear of the Gaz-51. Joel placed a wooden ladder against the lowered tailgate. Murph swept the canvas aside. Stoic faces and weapons at the ready, each uniformed man led a black-hooded "prisoner" down the ladder and onto the waiting aircraft. Dr. Berthold lay on a stretcher to hide his short, crippled legs.

After the prisoners and their bags boarded, Joel and Felix parked the vehicles off to the side.

Cajun strolled from the barley field, signaled Murph in the cockpit and said in Russian, "Switches off."

"Switches off," Murph confirmed.

Cajun rotated the propellers on both the left and right engine, removed the wooden wheel chocks, and unsnapped the ground line. After wheeling a large fire extinguisher with forty-inch steel wheels into position near the right engine, he waved to Joel in the copilot's seat.

"Fire guard in place," Joel announced.

"Fuel booster pumps ON," Murph said. When Joel acknowledged, he moved the carburetor mixture control to AUTO RICH, and cracked the throttle for the right engine.

"Clear prop," Joel shouted in Russian out his window. Cajun returned the call. The engine started easily. Cajun rolled the fire extinguisher to the left side and repeated the procedure.

With the second engine running and stabilized, Cajun walked around the plane climbed the short passenger ladder, pulled it in with its rope, and latched the door.

They taxied toward the runway. Dubov keyed the microphone. "Honor One, marked Yellow Three, taxiing to the active runway for immediate takeoff," he demanded in authoritative Russian.

"Aircraft calling, wait your turn," the tower responded.

"This is *KGB* flight Honor One, Yellow Three, taxiing to the runway for immediate takeoff," Dubov repeated, emphasizing KGB. "I'm not asking."

After a brief pause: "Honor One, cleared to the runway for immediate takeoff. All other aircraft stand clear."

Murph chortled. He lined the aircraft on the runway centerline. Dark clouds loomed to the west like roiling, gray mountains. "Just beating the weather," he said.

"Just beating a lot of things," Joel said, locking the tail wheel.

Murph stood on the brakes and ran up the engines. The aircraft shook, straining against the brakes. Murph released them and the aircraft lurched into motion.

"It accelerates slowly," Joel observed, urging the plane to go faster.

Murph said, "Even with a light load, this thing's heavier than a C-47. Russian engines don't make as much power."

The tail rose. They lifted off. Joel retracted the landing gear and flaps. He closed the cowl flaps slightly.

"Turn a little north," Cajun said, as navigator. "Fly dis headin' for 'bout ten, fifteen minutes, outta sight of da base, den turn south."

The Li-2 leveled off at ten thousand feet. Joel checked his watch, then yelled over the roar of the engines, "Long enough. What's the course, Cajun?"

"Right ta 150 degrees, toward Khabarovsk an' away from China."

"How far to Khabarovsk?"

"Four hun'erd fifty mile. Dere's a twenty-five hun'erd meter concrete runway. Don't t'ink we'll need a gas stop."

"Murph, what's our range?"

"The two main tanks are full, so we're good for about seven hundred miles, give or take fifty. I'm holding us to about a hundred fifty miles-per-hour to go easy on the gas. Khabarovsk is in range, about three hours."

Joel said, "I'll take over shortly, Murph. Monitor the radio. Let me know when they discover this plane didn't return. With any luck, they'll think we crashed. Radio our guys. Let them know we're heading home. Cajun, see what airports on your maps are at the limit of our range, say seven hundred miles from Magdagachi. Then check for airports on the coastline starting at Vladivostok and going north two or three hundred miles. I'll be back in a minute."

Joel unbuckled, and walked back to the plush passenger cabin. Susan slept under a KGB blanket in the general's expansive leather chair.

Ana curled up on a couch, asleep. He waved the others to join him near the rear of the cabin.

"Men, there's not enough gas to fly to Vladivostok."

Felix said, "Let's head to the coast and ask the Navy to pick us up. Vladivostok's a big naval base, with a large airfield crawling with fighters. Has a KGB regiment, too."

Joel said, "I understand, but Vladivostok is still our best bet because the coast line up here is so rugged. I don't want to risk a beach landing unless we really must. Any second now, they'll discover we stole this plane and the whole eastern coast of Russia will be on the look-out."

CHAPTER 104

NO SECURITY

Saturday, 16 September 1950
Magdagachi Air Field

"Is that my aeroplane taking off?" General Lieutenant Sergey Sauchenko asked as he left the senior officer's mess.

"I believe so, sir," his young aide-de-camp reassured him. "Testing the new engine, perhaps?"

Already disinterested, Sauchenko picked the remains of his sumptuous breakfast from his teeth. "We will prepare for the arrival of the KGB troops, Boris. I'll review my staff's recommendations on how to find the traitors. The sooner we capture them, the sooner we can leave this wretched place and return to Moscow. Now our meeting with the base commander begins."

Nearing noon, KGB General Lieutenant Sergey Sauchenko concluded his meeting—a painful, in-depth review of security at Magdagachi Air Field.

"So, we have determined you have *no* security here." His voice rumbled a quiet menace to the squirming, white-faced base commander. "An eight-year-old peasant leading a billy goat with a bell could wander onto this base and no one would notice or suspect. You *will* present to me a comprehensive plan for securing every aspect of this facility at 0800 tomorrow morning, after which you will be under arrest. You will be sent to Moscow for a Court Marshal for incompetence. Dismissed."

Two burly KGB men manhandled the terrified base commander from the room.

Sauchenko motioned to his aide. "We break now for luncheon. My other satchel is on the aircraft. Retrieve it for me."

As Sauchenko sauntered to the senior officer's mess he spoke with the local KGB commander. He praised him with a calm tone, "You did well to inform me, Colonel. I wouldn't have believed the lack of security had I not seen it myself. We are fortunate none of our enemies are nearby. We would fail to repulse even a small attack."

The lunch conversation remained stiff and polite. After Sauchenko's abrupt dismissal of the base commander, not one veteran KGB officer dared trifle with him. Tsarsko, despite being KGB, was absent. Relegated to the end of the table in disgrace, Lieutenant Colonel Yabitov fumed.

Sauchenko's aid interrupted the light banter. "I beg your pardon, General Sauchenko. Sir, there is a problem with your airplane."

The death knell of the young man's somber tone quieted the conversation, like spotless sheep silent before their shearers.

"Tell me," Sauchenko said. "What have you discovered, Lieutenant?"

"General, sir, there's a strange situation I'm looking into."

He shuffled through some papers searching for some notes. "Early this morning, sir, a Gaz and a truck entered the south gate using KGB credentials. Earlier an unidentified KGB Sergeant Major checked out a Gaz-51 truck and the Gaz Jeep from the motor pool. Later, they were found parked next to your aircraft tie down. Mechanics working nearby said KGB guards loaded several black-hooded prisoners onto your aircraft, including one on a stretcher. The tower confirms your aircraft took off this morning, but they don't know when or if it returned."

Sauchenko's eyes narrowed. "There are *no* KGB Sergeant Majors. No flight plan was filed?"

"No sir."

"Were other Li-2s flying at that time?"

"Yes, sir, several."

Yabitov asked, "Lieutenant, were there any women prisoners?"

"Two, perhaps three," the Lieutenant replied.

"Sir," Yabitov turned to Sauchenko, "I suspect the people who stole your airplane are the American spies and traitors."

Sauchenko regarded him with a cold stare. "Ridiculous." He turned to the lieutenant, "When the KGB troops arrive, we will begin investigations at the site of the train hijacking. Prepare transportation."

Colonel Yabitov quietly snuck from the meeting to search for Tsarsko and found him near the motor pool. "That fool General Sauchenko won't believe the traitors stole his airplane. He's going to start looking at the train site. So, *we'll* search for General Sauchenko's airplane. Bring that sergeant you mentioned and some corporals. I'm going to see if anyone spotted the stolen plane. Meet me here in a couple of hours."

CHAPTER 105

INTERCEPTED

Saturday, 16 September 1950
Northwest of Khabarovsk

"Joel," Murph shouted, lifting his headphones, "They've just realized this plane is missing. I've heard several calls for us to report in, even on the secret KGB frequency." Murph hooked his SCR-284(c) shortwave radio into the aircraft's electrical system.

"Do they know where we are?"

"No—wait. Uh, a pilot thinks he saw us turn south-east and fly out of sight. No heading. They're sending out SAR [search and rescue] flights. They think we crashed, 'cause the flight was only supposed to be thirty minutes."

Joel rubbed his chin. "OK, hopefully they won't put out an alarm right away. Ask Felix and Dubov to come to the cockpit."

Felix and Dubov crowded into the cockpit. "Dubov, could you buy us gas at Khabarovsk? How does KGB pay, in a case like this?"

"They sign a voucher, like everybody else. I could probably bully them into refueling us, especially if someone signs for the general."

"I could do that, Colonel," Felix said. "But I still think going to Khabarovsk is too risky. One phone call and we're caught. We should fly to the coast, even if means a beach landing. Don't forget Magdagachi has jets. So does Khabarovsk. They could be on us in half an hour, tops. Those little popguns on the roof won't help much against a jet fighter."

Cajun said, "Boss, lemme modify dat. If we turn now an' jus' head straight to da coast, we be in a desolate area, across from da Sakhalin peninsula. Not good. I t'ink we oughta fly to da water, den fly south along da coast. The closer to Vladivostok, da more likely we find a place. An' you know, we have da range ta fly ta Japan once we buy gas. Sapporo's only 'bout three-hun'erd fifty miles from the Russian coast."

Felix shouted, "Bandits! Eleven o' clock, our altitude!" A pair of camouflaged Yak-9 fighters flashed past in the opposite direction and began a tight turn toward the escaping Li-2.

Cajun scrambled to the Li-2's dorsal turret, peering out through the Plexiglas. "Coming aroun' fast. On us in twenty-five seconds."

Murph leapt to the radio. "What's the lead's call number?"

"White 12," Cajun shouted.

Murph tuned to the plane-to-plane frequency.

"White 12, White 12, this is an official KGB flight. Do not interfere. Break off and return to your base."

The thunder of the Yak-9's V-12 engines rumbled louder than their Li-2. The fighters perched off their left wing. The sleek lead plane's nose jumped a bit as its pilot spotted the gleaming KGB badge on the Li-2.

"Roger, KGB flight, White 12 breaking off." The plane and its wingman banked left and roared away.

"Dey're headed toward Khabarovsk," Cajun said.

In a grim tone, Joel said, "Murph, listen for a report. Cajun, give me a course to the coast."

In seconds, Cajun said, "Turn left ta 120 degrees."

Felix said, "Joel, that pilot will report us once he lands, even if he doesn't radio in. They'll be on us like ducks on a June bug."

"Not if I can help it," Joel said. He rotated the control wheel left and pushed it away from him, and brought the throttles to full power.

The airspeed indicator hovered near redline as they dove at close to 250 miles per hour.

Joel's maneuver and the louder roar of the engines jostled Susan and Ana awake.

"Where are we? What's happening?" Susan asked, her eyes wide. Ana white-knuckled the couch's armrest.

"We were intercepted by a couple fighters," Felix said, "but scared them off with the KGB emblem. We're flying to the coast, then we'll turn south and find a place to get gas."

"Do they know we stole the plane?" Ana asked.

Dr. Berthold said, "Do not be concerned, my dear. They believe this aeroplane has crashed. We have not been connected to it. Is this not so, Mr. Felix?"

"Yeah, according to the radio. If—when—they put everything together, we're in for some new grief."

The aircraft bounced and lurched in the worsening turbulence. Joel leveled off at one thousand feet and slowed down. A back spasm seized up. A sharp pain pierced his lower back. Joel's head pounded.

"How long to the coast, Cajun?"

"Two hours."

Joel glanced at the fuel gauges. *Two half full, the others empty. Fuel isn't a problem yet, but soon. We're gonna have to put down before that storm hits. That's going to be a challenge if the coastline is as rough as I think it is.*

"Felix, you guys take turns in the turret watching for aircraft and the storm."

CHAPTER 106

REBORN

Ana's stomach plummeted as her heart rate skyrocketed. Apprehension furrowed her brow as Ana's trembling hand white-knuckled Susan's wrist. Neither Ana nor Susan said a word until the plane leveled off. Over the engine's roar, Ana asked. "Susan, my friend, how do you remain so calm?"

"No matter what happens, I believe God is in control. If He wants to me to do more on earth for a while longer, OK, I can do that." She looked her tummy. "If He wants us to join Jesus in paradise, I won't worry, I look forward to God's promise of joyous rest."

Ana began with a mechanical tone, as if a programmed machine. "Our leaders do not believe in God. Lenin said, 'Religion is opium for the people. Religion is spiritual booze.' Poppa Joe said, 'You know, they are fooling us, there is no God.'"

"Is that what you believe, Ana, or are you just repeating what you think you must say?" Susan asked.

As if flipping a switch, Ana drunk with animus, blurted. "The Kremlin is drenched in alcohol. All Russia is. I think vodka is the Russians' opiate."

"Ana, how did you come to that conclusion?"

"Is not easy to cooperate with heartless leaders who play God. Stalin, Beria they break our spirits and for why? We are dead, although alive. Beria is alive, although dead. How does a leader preside over ruthless slaughter and remain sober? Lenin and Stalin *murdered* God and *danced* on His grave with their purges and revolutions."

"Guess Lenin and Stalin couldn't get it through their heads that no one's in that grave." Susan's wry remark turned earnest. "Jesus was raised from the dead, so we can have a brand-new life and everything to live for."

"I want a brand new life in America. My *Babushka* was Russian Orthodox before Stalin stomped one more brake on the squeaky wheel that overran her church. That's why my granny protested this silencing by naming me Ana Ksana. Like I told you before, Ana means 'one who will be reborn' and Ksana means 'praise be to God.'"

"I've heard the Russian *Babushkas* are quite a force in themselves."

"Yes, I miss my brave *Babushka*. She was full of wisdom and a peasant who suffered much hard times. When my taskmasters manipulated my terror of the grave to gain their corrupt power over me, I sighed for God so often in my oppression." Ana threw her hands against her face as her shoulders heaved with the sobs of a broken-hearted child.

"Ana, tyrants only triumph when they make you helpless by making you hopeless." Susan stroked Ana's arm as a mother calming her daughter. "Jesus suffered and died as He lived, living out an example of His Father's loving kindness. Jesus made suffering people whole. Those afflicted could be characters drawn from your Russian novels, outcasts and slaves, used and abused, the scum and dross of society."

Ana dropped her hands from her face. "I wish I had such faith in a God that drives fear away with hope."

"What are you afraid of, Ana?"

"Of believing the truth."

CHAPTER 107

HAVEN

Saturday, 16 September 1950
Northwest of Khabarovsk and Base R-117
The Soviet Forward Base

The worsening storm buffeted the Li-2. Murph pointed, "There's the coast."

"Whitecaps," Felix leaned on the back of Murph's seat. "Not a good day to sail."

"Goes double for flying," Murph said.

Joel banked right to follow the rugged coast southward, then slowed, watching for a landing spot.

The surf crashed against rugged rocks. Murph said, "I'm not seeing any beaches, boss, just a whole lot of big rocks."

"There's enough gas to be a little picky about where we set down. We'll keep looking."

Cajun stood on the turret platform watching for fighters. The bumpy ride smoothed out somewhat, which helped him maintain his balance and keep a good watch. Looking right, Cajun saw inland a few miles whenever the rain lifted. Several minutes later, the squall let up, revealing a long concrete runway stretching away from them. "Air field. Three o'clock, two miles. See it, Joel?"

Joel's heart sank. *Oh Lord, if fighters are on that field, we're dead meat. We came up on the Russian airfield so suddenly I couldn't avoid it.*

The squall swept past again. "I can't see. Did anyone see fighters?"

Cajun remained unflappable. "Didn' see any planes, boss. Jus' lots of runway an' buildings. A second runway goes almos' to da shore. No plane on it either. Maybe dis place abandoned?"

Murph strained to see past the thrashing windshield wipers with his binoculars. "No lights in the control tower cab. The airport beacon isn't lit. No trucks or planes on the ramp. Cajun's right. Looks abandoned."

Joel prayed under his breath. He raised the nose, added some throttle, and began a wary right turn to circle the runways. *No activity. This is weird, even for the Russians. Why's a big air field not being used?*

As they turned to the west, they saw a mountainous, black cloudbank as far as they could see in both directions. Lightning flashed and crackled all along the front.

Joel keyed the cabin intercom mic. "Folks, this rain is just the appetizer. The main course is coming, and we don't want to be airborne when it arrives. I'm going to land. Buckle up."

XOXOX

On the ground, they looked through the cockpit windows down the length of the runway. Felix said, "Joel, wait here. Murph and I will check things out. If we find something, I'll fire this flare pistol. If everything's OK, we'll wave."

Joel swung the tail to the side a little. He watched Felix and Murph run, crouched combat-style, toward the nearest hanger. With the engines idling, Joel said over the intercom, "Everybody on the right side, watch for signals from the guys."

Ten minutes later, Cajun walked out from behind the hanger and waved his arms. Felix ran to the next, larger hanger, his wire-stock .30 caliber carbine at the ready.

Felix ran through the rain, climbed into the plane and headed to the cockpit. "Big hanger's empty, Joel. Give me a couple minutes to open the doors."
Felix jumped back on the tarmac, and shoved open the huge metal doors. The Li-2 bumped across the door tracks and into the hanger.

Joel used the left brake, pivoting the plane around to face outward. *This hanger isn't big, it's huge. This is designed for the TU-270s. That's why it's so wide.*

He shut down the engines and climbed down after everyone else.

Felix and Murph closed the hanger doors, shutting out a torrential downpour.

Felix said, "Murph and I will check out the other buildings and try to figure why this place is abandoned. We'll see if there's anything we can use here. Tell the ladies the toilets and showers are in the back."

Felix frowned at Joel. "Boss, you're dead on your feet. Listen, take your lady to the private room in the barracks out back and grab some rest. Nobody's headed here during this storm. I'll make a guard schedule and wake you in the morning."

Susan's encouraging glance persuaded Joel. "OK. Wake me at daybreak."

CHAPTER 108

THE PITS

Saturday, 16 September 1950
Base R-117: The Soviet Forward Base

Before Joel and Susan could find their private room, Felix and Murph returned, soaked to the skin. Rain-whipped sheets rattled against the hanger's high windows. Murph shook the water from his hair. "This base isn't abandoned. It's a prepared forward position with lots of supplies—food, parts, ammo, everything needed for an attack. There are several other big hangers and barracks, too. The small ones must be for fighters. Don't know what they'd attack from here, though. Japan's only a few hundred miles away, but they're no threat."

Joel said. "This big hanger will park two or three of the TU-270s."

Dr. Berthold tapped his cane. "To me, gentlemen, the obvious targets are on the Korean peninsula. For some time, the Soviet propaganda apparatus has fomented against the Americans. A strike from this location would be unexpected and likely effective."

Cajun's eyes widened. "Dose TU-270s are long range planes. Dat puts our Alaska bases within reach. Prob'ly Hawaii an' Guam, too."

Joel's heart accelerated. "Guys, I want you to scout for bomb-loading pits. We need to know if they can load atomic bombs here."

"I'll look for the pits with Felix," Dubov volunteered.

Murph said, "Joel, I'll monitor the radio to see if they're looking for us. I want to find a weather forecast to see if this storm's gonna hang around. I also need to send a message home, too. I know where the radio shack is. I'll make their radios work."

CHAPTER 109

BORROWED

Sunday, 17 September 1950
Base R-117: The Soviet Forward Base

Somebody hammered on Joel's door. Waking from a deep sleep, Joel realized daybreak had passed. The rain still clattered against the metal roof.

"Wait a minute, Joel," Susan grabbed the cover and pulled it to her neck. Joel opened the door stepped out to face Felix, who clearly hadn't slept.

"We found a ten-man caretaker crew, drunk—passed out. They had quite a party. Vodka bottles littered the room. Snoring drunks plopped on the floor, lying on couches, and slumped over a table. We put 'em in the brig to sleep it off. A train with tank cars unloaded maybe 150,000 liters of jet fuel—about 40,000 gallons. We discovered two large, empty Avgas tanks nearby. My guess is they hold about 200,000 gallons together. If they're bringing in jet fuel and Avgas, people aren't far behind."

Joel absorbed the unwelcome information. "OK, Felix, go catch some shut-eye. You're relieved. I'll gather everybody together and plan what's next. Go."

✕◊✕◊✕

Joel performed a mental roll call of those gathered around a table eating breakfast. *Let's see, there's Susan, Ana, Dr. Berthold, Dr. Kalugin, Dubov, Cajun, and Murph. Felix is sleeping. That accounts for everyone.*

Dr. Kalugin placed a bowl of buckwheat porridge in front of Joel, and one for Susan, as well. "Thanks, Doc, I'm famished. OK, everybody, listen up. Felix informed me about the caretaker crew and the fuel train."

Murph spoke up, "More bad news, Joel. We found two bomb-loading pits, fortunately, no bombs. I spent the night in the radio shack, jiggering the teletype machine. We're receiving messages for every base around here. They call this base R-117. Looks like the Red Army and Air Force are about to launch a big exercise, not clear what it is."

Dubov said, "A '47 Ford bus is parked in the motor pool. An export model, a forty-passenger job with only 3000 miles. Dr. Berthold and Murph conjured up an idea that involves the bus."

"Before reacting," Dr. Berthold said, "please consider this plan, yes?"

"OK, I promise," Joel said.

"Very soon the Russians will reoccupy this base. Our aircraft is easy to identify and nearly exhausted of fuel, yes? The only petrol on this base is for autos. So, why do we not take the bus, which looks like all the other military vehicles, and drive south on the A-311." Dr. Berthold cocked his big head, waiting for Joel's reply.

Dr. Berthold glanced at Murph for support. "In addition, we can create a—ah, useful diversion with the KGB aeroplane. I can rig the empty aircraft to take off by itself and retract its landing gear. If we time things in such a way that the takeoff is seen, observers will assume we are escaping and send interceptors. Meanwhile, we motor south in plain sight in our fine motorbus."

Joel asked, "How? We don't a lot of time."

Berthold's eyes sparkled. "You are not counting on the magical bag of tricks our Mr. Felix has. You see, he has a fine collection of bungee cords, and he found more in the supply building. I can use them to hold the control wheel for a steady climb, stabilize the aircraft in roll, hold the throttles, and activate the landing gear control. We start the engines with the tail tied down. When the time is auspicious, we release the tail. The aircraft will fly itself off the runway. With Japan close by, the Russians will assume we are escaping. What do you think?"

"That's bold and the timing is critical." Joel said. "We'll have to do things exactly right to make it believable. You really think you can rig that plane to fly itself, Doc?"

"At the end of the war, the Luftwaffe often desired to send unmanned aeroplanes as bombs against allied targets, yes? I was consulted to design them. Most aircraft are stable in the air by design. This Li-2 is a fine example. The bungees will be used mostly for restorative control in the event of a gust-caused roll, or so. We must yet refine the means of retracting the landing gear and all is ready." Dr. Berthold stopped, allowing Joel to contemplate the plan. Long experience taught him a time arrives in every persuasive talk when the speaker should let his point sink in without additional words.

Dubov darted into the room. "Joel, the teletype says R-117 is the next base to be activated. Mechanics arrive tomorrow, about mid-day by truck. A flight of four MiG-9s will land a little earlier."

Joel nodded at Murph. "OK, bring the bus into the hanger, out of sight. Give those caretakers something to eat."

"Will do, boss." Murph said, "Let's be sure the bus is well off base before the trucks and planes arrive. There's a sidecar motorcycle in the motor pool. Felix and I will stay behind to launch the Li-2, then escape on the motorcycle."

"OK." Joel said. "Raid the supply warehouse and gather several days of food. Make sure to pack blankets."

CHAPTER 110

SOLID LEAD

Sunday, 17 September 1950
Magdagachi Air Field

Yabitov smiled when Boris Tsarsko returned with the men they selected. "Boris Arkady, I received a solid lead. I spent all morning checking around and found pilots at Khabarovsk, who encountered a shiny Li-2 with KGB badges flying south. And what do you suppose?" Yabitov snarled with contempt. "The Li-2 crew ordered them away. I talked to the wingman who told me he watched the plane turn east and fly out of sight. The approximate location is north and west of advance preparation base R-117. I think perhaps our wayward traitors discovered a temporary home."

Could they find the base in that driving rain and wind? Tsarsko mused. *Unlikely.*

As if reading Tsarsko's mind, Yabitov said aloud, "Well, Colonel, if they landed at R-117, they will find little to help them. Those bases won't have jet fuel until they are activated."

Tsarsko checked his notes. "They activate that base tomorrow, sir. If we move quickly, we may catch Joel Knight and the enemies of the people red-handed."

CHAPTER 111

UP, UP, AND AWAY

Monday, 18 September 1950
On the Road Toward Vladivostok

Joel glanced at a teletype sheet. "The planes arrive about 10:35. The trucks, about noon. We'll leave right away—drive at least twenty kilometers, before pulling over. We don't want anyone connecting the bus and this base. Okay, everybody, on board."

Dubov drove the '47 Ford bus from the hanger and headed south. Murph grinned at Felix. "Let's crank this baby up and get 'er out on the runway. Her last performance is about to begin."

The Li-2 sat on the runway, facing the sea. Bright sunshine surrounded them after the storm blew out to sea. Murph tied a heavy rope to the tail wheel strut. Felix sledgehammered a big pipe deep into the macadam. Murph fastened the rope on it. "Got the bolt cutters?"

"Yep, sure do."

Murph switched on the radio, set the frequency, and cranked, eyes closed in concentration. "ETA ten minutes. Let's do this."

Murph raced up the airplane's sloping aisle and plopped in the pilot's seat. He glanced at the passenger windows, each with the sunshade pulled down. Several featured pasted cutouts simulating a passenger's head. A partly inflated weather balloon with rough features bobbed in the cockpit.

The warm engines started immediately. Murph increased the power on both engines. The airplane shook against the rope restraint, anxious to fly to its demise. He locked the throttle and tail wheel and set the elevator trim tab to 4 degrees nose-up.

Murph slipped a strong bungee over the landing gear lever to pull it into the retracted position, the way Dr. Berthold told him. To counteract the bungee, he tied a shoestring around the landing gear lever to hold it in the 'down' position, then secured it to the base of the pilot's seat.

He removed a small glass vial from his pocket and with great care opened it, placing a single drop of concentrated nitric acid on the shoestring. The shoestring smoked as the acid burned.

Murph slammed the door and raced to the motorcycle. Felix grabbed the powerful bolt cutters and sliced the straining rope, then tossed the bolt cutters off to the side.

The Li-2 accelerated down the runway. The tail bounced once, lightly a second time, then the aircraft lifted off. Its graceful, shallow climb rose above the surrounding buildings, a breeze pushing against its tail. The aircraft weather vaned into the wind. As Dr. Berthold predicted, the bungees centered the control wheel. The Li-2 obediently turned toward Japan.

Murph and Felix mounted the motorcycle. Felix revved the motor. Felix slapped him on the shoulder, "Wait. Wait."

"What?" Felix yelled, panic in his voice.

Murph smiled. "I want to see the landing gear retract."

They watched the Li-2 climb over the ocean. Murph knew what was happening in the cockpit: The acid burning through the shoestring would release the strong bungee, snapping the landing gear handle upward. As they watched, the landing gear tucked away in the engine nacelles and Murph exulted. "Berthold knows his stuff."

"Here come the fighters." Felix shouted, then released the clutch and roared through the gate.

CHAPTER 112

SUICIDE MISSION

Monday, 18 September 1950

In the Sky Above Base R-117: The Soviet Forward Base

"Yellow Lead, Yellow Seven. Sir, a Li-2 is taking off. Could be the stolen KGB plane. Permission to investigate. Over."

"Do so, Yellow Seven. Take your wingman. Watch your fuel and report back. Out."

The two MiG-9s climbed out of formation and roared after the departing Li-2.

Within five minutes, the jet fighters caught the still climbing Li-2. The MiGs swept past the prop plane at a respectful distance. The pilot squinted and strained to see into the Li-2's cockpit, moving in as close as he dared. For long moments, he tried to see any signs of life.

He keyed his microphone. "KGB Yellow Three, this is Soviet Air Force Yellow Seven on your left wing. Do you read me? Over."

Nothing.

"Yellow Three, do you read me? Over."

Silence.

Twice more he called the shiny KGB aircraft.

No response. The pilot's head bobbed in time to an unheard symphony.

"Yellow Lead, Yellow Seven. The Li-2 has KGB markings, but they do not respond to radio calls. Over."

"Yellow Seven, Yellow Lead, check from both sides, Ivan. Get his attention. Over."

"Sir."

Yellow Seven flew along the right side of the Li-2, its pilot spotting only dark shapes in the cabin windows. He bumped his throttle and moved forward to look into the right side of the cockpit. Just as he peered into the Li-2s cockpit, its right engine backfired. Exhaust flame cascaded over the wing. The engine ran smoothly for a moment, then backfired again. Abruptly, the engine quit, the big three-bladed propeller slowing to a lazy turn in the slip stream.

With no pilot to feather the propeller or correct for the drag caused by the wind-milling propeller, the Li-2 began a right turn. Yellow Seven climbed to avoid a collision.

"Yellow Lead, they're turning. One of their engines quit. It—it looks like they're going into a spin!"

As the fighter pilots watched, the airliner shuddered on the brink of a stall. The right wing dropped and the aircraft slid into a clockwise rotation. The airliner spun around its vertical axis like a giant dinner plate, wings horizontal, nose a little high, faster and faster. The pilots knew any passengers inside were pinned against the cabin walls.

"They're going in."

The fighter pilots watched open-mouthed as the Li-2 smashed into the Sea of Japan. A huge spray of water shot out from the rotating airplane. It wallowed, broken, on the water's surface, barely afloat.

"Yellow Lead, Yellow Seven—they crashed. There's—there's a fishing boat coming. Maybe some of them can get out." He paused. "I'm BINGO on fuel."

"Yellow Seven, Yellow Lead. Find a landmark on shore to locate the wreck. Estimate how far out to sea you are, then get back here. Yellow Lead out."

CHAPTER 113

TOMORROW

Tuesday, 19 September 1950
Base R-117: The Soviet Forward Base

The IL-12 bearing false AEROFLOT Airline markings landed at Base R-117. As they circled to land, Yabitov spotted the line of trucks on Base R-117, then searched for the missing Li-2. Yabitov's fingernails dug into his palms. *The General's plane must be hidden. No Matter. I will find it. I will crush the traitors and Joel Knight.*

As Yabitov deplaned, a fatigued Army major in charge of the truck convoy met him at the bottom of the stairs. "Somebody *was* here, Colonel Tsarsko."

"The traitors?" Tsarsko asked.

"No way to know, sir." The major lifted a half-empty bottle of vodka to eye level. Perhaps the men in the brig—when they are sober—will provide information."

"It was them, Tsarsko. I'm sure that was General Sauchenko's aircraft." Yabitov's lip twisted with disgust. "There is no other explanation. Yet, why would they commit suicide on the way to Japan?"

Tsarsko, who did actual police work, viewed the situation from an evidence-based approach. "Until confirmed to the contrary, Colonel Yabitov, we must proceed on the evidence in hand. They appeared desperate to get somewhere. I agree that committing suicide is not in keeping with their previous behavior."

Yabitov snatched the vodka bottle from the major. "We will investigate further—tomorrow."

CHAPTER 114

RESTRICTED

Saturday, 23 September 1950, Late Afternoon
Alongside the Road

"I'd say, maybe, 'nother two hun'erd, two fifty miles ta Vladivostok, depend on how curvy da road is." Cajun pointed to a map location south of the R-117 base they exited three days earlier. The resourceful navigator had scrounged every road and aviation map on R-117 that he could find.

"We'd be lost without you, Cajun. Literally." Joel said. "Show me that little air field again."

An aviation map rattled as Cajun unfolded it. He jabbed at a spot marked by a strange symbol.

"Maybe 'nother seventy-five, hun'erd miles south-east. Hard ta tell what's dere, though. Don't know deir airport symbols. Could be jus' a 'mergency strip, no services, or a real airport. Located close ta dis town here—'Terney.' It's da only strip 'til we're way farther south, farther than we got gas for."

Overhearing Cajun's comment, Dr. Kalugin tapped his pointer finger on the map. "This symbol? This is no mystery. This is the symbol for the Ministry of Forestry of USSR."

"Like the U.S. Forestry Department? Not military?" Joel asked.

"Not military, but the Ministry of Forest employees *are* armed. Black bears, tigers, leopards, like that. They travel in pairs, spending a few days inspecting each site, then move on."

"This is a secondary road?" Joel pointed to a thin line on the map.

"Da, used only by the Ministry. Probably little more than a trail. The other access to this airport appears to be this road along the coastline from Vladivostok, but that's too far."

Joel said, "I think we've pushed our luck on this A-311 road long enough. Let's find the road to that airport."

An hour later, with the sun setting, they found the single-track road that wandered to the east. A rusty chain swung between two weather-beaten posts. A barely visible sign read, "No entrance. Restricted to Ministry of Forestry of USSR."

Felix picked the lock. The bus bumped over the rocky ground, leaving no tracks. Felix snapped the lock closed and hopped on the Ford bus.

The bus rocked and rattled over a low ridge until the main road was out of sight. Joel pulled the bus over and snuggled under tall pines. Low mountains stretched in all directions, rough mounds of granite thrusting through thin layers of soil.

"Those look like oversized construction debris, not real mountains," Joel said.

"Wait 'til we start driving over 'em." Dubov chortled. You'll believe they're real."

CHAPTER 115

RENOVATION

Sunday, 24 September 1950
The Sub-Siberian Forest

"Joel, a notice and description of our bus was sent by radio-telephone, calling for people to watch for us and report our location," Berthold reported after monitoring the radio with Murph.

"Took them long enough to discover the bus was missing. Felix was smart to steal their inventory sheets, which slowed them down. Well, I guess we can't hide in plain sight now."

"If I may, I have an idea in that regard, Herr Colonel." Always thinking about how to stay ahead of the dangerous chase, what Dr. Berthold lacked in stature and agility, he made up for in creative and logical thinking. "I propose we change how the bus looks by removing the center portion of the body, behind four rows of seats. Move the rear portion forward, leaving a . . . a what do you say? A flattened bed?"

"A flat-bed?" Joel stroked his chin. "We can disguise the front, too. Remove the grille, dent the fenders."

"I found some paint cans at R-117 and pitched them into the back of the bus." Dr. Berthold's eyebrows flinched up and down with mischief. "Just in case. Dr. Kalugin said there's no standard way of marking Ministry of Forestry vehicles. We'll hand-letter the sides. Who'll know? Maybe we can drive right into the airport."

They worked throughout the day using brute force to make the bus unidentifiable. Felix dug deep into his bag of tricks, finding a hacksaw and a box of self-starting sheet metal screws. Murph rewired the lights. They hid discarded center section of the bus and excess seats under the boughs of pine trees.

With the painted grille removed, a gaping hole exposed the bug-spattered radiator. Gray paint disguised the right fender. The headlight ring on the left fender disappeared, revealing the headlight aiming mechanism. Ana lettered "Ministry of Forestry of USSR" in Cyrillic letters on both sides of the bus with bright yellow runway paint.

"That is almost too perfect, Ana," Dr. Berthold admired. "You are more artist than sign painter."

Ana blushed at the compliment.

As they finished, Joel noticed jets high above—a *lot* of them. Joel strained counting the tiny specks and stopped at fifty. Multiple contrails streaking south etched white against the Dresden blue sky. A frown of concern curled downward on his lips. *The only big jets the Ruskies use are TU-270j's. Those are headed to China. Are they part of that October Victory mission? If they launch from north-east China, any Allied or UN target in Korea is in range of those bombers. They could reach all of Korea, and for that matter, Japan.*

Dubov called to everyone, "Listen, all. Time for firearms practice again. Let's check their condition and cleanliness, and your skills. We'll shoot a few rounds, to keep our hand in, so to speak."

He checked each person's weapon, admonishing gently when he found a speck of dirt. Finding every weapon's safety engaged, he smiled and erected a makeshift target. Revolver hammers all sat on an empty chamber.

To those with military experience—Joel, Dubov, Murph, Felix, and Cajun—the exercise the familiar routine of loading, firing, and clearing their weapons reassured them. But to Susan, Anna, and Drs. Berthold and Kalugin, who needed the practice, the unfamiliar routines unnerved them. After everyone finished target practice, Dubov directed each person to clean and oil their weapon.

CHAPTER 116

WASTED

Sunday, 24 September 1950
Base R-117: The Soviet Forward Base

Tsarsko tapped on the barracks door. No answer. He rapped on the door, a second time, then shoved the door open. The sickly-sweet stench of yesterday's alcohol and drying vomit filled his nostrils. Two empty vodka bottles lay in haphazard fashion on the floor, amid the litter of Yabitov's carelessly dropped uniform. The unshaven man himself lay in his underwear, flat on his back, mouth gaping open, snoring sonorously.

Tsarsko spat in disgust. Every Russian drank vodka, some to drunkenness, but Yabitov's binges were beyond the pale, especially for a senior officer.

The fool. He risks his career every time he lifts a bottle and opens himself to compromise. How can Beria tolerate such a security risk? Yabitov might wear general's pips by now if he'd stayed off the bottle. Perhaps that's best. He's not the smartest colonel I've encountered.

"Yabitov. Wake up." Tsarsko kicked the bed leg. "There is work to do."

Yabitov jerked upright, hair askew, bloodshot eyes blinking. "What? Who?" He looked around. "Where am I?"

Tsarsko snapped with a hard edge. "You drank yourself into a stupor—*again*. Get up now. Take a cold shower and meet me in the ward room. There are new leads."

Thirty minutes later, an irritable, hung-over Yabitov staggered into the ward room. He lurched onto a chair. An enlisted steward appeared by his side.

"Coffee," Yabitov ordered. "Black. And dry toast." Yabitov closed his eyes and massaged his temples with his fingers.

"Feeling better?" Tsarsko raised his voice just to watch Yabitov wince.

"Do not aggravate me, Tsarsko. What new leads?"

I have the upper hand. "The fishing boat captain, who climbed onto the sinking airplane, confirmed no passengers were onboard. It was a decoy. A Ministry of Forestry employee counting eagles' eggs, off all things, spotted the bus from his perch and noted the time and the bus's serial number. Then a motor vehicle refueling station three hundred kilometers south of R-117 reported a bus towing a motorcycle stopped for petrol. A man with KGB badges signed the voucher. The serial number on the voucher matches the stolen bus."

CHAPTER 117

BIPLANE

Monday, 25 September 1950
The Ministry of Forestry Airport

The rough, rut-filled track—not quite a road—forced Cajun to drive slow, as much for fear of damaging the bus as shaking its passengers into jelly.

"Man, Joel, I've driven on *loggin'* roads better'n dis." The bus dodged trees and jostled from one rocky outcropping into the next deep rut, slamming down, then pitching upward again.

"Yeah, driving across the prairie on my dad's ranch isn't *this* rough. I think we're almost to the airport. Is that a building?"

"Hope so," Susan said with feeling. "This is about all I can take." She held her swelling belly, her face pale and drawn. Ana patted her hand.

They drove onto level ground bordering a long, single concrete runway. Ugly, squat, buildings sprawled alongside the runway. Fuel tanks clustered nearby.

"Those are jet fighter revetments," Felix said. "This isn't a forestry strip. It's an auxiliary fighter base."

Other buildings loomed on the opposite side of the broad runway. A large, cabin biplane parked in front of a building.

Joel said, "What the heck is that? I've never seen a biplane so big."

Murph said with excitement, "That's a new Antonov An-2. The Russians nicknamed it "Annie." That thing's incredible. It will easily carry all of us to Vladivostok. Let's go hijack it."

"First, let's find the crew, then see if the thing is airworthy."

Dubov and Felix entered the building and surprised two Ministry of Forestry employees and a pilot drinking tea. They marched them into a storeroom and locked the door.

Murph and Joel inspected the biplane. Joel remarked in astonishment at the size of the flaps and big leading edge slats. "This thing must be able to almost hover. As far as I can tell, once the fuel tanks are topped off, it'll be ready to fly."

Murph grinned. "Colonel, CIA briefed me on this ship. It can fly as slow as thirty-five miles per hour. With a headwind, even slower. We received Intel that the Chinese and North Koreans trained troops to jump out of these without parachutes, can you believe that? They just skim along the ground and the troops roll out."

"*What?* How many did they kill?"

"Just a handful. If the troops remember to roll and drop their guns and entrenching tools separately, they mostly do OK."

"That's crazy."

The airplane's sparse interior came equipped with reasonably comfortable seats mounted near the pilot. Sturdy cargo tie-downs appeared along the aft portion of the cabin floor.

"You'd almost think they designed this just for us," Joel said. "What's its range?"

"Eats a lot of gas. Maybe five hundred fifty, six hundred miles, depending on the load and headwinds. Should make it to Vladivostok, though."

"Get 'er gassed up. I want to get outta here."

Murph and Dr. Berthold wired the SCR-284(c) radio into the Russian biplane's electrical system.

"Joel, I've contacted the USS *Valley Forge*," Murph said. "They know we'll need boats shortly. We're to let them know when and where, but the farther south the better. I reminded the Captain that

President Truman gave us priority over his regular mission. He's not real happy."

"I wouldn't want some Navy guy telling me how to handle Air Force planes and personnel, either," Joel said, "But these scientists are just too important to let service pride block things. We're fueled. Let's load this thing."

Dubov, Joel, and Felix stowed bags and supplies inside the An-2. When they were finished, Joel said to everyone, "Great job. Let's head back to the hanger and round up our exhausted troops and get out of here."

Felix added, "I'll remind everyone to carry their weapon until the aircraft is airborne."

CHAPTER 118

CLOSING IN

Monday, 25 September 1950

Base R-117: The Soviet Forward Base

"We are closing in on Joel Knight and the traitors, Ivan Semyon," Tsarsko placed the black mouthpiece of the clunky governmental telephone into its cradle and smirked at Yabitov. "Yesterday, a Ministry of Forestry worker reported a '47 Ford bus towing a motorcycle drove onto a restricted road fifty kilometers south of the petrol station. We need an airplane that can land on the main road. I'll obtain vehicles and troops to meet us at the junction. We shall capture them yet."

Hangover forgotten, Yabitov dialed the Chief of Aviation at Magdagachi Air Field. He recalled seeing a strange, high-wing airplane—he couldn't quite recall the name—that could land almost anywhere. Surely a major road would be no challenge.

Yabitov angrily invoked both the KGB Chief and Chairman Beria, before he finally pried a Shcherbakov ShchE-3 loose from the Chief of Aviation.

"You must understand, Comrade Colonel, only four such aircraft are assigned to me," the Chief of Aviation argued. "I'm supposed to have seven. You must return it promptly."

"You'll get the plane back when the KGB is finished with it," Yabitov's hand sliced the air with a dismissive wave.

XOXOX

The awkward-looking aircraft landed at R-117, the advance preparation base. A truck rumbled across the tarmac and parked beside the plane. Tsarsko climbed out and opened the tailgate. Sergeant Tokarev jumped down and shouted orders at two corporals and a pair of privates.

Tokarev armed himself with a PS 1943 submachinegun. The two corporals carried Kalashnikov AK-47 automatic rifles and the privates carried weapons Yabitov didn't recognize.

"What are these guns, Tokarev?"

"Comrade Colonel, you said we might need to fight in close quarters, so I equipped the privates with American Winchester Model 12 combat shotguns. *Very* effective."

Yabitov said, "Very good, Comrade Sergeant Tokarev, very good."

Tsarsko conferred with the youthful pilot about the approximate location of the Ministry of Forestry road. The young lieutenant appeared more concerned with the main road. "I require two hundred to three hundred meters of straight road to land on, Comrade Colonel. Sir, I may not be able to place you precisely at this junction."

Tsarsko couldn't tell if his concern was for his airplane or about displeasing Colonel Yabitov. "Land us as close as you can. We will thank you for our safety." The six men and the pilot boarded the Shcherbakov ShchE-3 and settled into their seats.

Any doubts that Yabitov or Tsarsko harbored about their young pilot's inexperience were dispelled as he demonstrated his mastery of the strange little twin-engine plane.

"The Pike is fun to fly, Comrade Colonel. So responsive. That is what will allow us to land on the road." The pilot was as good as his word. After two hours flying over the meandering road south, they spotted several waiting Gaz Jeeps. With crisp military radio work, the pilot verified this was their rendezvous.

The pilot reassured them, "The Pike will easily land on this road, sir." In moments, he landed them gently only a few hundred yards from the Gaz Jeeps.

Yabitov and Tsarsko strode to meet the drivers. Sergeant Tokarev supervised the corporals and privates as they unloaded their weapons and gear. The Pike lifted off and roared off to the north into the horizon, then disappeared.

Yabitov dismissed the drivers with an angry curse, seizing two of their vehicles. The troops he'd ordered remained more than two hours away.

"Now, *we* will capture the traitors ourselves. We must take them alive. I will take Joel Knight myself," Yabitov spat the words, "but just *barely* alive."

"Yes, Knight is important, but do not forget Dr. Kalugin. Him we must spare for special attention later," Tsarsko said. "Shouldn't we wait for the troops?"

"I cannot wait, not when my hands are so close to Knight's neck," Yabitov said through clenched teeth.

The seven men—Yabitov, Tsarsko, Sargent Tokarev, the two corporals and the two privates—climbed into the two Jeeps and began their pursuit, bumping over the same road the fugitives travelled earlier.

CHAPTER 119

VENGEANCE

Monday, 25 September 1950
The Ministry of Forestry Airport

Sergeant Tokarev raised his hand. The lead Gaz slid to a stop across the gravel a hundred yards from the runway.

Tokarev whispered to Tsarsko, "Colonel, the bus. They converted it to a flatbed. Look . . . The German dwarf! We found them."

Before Yabitov spoke, Tsarsko ordered, "Quick, move into the woods."

Yabitov flashed an angry glance at Tsarsko. "I disagree, let's run across the runway and grab them now."

Tsarsko grabbed the Red Army colonel's arm. "Not yet, Ivan Semyon. We'll enter that building through the back door, they'll have less time to respond."

Sergeant Tokarev's normal pre-combat jitters gnarled into gut-gripping fear. *I'm the only one with actual combat experience. The corporals and privates are kids, never served during the Great Patriotic War. Yabitov and Tsarsko? Both rear echelon officers. If these amateurs panic, we could all be killed.*

Sergeant Tokarev pointed to the privates, then held his arm up, palm toward his face and motioned for them to move out and follow him. Everyone crept in silence behind the sergeant toward the drab building. They crouched in a line below the windows.

Sergeant Tokarev glanced through a dirty window, then turned and whispered. "After you go through that door, spread out, so a lucky shot doesn't hit us. Advance as far as possible toward them without shooting. Do not shoot until you are shot at. We are to capture them, not kill them."

Even the Colonels listened. Tokarev noticed sweat beading on Yabitov's upper lip. Yabitov chewed his cheek. His eyes glazed with hate. Yabitov twitched and fingered the trigger of his Tokarev TT-33. Vengeance distorted his pale face. Sergeant Tokarev glanced at the perspiring junior troops, who lacked trigger discipline.

"Listen to me," Tokarev said again, with as much authority as he could muster. "Keep your fingers *off* the trigger until you're ready to shoot. You with the AK-47s, fire in three round bursts. Aim your fire. You men with shotguns, wait until you are closer before you fire, otherwise you waste rounds. Shoot deliberately, slowly. Is everyone ready?" He glanced from face to face. "Follow me."

They barged through the door and spread themselves two or three feet apart. Tokarev opened his mouth to tell them to space farther apart when . . .

CHAPTER 120

SHOT

Monday, 25 September 1950
The Ministry of Forestry Airport

"Enemy left flank!" Dubov shouted. He whipped his M1911A1 .45 Colt automatic from its holster and fired twice.

The green, Red Army troops fired, out of range. Shotgun blasts shattered the concrete. Shards ricocheted toward the escapees. AK-47s thundered on automatic, spraying rounds everywhere. Only Tokarev fired disciplined bursts, from his PS 1943 machinegun.

Felix's abdomen stopped a bullet's momentum, knocking him on his back unconscious. Ana screamed. A machinegun round slashed her right thigh. She crumbled to the floor.

Dr. Berthold rushed toward her only to be thrown to his knees by a blast of shotgun pellets and flying debris. Regaining his balance, he leaned over Ana with blood running into his eyes. He smeared the blood aside, along with a flap of his scalp.

Dr. Berthold swept aside Ana's blood-stained skirt. Blood gushed from her breached artery. Holding a thumb over the penetrating wound, he yanked off his belt and wrapped it around her leg. He snatched a still-smoking, brass cartridge, placed it under the belt, and yanked the belt tight. Ana groaned, as the bleeding stopped. He kissed her forehead with tenderness, and then whirled around like a German Rottweiler in full-on, killer-attack mode.

Tsarsko aimed his 7.62 mm Tokarev TT-33 automatic pistol at the dwarf's large head. Susan's S&W Model 10 .38 barked at a steady pace. She dropped Tsarsko with one shot between his eyes.

Shotgun fire swept through, blasting concrete shards into the air. She dropped to her left side, a bullet fragment bore into her right leg. Her right foot jerked as the next fusillade left her foot a shredded, bloody mess.

Joel grunted as a whining ricochet punched its way into his upper left chest. He rocked back on crossed legs, feeling no pain, but confused. His time-sense slowed in the face of the Russians' rapid-fire attack and blazing high-muzzle velocity weapons.

In exaggerated slow motion, Joel observed his right hand rise, his left hand moving to brace it. His M1917 Smith and Wesson .45 revolver thundered twice, somehow, on its own volition. The Red Army sergeant tumbled to the ground in a jumble of arms and legs.

No one stood between Joel and the onrushing Yabitov. The Soviet colonel bared his yellowed teeth like a pouncing wolf. His face contorted with hate. His scream was unintelligible. He waved his Tokarev TT-33 automatic like a club.

Joel's revolver cracked twice. Then once again. Yabitov stumbled. With a quizzical look, as if he couldn't quite understand, Yabitov stopped. Three red flowers blossomed on his chest. His body barreled facedown and smacked against the cement floor.

Cajun fired his M1911 .45, but was upended by a shotgun blast. Concrete shards peppered his left leg. A second blast struck his back, embedding a dozen pellets in Cajun's skin.

Murph's bolt-action M1891/30 Mosin-Nagant spoke in a slow, death chant. A Red Army corporal with an AK-47 dropped, his knees buckled.

A private wielding the combat shotgun pumped the action again and again, failing to comprehend that the American Winchester was out of ammo. Murph ended the private's confusion permanently.

The remaining private, still firing wild rounds, spun toward Murph. By instinct, Murph threw up his left arm. A shot shredded his sleeve and shattered his left hand at the same instant an AK-47 round tore across his right shoulder.

Dr. Kalugin surprised himself. *I will not allow these thugs take me or any of us alive.* Aiming the M1911 Colt .45 by instinct, Dr. Kalugin shot at the young man as the corporal's AK-47 pop, pop, popped. The corporal thudded to the ground like a felled dead tree. Kalugin staggered, wounded, his hands, arm, legs, and feet bleeding.

A sudden, intense silence engulfed the survivors. All seven Russians lay silent, unmoving. The air reeked of smoke and cordite. And blood.

CHAPTER 121

EVERYONE WOUNDED

Monday, 25 September 1950, Late Afternoon
Headed Out to Sea

"Susan's hit!" Joel checked Susan's wounds in a near-panic. He surveyed the bloodied group. "Anybody else?" His words sounded ridiculous even as Joel heard himself say them. Every one lay bleeding from their wounds. "Who's hurt the worst?"

Dr. Berthold—bleeding from his torn scalp—leaned over Felix's inert body. "He's wounded in the abdomen. Breathing is shallow. He's unconscious. Ana has a severe wound on her right thigh, with arterial bleeding. I used my belt as a tourniquet."

"Looks like we're all wounded, but nothing else life threatening." Dubov frowned. "Joel? What's all that blood on your shirt?"

"I don't know. I got hit, but nothing's broken. I'm OK. We gotta leave pronto. There's more Russians where those came from. Our only chance is to fly to the carrier. Murph, can you copilot for me?"

Murph glanced at his bloody left hand and gave Joel a brief nod.

"Cajun, can you navigate and work the radio with Murph?"

"Yeah, boss. I ain't bad hurt as y'all."

Murph and Joel gently lifted Felix and Ana and carried them onto the Antonov An-2 biplane that resembled a tractor with wings.

Susan needed help, but hobbled up the steps by herself and into the cabin that leaned distinctly rearwards. Joel watched as his wife limped to a seat and plopped down. *I so thankful the plane is fueled and loaded.*

Joel instructed Dubov. "Do first aid on everybody. Stop the bleeding first. Shrapnel can wait. Put a compress on Felix. Loosen Ana's tourniquet every few minutes."

Murph and Joel worked through the startup procedure and the slow-turning Russian radial engine started. Joel taxied onto the runway with exaggerated care.

This thing is heavy. Lots of inertia. The last thing I need is a ground loop before we can take off.

Sucking in a deep breath and offering a silent prayer, he shoved the throttle forward. The lumbering Antonov An-2 rattled down the runway.

SPLASHDOWN

Monday, 25 September 1950
Over the Sea of Japan

Murph helped Joel as he searched for controls in the unfamiliar cockpit. They leveled out at 1500 feet. Joel adjusted the trim tabs by trial and error until the plane flew satisfactorily. The Antonov An-2 responded in a ponderous fashion to control inputs.

I can deal with this. The plane has a good, solid, reliable feel. Thankfully, Susan's bleeding slowed down. He forced himself not to think about Susan. *I can't put her ahead of the others.*

He glanced at the clock. Almost 1700 hours. *Let's see, sunset's around 1945 or so. What's the weather doing? Can we arrive there in time?*

Looking north, he saw another storm brewing, coming in behind them. *Oh, great. Just what I need, a storm to complicate finding a ship in the open sea, flying an airplane I've never even seen before, landing us safely, and not losing any of my injured passengers. Gee, that's easy.* His pain drove the sarcasm.

Cajun shouted over the extreme noise of the engine: "Boss, I got da ship frequency dial up. You wanna call dem?"

"Yeah. We need their position and call signs."

"Da boat is PINE TREE. Y'all are PINE CONE. The ship is USS *Valley Forge*, CV-45, name for the Revolutionary War battle. She's flag ship of Task Force 73. Captain is Captain Steadman."

Cajun handed Joel the mic.

Joel sucked in a deep breath. *This won't be easy.*

Excruciating pain throbbed in his shoulder. The bumpy air, with the constant repositioning of the control wheel jerked Joel's wound back and forth. His shoulder bled, drenching his already blood-soaked shirt.

"PINE TREE, PINE TREE, this PINE CONE. Do you read? Over."

The answer came through the cheap Russian headphones, scratchy, tinny, a little faint, but clear.

"Roger, PINE CONE, this is PINE TREE. How do you read?"

"PINE CONE reads you about 4-by. We're airborne and need your current position ASAP. Over."

"Stand by, PINE CONE." Several minutes passed. "PINE CONE, this is PINE TREE. PINE CONE, why are you airborne and not on the beach? Over."

Without meaning to, Joel snapped with agitation. "Listen, things were hot for us and we escaped by air. Stop delaying and provide me that position. We have injured people aboard and don't have all the gas in the world. Over."

"Roger."

Another period of silence stretched out. Joel's imagination pictured every possible bad outcome.

"PINE CONE, this is PINE TREE. Stand by for coordinates."

Cajun monitored the conversation, ready to write down the information.

"Go ahead, PINE TREE."

"PINE CONE, fly to sector Juliet One Zero. That is J-ten. We are leaving box 35 for box 46. Do you copy?"

Some map genius had divided the area into five-mile square segments, identified by random coordinates. One hundred numbered boxes nestled within each five-mile square. Staring at the map, Cajun had to locate the ship's location, then figure out a rough idea of its heading.

"Roger, PINE CONE copies. Stand by."

Cajun bent over the Russian map that included the Sea of Japan. Muttering to himself, he found the latitude and longitude markings, then transposed the coordinates onto the map.

"Got it. Turn lef' ta course 095 degrees. Dey 'bout fifty mile or so."

Joel said, "PINE CONE confirms Juliet-ten. Over."

"PINE CONE, stand by for PINE TREE Boss."

The next deeper, older voice revealed the ship's captain, Captain Steadman. "PINE CONE, this is PINE TREE Boss. What the hell is going on?"

Joel spoke in a slow, concise manner, emphasizing every word. "PINE TREE Boss, be advised we were in a firefight. ROVER is wounded, repeat, ROVER is wounded . . . so is *every other* member of this party, including this pilot. Two of my people are in serious condition. We have nine souls on board who require immediate medical attention at your location. Over."

"PINE CONE, will you ditch at our location? Over."

The shrapnel digging deeper into Joel's shoulder screamed at him. With each movement of his arm, every piece of shrapnel announced its piercing presence.

"*No*. Negative, PINE TREE. PINE CONE will *land* at your location. Over." Joel hadn't thought about his response, which just occurred to him. *Murph says this thing can fly real slow. If the ship speeds up and turns into the wind, I'll set us right down on the deck.*

"Please repeat, PINE CONE. You intend to *land* at my location?" The Captain asked the incredulous question slowly and carefully.

"Roger, that is correct, PINE TREE."

"*Negative*. I will *never* allow a non-carrier-rated pilot to land on my deck with an unknown aircraft. You will ditch alongside. Over."

"Negative, PINE TREE! Negative! I say again, *every* soul on board is wounded. Two are critical. One is pregnant, another crippled. This is a fixed gear plane. Do you know what happens when a fixed gear plane ditches, Captain? They *always* flip over. I *will* land on your deck. Over."

The captain's voice roared like a bad Siberian winter. "PINE CONE, if you attempt that, I *will* order you shot down. Do you understand? Over."

Time to play my ace. Joel's voice replied iron-hard. "PINE TREE, be advised, PINE CONE has the *full imprimatur* from CACTUS, repeat, full imprimatur. I have been given command authority. You *will* comply with my direction. Do you understand? Over."

Joel knew Captain Steadman was aware that President Truman chose CACTUS as his code name for the mission. With orders from his Commander in Chief to comply, Captain Steadman had to obey whatever Joel requested.

The hiss of the radio's carrier wave grew louder in the intervening moments. *If he refuses, we'll all die.* Cold sweat trickled down Joel's arms, his breath came in gasps. Joel didn't envy the captain. And didn't care.

An honorable man reluctant to obey an order he detested and one he knew put his ship and its company in danger, the captain's strained voice came back. "PINE CONE, this is PINE TREE Boss. I understand and will comply. Stand by for PINE TREE Air Boss."

Joel breathed a sigh of relief and a quiet prayer of thanks.

"PINE CONE, this is PINE TREE Air Boss. Describe your aircraft type. Over."

For ten minutes, Joel and the PINE TREE Air Boss traded questions and answers. At last the Air Boss understood the basic concept of the An-2 and its unusual flying characteristics. Cajun calculated their position, which Joel passed to the ship.

Monitoring the Red Air Force fighter frequencies on the plane's radio, Murph slapped Joel's arm.

"Boss, they discovered we stole this thing. Vladivostok launched fighters with orders to shoot us down."

"MiG-9s?"

"Yeah, or MiG-15s."

"I'll advise *Valley Forge.*

XXXX

"PINE CONE, PINE TREE is launching four flights of two for CAP. They will do a fly-by when they're on station. Over." CAP stood for Combat Air Patrol, fighters flying protective cover over ships in the Task Force or, in this case, Joel's aircraft.

A deep sigh of relief rushed from Joel's chest. The launch of the CAP proved that the PINE TREE Boss took him seriously.

"PINE CONE, repeat your wing span."

"PINE TREE estimates sixty feet. I just remembered: the NATO code name is COLT. Over."

"COLT. Understand. Say again minimum landing speed and distance."

"PINE CONE advises the handbook says about thirty-five miles per hour and about seven hundred feet. Over."

"That's a problem, PINE CONE. PINE TREE doesn't have seven hundred feet of unobstructed deck."

"PINE TREE, if you can reach twenty-five knots or more, I can almost hover this thing over the deck. Do you understand?"

A pair of dark blue Vought F4US Corsairs roared by, rocking their wings.

"PINE TREE, be advised, CAP just arrived."

CHAPTER 123

ARMED

Monday, 25 September 1950
Over the Sea of Japan

T he four, bent-wing F4U Corsair prop fighters stayed low to surround the An-2. At high altitude, Section Leader Marine Captain John "Scotty" McGee signaled his wingman with his hand. The four sleek, dark blue Grumman F9Fs Panthers—the Navy and Marine Corps' latest jet fighters—had yet to be blooded. And they were hungry.

McGee's radar showed Soviet fighters racing toward them. His orders said he was to prevent the Russians from approaching the stolen airplane without shooting them down, if possible.

Those are the orders, but I sure hope I get a chance to splash a couple of Russians.

A six-kill WWII ace, he wanted to add to the total in this new war. Like a good Marine, though, he followed orders. He watched the Corsairs turn toward the Russians, warning them away. His fellow Section Leader and his wingmen circled high above, waiting like hungry hawks stalking plump rabbits.

✕✕✕

Soviet Air Force Captain Ivan Ivanovich had his orders, too: Shoot down the stolen An-2. Kill the traitors and spies in the plane, no matter the cost. With no restrictions on what to do with the enemy aircraft, Captain Ivanovich intended to kill them all. *I will give the Americans a bitter lesson.*

Nineteen MiG-9 Fargo jets flew in formation, all flown by experienced pilots. The new jet-powered Grumman F9F Panthers were unknown to Captain Ivanovich. He expected to encounter WWII vintage Vought F4U Corsairs, or perhaps even some Grumman F8F Bearcats.

XOXOX

Navy Lieutenant Jonathan "Ringo" Barnes turned his big gull-winged prop fighter toward the Russians to be sure they saw him. Then he realized they had no intention of just threatening the stolen airplane—the Russians intended to shoot the biplane down. Cannons winked along the nose of two of the MiGs.

"Hostile fire! I repeat, hostile fire! Get 'em!" Ringo shouted. He and his wingmen lined up on the straight-wing Russian jets. The closing speed between the two groups of aircraft was nearly a thousand miles per hour.

MiGs and Corsairs alike fired their weapons with no visible damage to either. In seconds, they flashed past each other. The Corsairs had no hope of turning to catch the much faster MiGs.

Ten thousand feet above, Scotty McGee watched the clash and heard the radio call. He and his squadron mates nosed over and dove behind the unsuspecting Russians.

All four pilots armed the 20mm cannons in the noses of their sleek Grumman F9Fs Panthers. The green ARMED light glowed in each cockpit.

Scotty McGee pushed his throttle as far forward as possible. In level flight, his plane could fly as fast as 500 knots [575mph], approximately 0.65M. M stood for Mach, the speed of sound, which was 760 mph at sea level.

As he dove, the Airspeed indicator rotated past the cruise speed indication of .63M. An angry red line marked the Vne speed [Velocity Never Exceed] for the Panther at .95M.

Faster than .95M, the aircraft experienced Mach-tuck and other nasty compressibility issues. McGee held his speed just below the red line.

The four diving Panthers caught the MiGs in seconds. Each Panther pilot chose a target. Opening fire, the 20mm cannons thundered. Two MiGs burst into flames and plunged into the troubled, green-gray sea.

With a speed advantage of more than one hundred fifty miles per hour, McGee's Panthers experienced little trouble forcing the MiGs to turn away from their attack. McGee climbed and turned toward the now-fleeing MiGs.

With a grimace, he sprayed the closest MiG with cannon fire. A burst of black smoke rose into the sky, as the Russian dove straight into the ocean, creating a huge splash. McGee rolled and walked his cannon fire across the canopy of another ill-fated Russian craft. That aircraft impacted the Sea of Japan inverted.

To his right, a MiG exploded in a ball of angry, orange flame. Parts from the ill-fated MiG nearly engulfed the Panther that shot down the doomed craft. Yet another MiG banked away, exposing the Red Star on its flank. Black smoke and fire poured in gouts from its engine. The pilot ejected into the unforgiving sea. Several wounded MiGs met their fate at the hands of the hungry, waiting F4U Corsairs.

McGee slowed, viewing the scene through the increasing rain— a depleted Russian formation, scattered, broken, and eliminated as a combat force. The remaining MiGs retreated toward the mainland, unable to resist the speed and firepower of the American warplanes. A wounded F4U Corsair trailed oily, black smoke on its way back to the carrier.

CHAPTER 124

TOUCHDOWN

Monday, 25 September 1950

USS *Valley Forge*, CV-45

The sun touched the horizon and danced below the grey storm clouds. Joel watched the whitecaps increase as the light dimmed. *One way or the other, this little adventure is about over.*

"PINE TREE, PINE CONE has you in sight. Please advise your escorts we're friendly."

"PINE TREE, Roger. Report when you are two miles out. The ship is turning into the wind. Over."

Joel hashed over the landing process and signals with the LSO. The Landing Signals Officer irritated him. *Why didn't they listen to me?* He shook off his frustration. *I have to make this work.*

"PINE TREE, PINE CONE. Please advise CAESAR we will visit him ASAP, over."

CAESAR, General MacArthur's code name, commanded the U.S. and UN troops in Korea. Joel chuckled at the irony of MacArthur's code name, given the man's tendency toward grandiosity. MacArthur, who stayed in Inchon following the successful invasion, directed the Allied push north toward the Chinese border. *MacArthur has no idea what Chairman Beria has in mind for him.*

"PINE TREE, PINE CONE is within two miles. Over."

Flying over the escorting destroyers and cruisers, Joel spotted the massive aircraft carrier's broad wake. *Valley Forge* turned to the right.

"PINE TREE, I'm turning on every light I have. I'd appreciate returning the favor. Over."

Joel and Murph switched on every light, including the landing lights. Ahead, the aircraft carrier's deck suddenly illuminated. The night was not quite dark yet. The steely twilight appeared more metallic and unreal by blowing spew and gusty rain. The storm raged close by.

"PINE CONE, this is LSO. I have you in sight. Follow my directions." Joel concentrated on aligning the bulky biplane with the deck, thankful it wasn't pitching and rolling too much. His concern remained the gusty wind. He backed off the power. The aircraft settled into a steady, stable descent.

With a startling clank, the An-2s leading edge wing slats automatically deployed, activated by their strong rubber cords. The open slot along the front of the wing allowed air to flow smoother over the entire wing, permitting the aircraft to fly even slower.

The ship's wake grew deeper and whiter as the stern sank a little under increased power. The massive bow wave curled away from the ship in an almost artistic curve. They bumped in the swirling air behind the huge ship.

Murph called out airspeeds so Joel didn't take his eyes off the deck. "Forty-one knots, now thirty-eight. Steady, you're doing fine. Good. Keep slowing."

With the plane slowing, the ship accelerating, and the storm-generated wind blowing over the deck, the speed differential between plane and ship shrank quickly. As the An-2 crossed over the ship's stern, their relative speed dropped to less than ten miles per hour.

Joel let thirty feet of the deck pass under them and then cut the power. The An-2 smoothly dropped six feet in a gentle touchdown on the wooden deck. They rolled less than ten feet.

CHAPTER 125

ONBOARD

J oel watched as Navy corpsmen scrambled to the An-2's door before they opened it from inside. The corpsmen carried Felix, still unresponsive, out first. A CPO [Chief Petty Officer] wearing medical insignia immediately inserted a plasma needle in his arm, replacing lost blood. Two sailors lifted Felix onto a metal litter. A third man held the plasma bottle high, as they sprinted toward the ship's hospital bay. A full ER crew waited below decks.

Next came Ana, her complexion pale, almost gray. She gave the men a wan smile. They eased her onto a litter. The CPO administered plasma to Ana. Berthold watched with agony etched on his face, as they carried Ana to the hospital bay.

Joel helped Susan limp out the door. She winced as the shrapnel jabbed her upper leg. Her blood-soaked skirt hung in tattered ribbons. To the sailors' astonishment, the beautiful woman was not only wounded, but pregnant. The walking wounded from Joel's crew followed the litter-bearers.

Dr. Berthold scurried in his clumsy, painful way, toward the An-2's nose, his cane thumping. Several sailors viewed the aircraft, trying to decide what to do with the ungainly Russian biplane.

Berthold beckoned to one. "Come. I will show you. This aircraft can fold its wings, yes?"

The sailors looked surprised that the little man with a hideous wound on his head spoke with such authority. In English, no less, with a German accent, not Russian.

Berthold stomped over to where the front of the lower right wing connected to the fuselage. The wing root loomed above him. "Push on that." He pointed his cane at a triangular metal cover at the intersection. "You will see a hinge with a removable pin, yes? Do you see?"

A sailor stood on the right main landing gear tire and pushed on the cover. The cover obligingly rotated into the fuselage.

"Yeah, there's a big pin here, just like he says."

"*Jawohl*, this is so. You will find also another at the top wing intersection. Position two men at the trailing edge of the lower wing and remove both pins at the front. The wings will pivot easily to the rear. As they do, release the red interior strut and reposition the control cables. Move the wings all the way back and secure them near the tail, yes?"

A scowling Petty Officer watched. "Don't bother, boys. Soon as all the people are off this ugly Russian tub, it's going over the side. We got aircraft to recover."

"As you were, Petty Officer," Dubov snapped. "The CIA wants this plane. You *will* fold its wings and you *will* stow it on the hanger deck."

With their mouths agape, the PO and the sailors stared at Dubov's bloody face and blood-soaked clothes. There was no mistaking the authority in his voice.

"Yes sir. We'll have to make room for it, it's so big."

"Yes, that's what you do, I'm told." Dubov turned and limped toward the passageway, his lips curling into a slight smile.

CHAPTER 126

DESTINY

Monday, 25 September 1950
The Kremlin, Moscow, USSR

Lavrenti Beria reread the radio dispatches. Anger reddened his neck. He clinched his fist. *So the Americans escaped again, did they? Well, not for long.* He whirled the dial on his safe, like a spinning top, then removed the October Victory execution document. He scrawled his signature on the document, not caring how it looked.

"Transmit this at once." His words slurred. "Highest priority." Beria's hand trembled as he handed the document to a courier, who scurried to the transmitter room. Two minutes after Beria affixed his signature, a powerful radio signal broadcast the orders.

Beria rose, his stomach writhing. He stumbled, then paced with a limp back and forth across the expansive, empty room. Beria gestured and lectured an unseen audience. Nervous, anxious thoughts raced through his head. *Will this plan work? They will be caught by surprise, but will the Americans believe the Chinese attacked them? Yes! Yes! They must. They must fight and defeat each other. Then I'll rule the world, my destiny!*

An avalanche of massive pain attacked without warning, like a red-hot steel spike impaled in his head. He couldn't see the open window. His right arm dropped. His right leg collapsed. A hurricane of unbearable pain whirled through his body. He plunged face first onto the exquisite parquet flooring. Lavrenti Pavlovich Beria lay paralyzed, dying, the unconscious victim of a massive stroke.

CHAPTER 127

HOTSHOTS

Monday, 25 September 1950
Flight Deck, USS *Valley Forge*, CV-45

A delicate ballet on the flight deck engrossed a dozen sailors as they manhandled the over-sized An-2 onto the ship's elevator. The big Russian biplane's tail barely cleared the edge of the wooden flight deck on its way down to the hanger deck when the first CAP aircraft landed.

The damaged F4U Corsair still smoked as the pilot shut down the engine, and rolled to a stop. Three sailors emptied fire extinguishers into the airplane's engine cowling. The smoke became white, the fire extinguished. Sailors pushed the wounded plane aside as the pilot folded the wings.

With the damaged Corsair safely out of the way, the four F9F Panthers landed in rapid succession. The gas-guzzling jets teetered on the verge of fuel starvation. Slicing rain swept across the USS *Valley Forge's* deck as the last of the Corsairs snagged the Three Wire.

The Commander of Combat Air Group watched from the control deck. A smile of satisfaction spread across the CAG's face.

Eight sent out. Eight came back. Only one damaged. And these hotshots think they splashed at least seven Ruskies. Good mission.

CHAPTER 128

J oel watched the frantic, but ordered, activity with amazement as corpsmen in the ship's sick bay dealt with the unexpected inrush of nine wounded people. A surgeon and two male nurses worked frenetically on Felix under glaring white lights. Their intensity reflected the seriousness of his condition.

Two men, dressed head-to-toe in white, sutured the sliced artery in Ana's leg. Her leg returned to its normal healthy pink, signaling success. They bandaged the leg and rolled her toward a recovery area. An IV delivered plasma into a vein in Ana's arm.

A tall, black corpsman, with the hands of a musician, centered his attention on Susan. In a quick, skillful movement, he extracted the small piece of shrapnel from her upper leg and dropped it with a clang into a steel pan.

"That won't bother you any more, ma'am," he said kindly. Three skillfully placed stitches closed her wound.

"You're real lucky, Ma'am. You didn't lose much blood, just looks that way." He swabbed the wounded area with iodine and placed surgical dressing on it. Although painful to watch, Joel watched the man extract the shotgun pellets and tiny bits of concrete from her leg and right foot. Susan stoically endured the probing, occasionally twitching when the corpsman touched a particularly tender spot.

"Seems like quite a shootout you were in, Ma'am. Hope everyone recovers quickly."

A sailor directed Joel toward a sheet-covered table. "Let me look at that shoulder, sir." Using a huge pair of utility scissors, the man cut off Joel's borrowed Russian jacket and shirt before he could protest. He discarded the bloody compress and examined the wound with gloved hands. The slightest touch felt more like a prod with a red-hot fireplace poker.

"There's some deep muscle damage here, sir. We'll need the surgeon. Doesn't look like any bone damage, though. Does this hurt?" He raised Joel's arm. Stabbing pain streaked through his shoulder.

Joel gasped. "Oh, yeah, that hurts. Listen, just put a dressing on for now. I gotta make a Priority One call." Blood streamed down his arm and chest again.

"Oh, no, sir. It's medical necessity to stop that bleeding and repair the damage." Joel winced at the hypodermic needle's prick. "This will help you sleep, sir, while the surgeon repairs things."

"No, wait . . ." Joel slipped into drug-induced coma.

)(O)(O)(

Joel awoke, unsure where he was. The white room swirled. He gripped the edge of his bunk. The deep throb of the ship's engines brought everything back, and he remembered. *I've gotta get to the radio room.* He swung his legs out of the bed.

"Wait. Stop. Hold on, sir." A young corpsman rushed toward him. "The doctor hasn't released you."

"Young man, I am *Colonel* Knight. It's vitally important you take me to the radio room immediately. Get me an escort. And some *pants.*"

Swaddled in bandages, Joel's left shoulder and arm were immobilized. His upper torso and arm hurt. Bad. He bit his lip and allowed the corpsman help him into some trousers. Every place on his legs and feet where the docs removed shotgun pellets and cement debris stung like mad. *I feel like a human pin cushion.*

"Where's Dr. Kalugin? How badly was he wounded?" Joel asked the sick bay clerk. "He's the balding, older gentleman."

The clerk rustled through the papers on his desk. "Sir, we treated him for superficial wounds on his left hand, face, and scalp. The wounds on his legs and feet were more severe. Like the rest of your group, sir, we gave him penicillin against infection. Our on-going concern, though, is his heart. We put him on oxygen. While you slept, the COD [Carrier On-board Delivery] plane brought special drugs, which appeared to help. Doctor has him on bed rest until we transfer him to a stateside hospital."

Joel asked, "What about Felix—uh, Mr. Harrison?"

"I can answer that, Colonel." A man walked into the compartment. "I'm Commander Collins, your surgeon and his. The shrapnel that hit you was a 7.62 round. Must have ricocheted, 'cause it spun and cut like a buzz saw. We repaired muscle and tendon damage. Find a good physical therapist stateside to prevent *permanent* restricted movement."

"What about Mr. Harrison?"

"Your friend, Felix, lost a lot of blood and several feet of intestine. He suffered a nick on the liver that'll heal. One kidney received damage, so I removed it. Abdominal wounds heal slowly, especially when there's significant muscle damage, as in his case. Give him ninety days, at most six months, and he'll be back in fine fettle."

"Thanks, doctor."

"Sir," a Navy lieutenant said through the door, "I'll escort you to the radio shack." As they walked down the passageway, the lieutenant said, "The Captain briefed me about the security level of your message to the White House, sir. All of my people are cleared to the appropriate level. General MacArthur has been notified regarding your visit."

CHAPTER 129

CABLE

Monday, 25 September 1950

USS *Valley Forge*, Radio Shack

Joel composed the cable with great care. *It's not every day you personally report directly to the Commander in Chief, and it's even rarer to make the requests I'm about to make.*

JUMPER reports to CACTUS:

1. Mission BASKET concluded with success on 25 September with arrival of ROVER at location PINE TREE. Two ROVER associates accompanied. Also at PINE TREE are JUMPER II, CAT, ALLIGATOR, and MINER.

2. All, repeat, all, members of BASKET wounded. CAT and ROVER associate in serious medical condition; JUMPER II also wounded, secondary condition unaffected. All others walking wounded.

3. ROVER materials intact and being forwarded soonest. Written reports on observations to follow.

4. JUMPER requests following:

I. Advise CAESAR of urgent purpose of JUMPER briefing. JUMPER to be given authority to cause evacuation.

II. Request brevet promotion of JUMPER to O-7 to facilitate discussions in 4. I.

JUMPER ends.

As Joel handed the handwritten cable to the waiting radio man, sweat rolled down his back.

I'm really pushing things. Even if Mr. Truman gives me what I want, I don't know if MacArthur will evacuate. What a crazy way to make general. How do I get myself into these things?

CHAPTER 130

CLASSIFIED

Tuesday, 26 September 1950
The White House, the Oval Office

"**M**r. President, please excuse me. You have an urgent cable from the *Valley Forge*."

Harry Truman looked up from the legislation on which he and a Democrat Congressman were finessing the language.

"Please excuse me, Mr. Congressman," Truman said. "This is important and secret, I have to ask you to step outside for a moment."

The politician closed the door to the Oval Office, and Truman asked his military aide. "Is this a battle report, George?"

"No, sir, it's something I never thought we'd see—a final mission report from the last of the Project Jubilee team."

"Really? I feared we'd lost them all after that Mongolian plane crash. I never trusted the radio reports after that. Always appeared too much like Russian tricks."

Truman folded back the cover concealing the classified contents. His eyebrows curved up and his jaw slacked and his mouth hung open.

"Well now, that Colonel Knight is more stubborn than a Missoura mule. I can't wait to hear how he pulled *this* off. Sounds like his wife's OK, too. That's sure good news. So, we got our man and a couple to spare." He pored over the cable in a slow, precise way, and chuckled when he read Joel's requests. "Well, I'll give him whatever he thinks will help force MacArthur to move out of harm's way. If all it takes is a star, well, he's got it. I doubt it'll help much, though."

CHAPTER 131

CAESAR

Tuesday, 26 September 1950
USS *Valley Forge* Radio Room

Joel returned to the radio room to read the cable from the White House.

CACTUS replies

1. Strong message to CAESAR per request.

2. Permanent promotion to 0-7 granted.

3. Remove CAESAR by force if necessary, repeat, if necessary.

4. Good Luck, God speed.

CACTUS ends

Joel released the breath he didn't realize he was holding. *OK, he gave me the authorization. Let's see if I've got the ability. Nothing quite like sticking your head in the lion's mouth.*

Murph caught Joel leaving the radio shack. "Sir, I need to tell you a couple of urgent things." They stepped back inside the secure compartment. "Radio Moscow reports our buddy Beria met an unfortunate end. Sounds like it was 'natural causes.' But knowing how the Ruskies play propaganda games, who knows? Know what's weird? They're floundering over who's next in line. No such thing as "vice-chairman." We don't know who'll pick up the reins." Murph cleared his throat.

"The execution order for 'October Victory' was sent out over the KGB frequency. The start time and date are in code. The crypto guys on board are working to decipher them. We only have hours, perhaps a day or so at most before they start bombing. It's about to hit the fan."

CHAPTER 132

STANDOFF

"Here's what's happening, Susan." Joel slipped his hand under Susan's soft palm. "Gotta hurry, 'cause I don't have much time. We intercepted a Russian broadcast. They're attacking within the next few hours. I'll brief *Valley Forge* pilots who'll probably see flying wing attacks from R-117 and other bases. Then I'll catch a plane to Kimpo Air Field, near Inchon. I have to convince General MacArthur to evacuate and brief the fighter jocks there. MacArthur will send evac notices to Ascon City, Yongdong, and Seoul as well, 'cause the Russians may try to hit them."

He held her hand as he caught his breath. "From Kimpo, I'll fly to the carrier USS *Philippine Sea* in the Yellow Sea to brief her pilots. Those Chinese-marked TU-270s will probably come out of air fields on the Chinese coast."

Susan appeared pale even against the white sheets, her blond hair splayed over the pillow. Her vulnerability tugged at his heart. "How're you feeling, hon? How's our boy doing?"

Drowsy from medications, her weak smile affirmed her resilience. "I'm awful sore. Those shotgun pellets really sting, like squeezing searing metal balls from an infected blister, especially on my feet." She cradled her belly with both hands. "The doctor said our baby's just fine and he sounds healthy."

She stopped. Her eyes closed for a moment. "What are they going to do with us? We can't stay on this ship during fighting, can we?"

"They're gonna transfer you to a cruiser and transport you to Japan. In a day or so, you'll be on your way home. Ana and Felix need to stay onboard until they're stabilized."

Susan's right eye twitched. Her eyelids flickered closed, then open. She squeezed his hand. "Be careful, flyboy."

"See you soon, sweetheart." He kissed her lips, headed to the door, then paused to glance back at Susan sleeping.

CHAPTER 133

GENERAL

Tuesday, 26 September 1950
Kimpo Air Field, Seoul, South Korea

Joel braced for takeoff, worrying about his injured shoulder, then remembered. *The Douglas A-1 Skyraider doesn't need a catapult.* The small compartment below the pilot felt claustrophobic, as he sat in a radar operator's chair. The small, round window in the single, side door comprised his only view out as the huge piston engine aircraft pounded toward Inchon.

Well, no need to sight-see. I need to consider what to say to the highest ranking military man in the Far East. God, I need your wisdom. This'll be a real test of whatever diplomatic skills I possess.

XOXOX

At Kimpo Field, Korea, an Army lieutenant handed Joel an Air Force officer's dress blue uniform blouse with the correct sleeve markings. "We didn't know the appropriate decorations, sir." Displayed on the uniform's left breast was a pair of Command pilot's wings, under his name tag. Never before had Joel seen a uniform with his name on it and a star on each shoulder.

With Joel's shoulder tight binding, the lieutenant helped him change from the borrowed tan *Valley Forge* uniform into the blue one. His arm in a sling, the left arm of Joel's uniform hung limp, empty. His forehead sported bandages.

Like a mechanical dragonfly, a Sikorsky H-5 helicopter waited to transport him to MacArthur's headquarters. Other helicopters would meet him there to evacuate the headquarters staff. Joel had also requested a squad of uniformed Military Police to wait for him outside General MacArthur's headquarters. *I pray I don't have to use the MP's to force MacArthur to leave.*

The noisy, vibrating machine landed with a soft bump next to a brick building with a sign that read: Headquarters, Supreme Allied Command, United Nations and U.S. Forces.

An Army Captain wearing the rope of a general's aide waited to escort him to the big man's offices. "Good morning, General Knight. I hope your flight was pleasant. If you would follow me, sir?"

The man's squinty eyes and wide swarmy smile turned Joel's stomach. Joel followed the Captain through the busy office. *They know.* Joel noticed more than a few hostile glares. *Obviously, the Army grapevine still operates.* Outsiders were unwelcome in MacArthur's inner sanctum.

The Captain opened the outer office door. Inside, uniformed people worked industriously. A steely-eyed, unsmiling Major presided at a desk, guarding the door into MacArthur's private office. He ignored Joel and motioned to the Captain. "He's waiting."

General Douglas MacArthur leaned on his elbows behind an impossibly huge, antique oak desk dominating the room.

The thing looks like a throne. The size and position of the furniture's clearly designed to intimidate the 'supplicant' coming before the court, just like Susan said. Bet he shortened the legs on the chairs so I look up at him.

"Brigadier General Joel Knight, reporting at the direction of the President, sir." His salute mirrored a West Point how-to illustration.

MacArthur wore his gaudy, crushed officer's cap with its gold "scrambled eggs" and the tan summer uniform known round the world. Five gold stars gleamed on each shoulder epaulet. Taking his famous corn-cob pipe from his mouth, he said with a blank face, "So you're here to throw me out of Korea, are you, 'General'?"

The emphasis on his new rank galled Joel. Joel maintained eye contact. *He didn't deign to return my salute, another insult.*

"General MacArthur, sir, before I left *Valley Forge*, I was informed we intercepted radio signals ordering the Russian bombers to launch atomic attacks on this headquarters and the Korean capital. If they've already launched, no more than three hours remain to evacuate this headquarters and the surrounding towns. I am here to facilitate the transfer of your command to your choice of the carrier USS *Philippine Sea* or the battleship USS *Iowa*, sir."

"Oh, I really don't t'ink the situation is all that serious, General Knight," interjected Colonel Charles Willoughby, MacArthur's sycophantic, intelligence officer, in his German accent. "Ve haf heard of no such information."

"Is it your habit, *Colonel* Willoughby, to interrupt general officers when they speak?" Joel retorted. The man's mouth snapped closed.

"Sir," Joel faced MacArthur, "less than two days ago, I was in Russia." He lifted the elbow of his bandaged arm. "I was wounded bringing you this information. I saw the aircraft they'll use. I observed them practice-load atomic weapons. I personally read orders in Russian directing the bombers at Magdagachi Air Field to China to prepare to attack this headquarters. I also observed at least sixty heavy bombers flying toward China. There's absolutely no question in my mind that Russia presents a clear and present danger to you, your staff and the surrounding cities. You need to depart immediately, sir."

MacArthur puffed away on his corncob pipe as he listened to Joel. Then with a sudden jerk, he set his steel jaw and upped his famous chin in defiance. "I am disinclined to uproot my headquarters and disrupt my war planning on the basis of uncorroborated, fantastic reports, even if they are made by a shiny new general." MacArthur stared down Joel as if only playing chess and it was Joel's move.

He's calling me a liar. "Fantastic or not, General MacArthur, my report is corroborated by radio intercepts, as well as statements from a high-ranking member of the Soviet atomic weapons bureau who defected with me. Your life, sir, and the lives of every person here hang in the balance. I urge you, sir, to leave *immediately.* Helicopters await to transport you and your staff to whichever ship you designate." Joel paused and stared in MacArthur's eyes. "You must act now or die."

"I remain unconvinced. Masters of intrigue, the Soviets play us for amusement. Why would they launch their bombers from China?"

"General, the CIA holds intelligence indicating Soviet Chairman Beria intends to blame China for atomic attacks on Korea with the hope that China and the U.S. will go to war, and Russia will wait to pick up the pieces. Sir, we *must leave now.*"

General MacArthur sniffed in disapproval. "China? The 'CIA has intelligence'? I don't trust the CIA, never have. I know the Chinese. The Chinese are far too busy consolidating their revolution to involve themselves in Korea. They have no atomic weapons and this makes no sense. I will not leave. You are dismissed."

He wants to play chess? Here's checkmate. "General MacArthur, sir, the President has stated that your death would be a serious blow to the Allied cause and must be prevented at all costs. Sir, this is very difficult, both because of my respect for you and for your rank. Sir, by order of the Commander in Chief, President Harry S. Truman, I am ordered to remove you from this facility, by force, if necessary. Sir, I know you're in receipt of similar orders from the President. If you refuse to leave on your own, a squad of Military Police stands by to 'escort' you. Please don't make me do that, sir. I assure you, General MacArthur, I *will* obey the President's orders."

Willoughby gasped. MacArthur digested Joel's remarkable statement. "I am not accustomed to taking orders from a Brigadier General."

Joel said with all the firmness he could muster, "With respect, General MacArthur, my orders—your orders—are from President Truman, our Commander in Chief. I believe to the core of my being what I've told you is fact, sir." He eyeballed the aging general, believing to do otherwise was cowardice . . . and foolishness. "With the deepest respect, sir, I must ask: Will you comply, sir? Or must I subject us all to the humiliation of placing you under the 'protective custody' of the Military Police?"

A flare of rebellion flashed in MacArthur's eyes. "You dare to take that action?"

"Absolutely, sir, to save your life."

MacArthur's eyes narrowed as his head jerked back and his chin tucked into his neck.

He's weakening. "Sir, I personally counted no less than two dozen atomic bombs at Magdagachi Air Field, Russia. Each Soviet bomber can carry at least two of the Hiroshima/Nagasaki-class weapons. I respectfully remind you, sir: Soviet Air Force protocol is to bomb each target at least twice to assure destruction. Inchon and your headquarters are primary targets."

MacArthur's jaw ground his teeth behind a bitter expression. He slumped in the chair, his eyes those of an old man, beaten, at least for the moment. He removed his cap, his thin hair emphasized his age.

Check mate.

MacArthur tipped his chin up. "For the sake of the morale of the troops, I cannot allow you to place me in custody. We must execute a planned tactical maneuver, a deliberate repositioning of my command headquarters. We'll do so as quickly and efficiently as possible."

MacArthur appraised his office, with its sumptuous decorations, many from Japan. "To leave all this—" His face once more became resolute. "General Knight, I shall be at your disposal in ten minutes.

Willoughby, prepare the senior staff to leave with me. How many can you take by helicopter, General?"

"No more than six, General," Joel replied.

"Very well. Willoughby, limit the senior staff to me, yourself, and four others. Order the Public Affairs officer to send an urgent, emergency announcement to all the local governments to evacuate immediately. Send the evacuation orders to everyone in this headquarters and the rest of the base, as well as Kimpo Field and the Navy docks. All classified documents are to be destroyed per Standard Procedures. Go. Make it happen. *Now.*"

CHAPTER 134

GODSPEED

Tuesday, 26 September 1950
Tarmac at Kimpo Air Field, Seoul, South Korea

With an air of hubris, General Douglas MacArthur strode toward the waiting helicopter. Joel overheard him direct a scrambling captain. "Contact the Public Affairs office. Release a press statement. This headquarters is repositioning for tactical reasons. Give no details. We will issue a statement later."

Joel stood to the side as an Air Force war photographer's 4×5 Speed Graphic camera captured a photo of MacArthur. *Someone's always taking his picture. He's always posing. That's part of his problem.* MacArthur halted and pivoted toward Joel interrupting his thoughts.

"Well done, General Knight. Godspeed on your mission."

All the emotions Joel stifled drained away as the helicopter carrying Douglas MacArthur lifted off on its way to the battleship USS *Iowa*. Two other H-5s lifted off, clattering after MacArthur's helicopter and blowing gritty dust everywhere.

Joel turned to the pilot of the remaining helicopter. "OK, Captain, fly me to Kimpo Field as fast as possible to brief their fighter pilots. Radio ahead. Make sure a plane's waiting to fly me to the *Philippine Sea* to brief them."

Twenty minutes later, Joel stood in an auditorium at Kimpo Field. Pilots in flight gear filled the room. Their grim faces reflected what they sensed coming.

Joel said, "Men, in a few hours, you will be thrown into a desperate battle to defend this base, Inchon, Seoul, and Korea itself from Chinese-marked, Russian bombers carrying atomic weapons. They're not reverse-engineered B-29s. They're updated WWII vintage German-style, flying wings."

Murmurs of disbelief rippled through the crowd.

"The aircraft carrying atomic weapons will be mixed with flying wings carrying conventional bombs. The atomic bombers are equipped with podded jet engines under their outboard wing sections, and a pair of vertical stabilizers on the trailing edge. Attack them first."

Joel looked at the base commander. "I understand that none of your F-84s have rocket guns, is that correct?"

"Yes, sir, that is correct," the colonel answered.

"Well, the Russian atomic bombers carry rocket guns and so do a fair percentage of their conventional bombers. I doubt they'll commit jet fighters to protect the bombers due to the range involved. The Russians still have lots of Yak-9s, which have the range to escort the bombers. Don't be surprised if they have some tricks up their sleeves.

"I know you're all well-trained, but this is different than anything you've faced before. You've heard how the WWII German versions of these planes folded like a butterfly if you hit them in the center section. I can testify that while the German ships had that problem, the Russians engineered that weakness out. To attack *these* flying wings, shoot at the embedded recip engines and set 'em on fire. Aim fifteen or twenty feet ahead of the props. Their cockpits aren't armored, so they're vulnerable, too.

"I know you know the rocket guns can reach you before you're in range for your own cannons or machineguns. But their rocket guns are manually aimed and traversed, so high-speed runs help. Approach in pairs, but maneuver separately. The gunner can aim at only one of you at a time. I don't know how well-trained the gunners are at protecting each other's planes, but probably not well. Hit 'em hard, wound them, leave them for the prop fighters to finish off."

He stopped and scanned the faces in the somber crowd. "Look, I don't want any heroes. Don't make more than one pass on the same plane. Look for vulnerabilities, but don't sacrifice yourselves or your planes. The Ruskies built a *lot* of these flying wings. We may be in for repeated attacks. The Air Force is keeping the few F-80s in Korea at Pusan, so your F-84s are the only jets here, beside the handful of Navy F9Fs. Reinforcement fighters are coming from the States, but won't be here for several days. You guys and the Navy are our first line of defense. You can do this, men. You must. We're all depending on you."

Joel answered a few questions then raced for the flight line. An aging Grumman TBM waited to fly him to the USS *Philippine Sea*. As the old torpedo bomber thundered along, Joel checked his watch. *At best, there's only another hour and a half before the Russians are overhead. He breathed deep and expelled a heavy sigh. This'll be close. I don't know if we have enough fighters between the Navy and the Air Force to hold them off. Oh, Lord, be merciful to all those evacuating civilians. They've suffered so much already. Give us the victory, Lord. Please.*

)(O)(O)(

After Joel finished briefing the Naval aviators aboard the USS *Philippine Sea* a sailor handed him a radiogram. "Sir, you are ordered to fly to Pusan immediately." An idling TBM waited as Joel sprinted across the deck.

A speaker blared, "Battle Stations. Battle stations. All hands, man your battle stations."

CHAPTER 135

EVACUATE

Tuesday, 26 September 1950

Inchon, Korea

Every day, Jung Kim listened to his radio at work, attentive for bad news. *Dear God, MacArthur's announcement said "nuclear bombs."*

The evacuation announcement from MacArthur's headquarters launched him out the door like a cannon ball. For weeks, Kim and his wife worried, jittery about another invasion from the North.

His family's pride, Jung Kim was too young to serve during WWII. He distinguished himself with a post-war degree in finance from UCLA. The resurgent South Korean economy needed capable men in her recovering banking industry.

With the current fighting, somehow, their home avoided destruction by the marauding North and the invading Americans. Kim's rapid advance at Inchon's largest bank left Kim in a high-tension tug of war between his prestigious job and his family.

For the past month, Kim and his wife had taken 'pleasure drives' to scout escape routes—just in case. At a moment's notice, his wife, Cho, remained prepared to evacuate. Now, their planning paid off.

After Jung's quick call from work to his wife, he raced toward his family in his cherished, if battered, pre-war Ford. Cho Kim gathered her four-year-old daughter Sun, and two-year-old son Gi, and waited. When her husband arrived, Cho bundled their children into the back seat. Jung loaded packed boxes containing food, clothing, a few toys, and a small ex-Army tent.

As Jung drove south to escape from Inchon, he inched through irrational crowds of civilians retreating in full flight nearly 17 miles northeast to Seoul, the nation's capital. Jung honked for people to clear a path.

At last he broke past the panicked throng and onto the uncertainties of the day. Kim continued his tortured drive south and west toward the coastline overlooking the Yellow Sea lying between mainland China and the Korean peninsula.

Kim's original plan involved driving 103 miles south to the tiny fishing village of Kunsan where an old cabin powerboat waited to take them to Japan. *Japanese may hate us Koreans, but hatred is better than murder by Kim Il-Sung's merciless soldiers. I've got to find a sturdy rock between my family and the bomb that will surely drop on Inchon.* As he followed the route down the coast, he searched for a granite ridge to protect them.

From the corner of Jung's eye, he saw Cho's head bowed, her beautiful, delicate hands clasped in prayer. As he steered his Ford on a winding, dirt track that meandered down the bumpy slope to the shore, he prayed. *Oh, God in Heaven, please show your mercy and grace to my wife, my children and me. Let us find cover before . . . before . . . please show your mercy to those still in the city.*

As the second hand of destiny ticked down, Jung Kim snuggled the old Ford within a foot of the wall of granite by the sea and left the car's radio on. He recalled the stories of a single bomb destroying Hiroshima and Nagasaki. Madness, how was that possible?

As his family huddled beside him, he covered his family with a blanket. The radio repeated the evacuation warning, then stopped mid-word.

CHAPTER 136

RUINED

Tuesday, 26 September 1950
Inchon, Korea

A ir raid sirens wailed and an eerie, barren gloom settled over the city of Inchon. Dry, gusty winds scattered dust through the near-abandoned streets. After the warnings from McArthur's headquarters three hours before, the disciplined Korean population quickly obeyed.

All through Inchon, huge crowds of people escaped by walking, running, or driving every sort of conveyance from automobiles to scooters to ox carts. Only the unbelieving, the aged, the infirm, and the opportunists lagged behind.

High above Inchon, three jet-propelled TU-270j's with Chinese markings soared in the clear blue sky toward the emptying city. One at a time, each dropped a huge, grey mass, and banked away.

The first A-bomb exploded at 1,500 feet with a super-brilliant, blinding light above the Navy quay. Seconds later, the other two bombs erupted like a demented Fourth of July display, fulfilling the Soviet doctrine that demanded multiple bomb strikes on each target. The phenomenon of atomic fratricide—bombs exploding in close proximity and time cancelled a portion of each bomb's destructive power—lessening slightly the horrific blasts.

Fireballs, as hot as the sun, and massive dome-shaped shock waves bursting from each bomb, raced without mercy across the city, vaporizing everything in their paths. The shock waves collided and whirled into horizontal tornadoes of destruction.

Hellish lightening flashed in the clouds of debris and smoke over the wasteland. Three tormented mushroom clouds roiled upward and collided. Twisting into a writhing, incandescent nightmare of shapes, they climbed skyward toward eternity.

The monster mushroom cloud paused at 51,000 feet, then swept seaward. The dust of irradiated flesh pursued by pulverized, radioactive debris—rocks, buildings, automobiles, ships—nearly obliterated the light of the morning sun. Torrents of falling ash rained still as death in a dismal cascade over a nightmarish, burnt-over plain.

Seventeen miles to the north-west, terrified residents of Seoul heard the triple-tympani thunder of Inchon's agony and felt the earth shake by the force of the blasts. The previous orders of evacuation to their designated 'safe areas' propelled Seoul's population into panic.

Like the wrath of an ancient god, the visible mushroom cloud towered over their luckless neighbor city—now invisible—burned alive and blown away to nothing but residue.

CHAPTER 137

A-BOMB

Tuesday, 26 September 1950
The wall of granite by the sea, Korea

"**C**lose your eyes, tight!" Kim shouted and wrapped protective arms around his family to hold them close to him.

A silent iridescent white flash penetrated the blanket with otherworldly light. Jung peeked out the car window just as the second and third weapons detonated. A brilliant, yellow light dazzled his eyes as he threw the blanket back over his head.

His restless young children attempted to wrestle out from under the blanket. The thunderclap from the first bomb drowned out Kim's shouted—"No, stay."

The shock wave roared over the top of the rocky wall, showering the car with gravel and sand. Seconds later, the combined shock waves from the second and third bombs rattled the car with a sound like the torments of Hell. The children screamed in terror.

Kim's momentary gratitude of surviving the flash, the boom, and then the roar was washed away by an icy thought: *fallout.*

"We must go to the boat. Fallout is coming. Hold on."

The engine roared as he drove his old Ford up the embankment and swung southward on to road toward Kunsan. His heart raced as fast as he drove to escape the fallout hurtling their direction.

CHAPTER 138

BRIEFING

Thursday, 28 September 1950
Pusan, Korea

"**G**entlemen, the latest information from Navy and Washington reports that Inchon City essentially no longer exists, as of 1830 hours local on Tuesday." A bespectacled Army Lieutenant Colonel stood in front of a microphone shuffling a thick sheaf of papers. He, like everyone, wore the same bedraggled expression as Joel: Too much tension for too long coupled with too little sleep.

Joel slouched in an old chair in the battered Army Intelligence Headquarters building in Pusan. His eyes burned from lack of sleep. His wounded shoulder pulsed. Aspirin hadn't helped. Cigarette, cigar, and pipe smoke hung in a dank cloud in the crowded room. One wit tagged it *stratus tobaccus*. Joel stifled a yawn as he stared at the projected photos of smoking ruins with no standing buildings visible.

The Lieutenant Colonel continued the briefing. "The radiation cloud headed out to sea, toward Shanghai, which the British are evacuating. Preliminarily, we estimate at least ninety-five percent of all buildings in Inchon were destroyed, and the remainder rendered uninhabitable. At this point, we know of no military causalities. Our timely and effective evacuation kept civilian causalities low, despite three nuclear bombs exploding over the city and environs. The majority of citizens evacuated into the countryside. No bombs detonated over Seoul. Our fighters held the Russians back, but it was a near thing."

The Colonel adjusted his gold-rim glasses. "Korean officials will keep citizens out of Inchon until its safe. President Syngman Rhee is sending several military police companies to help and has promised more if needed. Inchon's port facilities, including the stone piers, were functionally destroyed. Navy Seabees are checking radioactivity levels. They'll start rebuilding as soon as possible.

"Our losses are skyrocketing, I'm afraid. Navy reports they lost eleven F9Fs based on the USS *Philippine Sea* and thirteen F4U Corsairs. Sixty-plus Russian bombers attacked Inchon and Seoul. We dropped or damaged at least forty, probably more, between Air Force and Navy fighters. Air Force F-51 units provided yeoman service, with large losses as they performed the coup de grace on damaged bombers. Amazing bravery on their parts. Incomplete loss reports from Air Force F-84 units aren't quite as bad. They may have suffered twenty percent losses. With Kimpo Field destroyed, surviving F-84s are scattered all over the country, so it's possible losses are a little less. Navy is patrolling the Yellow Sea and the Sea of Japan. They've rescued many flyers in rafts, so the final story hasn't been written. We also captured about a dozen Russian crew members."

The anger welling up in Joel's chest gripped his throat. *I tried so hard to warn everyone. I was naive to think we could turn them all back. Those American pilots did so well, but what a cost.*

The colonel's grim face scanned his audience. "It would seem, sirs, we're relearning the hard lessons of WWII about rocket guns. Our machineguns and cannons still can't match their range. The Russians improved the German designs, while our rocket guns, I am sad to report, sit in storage. Editorial ends."

Every airman knew the colonel was right.

Joel's teeth involuntarily ground together. *I tried to convince the Air Force and Navy to adopt those rocket guns we used with success during the final days of the war, but no. The decision makers stayed with the safe and the cheap. Now our guys are dying to show them how wrong they are. Will the bureaucrats ever learn?*

The lieutenant colonel continued, "Fighters from USS *Valley Forge* countered Russian attacks from Vladivostok and the northern bases. *Valley Forge* lost the equivalent of an entire squadron, thirty planes. Despite escorting MiG-15s, they held back the attack. Not a single atomic bomber got through to their target, the Marines at Chosin Reservoir. Thank God for that. Their conventional bombers accounted for little substantial damage. There's even a report that a very determined Navy AD-1 attack plane took down a TU-270.

"Reports from Washington about Moscow reflect the chaos. With Chairman Beria confirmed dead, and no known succession plan, the Soviets are scrambling to decide who's in charge. At the moment, a guy named Nicolai—check that, *Nikita* Khrushchev—appears on top. With at least half-dozen candidates, no one knows who will end up actually wielding power. Our difficulty, of course, is who do we listen to? This Khrushchev character released and then withdrew a statement apologizing for the attacks. CIA says the Soviet politburo is meeting in emergency session. Remains to be seen what will comes of that."

He shuffled more papers, then looked out at the assembled colonels and generals, including British officers as well as Turks. "The civilian population of D.C., and much of the country is in a panic. Afraid the Russians will attack, roads everywhere are clogged with people fleeing the cities. The American press and public are howling for a declaration of war against Russia. For a change, Congress is showing restraint, and President Truman is doing all he can to slow our reaction. The last thing he wants is a full-on nuclear war. Since we don't know the total Soviet inventory of A-bombs, an attack on the Russian capitol could bring atomic fire on our unprotected troops here, to say nothing of those panicky civilians at home." A murmur of concern swept across the room.

"Air Force sent RB-45 jet photo ships to photograph known Red Air Force air fields here in the Far East. Two new RB-47 jets are being readied, since they can penetrate a lot deeper than the RB-45s. Our planes have been unopposed. So far, recon shows Soviet air fields standing down. We can only hope and pray they stay that way.

"Allied–British air forces continue to patrol the borders and sea corridors. They're under UN orders to defend themselves, but not attack. Some in the Pentagon are pushing hard for strikes deep in Soviet territory. So far General Lemay's being held back. He wants to hit 'em with every B-36 and B-50 in the inventory.

"General MacArthur continues his push north, with mixed success and heavy fighting. Initially, the Chinese fell back, but resistance has stiffened considerably. They continue to deny any complicity in the atomic attacks." He raised a skeptical eyebrow. "The Joint Chiefs seem to believe them. General MacArthur's strategy is to push to the Chinese-North Korean border and hold there. He says it will be a matter of days. That remains to be seen. Whether we advance into China when they get there depends pretty much on the Chinese. If they don't attack, we probably won't go in after them. President Truman has ordered General MacArthur not to cross the border. However, he can respond to cross-border shelling.

"Our Marines pushed out of the Chosin Reservoir area with great heroism, and heavy losses, led by General Chesty Puller. Chinese forces are falling back in confusion. They don't understand how to retreat. Marine Major General O. P. Smith is concerned they'll consolidate on high ground and stop our advance.

"Our recon flights show thousands of Chinese troops and a lot of materiel at holding bases several miles behind the border. So far, they're not being moved up. If the Russians don't attack, we may head toward a stalemate at the border. That's all I have, sirs. Any questions?"

A burly Marine general asked in a deep Texas accent, "What's that Chairman May–O sayin' about the Chi–nese markin's on Ruskie bombers and the fact they launched from Chi-nese territory?"

"Sir, it's Mao, spelled M-A-O. They deny they knew the Soviets planned to launch *atomic* attacks from their territory. Seems pretty clear they expected them to launch conventional attacks. Sounds like a difference without a distinction, to me. They claim the Soviets used Chinese markings without permission. The Soviets also claim they wouldn't have given it had they asked. The so-called China experts at State Department believe Mao is telling the truth. They point to the fallback of Chinese troops as evidence. A more cynical view has it that the Chinese don't want us to have any excuse to bomb what little industrial infrastructure they own. I'm inclined to agree with that view."

An Army general asked, "Colonel, what's the status of reinforcements and replacement equipment? My boys are using up tanks and artillery tubes like mad."

"General, I'm pleased to tell you that two full divisions of regular Army are coming, a Marine division as well. Close to a thousand tanks and two thousand artillery tubes are either on their way or will sail shortly. Replacement aircraft for Navy, Marines, and Air Force are pouring into Hawaii and Japan. The Royal Australian Air Force is sending two squadrons of Venom jet fighters. Two more *Essex* class carriers and four *Independence* class carriers are on the way. The first arrive in about two weeks.

"Ammo for everything from handguns to 155mm howitzers is on hand. Limited port facilities are slowing things. Air Force C-46, C-47, C-119, and C-123 aircraft are flying ammo to MacArthur's troops and the First Marines. In critical cases, helicopters ferried in supplies and ammo. We continue to evacuate wounded by the same helicopters. As soon as we secure enough roads, we'll convoy by truck. Our Australian allies sent the hospital ship AHS *Manunda* to complement USS *Haven*—soon to arrive off of Inchon."

Joel sensed the grim determination in the room. *The last chapter on this war remains to be written.*

CHAPTER 139

NEGOTIATION

Tuesday, 3 October 1950
East-bound from Clark AB, Philippines

The MATS C-54 military transport carrying the Soviet scientists reached cruise altitude and the engine noise lessened. Joel, Susan, Felix, Murph, and Dubov followed on a second plane.

The seat belt sign went off. A sandy-haired man moved to sit beside the solitary Dr. Kalugin. "Sir, my name is Henry Aldrich, with the CIA. I'll escort you to California by way of Hawaii." His Russian was flawless. That he used the name of an imaginary teenaged radio comedy character was a cultural subtlety lost on the Russian physicist.

"When will I see my wife and son?" Kalugin's drawn countenance expressed his anxiety behind his oxygen mask.

The man placed his hand on Dr. Kalugin's shoulder. "Your wife and son are waiting for you in California. They escaped through Finland without incident. They are safe, well, and anxious to see you again. You'll spend a day with them, then we'll begin debriefing you."

"What is this 'debriefing'?" Deep fears racked Kalugin. *Will they use KGB techniques, or threaten to torture my family to force me to talk? What if I can't tell them all they want to hear? Have I exchanged one death sentence for another?*

"We want to learn all you can teach us, Dr. Kalugin. Some nuclear physicists want to ask you questions and review your documents. This process may take several weeks. We want to be sure we understand the nuances and subtleties."

Aldrich failed to reveal to Dr. Kalugin that his every word would be recorded, his every gesture photographed and analyzed. Dr. Kalugin remained guilty until proven innocent. The great, unspoken fear of American intelligence was an unwitting mistake—bringing a double agent, a mole, into their confidence.

"What will become of my team?" Deep lines furrowed in the Russian's forehead.

"Each person will be questioned like you, Dr. Kalugin. Then, we'll bring all of you together for some joint sessions as well. We want to understand things in a broad picture sense."

"They promised American doctors, for my heart condition. When will this happen?" *Did they promise me this just so I would seek asylum? Am I a fool to trust them? Will I die as I might have at home?*

"Ah, yes. Military doctors will meet us at Hickam Field in Hawaii, our next stop. They'll fly with us to California and examine you along the way. All of your team's wounds will be reexamined and treated, as well. Once the doctors decide on a course of treatment for you, we'll make allowances for hospital visits during your interrogation. *We* want you to be healthy for a long time, sir.

In a tight, brittle voice, Kalugin said, "When you have satisfied yourselves that I have told you all I know, what then will become of my family and myself?"

The CIA agent leaned back in the upholstered airline-style seat and spread his hands in a welcoming gesture. "If all goes well, and you and your wife agree, we'll help you settle into productive work again. This will entail changing your names for your protection. Several advanced physics facilities are already bidding for your services. The same goes for your colleagues."

In another portion of the cabin, a second CIA interrogator spoke with a terrified, weeping Ana Ksana Bakhtina. Throwing up her shaking hands, she squirmed away from him. "I–I know wh–what you will do to me." She stopped to catch her breath between sobs. "I–I will tell you everything. Do not hurt me."

Dr. Berthold glared at the CIA man. Dr. Berthold patted her hand. "These are not KGB." Ana clung to his hand as a drowning woman clings to a life preserver. "Ana, listen, please. They will not torture you or kill you. They need to understand why you escaped with Dr. Kalugin and learn what you know about the bombs. I will do all I can to protect you. Please, don't cry."

"Please, Dr. Bakhtina, listen to Dr. Berthold. We have no reason to hurt you. We don't work that way. We just want you to answer a few questions. That's all. You will surely be granted asylum when we finish. Your future is bright in America." His smooth words gently spoken calmed her. He motioned to a Navy medic who administered a mild sedative.

Another CIA man touched Dr. Berthold's shoulder. "We need to talk, sir." They moved a few seats away from Ana, who fell asleep.

The CIA man eyed the diminutive man. *He seems an unlikely spy.*

"I'm Joe Smith, Dr. Berthold. You're in a little different category than the others. How did you come to work with the Russians."

"I was taken against my will, yes? Kidnapped, to be precise. The Russians told me: Work with them or be shot. The choice, then as now, was obvious. In view of my physical condition, you will agree I had no expectation of escape, is this not true? In fact, I have done little directly on the atomic bomb project beyond designing adaptations for aircraft to accommodate them."

His intelligent eyes bored into Joe Smith. "I claim asylum in the United States on the basis of being a POW, yes? Despite my Russian captivity, I point out my citizenship remains German. I demand to see German embassy officials as soon as we arrive in the U.S., yes? I believe you will discover no legal grounds to detain me. Or, we could avoid such uncomfortable questions the German embassy might ask if I should be allowed to remain in the U.S., yes? We will agree not to discuss my—adventures, shall we call them—before I arrived?"

Joe Smith swallowed and swore to himself. *The smart ones are always the most difficult. He's right. The State Department will never let us keep him. At worst, he's a DP [displaced person], a victim of Russian terror squads. If he asks for asylum, he'll get it, sure as rain.*

"I reckon what you're saying is right, sir. People from the State Department will be waiting for us when we arrive at Hickam. I'll check for you then."

CHAPTER 140

OPERATIONAL DEBRIEF

Tuesday, 3 October 1950
Aboard USAF C-121 49-0881

The agents worked on writing first their drafts of what would become their official statements about the mission and its events. When completed, joint sessions would be conducted to take advantage of what Langley called "corporate knowledge."

Joel's engineering background revealed itself in his report organization. After listing the major events in outline format, he filled in details under each heading, making frequent references to his notes. *I was so busy during some of the more exciting episodes, I couldn't make notes. I hope memory serves.*

Joel spent extra time on details of Soviet aircraft, including individual tail numbers. *The guys in FTD will have a ball with the half-dozen operational aircraft we didn't know existed. Except for maybe the MiG-15, none seem especially advanced, though. From what I saw, their training is old fashioned. I guess the USAF isn't the only military organization that's slow to develop new strategies for new technologies.*

Susan approached the report-writing task polar opposite to her husband. Arranging her report by individual names, including those lost in the crash, her colleagues would be most interested in why each Russian scientist decided to defect.

They'll want to know their backgrounds and how each person coped with the stresses of being pursued. Hmm . . . there will be a nice book from all of this, even if it remains classified. Maybe the old fossils at CIA will give us psychologists a little credit.

She tapped her pencil on the tablet, then began writing her thoughts. *Ana avoided recognizing how dangerous our situation was. "Denial." She tried to cope with each day's problems and didn't worry about the outcome. That's an interesting defense mechanism. I don't think it worked out too well for her. As time passed, she relied more and more on emotional support from Dr. Berthold. Did he become a father figure for her? Or more of a "Prince Charming?"* She chuckled at the mental image of Dr. Berthold in costume as the fairy tale hero.

The collective farm. What an eye-opener. What we found at the collective farm will intrigue my CIA colleagues. She added notes to the side.

Roger Dubov. His story is a book by itself. How did he compartmentalize his American experiences so well while undercover that his Russian bonafides were never questioned? How did Dubov then leave his Russian self behind and switch back into his American persona when he met Felix and his team? What story will we give him to explain where he's been all these years? That's another whole layer of deception.

Susan delayed until last her description of Joel's role in the mission. *I must exercise my best professional detachment. This will be my biggest challenge of all.*

Writing about Joel's wounds and his mistakes emotionally jarred Susan. *Keep everything clinical, Susan. Somebody else will make the critical determinations about Joel's performance. Against incredible odds, he got us home safe and mostly sound. That's big for me and the rest of the team, I suspect. He overcame his fear of leading men. That boogie man is buried.*

Alexander Daniels, CIA Senior Deputy Director for Far Eastern Affairs, stood with arms crossed against his chest. Daniels scrutinized each agent writing their mission report.

Dr. Knight isn't an agent. She's a senior analyst, as if that made any difference on this mission. I can't believe any of them survived, let alone managed to bring the Soviet scientists back with them. This one will go down in the history of the Agency, that's for sure.

The Senior Deputy Director's gaze moved to Roger Dubov. *How did he maintain his cover so long? He's amazing. Dubov's knowledge of the Soviet army will be almost as valuable as what the scientists tell us. Is the Red Army still the formidable force we saw during the war, or has it decayed like our own? What about unit cohesiveness? Oh, I would love to sit in on his debrief. Dubov went undercover in '43. He's got seven years back pay coming. Wonder if they'll pay him as an NCO or as a field agent? I'll push for field agent. God knows, we can never pay him enough.*

CHAPTER 141

TV ADDRESS

Friday, 13 October 1950
The Oval Office

The makeup artist patted the TV-7N Pan-stic makeup with the palm of his hand against Truman's close-shaved beard to give the President that fresh-from-the-barber look.

Harry Truman scoffed to Monte, the man with the brushes, pancake powder, dry rouge, eye shadow, and moist lip rouge. "No self-respecting *man* wears makeup," Truman squirmed in the portable make-up chair.

"For television you must, Mr. President. We don't want your beard to appear dirty or for your skin to look spotty or ghostly white. You must look your best, sir."

"Damn foolishness," Truman groused not quite under his breath. He waved the man away and read through his notes again. Not his first time in front of the TV camera, Truman was proud to be the first president to appear on TV on October 5, 1947—the dawn of a new age.

"Standby Mr. President, ten seconds," somebody called, "and live."

Off-camera a deep male voice announced, "Ladies and gentlemen, the President of the United States."

Truman stared into the RCA TK10 television camera. "Good evening, my fellow citizens. Tonight, I'm addressing you from the Oval Office in the White House. You deserve an unbiased report from your President about the momentous world events of the past ten days.

"As reported by newspapers and radio stations, warplanes of the Union of Soviet Socialist Republics attacked American and United Nations forces at Inchon, Korea, with atomic weapons. This second atomic attack is an awful blot on mankind's history. Our hearts and prayers go out to the families of those injured and killed. At this point, we have not retaliated. Despite the emotions in the newspapers, if I have my way, we will not, for reasons I will explain.

"Russian forces in and around Korea have ceased combat operations. We are allowing Russian units to retreat back across the North Korean border unmolested. I'm sad to say, I cannot say the same for the armed forces of the People's Republic of China, who remain engaged in deadly combat with American and UN forces.

"A great cause of difficulty in dealing with this situation is the chaos in Moscow following the death of Chairman Lavrenti Beria. We've received conflicting messages from the Kremlin, first apologizing for the bombing, then retracting the apology. We are concerned that a successor to the Chairmanship of the Soviet Union still has not been named. Unlike America, they have no constitutional succession plan for senior leadership of their government.

"From the outside, it looks like the dogfights I saw on the streets as a kid back in Independence, Missouri. Occasionally, a head pops out, and is dragged back into the fray. Senior Red Army officers are holding things steady until the politicians iron things out. Red Army generals, who hold the reins of power, understand that further aggression on their part could lead to all-out atomic war, which neither country wants.

"We received timely warnings of the Russian attacks and General MacArthur quickly moved his headquarters and the troops stationed at Inchon, so we suffered few military casualties. We also warned the Korean government of the impending attacks. I deeply regret the several thousand reported casualties among the Korea civilian population. Civilians aren't as organized as the military, and too many, reacted too slowly.

"The Navy, Marine Corps, and Air Force pilots heroically defended against the Soviet atomic bombers, but sadly, at a great loss of fliers. We and the Korean people owe them a great debt of gratitude.

"If the Russian government is confused, so are the Chinese, who claim they weren't party to the atomic attacks. Yet the Chinese allowed Russian bombers to launch against us from Chinese soil. Chinese forces continue to stoutly resist our advances, even though Russia has stopped providing them arms. How long can they keep fighting? I don't have an answer.

"General MacArthur's troops are advancing northward against heavy resistance in the bitter winter weather. I regret the many casualties. Marine Major General O.P. Smith's forces moving northward out of the Chosin Reservoir area continue to demonstrate great heroism and determination. They, too, are suffering casualties.

"Our strategy is to drive northward until our forces reach the China-North Korean border." Truman paused in silence for a moment. "To be clear, it is neither my intent nor my desire to engage U.S. forces in a protracted land war in Asia. We will avoid moving troops onto Chinese soil, but we *will not* tolerate Chinese troops in Korea. I will bring as much pressure as possible, both diplomatically and militarily, against the Chinese government and their armed forces to bring a speedy end to this sad episode.

"General MacArthur says UN and American forces will be at the border by years' end. He cautions that wartime plans often don't work out. World opinion is strongly against the Chinese. Whether that will sway Chairman Mao and his generals, it's too soon to say.

"The Chinese have millions of men under arms, and as our generals will tell you, they are ferocious fighters. Nonetheless, they are in a precarious position, having lost the supply of arms from their former

Russian allies. As I know only too well, warfare uses supplies at a prodigious rate.

"As I stated moments ago, I will not commit troops to a land war in China. I am willing, however, to commit massive numbers of heavy bombers to destroy what remaining supplies the Chinese possess. If that fails to accomplish the job, we have other, more powerful tools to persuade them to stop their aggression." He left the threat unspoken, but knew everyone understood: America had the will to use atomic weapons.

"Our United Nations allies join me in this declaration: China must stop fighting and lay down their arms immediately or suffer the consequences. The armed forces of the free world stand ready to join America in the destruction of the Chinese means of war, which includes Generalissimo Chiang Kai-shek's formidable forces on the island nation of Formosa.

"If, within the next forty-eight hours, we have not received a definitive, positive response to our just demands, I will instruct Air Force General Curtis Lemay to prepare our long-range Strategic Air Command B-36 and B-50 bomber fleets for immediate use. The U.S. Navy will also prepare to interdict Chinese shipping worldwide and commence shelling and aerial attacks on Chinese port facilities.

"The air and naval forces of Great Britain, France, Australia, and Turkey, as well as others, are prepared to join us. The effect on China will be overwhelming. Ladies and gentlemen, the world stands tonight on the precipice of a great world conflict unlike any other. The Chinese government, alone, holds the key to whether this dreadful event occurs—or not. Pray God they make the right decision.

"Thank you, and good night."

CHAPTER 142

SURRENDER

Saturday, 14 October 1950
TV Studio

A stone-faced television commentator stared into the camera. "Ladies and gentlemen, I can report to you that in the hours following President Truman's speech last night, telegrams and telephone calls backing the President deluged the White House and Congress.

"Widespread sentiment across the country is that someone must pay for the outrageous actions in Korea. With Russia fading from the scene, the Chinese are now the focus of America's anger.

"Our correspondent in China tells us there's a great deal of turmoil in Peking tonight. Unverified reports say that Chinese General Secretary and President Mao Tse-tung is being urged to capitulate to Mr. Truman's terms or surrender his position. State Department spokesmen are concerned about violent demonstrations.

"According to my clock, Chairman Mao has less than 16 hours to respond or suffer the consequences. As the deadline draws near, this network will report again and will, of course, break in to regular programming should that be necessary."

CHAPTER 143

PARENTHOOD

Tuesday, March 20, 1951
Base Hospital, Norton AFB, California

*H*e's so perfect. Look at those tiny, perfect fingers. His hair is so blond it's almost transparent. Like most first-time fathers, the wonder of new human life enthralled Joel. He beamed as Susan nursed their day-old son.

"So what do you think of your son, Daddy?" Susan stroked the baby's blonde hair.

"He's—amazing! I'd forgotten how tiny newborns are. Do you think his eyes will always be so blue?"

"Well, we both have blue eyes, so there's a good chance."

"Micah Johan Knight—that's a big name for such a little guy."

Their firstborn's name continued the Knight family tradition of naming sons after biblical men. The baby's middle name honored Susan's father.

"But then, of course, he *is* heir to the vast Knight family fortunes."

They both laughed. Joel's "fortune" consisted of one-third of his dad's ranch in Colorado and whatever pension the Air Force might grant him some day. All that faded in the face of life's real treasure—a precious new life.

Someone cleared his throat. "Excuse me, General. A dispatch, sir." A fresh-faced lieutenant handed Joel a folded sheet. Joel stepped into the hall to read it. When he returned, his face was somber.

"What's happening?" Susan asked. The baby slept in her arms.

"General MacArthur has been relieved for medical reasons and flown to a hospital ship. They think he suffered a heart attack. Looks pretty bad. He may not make it. General Matthew Ridgeway has been named to replace him. That's almost ironic. Most of us believe the President was about to relieve MacArthur for cause anyway. MacArthur just seems to think he doesn't have to obey the orders of the Commander in Chief."

Joel glanced at his watch. "Gotta run, my love. Red Garret wants to see me at 1100 hours."

EPILOGUE

CONGRATULATIONS

"**C**ome in, Joel. Congratulations! I don't think I've ever heard of anyone in the Air Force getting his star on a Navy ship. And congratulations on the mission. I read your report. My goodness, it reads like an adventure novel. Please have a seat, General. How are Susan and the baby? Doing well, I trust? My Maggie's going to drop by and see them this afternoon."

As Red chattered, Joel wondered, *What's this really about? He didn't call me in to congratulate me. Something's up.*

Red settled against the back of his chair. "The way we've pounded the Chinese the last two months, I think this may be over soon. Since the Chinese threw out Mao, the truce talks seem to be going well with Joe En-Lai running the show. And there's some news for you, Joel—two pieces of news, in fact. First, remember that application you turned in more than a year ago to attend Stanford for your PhD? It's been approved."

"Kind of unusual for a shiny new brigadier to be shipped off to school, but the Pentagon thinks the Air Force of the future will need lots of smart, well-educated officers, instead of a bunch of old fighter jocks like me. They want you there the beginning of September for orientation, then you'll start classes. I've got your orders, including a nice move package, and a housing allowance while you're in school. In the meantime, I'll work your fanny off flying test stuff at Edwards."

"Wow, that's wonderful, sir. I'm glad I'm not going to the Pentagon."

"Believe me, nobody wants *that* assignment, especially pilots. Flying a desk." He made a disgusted noise. "I'm afraid it's inevitable, though."

Red's face brightened. "Listen, there's more good news." He keyed his intercom. "Please send them in, Janet."

Garret's door opened and in limped Chappy, using a cane. Behind him trailed JD.

Joel leapt from his chair and hugged his old friend. "We all thought you were dead, man. I can't believe it, Chappy. And JD, too. This is amazing. Who else made it out?"

Chappy winced, only partly from his wounds. "May I, sir?" He indicated a chair.

He settled gingerly in the chair, wincing at the pain. "Joel, I'm sorry, everyone else died in the crash. JD and I still don't know how or why we survived and they didn't. It was only by the grace of God we weren't killed, too."

"How did you guys escape?"

"This sounds like some corny movie," JD laughed. "We were rescued by Luthor Tömörbaatar, who travelled with a roving band of merchants. They hid us in their camel caravan and carried us to Hami, China. Most of the time we were both unconscious. Later, Chappy borrowed a funny little Brit plane—what was it, Chappy?"

"A Percival Gull. Some smuggler's. Nice little low wing, all metal four-seater. Took us to Tashkent. We hid out there, then the CIA flew us to Tehran. We spent a couple months in the Shah's hospital before they let us return home." Chappy glanced at Red McNeil. "General, they haven't told us. Did the scientist and his materials get out?"

"He sure did, and the Intel was better than any of us dreamed. Besides the atomic bomb details and three scientists, they brought unbelievable Intel on Ruskie atomic bomb bases and aircraft. You knew Joel and his team were all wounded escaping?"

"No? Is Susan OK? Was she hurt?"

Joel said, "She was struck in the leg and feet, but she's recovering. The baby came through just fine."

"A baby? What? Boy or girl?"

"Boy. Nineteen-and-a-half inches long, seven pounds, four ounces. Micah Johan Knight."

"All right, boys, time for me to break up this little party and get some work out of this guy. Chappy, you and JD will fly home shortly. Consider yourselves debriefed as soon as you sign my papers. CIA wants to debrief you next week in DC. Call your contacts and make that happen. Feel free to use my government phone. Now, you're all dismissed with my deep gratitude."

ABOUT THE AUTHOR

A Northrop Institute of Technology (NIT) ad in *Air Progress Magazine* captured ten-year-old Jeff Kildow's passion. He wrote a letter to NIT and received a kind, gentle reply: Study hard. Apply to college after high school. Twenty-eight years later, Jeff received his diploma from the flying wing pioneer, John K. 'Jack' Northrop.

Coloradan Jeff Kildow listened to his father's WWII tales of the magnificent aircraft that the Army Air Corps flew. Following his father's lead, Jeff joined the Air Force to become a pilot—a dream grounded by poor vision. Undeterred, if Kildow couldn't fly planes, Jeff determined to design them. In the Air Force, Kildow trained as a missile maintenance technician, working on the then-new AGM-28 Hound Dog.

After serving his country for four years, Jeff continued to pursue his dreams and earned his engineering degree. At Huntsville, Alabama's Marshall Space Flight Center, Jeff worked on NASA's Sky Lab program, first as a mission planner, then as part of the operations team. His 34-year career as an aerospace engineer included assignments involving deep space probes, launch vehicles, and satellites.

Kildow loves vintage airplanes and cars. Jeff often builds scale models of the aircraft in his stories and in the '80's he built a 1937 Chevrolet. His extensive aviation library of over 200 volumes includes signed biographies of WWII pilots by such notable figures as German General and fighter ace, Adolf Galland, USMC Colonel Gregory "Pappy" Boyington, and Robert "Bob" Hoover. Jeff is married, with two adult children and six grandchildren.

ACKNOWLEDGEMENTS

The completion of the novel *Red Menace* is due in large part to the outstanding help I received along the way.

Thanks to my beta-reader, pilot friends, Randy Meathrell and Don Shipman, for their thoughtful advice and recommendations about my descriptions of flying sequences. Special thanks to fellow author and historian Charles Patricoff, who kept me on the straight and narrow. *Red Menace* is the second novel my friend and prolific author Mike Carroll has guided me through—heartfelt thanks, Mike.

I extend my grateful thanks to long-time friend Elaine Radney for her precise corrections of my grammar, spelling, and punctuation. Best-selling author and editor extraordinaire Robert Liparulo showed the patience of Job during his year-long content edit. The resulting story is infinitely better, due to his insights and recommendations. I'm deeply grateful, Bob.

Throughout the ups and downs of the writing process, my friends and fellow authors at the ACFW Denver South Chapter, Mile High Scribes, encouraged me. To them, my hearty thanks.

FRONT COVER PHOTO CREDITS

Clock: thomas-bormans-JsTmUnHdVYQ-unsplash.jpg

A-Bomb: Gerd Altmann Pixabay atomic-bomb-1011738.jpg

MIG: MiG-15 RB2.jpg, photo by Radomil, 6 June 2005, Poznan, Wikimedia Commons

AIRCRAFT IN RED MENACE

A1: Large American single-engine attack aircraft manufactured by Douglas Aircraft

AN-2: A single-engine Russian utility biplane produced after WWII by Antonov; NATO code name COLT

B-25: WWII twin-engine light bomber with twin tails manufactured by North American Aviation

B-29: A four-engine propeller American heavy bomber from WWII, built by Boeing

B-36: Six to ten-engine heavy American bomber manufactured by Convair (some versions included four jet engines in addition to six propeller engines)

B-50: A later, up-engined and improved version of the B-29, used as America's first strategic bomber

CONVAIR 240: American passenger airliner, post-WWII

C-46: Large WWII twin-engine cargo/transport manufactured by Curtiss

C-47: WWII twin-engine cargo/transport; militarized version of Douglas DC-3

C-54: Large four-engine cargo/transport; militarized version of Douglas DC-4

C-119: Large, powerful twin-engine transport manufactured by Fairchild

C-121: Large four-engine cargo/transport; militarized version of Lockheed Constellation

C-123: Mid-size, twin-engine transport manufactured by Fairchild

DC-2: All metal twin-engine airliner developed by Douglas Aircraft; predecessor to DC-3

F4U: WWII/Korea single-engine fighter, characterized by a gull-wing design; manufactured by Chance Vought Aircraft

F6F: WWII U.S. Navy single-engine propeller fighter manufactured by Grumman

F8F: Powerful WWII single-engine propeller fighter manufactured by Grumman; U.S. Navy

F9F: Early straight-wing jet powered fighter, U.S. Navy manufactured by Grumman

382 | JEFF KILDOW

F-51: A re-designation of the USAF P-51 single-engine piston fighter of WWII

F-80: America's first production jet fighter, extensively used in Korea by the USAF; manufactured by Lockheed

F-84: A single-engine straight wing jet fighter flown by the USAF, developed by Republic Aircraft. Used extensively in Korea as a ground attack plane.

GO-460: Fictional WWII Germany six-engine flying wing bomber

HE-162: Small WWII single, jet engine plywood fighter manufactured by Heinkel

HUDSON. A version of the Lockheed Lodestar airliner militarized and sold to Great Britain as a light bomber

IL-12: Russian propeller cargo/transport aircraft manufactured by Ilyushin; NATO code name COACH

JU-252: WWII German three-engine cargo plane manufactured by Junkers; fictional NATO code name CRANK

LI-2: Russian license-built version of the Douglas DC-3, manufactured by Lisunov; NATO code name CAB

MARTIN 404: Post WWII commercial airliner designed by Martin Airplane Company

MIG-3: Late WWII Russian propeller fighter manufactured by the Mikoyan-Gurevich Design Bureau

MIG-9: Early Russian single-engine jet fighter manufactured by the Mikoyan-Gurevich Design Bureau, using a German-designed BMW engine. NATO code FARGO

MIG-15: Late 1940's Russian fighter used in Korea and beyond. NATO code name FAGOT

PERCIVAL GULL: British all metal low wing private aircraft seating four passengers

PV-2: WWII U.S. Navy twin-engine patrol bomber manufactured by Lockheed named Harpoon; an advanced second military variant of the Lockheed Lodestar airliner of the 1930's

RB-45: A photoreconnaissance version of the North American B-45 four-engine jet bomber; the "R" prefix designates photoreconnaissance

RB-47: A photoreconnaissance version of the Boeing B-47 strategic bomber

RB-50: A photoreconnaissance version of the Boeing B-50 four-engine propeller bomber developed from the WWII B-29

RB-36: A long-range photoreconnaissance version of the Convair ten-engine (six propeller, four jet) heavy bomber

SHCHE-3: A fictional version of the post-WWII Russian light utility aircraft featuring a high wing, two small piston engines, and a wooden fuselage

TU-4: Russian copy of American Boeing B-29, accomplished by reverse-engineering a captured copy; NATO code name BULL

TU-270: A fictional Russian-copied version of the equally fictional WWII German GO-460 six engine flying wing bomber; fictional NATO code name BLAZER

TU-270J: A fictional version of the TU-270 with added jet engines. No NATO code.

YAK-9: A single-engine WWII Russian fighter designed by the Yakovlev Design Bureau. No NATO code.

OTHER BOOKS BY BLACKSIDE PUBLISHING

The Orphan Maker's Sin by Holly DeHerrera

Fifteen years have passed since a car bomb blew up seven-year-old Ella's father, a colonel in the Air Force. One minute her daddy was there. The next? He disappeared, leaving only a charred shell of a vehicle and a burnt hubcap clacking down a Turkish street. Gone. As if he never existed at all.

The percussion of her father's violent death still ricochets in the present. Ella yearns for healing and peace from the emotional shrapnel embedded in her heart. Drawn back to Turkey—a place she swore she left behind—Ella seeks to solve the mystery of who killed her father—and why.

When she meets Murat, a handsome Turkish man, she almost hopes for a new beginning—until she discovers family secrets that torture Murat and shake Ella to her core. Will the war in her soul close her heart to receive or give love—or forgiveness?

Ella faces two choices. Stay anchored to a bitter past or seek a new ending. Can Ella move past old wounds? Or, is the damage too shattering, making healing impossible? *Available in both paperback and e-book.*

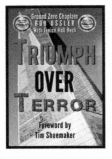

Triumph Over Terror by Ground Zero Chaplain Bob Ossler with Janice Hall Heck. Foreword by Tim Shoemaker

When terrorism, politics, and violence lunges too far, heroes arise. What happens when an ordinary American shows up in Manhattan after the worst terror attack on America soil since Pearl Harbor?

The day that changed the world—September 11, 2001—propelled America into the long war, the Global War on Terror. Like many Americans who serve our country, Chaplain Bob Ossler donned his firefighter turn-out gear, boarded a plane, and made his way to Manhattan to help in any way possible. He was escorted onto the smoldering, quaking heap, dubbed "The Pile." Entering into the Gates of Hell—the crematorium and morgue for nearly 3000 beloved souls—an electrifying chill of horror shot through him.

Trained as a professional first responder, Ossler served five tours of duty during the cleanup at Ground Zero after 9/11. Bob's eyewitness vignettes recount the questions, fears, struggles, and sacrifices of the families and workers overwhelmed by despair. Chaplain Ossler conducted over 300 mini-memorials for the fragmentary remains carried off the Pile. He comforted the mourners, the frightened, and the heartbroken laborers sifting through millions of tons of carnage for the remains of their friends, the unknown dead—and their faith.

From the broken fragments of glass, steel, and men, Chaplain Ossler's mosaic of God's grace unveils the outpouring of generosity, heroism, and unity from people who stepped up to do "something." Ossler honors the ultimate sacrifice and bravery of first responders who rush toward terror to save lives.

Chaplain Ossler chronicles the best of humanity—acts of courage and goodness in the midst of chaos, personal tragedy and unimaginable devastation. As terrorist attacks continue to assault humanity, Ossler reveals how your spirit can triumph over terror's reign, and how you can help others suffering from trauma and loss. *Available in both paperback and e-book.*

A Soldier to Santiago: Finding Peace on the Warrior Path by Brad Genereux. Foreword by Heather A. Warfield, Ph.D. Afterword by Dr. Christine Bridges Esser

"I gave the best years of my life to a cause—to a belief that proved false. I loved living on the edge. The thrill of standing the watch. Rushing into harm's way on behalf of my country. For over 22 years and with pride, I represented America by wearing the cloth of the nation. When my service

was all over? Life had passed me by and . . . I fit in— nowhere."—Senior
Chief Petty Officer Brad Genereux.

Is forgiveness and peace within the grasp of those who spent their lives pursuing the next mission on behalf of their country? Brad Genereux traces two parallel journeys—one through the inferno of war in Afghanistan, and the other through the healing purgatory of the Camino de Santiago. Juxtaposed between a combat zone and The Way of Saint James, experience two adventures and the two lives of one man. Willing to sacrifice his life to aid the Afghanis, Brad's candid account chronicles the challenges to carry out missions while operating under a complex chain of command, Afghani corruption, and deadly sabotage by the Taliban.

After Genereux retired from the military, he faced the arduous pursuit to assimilate into civilian life and to make sense of the unexpected deaths of three family members. Brad revisits dark demons imprisoning his spirit and the healing peace unlocked on The Way of Saint James. This book shadows the reflections of a war-hardened man devoid of identity and purpose and his search for answers, hope, and himself on a 769-kilometer trek over the Pyrenees and across northern Spain.

Are you searching for peace and purpose? Are you suffering from isolation, hypervigilance, nightmares, or insomnia? Experience the camaraderie of warriors deployed to the battlefield and the *esprit de corps* of Camino peregrinos as they triumph over the inner battles of the spirit. *Available in both paperback and e-book.*

The Ghosts of Babylon by Jonathan Baxter. Foreword by Leo Jenkins.

The haunting poetry of The Ghosts of Babylon is as near to the crucible of war as you can get without wearing Kevlar and camouflage.

Every war triggers the question—what's war like? *The Ghosts of Babylon* offers eyewitness accounts of warriors who lost their innocence dueling in the sands of the Iraqi inferno or fighting in the chilling Afghan mountains or on the khaki-colored plains. Wounds enshrouded under the bandages of headlines and sound bites will never bridge the gap between soldier and civilian.

Only a soldier poet lays bare the honor and horror. Only a veteran reveals the physical and mental battles waged by the warrior caste. Only the war poet distills the emotions of those who tasted bravery and terror, love and vengeance, life and death. Based on the experiences of a U.S. Army Ranger turned private security contractor, these powerful poems capture the essence of Jonathan Baxter's twelve military and civilian deployments.

Jonathan reveals the contradictory nature of deployment in a war zone—exhilaration, monotony, ugliness, and occasional beauty. From ancient times to present day, war poetry telegraphs a dispatch across the ages about the universal experiences of war—brotherhood and bereavement, duty and disillusionment, and heroism and horror. No history mirrors the brutal realities and emotions of armed conflict than the shock of war erupting from the warrior poet's pen.

Jonathan resurrects the ghosts and gods of soldiers past. His poignant memorial to fallen brothers transmits the shadowy presence and ultimate sacrifices of the coffined to the fortunate un-coffined. *The Ghosts of Babylon* strips away the cultural varnish of the 'enemy,' painting the bitter irony of every day lives caught in the crosshairs of terror, chaos, and death. From moving to startling to soulful, these masterpieces provoke you to think about the truths and consequences of those who risk their lives on the frontline of freedom—for you, their friends, and our country. *Available in paperback.*

The Middlebury Mystery Series for Ages 7-11 includes:

Available in print and e-book. Middlebury Mystery Book Club Questions. A closed Facebook group, Middlebury Mystery Book Club, to provide homeschoolers, teachers, tutors, and grandparents with ideas to inspire great conversations about this mystery series and to explore important life-application principles. 3-D Reading Activities for Homeschoolers and Creative Parents Old-Timey Mennonite recipes in *The Root Cellar Mystery.*

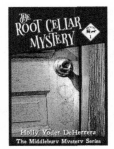

The Root Cellar Mystery by Holly Yoder DeHerrera: Old Order Mennonite cousins, Poppy and Sadie, suspect "A re-e-a-a-al criminal" is staying at Aendi Hannah's bed and breakfast. A missing dog, a mysterious code, creepy creaks, and a floating light in the dark of night only make Poppy and Sadie more jumpy and suspicious of their strange, elderly guest.

After spotting wads of green bills in the snowy headed guest's large trunk, the sleuthing cousins wonder: *Was Ms. Lindy just released from prison and is she a thief?* To figure out what this little old, Mennonite grandmother is up to, the junior detectives spy on their mysterious guest. Confused by Ms. Lindy's odd behavior and an accidental discovery in an old-timey recipe journal, the nosy amateur sleuths hit a dead end. *Why has Ms. Lindy come to Middlebury, Indiana, and what is the puzzling stranger searching for in Aendi Hannah's root cellar? Will Poppy and Sadie's snoopery solve the mystery surrounding Ms. Lindy's past in this cozy mystery in the children's Middlebury Mystery series?*

The Key in the Wall Mystery by Holly Yoder DeHerrera: A bad back laid up energetic Aendi Hannah, who's likely going stir crazy. Poppy and Sadie fix up the rooms for guests staying at the Aendi Hannah's bed and breakfast in Middlebury, Indiana. While cleaning, Poppy and Sadie discover a key behind a broken baseboard in the guesthouse. *Who hid the key that looks like a skeleton's bony finger, and why?*

Their crazy quilt clues—an old cast iron key, 70-year-old letters promising a great treasure, a lost, buried time capsule, and a hidden, secret room—lay out no real pattern or direction. The trail grows cold, like the back burner on Aendi Hannah's big, old gas stove.

Twelve-year-old, amateur sleuth Poppy worries: Will their snoopery discover any new leads to follow? And how will the Old Order Mennonite, junior detectives find time to solve this mystery while attending school, cooking meals, and taking care of a household, plus guests? Are the mystifying lock and treasure lost forever? Or are Poppy and Sadie on a wild goose chase in this cozy mystery in the children's Middlebury Mystery series?

The Covered Bridge Mystery by Holly Yoder DeHerrera: *What kind of creep lurks just waiting to steal from Mammi or Dawdi?* Poppy and Sadie never expected a real, honest-to-goodness burglar to strike in their close-knit, Old Order Mennonite community in Middlebury, Indiana. The pie-swiping culprit mystifies everyone by stashing all the stolen evidence inside the dusky-dark, covered bridge near Dawdi's farm.

Is the thief-on-the-loose tempting the suspicious cousins to catch him—or her? Jonah, who's developmentally disabled and distraught, fears the burglar will hurt his grandparents. And to make matters worse, Mammi and Dawdi refuse to lock their barn and house—even at night. Using an apple pie as bait, the junior detectives set a trap. Will these amateur sleuths nab the criminal or will the bandit remain on the run in this cozy mystery in the children's Middlebury Mystery series?

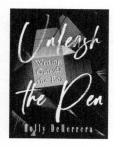

For Middle School and High Schoolers: Unleash the Pen. Writing Outside the Lines by Holly Yoder DeHerrera: Too often Holly DeHerrera hears kids say, "I hate writing," or parents say, "I'm so frustrated. I have to force my child to write."

Discover the power of language and the joy of writing. Writing involves far more than mastering the mechanics. Like that old saying, "Putting the cart before the horse," if a student doesn't love writing, or entertain at least a joyful tolerance, stressing rules without free expression chokes imaginative creativity and critical thinking skills.

A student's ability to write affects student achievement in all subject areas. *Unleash the Pen. Writing Outside the Lines* ignites a love for writing and self-expression through words. DeHerrera's positive vision of writing lays out an alternative plan to teach writing that combines writing instruction with diverse, creative writing projects.

Students dive into a topic of their choosing, while experimenting with a variety of fun writing assignments with authentic connections to their lives and their studies. Each self-guided, creative writing incentive leads the student to learn by writing.

Unleash the Pen. Writing Outside the Lines is designed for students to independently work at their own pace, or over the course of a 36-week school year. This teacher-friendly, multi-genre curriculum motivates your students to leap into the adventure of writing. *Available Winter 2020.*

Made in the USA
Coppell, TX
17 January 2021